S0-ALH-300

THE DARE

LAUREN LANDISH

Edited by
STACI ETHERIDGE
Edited by
VALORIE CLIFTON

Copyright © 2019 by Lauren Landish.

All rights reserved.

Cover design © 2019 by Coverluv.
Photo © LightField Studios, Shutterstock

Edited by Valorie Clifton & Staci Etheridge.

No part of this book may be reproduced in any form or by any electronic or
mechanical means, including information storage and retrieval systems, without
written permission from the author, except for the use of brief quotations in a book
review.

This book is a work of fiction. Names, characters, places, and incidents are either the
product of the author's imagination or are used fictitiously, and any resemblance to
actual persons, living or dead, events, or locales is entirely coincidental.

The following story contains mature themes, strong language and sexual situations.
It is intended for mature readers.

All characters are 18+ years of age and all sexual acts are consensual.

PROLOGUE

ELLE

"*W*hen you're ready, gimme that nod, darlin'!" The guy's voice is loud over the din surrounding me and there's definitely a false note to his twang.

Poser . . . but damn, does he look great in those skintight jeans that leave nothing to the imagination. He's going for the 'what you see is what you get' look and it's serving him up to every pair of eyes in this place.

No judgement, though. It's not like I'm any different.

I watched a YouTube video to get my cutoff shorts just right, I borrowed a pair of cowgirl boots with actual fringe, and I'm wearing an add-a-size pushup bra to make my breasts look bigger as they nearly bounce out of my low-cut tank top. I look like Daisy Duke and a Dallas Cowboy cheerleader got together, and I'm their style-baby creation for a reality television show called *So You Wanna Be a Sexy Cowgirl?*

How did I end up here, anyway?

Here is a honkytonk on the rough side of town, when I don't even know how to two-step or line dance or any of the other stuff I've been doing all night.

Here is with my long legs wrapped around the vinyl of a mechanical bull and a cowboy I don't know straddling me from behind. Apparently, we're riding together, which seems unprofessional but also completely improper, so I'm down for it.

Here is in that moment I live for. I wait for my blood to sing through me and to feel its hot burn from the top of my head to the tips of toes and everywhere in between.

Anticipation. Excitement. Restlessness.

All so loud inside my head that everything else is shut out. There's no real world, no pain, no doubts, only hope that the next dare will leave me adrenalin-filled and buzzing, high on the danger and risk.

It's my favorite moment, right on the edge of greatness.

Another voice whispers in my ear, "You're not having second thoughts, are you? Give the man his nod and let's ride, baby."

I'm not this guy's baby, but the high flows through me and I look to the bull man. His eyes are hungry, whether for me or to watch me fall off this thing, I'm not sure, but it's all the same.

I nod, and my last conscious thought is that he has a pretty smile before everything in my head becomes a shout.

Hang on! Squeeze with your knees! Grip the rope!

I've got the knot of the length of rope in one hand, my free hand waving around like a maniac for about zero-point-two seconds. Then I give in and grab the knot with both hands. It's not pro-style, but I don't give a shit as I hoot and holler and hold on for dear life.

Behind me, the cowboy whose name I don't even know has his arms wrapped around me to fist the base of the rope, which suddenly seems very phallic with both our hands gripping it. His thighs squeeze me as he pulls me back against him with every jerking move of the machine beneath us. I can feel him, hard and long against my ass when we bump together, which has to hurt because we're not talking an easy jostling here.

But the operator must be in cahoots with Cowboy because the rhythm becomes less jerky. Instead, we spin a bit but the forward and backward movement is smooth and wavelike. Cowboy's grunts don't sound so much like work to hang on now. Instead, he's groaning in my ear like he's enjoying this a little too much.

But still, I hold on, praying for the eight.

Bump-bump-bump.

One last maneuver has Cowboy bouncing against my ass, and if there weren't two layers of denim between us, I have no doubt he'd easily slip right inside me with those thrusts.

The thought makes me unsteady, and I lose my grip, slipping off to the side. Cowboy tries to save me, but I fall from the circle of his arms, my legs flying up in the air as I bounce to the cushions below the bull.

The crowd cheers all around me, and my eyes jump to the digital readout.

Nine point five.

I wait for the second-best feeling to wash through me. Success, accomplishment, power.

Son of a bitch, I made it! Plus overtime!

I jump up and make a high-kneed victory lap around the padding, slapping hands as I go.

When I get to my bestie, she grabs my shoulders and shakes me almost as hard as the bull did. "Oh, my God! You did it, you crazy bitch! That was epic! Awesome! Hell, yeah!" she calls out in a fake twang of her own, and everyone around us cheers again as they hold up their beers.

The smile on my face is so big my cheeks hurt.

"That was some ride. What's your name?" I turn to face the deep voice behind me. Cowboy is looking me up and down like a snack. Like we're already halfway through foreplay and I'm a foregone conclusion.

I consider for a quick moment. He's ridiculously hot. After all, I know what he's working with since I felt it against my ass, and he was good with that bull-riding motion, which tells me he's probably at least decent in the hay.

I giggle inside at my own countrified joke.

Tiffany grabs at my arm, digging her nails in a little too hard. The universal girlfriend code of *no, no, no, abort mission!*

I don't even have to look at her to know her eyes are yelling at me, so I give Cowboy my sweetest smile. "Cindy, but I've got to go." It's our play on Cinderella, an inside joke that roughly translates to 'run for it like it's midnight.'

With that, Tiffany helps pull me over the polished wood railing around the bullpen and we take off, laughing as our hair flows behind us like perfectly curled banners.

"Sorry!" I call back to Cowboy, who's yelling at me to wait.

I laugh harder, smile bigger, and dodge a waitress with a tray full of beers. We're in the parking lot, Tiffany pulling into the street before I can ask why she didn't let me give Cowboy my real name.

"He was hot, Tiff. He could've ridden me all night!"

In the passenger seat, I buck my hips like I'm back on the bull and bite my lip like I'm definitely somewhere else. Namely, beneath Cowboy.

"You know that's not how this works," she admonishes.

She's right. We dare each other to do crazy things all the time. It's a big part of our fun friendship.

But we have limits.

Nothing that could hurt someone, no sex, and nothing *really* illegal. A little illegal is sometimes okay, like the time we trespassed on the roof at school to underage drink and smoke, but nothing seriously over the line.

"So sex with Cowboy couldn't be part of the dare. It could've been my own fun after smashing that dare successfully. Did you see me ride that bull? That was no beginner's luck. Maybe my streak could've continued all night long." I'm back to teasing her even though I've mostly already forgotten Cowboy in favor of my delight at winning the dare.

"Maybe, but you didn't see the waitress eyeballing you two. I figured out pretty quickly that if you got off that bull and onto Cowboy, you were going to be in a catfight in less than those nine-point-five seconds this time." She says it seriously, but there's a tiny bit of disappointment in the words. Like she would've paid good money to see me catfight in a cowboy bar.

But she's a great friend and saved me like the rule follower she is. Which is to say that she dances all over the rules, tapping her pretty booted feet on both sides with regularity, but that's pretty in line with me, so we're golden.

"Oh, no. I didn't see that. Thanks for saving me then." I reach across the console and hug her shoulders, careful not to distract her from driving.

When I'm back in my seat, she glances over at me, a smile already blooming. "But dayum, did you ride that bull, girl! Whoo hoooo!" she yells out into the night through the rolled-down windows.

"And yeehaw!" I answer just as loudly.

Dare done.

We pull into the dorm parking lot with our lights off so security hopefully won't see us, because bull riding wasn't our only dare of the night.

Hours ago, I was the one who dared Tiffany to sneak out, so

she's got a successful dare done tonight too. As long as we can sneak back in after curfew without getting caught.

We park and get out, staying low between the cars. I'm not sure why, but it seems like the sneaky thing to do. We're probably too loud as we shush each other, giggling quietly, but we manage to make it all the way inside the building and to our dorm room without getting busted.

As I lay in bed, my face scrubbed clean and in my PJs, I replay the night. Fuck, that was fun.

A tiny voice tries to butt in, telling me to be safe, take things seriously, and be good. It's my dad's voice, living in my head, quoting all the things he's said to me an infinite number of times over the years. He still thinks of me as his good little girl.

But when I set his prerogatives on the scale against the exhilaration I feel doing things that are a little crazy, Dad loses every time. Mentally, I can tell him to shut up and do what I want, though I'd never tell him that in person. I love him way too much for that.

I just love doing daring things too.

CHAPTER 1

ELLE - FOUR YEARS AND 1500 DARES LATER

"Ow!" I yelp right out of my sleep as Taylor Swift jolts me awake and causes me to bang my head against my headboard.

Rumbling irritably, I slap the alarm next to my bed. But it doesn't go off. It gets even louder as it falls off the nightstand and into bed with me, Taylor sassily telling the guy she's singing about that they're never, ever getting back together. Great news, but I could really, really use another half hour of sleep before discussing your love life drama, Tay-Tay.

Grumbling, I mash the button again and Taylor goes up another octave, making my head pound. Why did I buy an alarm clock with such tiny buttons again?

It takes several more mashes and a well-placed karate chop to silence the alarm. I make a mental note to buy a new one because I might've actually just broken it, and if not, something with a big-ass snooze button would be nice.

"Gee, thanks—" I begin to growl but then stop, choked as I breathe in a . . . ball of cat fur? Hacking, I wipe at my mouth, disgusted and unfortunately not all that surprised. "Sophie!" I complain, "Have you been sitting on my chest while I sleep again?"

My black and white Persian cat, Sophie the Magnificent—and in her mind probably a lot of other titles—gives me an imperious, I-give-zero-fucks look from where she's perched on my desk before licking her paws. If I didn't know any better, I'd almost be tempted to think her incapable of being responsible for the fluff-ball that oh, so conveniently found its way into my mouth.

But looks can be deceiving.

Sophie can be a sweetheart most times, but she can also be my worst nightmare. Besides costing me a rather nice chair earlier in our relationship, I swear she hops on my chest while I'm asleep. The sweet side of me likes to think she's guarding me, making sure I'm breathing all night. The not-so-sweet side is certain she's trying to suck the life out of me.

But I know better than to expect further response from my feline companion, so I get up and stretch my arms. I mentally cycle through all the things I have to do to get ready for work. Shower, shave, makeup, get dressed, and then off to pick up my bestie, Tiffany Young, for carpooling, but I talk to Sophie the whole time. That's one of the main reasons I have her—so that I don't look like a lunatic talking to myself.

"If you keep leaving me hairballs for breakfast, you're going to see me use up every last one of your nine lives—" My voice fails me as I step forward and fall into a tangled heap. "Dammit!"

Damn, am I usually this clumsy?

I glare balefully at Sophie, who's still sitting pretty on my desk, but I can see the laughter in her eyes. She's enjoying my morning clumsiness. I kick my feet, messily getting untangled from the pair of jeans I shed as I fell into bed last night. I know there's a trail of clothing from the front door leading to this last puddle right here, meaning I'll have to watch it so I don't fall again. At least I managed to not knock last night's wine glass off the nightstand with my alarm clock battle *du jour*.

Yeah, last night was epic. If you consider one and a half glasses of wine, my favorite book boyfriend, and falling asleep immediately after jilling off to be a great night. To be fair, sometimes, I do. Others, like now, I think I really, *really* need to get a release with a pulse. Wait, make that a heartbeat because Maximus, my battery-operated boyfriend, does have a pulse mode. A really good pulse mode.

"Don't you *dare* laugh at me," I warn Sophie, shooting her a murderous glare as I climb carefully to my feet. Meanwhile, she's unperturbed by my death gaze, even offering a soft meow that belies her evil nature. "I swear someone's got a voodoo hex—"

"Papa don't preach—"

The music is back again. This time it's my phone, and fate must be screwing with me today on the music choices.

Shit. I do not *need this right now.*

Part of me wants to blow it off and go about getting ready for work. But another part of me feels guilty for even thinking that. There are people you can ignore and people you can't.

And if you don't answer, he's liable to get so worried he might send the "boys" to check on you.

Just the image of my two lumbering, overprotective hand holders, also known as my cousins, showing up at my door is enough to change my mind, and with a sigh, I press *Accept*.

"Dad," I complain as my father, Daniel Stryker's, handsome face appears on my phone's screen. At forty-six, he's what my best friend crassly likes to call a D-I-L-F. I have to constantly remind her that's the last fucking thing I want to hear. Yuck.

His strict diet and workout regimen help him exude a youthfulness of a man almost half his age. If that weren't enough, he's a vice-president at Fox Industries, a multi-billion-dollar Fortune 500 Company, making him the most desirable middle-aged bachelor in the city. And that's according to several magazines, not just his own ego.

I mean, it's kinda nice to know I've got the genetics to age gracefully myself, but it's also really, really strange when you have to use a bat to keep your female friends at bay. Surely, they can work their daddy issues out with someone who isn't my actual dad, right?

"I'm trying to get ready for work. Is it important?"

"Ah!" Dad exclaims, ignoring my complaining, his handsome mug lighting up like a Christmas tree as my face appears on his screen. "There's my beautiful little princess!" He suddenly recoils sharply from his screen, his face twisting in horror. "Damn, baby girl, Medusa's got some competition going!" He pops a raspberry into his mouth, talking to me and prepping his breakfast at the same time.

"Very funny!" Despite my irritation, I laugh, not offended in the least. He's always teased me about my bed head. It's been an ongoing joke since I was a little girl when he'd have to painfully, patiently get the tangles out before school. It got so bad I started wrapping my hair in silk wraps in my teen years to help control it, but that never seemed to work since apparently, I roll around like the possessed girl from *The Exorcist* in my sleep.

Eventually, I said to hell with it and just started fixing it with a shower, heavy conditioning, and a quick blowout in the morning.

"Not everyone can wake up looking picture perfect like Your Highness," I tell him, stroking his ego. "And I just rolled out of bed, so I have an excuse."

"You're definitely right about that," Dad agrees, smoothing back his already impeccably slicked back hair. But there's a hint of laughter in his eyes, letting me know he hasn't gone totally arrogant in his not-that-old age. "But you're just getting out of bed? Honey, you really do need to make time for yourself. Early to bed, early to rise, get a workout in and a healthy breakfast to start your day right."

It's advice, but it's also a recap of his morning as he holds up a glass containing green glop. He takes a good gulp of the drink, and I cringe. That stuff tastes like grass, and I refuse to drink it anymore now that I can make my own coffee and Pop Tart breakfast.

I roll my eyes in an exaggerated enough manner to make sure he sees it. "Give me a break. I've had a rough start this morning. Sophie's been playing soul stealer again, and I damn near tripped and broke my neck before you called. The only thing that could make it worse is that Peeping Tom I caught outside my window a couple of nights ago."

Dad frowns and leans forward to get closer to the camera, suddenly serious and on edge. "Peeping Tom?" Dad's breath escapes him in a huff. "Should I send the boys to check everything out?"

I let out a groan.

But Dad's on a roll now. "Security system, with door and window alarms. Maybe have the boys sleep over for a few nights to see if they can catch the fucker . . ."

My cousins, Billy and Ricky, or as Tiffany likes to call them, Bebop and Rocksteady, are like my dad's adopted sons. More meat than brains, they've been a thorn in my side ever since I could remember, with Dad having them watch over me like hawks.

Their primary mission? Keep me safe, which leads conveniently into their secondary mission, no fun for Elle. And now I'm talking about myself in the third person like I'm crazy. Thanks, Dad!

At least I've always been able to outsmart Billy and Ricky so they haven't been much of a hindrance to my shenanigans.

"Dad, didn't we already have this discussion?" I ask in a tired tone and giving him the 'look' through the camera. "I'm a grown woman. I don't need anyone to come looking after me just because I'm having a rough morning. Besides, I was just joking about the Peeping Tom thing. Payback." I stick my tongue out, disproving my claim of being an adult.

"Seriously? That doesn't stop me from worrying about you, El," Dad says, not amused by my little joke. "No matter how old you get, I'll always worry about you. It's my job."

The sincerity in his eyes and the worry lines etched in his brow pull at my heartstrings, and for a moment, I empathize with him.

After all, his worry isn't totally unfounded, given our family's history. Our life had seemed pretty picturesque, but then came the fateful day where Mom up and left with no explanation. No goodbye letter. No telling me, or him, that she loved us.

Nothing.

She just disappeared one day, never to be heard from again.

At first, we'd thought the worst and Dad had even called the police to report her missing. But she hadn't been missing. She'd just left us. To say Dad was devastated is an understatement. His entire life, his partner, his heart had been ripped out of his chest.

We later found out that she was having an affair with an old college flame, and he was tired of being the side dick, so he gave her an ultimatum. Him or her family.

She chose him, and I've never even gotten a birthday card since.

Dad reacted by going insular, focusing on me and work, in that order. For a while, I reveled in being his main focus. He made me feel safe, comforted, and loved in the face of my mother's rejection, which was no small task. And somehow, he managed to still be a machine about work. When I learned what the word *efficient* means, I immediately saw Dad. He'd drop me off at school at eight, and while I would catch a ride home with my cousins or a friend, he was always there by five thirty to take me to ballet class, Girl Scouts, or whatever. He even cooked, and he cooked good stuff too. No spaghetti from a can in my house. He balanced it all and made it seem effortless and easy.

But as I got older, things changed.

I coped rather oppositely, deciding that living safe was no guarantee of a happily ever after, so why not try YOLO instead? If I'm only living once, I'm going to make the absolute best of it.

Okay, so that led to a couple of scares. I might've jumped off the roof into the pool once or twice, and I sorta got into it with a curb and broke my nose after spinning around a bat a few dozen times. And there was the time I decided I could handle hard liquor even though I'd never so much as had a beer. And those are just the things Dad knows about.

Eventually, I wouldn't say no to any dare, no matter how crazy it was. If someone said those magic words—*I dare you*—I was in.

"Well, stop worrying about me," I tell Dad, shaking myself out of my reverie. "I can take care of myself, remember? Lord knows, Billy and Ricky made sure I knew how to squash a guy's nuts like a pumpkin pie as soon as I was old enough to swear."

Dad's answering grunt sounds a bit pained, as if the summoned imagery makes him think of his own family jewels getting crushed, but he murmurs something that sounds suspiciously like, "Good boys."

I cut him off, wanting to change the subject from the one we've beaten to death, reanimated like a zombie, and beaten to death again. "I've got to get ready. But quickly, before I go, how's the search for Fox's HQ2 coming along?"

Dad brightens, straightening his shoulders and steepling his fingers beneath his chin, his eyes brimming with excitement. If there's one thing he loves almost as much as me, it's work. And with my 'leaving the nest', first for college and then getting my own apartment, he's been able to rocket up the corporate ladder even faster.

The recent announcement that Fox Industries would be acquiring a second headquarters, along with a Regional President to run it, had every top executive scrambling to produce the best location for the company.

Rumor has it, Dad's plan is top on the company's list.

"Great! The board is still hearing presentations, but I think

THE DARE

they're close to voting. If everything goes to plan, you're looking at the new President of Fox HQ2!" Dad gloats.

I clap my hands and let out a whoop, causing Sophie to jump at the sudden noise. "Wow, that's awesome! I'm so happy for you!"

Dad beams, but then he leans forward, looking at me expectantly. Even through the screen, his gaze is heavy and meaningful. "If I land the deal and get promoted, you know what that means, right?"

I know exactly what that means.

Come work for me.

He might have let me live in the dorms in college and of course have my own apartment . . . but he still wants me to be within arm's reach. I'm his little girl, after all.

But though it's something I feel torn about, I can't tell him that now. Not again, when we've had the discussion several times already about how I want to pave my own way, not get by on his last name.

Knowing I don't have time to argue, I take a different tact, striking a button I know he refuses to discuss with me. "Yep! So, does this mean you're gonna finally find a lucky woman to share all this awesome success with?"

He immediately looks over his shoulder and then coughs before looking back at the camera. "You know what? I should start preparing for that meeting," Dad says. "Have a great day, kiddo."

With a wink, he's gone and my phone's screen blank. "Can you believe that, Sophie?" I say, not surprised by my dad's reaction. He always gets skittish when I press him about finding a partner, and I sometimes use that knowledge to my benefit. "He wants the play by play on my private life, but as soon as I try to get the scoop on his, he turns into Casper and ghosts."

Naturally, Sophie doesn't answer, and I glance at my clock.

8:05 . . . less than an hour to get ready, pick up and Tiff, and rush to work.

"Holy shit!" I hiss, cursing Dad for calling me and wasting precious time. "I gotta get ready!"

I hop over the bed, nearly falling and busting my head on my dresser, and I'm in the shower in a jiffy. I only have time for a quick shave of my legs before I'm toweling off. I decide to use my fallback hairstyle of a slick bun because my condition and blow-dry routine is too time-consuming after Dad used up all of my spare minutes this morning.

I apply a light layer of makeup, focusing on my lashes and a matte red for my lips, a few spritzes of my woodsy perfume, and then pull on a white dress shirt and a tight black pencil skirt. Red heels complete the look, making the almost-uniform seem chic and stylish.

"All right, Sophie," I tell her as I check myself over in the mirror.

I look pulled together and professional, like Professional Barbie with my blonde locks, big blue eyes, and boobs too big for my frame—thanks for that, Mom. But I know how to use those attributes to my best advantage too. People don't often expect a brain like mine to be housed in this packaging, and I'm more than happy to let them underestimate me while I mow right over them, kicking ass and taking names.

"I need you to hold down the fort." I grab my purse and work keys off the dresser and head for the front door while saying over my shoulder, "Try not to tear down the house while I'm gone, 'kay?"

She meows . . . but that could be a good or a bad thing.

It's all hustle and bustle to get to Tiffany's apartment with me nearly getting into a fender bender as I burn rubber across town. But she's nowhere to be seen when I pull up to the curb, which is unusual for her because she's always outside before I show up.

I wait a few minutes before rolling down my window and honking the horn while yelling, "Come on, Tiff, we need to go!"

When Tiffany fails to appear, I grumble angrily as I jump out of my car and walk up the first-floor walk, ready to pound on her door. I only make it a few steps before I hear booming bass and a voice yelling, *"Shake your ass! But watch yourself."*

"What . . . on . . . earth?" I mutter as I walk up and pound on the door. "Tiffany!" I yell over the music, seeing several neighbors peek out from behind their curtains. "You've got three seconds to come out or I'm leaving!"

As if in response, the door swings open, and instead of Tiffany, I see Ace Young, Tiffany's older brother, standing there in unbuttoned jeans and no shirt, a can of Coors in his hand.

Once upon a time, he'd been hot, and I'd told Tiffany so during one of his visits to our college dorm. Hell, the first time I saw him sprawled out on her bed, I'd thought she was hooking up with him and was thinking my girl had done *good*. I'd been delighted to be wrong, even though girl code dictated that he was look-don't-touch level only.

But his glory days are gone.

What the hell is this fool doing, drinking this early in the morning? I think to myself but then decide I don't want to know as the smell of his beer breath hits me. He looks like a total mess, his once flat as a board stomach now bloated and soft.

"Elle?" Ace asks, looking absolutely wasted and making me wonder what the hell is going on with him. Last I knew, he'd landed a good job up north and was seeing an awesome girl with wedding bells on the horizon. But a month ago, he mysteriously returned, much to Tiff's dismay, sullen, tight-lipped, jobless, and very single, to crash on her couch.

And he's been driving her absolutely crazy ever since.

"How's it going?"

"Hey, Ace, where's Tiff?" I say loudly over the still bumping music, ignoring his question because I don't want to get drawn into a conversation. "We're running late for work." We're not really late, but any cushion on the clock is gone and we need to go.

Ace begins to reply but is shoved aside as a familiar voice growls, "Move!"

Tiffany, my best friend and partner in crime since freshman year dorms, appears looking frazzled, her dark hair pulled back behind her in a messy ponytail and her dress shirt rumpled and buttoned wrong, leaving one tail long and one short. Never mind the fact that it should be tucked in to begin with.

With her bright, mischievous eyes and brisk demeanor, some people might think we make an odd couple. Friends are supposed to keep you out of trouble and give you sage advice when you're about to do something stupid.

Tiffany's the exact opposite.

I was already a small-time daredevil in my own right when

we met, but she became my main instigator, always upping the ante on me with the dares.

She's become something of a devil on my shoulder.

The Thelma to my Louise.

And I love her for it because we've had some great times. Some really great times.

It's unlike Tiff to come out of the house looking barely put together, though, because she's also the organization to my chaos, so I know whatever delayed her must have been one hell of a reason.

I open my mouth to ask her what took her so long, but she brushes past me, rushing toward the car, throwing over her shoulder, "Let's go. I'll explain in the car."

"Bye, Ace," I say quickly, turning to rush after Tiffany.

"See ya, Elle," Ace replies, watching me through bleary eyes. Behind him somewhere, the music begs me and everyone in the building to 'show me what you're working with!'

Classy AF, Ace. Really.

Tiffany yells back over her shoulder, "Turn that shit down before my neighbors call the cops!"

He does at least look chagrined, and before we even close the car doors, the music quiets.

"What the hell was that all about?" I demand as we pull away from the curb. "Drinking this early in the morning?"

Tiffany bangs her head against the headrest, her eyes closed. "I'm going to kill him. He was up all night and then commandeered the bathroom for forty-five minutes this morning, doing God knows what, because he sure as hell wasn't taking a shower." Her nose crinkles cutely even though she's talking about Ace's stale body odor.

"Jacking off?" I offer.

Tiffany makes several retching noises. "Ew! But seriously, I don't know what to do with him. He goes off like he's going to conquer the world, then comes back a shadow of his former self, refusing to talk about what happened . . . all while making my apartment living room his official man cave." Tiffany growls, but her fire is dimming, replaced with sadness. "It's almost as if he met some crazy succubus out there that sucked the life right out of him and replaced him with . . ."

She loses her voice for a moment, shaking her head. At the

worried look in her eyes, I feel a pang of sadness too. I know Ace is in pain, and whatever is going on with him hurts Tiffany too because she loves her brother like I love tacos and cake, which is a lot. Complaining about him to me is her way of dealing with it, and I suspect, her way of coming up with a plan to fix whatever mess he's in.

That's Tiffany's way of showing love. She'll fix your shit right up, whether you want her to or not.

"Maybe you should try getting him some help," I offer gently. "Looks like whatever's going on with him, it's not healthy."

"You're telling me," Tiffany mutters, "except I'm pretty sure he'd just tell a therapist to fuck off as it is right now."

She looks sad and lost in thought as she nibbles her lower lip. "I do worry about him, though, which is why I'm putting up with it . . . for now."

I reach out and gently pat her hand. "Everything's going to be okay, Tiff. He'll come to his senses eventually."

"I hope so," Tiffany sighs. "I really do. Because if he doesn't get his shit together soon, I'm going to have to put my foot down."

And that's one thing I love about Tiffany. She might be a shit-stirring, grade-A professional instigator who likes to play around, but when it comes to serious issues, she can show a surprisingly level of maturity.

"Anyway," Tiff says, waving a hand and wiping at her eye in one flourish while appearing to simultaneously brighten up, "did you get your usual call from Daddy this morning?"

"Tiff!" I protest, glaring daggers at the nickname she's adopted for my dad. Tiffany has disturbingly let me know that she has a crush on my dad.

I let her know just as certainly that he is off limits because it gives me the heebie-jeebies whenever I think about it. I love my dad and I want him to find a woman who's a perfect fit for him. Grown up, professional, a woman who can be his equal.

And while I love her to death, Tiffany is none of those things.

"What?" Tiff asks innocently as I keep glaring at her.

"Stop calling him that! Maybe Ace isn't the only one who needs a therapy appointment." I throw my voice into a caricature of my professional tone. "Daddy issues . . . right this way, please."

"I'm just playing. Chill."

"Yes, I did talk to him this morning . . . and no, he didn't ask about you."

"Whatever." Tiffany laughs, knowing not to press my buttons any further on the issue.

Everything's good until we get off the freeway and run smack dab into traffic.

"Ugh!" Tiffany groans as we watch four cars get through the intersection ahead before stopping. "It's like everyone and their grandma is in the way!"

"What do you want me to do?" I ask, drumming my fingers on the steering wheel. "There's a garbage truck ahead, you know."

"So?" Tiffany asks.

"What the hell does that mean?"

Tiffany grins, pointing to the oncoming lane which is currently empty. "Pop it."

I look over at her grinning face, her perfectly white model's smile tweaked into that little tilt that I know way too well. "Are you nuts? Intersections like this, you know the cops—"

"Just skip ahead. I dare ya."

The words hang in the air, and Tiffany's grin widens as I turn my attention back to the road, my hand resting on the gear shift. "Fine . . . on the green."

Up ahead, the light goes green and I floor it, throwing my Camaro into first while jerking my steering wheel to the left. Adrenaline rushes through me, filling my blood as we rocket through the intersection and beyond. Up ahead, I see the problem—a city sewer repair truck—but I'm committed now.

"Elle, there's—" Tiffany yells, but I see it. A flagman, traffic . . . oncoming traffic.

I push it a little harder, shooting the gap and jerking my wheel back to the right just in time to avoid getting my bumper clipped by a soccer mom in an oversized SUV. "Yes!"

I don't let up, making a quick right and then a left a block later to try and not be followed by the cops before I merge back onto the main road and slow down like everything's normal. "That was fun." I pat the dashboard of my baby. "Good girl, Cammie."

Next to me, Tiffany looks like she's ready to lose her breakfast, and I'm betting she only had coffee. Wiping the sweat off her brow, she gasps. "Damn, girl. That was close."

I grin like I just did something amazing. It really wasn't even that close. It was definitely a bitch move to make, and those folks had every right to honk at me, but it wasn't nearly as dangerous as Tiffany's making it out to be.

Dare done.

And that adrenalin wears off, leaving me buzzed and fizzy inside, ready to tackle another day.

CHAPTER 2

ELLE

ox Industries headquarters is one of those rare things in the corporate world, a headquarters that doesn't *look* like a headquarters. Oh, don't get me wrong. Nobody who drives by the five-story, half-mile-long building is going to think it's just your average business park.

It's built into a hillside. On the side that you park on, only the top three floors are visible, each one surrounded by a wide, shaded walkway that you can use to get from one end of the building to the other while getting some fresh air if you want.

But on the other side . . . well now, that's where it gets truly impressive. From that side, you see all five floors overlooking a wide, shallow half canyon that opens up into a view of the entire valley below us.

If you didn't know better, you'd think the building was a hospital, or maybe a technological college. But for forty years, it's been the Fox headquarters, and as we walk into the lobby on the 'ground' floor, I'm once again glad to work here.

Just not under Dad.

Well, technically, I guess I do work for him. Tiffany and I work for everyone in the company. Every executive has their own team, but the business assistants like Tiffany and I get the grunt work.

Answer the phone? Yep. Give tours? Every day at ten and two if there's someone here who wants a peek behind the Wizard's curtain. Make copies, file paperwork, create binders for presentations, act as a courier from one end of the building to the other, and plug numbers into spreadsheets for data analysis? Yes, yes, and yes to all that.

It's not exactly what I thought I'd be doing with my business degree, and definitely not what Dad wants me to do. He offered me an unpaid internship as an analyst in his department straight out of school with near assurances that it'd become a permanent job after the twelve weeks. And while the brainwork of that had definitely appealed, I want to earn my positions myself, so we'd compromised that I'd work at Fox in a role where he doesn't hold any sway. And in a job where I'm not being subsidized by his bank account. I might not make much, but I earn every penny myself and that's important to me.

One day, I'll make my way up the ladder myself and get to use the intelligence I inherited from Dad, but in the meantime, I'm paying my dues and enjoying my work. It's busy and constant, but I could do it with my eyes closed and both hands tied behind my back while hopping on one foot.

Hmm, maybe I'll dare Tiffany to do that later and see how it works out?

Unfortunately for Tiffany and me, we're ten minutes late, and as we come in, we see the current bane of our existences, our boss Miranda, manning the lobby phones, looking like the proverbial chicken with her head cut off. She used to answer the phones and worked her way up herself, but I guess it's been a while since she was in the trenches.

She's perfectly put together, her brown hair frosted just enough to accentuate her maturity while her super-tight-even-after-two-kids body's tucked into a form fitting mirror of our own business professional outfits.

I wonder if she'd be a good fit for my dad? Then I remember that her kids are barely teenagers and mark her off the list of potentials. Dad doesn't need that, and besides, he already knows Miranda, so if there were sparks to be made, he'd have already seen them.

There's definitely some sparks right now, though, her eyes blazing behind the lenses of her glasses as she hisses at us, "Where have you two been? You're late."

"Her fault," Tiffany immediately says, casually hooking a

thumb in my direction. "So much traffic and she drives like my Grandma," Tiffany says before covering her mouth.

Miranda gives her the stink eye then instructs us, "You two get to work. I've got to brief Mr. Wolfe in half an hour and I'm not ready, thank you two very much."

Miranda walks off, leaving us to work at the desk alone. Not that we can't handle it. Most of the job involves coordinating interactions when visitors, delivery people, or outside contractors come in.

The most common problem we have is explaining to a new visitor that yes, while they are in the lobby and yes, they just walked in the front door, they need to take the down elevator to get to the first floor.

"Why did they do that, anyway?" Tiffany asks me after escorting a lost coffee delivery guy. I'd dared her to use an accent of her choice and she'd used a pretty good fake Spanish accent for the trip to the elevator. Back in her usual voice with no rolled Rs, she says, "We've been working here over two years, and I still don't know."

"Dad told me that some of the people working on the bottom two floors were threatening to strike," I reply as I check the pile of mail in front of me for proper postage and labels. "They were pissy about working in the so-called 'basement' by having negative numbers. So the board renumbered the elevators and repainted the numbers in the stairwell, and the strike threat went away like that." I snap my fingers to emphasize the point. "People are stupid," I say with an exasperated sigh, but I get that sometimes, little things like that can be a sign of something deeper, so I don't begrudge the complainers too much.

Except when I have to answer the same question for the umpteenth time in one eight-hour shift.

I turn my mind back to checking the mail, ignoring Tiffany for a bit. While I love my job, it can be boring and monotonous, like checking outgoing mail for stamps and labels. Tiff helps me keep it fun by daring me to do silly things from time to time, like wearing a pink sticky note on my butt when I go to get a coffee.

"Oops, how'd that get there? Thanks!" I tell the lady who whispers to me about it like it's a gross misstep of proper civility.

I laugh lightly as I sit back down at my desk. There isn't much time to do anything too crazy, which is probably for the best.

Instead, we answer phones and take questions and operate as information central for pretty much the entire building.

Just after lunch, I see a large group of suits walk in, talking animatedly among themselves. Nothing unusual about that, either the suits or the talk. Fox is so successful because it doesn't treat their workers like robotic morons, and a lot of the workers are passionate about their jobs.

There's one suit, though, who lags behind the rest, and Tiff jostles my elbow as she notices who it is. "Oh, shit."

My eyes follow hers and I see him. Miranda's boss. I guess technically, *my* boss too, since he oversees internal operations.

It's The Big, Bad Wolfe.

Colton Wolfe.

Tall, dark-haired, and handsome . . . with the sexiest British accent I've ever heard. He's the poster boy for the new generation of Fox executives, the man who's got it all. Brains, guts, and he's sexy enough to make even a double-breasted gabardine suit look good.

He never says anything when he comes through the lobby. He doesn't even look at me, though I've tried I don't know how many times to get his attention.

Including offering him a good morning coffee, faking a sneezing fit, and once, dropping a folder right in front of him and bending down to retrieve it. All dares from Tiffany, of course.

I gave up after the last one, where he literally walked around my swaying ass without so much as a glance.

To say he's handsome is an understatement. And the fact that I work in a department that he oversees . . . that I work *under* him . . . yeah, I've had a few fantasies with that phrase having a whole different meaning.

But he's never said a word to me. Two plus years with the company, if you count summer internships, and the most he's done is give a little two-minute welcome speech at a new hires meeting my first day on the job.

"I dare you . . . to go talk to him."

I turn to Tiffany, who's grinning as she looks at me. I guess I can't blame her. I give her so much shit about her crush on my dad, so she can't be blamed for trying to get me on my DL crush on Colton. "Tiff, we've talked about this. Remember the ass-waving incident? He's a no-go."

"I'm serious," she says, still grinning like she's just this side of the nuthouse. "You've been checking him out since you first laid eyes on him, and he just hasn't *seen* you yet. Here's your chance. If he acknowledges you and then moves on, you'll know for sure. But until then, it's just no guts, no glory on your part."

"Tiff," I plead, knowing she's dared me and how hard it is to turn a dare down, "he's our boss. Or Miranda's boss, which means if I make an ass of myself, she's going to chew it right off before the end of the day. And this is bordering dangerously close to rule number two—no sex dares."

Tiffany isn't swayed, though, and she crosses her arms over her chest. "I'm not daring you to fuck him over the desk. I'm merely strongly suggesting that you talk to the man. Face to face, eye to eye. I double dare you to go tell Colton Wolfe your name and that you think he's sex in a suit."

A double dare. Fuck. I can't. I can't. It's stupid, though her words paint a rather sexy picture of the two of us. Still . . .

He walks by, my heart pounding, and before I know it, my mouth's open. "Good morning, Mr. Wolfe! Nice suit!"

I try to keep my voice casual, not giving in to Tiff's suggested words because I'm a daredevil, but I'm also not looking to get fired for sexual harassment by telling him the filthy thoughts really running through my mind when I see him.

See? I have boundaries. They're just really far and wide.

My cheeks are burning and my gut's churning. I expect him to turn and look at me. To say something, anything.

But he just grunts and keeps on his way as if I don't even exist.

"Seriously?" Tiffany asks as Colton disappears into the executive elevator. "Nice suit? I am so disappointed in you."

Okay, so maybe that dare doesn't count as done. But even in the failure, my heart's soaring and I get that fizzy feeling, so it's not a total loss.

"THERE HE GOES AGAIN."

I don't even say anything, knowing Tiffany's going to get me in trouble if I even acknowledge her.

She's already dared me to eat a double chocolate orgasm

donut from the shop next to Starbucks this morning. Well, that wasn't the dare, exactly. It was more to fake the orgasm the donut incited, right there, *When Harry Met Sally* style in the donut store.

Dare done.

Embarrassingly so, and with giggles, but done. And the donut was really good, so I'd tipped the smiling lady at the counter an extra couple of bucks for putting up with our craziness as I bought a dozen to share with the people at work. Billy and Ricky had eaten three each, and Dad had declined with a pat of his flat belly. Even Miranda had eaten one with a groan of thanks.

But even as I know I should ignore Tiff, I look up and see Colton crossing the lobby with a couple of the other high up executives in the company.

I know their names, have probably had dinner with them at some point when I was younger. But much as they now overlook me as 'the help', I can't tell you more than their names and positions on the organizational chart. I curse my younger, clueless self for not taking better mental notes of who liked opera, who preferred chardonnay over whiskey, and what role everyone who sat at Dad's table played at Fox. I can almost hear Dad whispering about the 'wasted opportunity', but I shush him with a blink.

Because mostly, my eyes are focused on Colton.

Today's suit is even sexier than yesterday's, in my opinion, the navy-blue matching well with the deep blue of his eyes, and I swallow despite myself.

And it's been that way for years, ever since I started at Fox. Just when I think my poor ego and libido can't take another upgrade to my fantasies, he takes it up another few notches.

Still, he's never even looked my way. "Yeah."

"Think he'll say something to you today?" Tiffany asks me, hope springing eternal. "I mean, after being such a big, throbbing dick and ignoring you?"

And now I'm thinking about throbbing dicks and reminding myself that I decided I needed a lay with an actual heartbeat.

Colton's got a heartbeat. I bet he's got a big, pounding . . . heartbeat.

"Ms. Carter?" a decidedly British voice says. Honey over ice is what he sounds like, I decide dreamily before realizing he actually spoke. Though it's not to me, unfortunately.

Tiffany and I look up in shock, realizing Colton's stopped right in front of our desk. Miranda, who's been looking through the visitor sign-in log, looks up in surprise. "Yes, Mr. Wolfe?"

"A moment, please," he says, leading Miranda over to a cutout near the elevators. He pushes the button, letting her know this will be a quick conversation, and then begins questioning her fiercely. Even though he's trying to follow the classic leadership rule of *praise in public, chew ass in private,* a trick of the lobby's acoustics brings his voice to us.

"What was the purpose of sending that outbound shipping report to my office?" Colton asks, all honey gone and pure ice in his tone. "What would I care how many packages are sent out?"

I remember that report. I took it upstairs myself . . . on Miranda's orders.

"You said that you wanted an overview of the shipping practices, sir, during our last meeting, and—"

"And what you sent was a load of spreadsheets and figures," Colton growls. "I don't need data to analyze myself. I expected you to do the analysis and send a single-page summary as we discussed. I need bottom-line figures of shipping expenses by department, and if you can conceive of a way to cut costs, please feel free to include that in your breakdown."

"I . . . I apologize, sir," Miranda says. "I thought—"

"By the end of the day, Ms. Carter."

The elevator dings and opens, and Colton disappears inside, leaving Miranda standing there with her head bowed.

As the doors close, I see that Colton already has his nose buried in his phone once again. Miranda turns around, her face tight with anger and maybe a little embarrassment from her fresh ass reaming.

"Are you two still wasting time?"

Her question catches me by surprise. After all, I was just the delivery girl, not the report writer. But she's lashing out at the closest targets . . . us.

I stand, stumbling as my left high heel slips on the carpet and my ass bumps against the long desk Tiffany and I share, but I hold on to the stack of papers in my hands. "Miranda, I was just taking these—"

Miranda has zero interest in listening. "Girls, the FedEx man will be here soon. You keep him waiting, and I'll show you what Fed Up means."

She walks off, and behind her back, Tiffany scowls at her before rearranging her face into her usual professional soft smile. "At least he stopped by and spoke. He had to have seen you this time. He was right in front of you!"

"Well, if he did, he was unimpressed. No professing his undying love and questioning where I've been his whole life." I throw my forearm up to my brow like I'm a Victorian-era debutante about to faint. "Poor me, whatever shall I do?"

Tiffany's eyes get wide, and I know she's already coming up with ideas.

"Rhetorical question, little missy." I point a finger at her and then the stack of boxes visible through the open door of the mailroom. "Get to work or I'll give you a dare with Arnold." The threat holds weight because our FedEx driver is downright mean and always in a hurry. We learned to never delay him the hard way when he left our packages over a long holiday weekend without a second thought, even though our pickup time was still thirty minutes away. After that fiasco, we started calling him Arnold the Asshole.

But it works, because now we're always ready at least an hour before he's scheduled to appear.

We work the day away, Arnold comes and goes with all the boxes, and I give a tour to two cute little old ladies who want to talk about the architect who designed the building. The phone rings non-stop and I make about a thousand copies of some annual report for the upcoming shareholders' meeting.

Late in the day, Miranda finally makes an appearance. I'm pretty sure she skipped lunch because she's been holed up in her office all day, licking her wounds.

"Elle, can you take this upstairs, please? It's very important." She doesn't say it's the summary Colton demanded, but we all know it is. "I've got to go because my daughter gets out of volleyball practice at five thirty sharp." She glances at the huge wall of clocks in the lobby foyer that highlight six different major time zones over the globe.

Miranda's not all bad. I can see that in the way she prioritizes her kids, just like Dad did for me. I still don't think she'd be a good fit for him, though. He's done his time raising kids, and I was not an easy child. He deserves someone past that stage, I think, someone he can travel with at the drop of a hat, sip wine with, and enjoy the finer things mid-life can offer.

I take the report, a single sheet of paper. I turn to grab a file folder and slip it inside, letting Miranda know that I recognize the importance this paper holds for her. "Sure thing, Miranda. Hope Isabella's practice goes well. Have a nice night."

She nods her head, a grateful smile on her face. A moment later, she's got her purse on her shoulder and is booking it for the doors.

Most people leave around five, though it's not a strict eight-to-five workplace. Tiffany and I usually work until six to make sure any last mailings hit the post office and to be backup if any executives need clerical help after their own assistants leave.

The last hour of our day is usually easy-peasy with less phones, less people, and less work. Which means we can get into more trouble, but not today.

"I'm going to run this up to Mr. Wolfe's office. Be back in a second," I say. I'm going for a no-big-deal tone, but inside, my belly's flip-flopping in excitement.

When I delivered the report before, the one that got Miranda in trouble, it'd been to Mr. Wolfe's assistant. Now, with it being just a smidgen after five, there's a chance she'll be gone for the day and I'll get a peek inside his actual office.

I wonder what it looks like? Sleek and modern like the building? Traditional and dark like an English pub? Or somewhere in between?

The thought of finding out thrills me.

Or maybe the assistant's gone and he's in his office, and he calls out to me to bring him the report. And he lays eyes on me and falls hopelessly in love—or lust, I'm not picky—as soon as he sees me.

"Not so fast," Tiffany says sharply. "This is your chance, a once-in-a-lifetime shot. You need to take advantage of this."

I quirk a perfectly sculpted brow her way. "Advantage of what?" I question like I wasn't just thinking that I might learn something about Colton by seeing his office. And definitely not like I was fantasizing about him swiping all the contents of his desk onto the floor in a mad rush to make room for me to stretch out so he can take me.

"Okay, here's the deal. If Colton is there, I dare you to actually talk to him, flirt for real, make it obvious and apparent that you are thirsty as fuck for his dick. Sit on his lap or something," she says, thankfully laughing because I'm definitely not doing that. "If he's not . . ."

She hums, tapping a burgundy-tipped finger to her lip, and I wonder when she got her nails done because we usually go together. But then I remember her saying she had to get away from Ace over the weekend and figure she must've gone then.

"If he's not there, I dare you . . . to leave a mark," she says finally.

My brows knit together. "Huh? Leave a mark? What does that mean?"

She nods like a bobblehead, her bun threatening to topple off her head. "Dealer's choice, but the reward is congruent with the risk." She steeples her fingers like a maniacal villain, the architect to my fun. "Leave your panties on his desk or in his chair? I'll buy drinks all weekend and brunch on Sunday, plus get your next mani-pedi. Ass print on the desk? Drinks on Friday. Selfie in his chair? One drink. Or go evil. Move everything one inch to the left, and I'll give you a mani-pedi for that if you can pull it off. Put a mustache on the fancy self-portrait he's got on his wall. That's worth a drink. Or come up with your own idea. I can't wait to see what you do!"

Her excitement is contagious, alarmingly so.

"How do you know he has a self-portrait on the wall?" I ask, a good dose of jealousy already licking through my veins.

Tiffany smirks. "I don't, but I'm thinking it's a damn good guess. You in?"

She holds out her hand.

I know she's serious, but still this isn't a silly dare. This could cost me my job.

I can feel my heart speeding up. Anticipation and excitement, danger and risk are playing against sanity and brains.

I already know which one is going to win, so I shake her hand.

CHAPTER 3

COLTON

*T*he canyon stretches out before me, the morning sun casting the oak trees and grasses in a soft golden glow that ironically reminds me of home. It makes no sense. The family estate is in a part of England that is much, much greener than the vista outside my office . . . but the connection's still there.

Maybe it's the smell?

On mornings like this, the dew just starts to evaporate off the oak leaves right when I take my morning tea break on the balcony outside my office. It carries with it a scent that reminds me of home, with its thickets of oak so dense that you couldn't walk through them without wearing trousers and a long-sleeved shirt.

I only have a moment to gulp my tea down with the busy day ahead, and I should be focusing on this afternoon's important meeting. But somehow, my presentation isn't what's running through my head as I stare unseeingly across the expanse of green.

"Bloody hell, Colton," Father growls, looking me up and down. "Out on the town, and you get yourself completely arseholed in front of the paps. Just how long do you plan on this gallivanting, anyhow?" He holds up the sleazy tabloid with my face plastered across it. It's page twenty-two, not like it's the cover, but that makes no difference to Edwin Wolfe.

"It wasn't like that," I protest, keeping my back ramrod straight.

Slouching in front of Edwin Wolfe is something I learned not to do at a very young age. "I didn't even finish the pint!"

"You were photographed in a pub!" Father shouts, a vein in his fore-head bulging grotesquely.

And that's the crux of it. It's not that I was there, it's not that I was drinking. It's that I was photographed doing so. Image is everything, after all. At least to Father.

"Edwin!" Mother protests, and for a shining moment I think she'll be on my side. A voice of reason in the fray. I should know better by now. "Don't let Colton stress you out, dear. Your heart, you know."

There's nothing wrong with my dad's heart. He's healthy and robust, definitely enough to give me what for. But our shouting stresses Mother, though she'd never admit it.

She turns to glare at me, disappointment written in the tremble of her lips. "Why can't you just do as expected? Like Eddie?"

Ah, yes, my brother. Edwin Wolfe the Third, or Eddie, as he chooses to be called. As if that's a proper English name. But he can do no wrong in our parents' eyes. The good son, the obedient son . . .

The two-faced bastard who got me into my most recent cock-up because I was at the pub to get his knackered ass out at the bartender's behest. Just my luck that he'd been taking a piss when the pap came through.

"Very well, Mary," Father says, tossing back the remainder of his scotch and setting the empty tumbler on the blotter of his desk. "Colton, I don't know what I'm going to do with you just yet . . . but I cannot let you besmirch the Wolfe name any longer, boy."

The dismissive nickname rattles me out of my dark memories as it sends a bitter heat through my heart. I know I wasn't perfect, but I was hardly the hellion that my parents made me out to be, no more than Eddie was the saint they painted him as.

Still, I knew when it was time to go, and go I did. I jumped over the pond to make my name and my own fortune, intent on returning home triumphant to toss my success right in Dad's smug face.

Today is a large step in that victory and what I should be focusing on. Not the past, but the future and the opportunities it holds.

"Sir?"

As I leave the freshness of the morning outside for my air-conditioned office, I turn to see my secretary, Helen, standing in the doorway. A professional and very competent woman, I honestly couldn't imagine the business success I've had here in the States without her assistance. American business etiquette can be very . . . confusing. Though I occasionally use the slight cultural differences to my advantage. My father might have been a difficult man to grow up under, but if there's one thing he taught me, it's how to use power to benefit myself.

"Yes, Helen?"

"It's time for the meeting." She's holding out a stack of bound presentation files, the framework for my pitch to the board.

"Thank you, Helen. Wish me luck." I don't need luck. Fortune favors hard work and preparation, but the American saying amuses me.

I SIT DOWN IN THE BOARDROOM FOR OUR WEEKLY MEETING. I HAVE A flash of Father's face talking down to me. Once, it hurt me deeply. Now, I use it.

It fuels me, motivates me for what I'm about to do, and in my lap my fist clenches. I've been banging away at my computer for weeks on this seed of an idea.

I know I can do it.

I'll see you soon, Father.

Up at the front of the room, Daniel Stryker, who all but thinks he's going to be the new HQ2 Regional President, is pitching his idea.

"So just as HQ1 is strategically positioned for the best coverage of the West Coast, setting up HQ2 in my proposed site allows us better connections throughout the East Coast and even into Europe with the localized shipping hub. And with the current business friendly administration in the State House, I just can't see why we'd pass up *striking* when the iron's hot, so to speak."

His last little joke, a not-particularly-clever dad joke twist on his last name, earns a chuckle, and around the table, there's polite applause as Daniel tries not to look too smug. He's failing spectacularly at it, might as well be waving like the bloody queen as he sits back down.

At the head of the table, Allan Fox, Chairman and CEO of the company, beams. "Very interesting, indeed. Thank you, Daniel."

I can read the room and know that this decision is already half-made before I even begin my presentation. But I believe in what I'm proposing, for more reasons than I'll discuss today. Still, it's time for me to shine.

Allan meets my eyes, and I swear there's the smallest hint of pity there, but he perseveres. "Colton, I believe you're up next."

I stand up, reaching into my pocket and pulling out the thumb drive I've copied my presentation to before slipping it into the USB slot on the laptop connected to the screen behind me. The bound packets Helen worked so hard to put together work their way around the table simultaneously, and as my fellow board members open the cover and see the first notes of my plan, in front of them and behind me, a murmur begins to work its way through the room.

"Gentlemen, if I may?" I ask, lifting an eyebrow and hushing the room. Allan nods, and I begin. "The facts are in. Despite the comfort and ease of staying local, the world is more interconnected than ever. And while the Internet has allowed us to shrink the world exponentially from what it used to be, we need to grow beyond the comfort of American backyards. We are a global organization, and acting as such will only serve to grow our market share. But to effectively do so, we need to look at the big picture. We need a more local presence overseas."

I click to the first slide, which is a simple listing of time zones. "Case in point. No offense, you all work hard, but it's sometimes damned difficult to try and work with a European customer when they're just finishing up their day as we're finishing our morning coffee . . . or tea."

My self-referencing joke earns a small smirk from Allan, who nods. I click to the next slide, running through my ideas quickly, how an international HQ2 would give Fox better impact in foreign markets, how it'll connect us to our customers better, make us more efficient, and more.

"And perhaps I'm being a bit biased here, but I believe that the London area would position us best for this opportunity," I continue. "With the ability to draw on the Commonwealth's business connections . . . well, that's fifty-three nations and roughly two and a half billion potential customers we just plugged into."

The last sentence drops, and silence reigns over the entire boardroom.

"Colton, that's a remarkable idea, but how many of these countries are financially relevant to our pursuits?" Jim Roberts, one of the board members who's just slightly younger than Jesus, asks. Hence his less than politically polite terminology.

"Jim, they all have something to offer," I promise him. "Either as customers or as potential suppliers of materials, goods, or even information. We already ship approximately twenty-five percent of our large-scale sales to our European customers, and if we had a local presence, that could be exponentially larger. The key is a London HQ2. And if we pass them up, we're giving up, well . . . a lot of money."

And now I'm speaking their language. Nerves and change are one thing, a hold back to progress. But bottom-line financials can overcome a lot of resistance. The board members' faces look significantly more interested now.

Daniel, who's been quiet this whole time, speaks up. "And just how do you know that we can find a headquarters in London that won't break the bank? It's not exactly a city known for inexpensive real estate."

I flash him a respectful smile, one brow jumping up before I school myself. Daniel is a worthy adversary in this situation, both of us wanting what's best for both Fox and ourselves.

"To an outsider, maybe. I do have rather useful resources there, however. I even have a couple of locations in mind that would be more than suitable for Fox HQ2." It's as much as I'm willing to divulge just yet, though I can see the interest flare in Daniel's eyes. He'd love to scrutinize the sites I have in mind, no doubt about that.

"And I assume you'd want to be the president of this venture?" Allan ventures.

I chuckle lightly, looking him in the eye. "Well, I would certainly toss my hat in the ring on that. At least I can properly say that I know how to use a roundabout. Though I'm sure you'd make the decision based on many factors." It's a kindness of formality because we all know I'd be the best fit for a leadership position in London.

There are murmurs around the room and conversation quickly breaks out. "I know that globalization wasn't exactly what you'd expected with this HQ2 proposal. But this is an idea we should consider carefully, along with the remaining locations. As Daniel pointed out, London can be expensive, and we don't want to lose our bollocks in a bad deal."

I lean forward, placing my hands on the table and meeting each pair of eyes around the table. "This has the potential to revolutionize Fox Industries, so I challenge us all to think big, think toward the future, and be brave."

Allan nods. "I think that's a fair request, Colton. Okay then, that's the last of our location proposals, but I move that we delay the final vote on the HQ2 site until we have some time to do further research. Colton, I'd like the exact figures on our shipping and customer base in the UK specifically and then Europe at large."

I dip my chin in recognition, wishing I'd had the exact figures and not an approximation for this initial presentation. Internally, I curse the reams of spreadsheet figures Miranda brought me, useless drivel that I couldn't sort through in time for the meeting today.

But his desire for the numbers to crunch, and his openness to even the idea of going abroad, is greater than I could've hoped for.

When the meeting's over, I feel more secure than ever as I listen to the post-meeting chatter and head out into the hallway.

"Colton!"

I pause, turning around to see Daniel just emerging from the boardroom, a tight smile on his face. He offers his hand, though, shaking mine politely. "Daniel . . . nice presentation in there."

Not that I think he really cares about meaningless compliments, especially from me, but a gentleman's always polite in the face of his rivals.

"Thanks. You too," Daniel, who's always a cool customer, says. "Actually, I wanted to congratulate you. That was impactful and passionate, if not unforeseen." There's a small dig in the words, but it's almost like he's furious with himself for not predicting my play.

"I do believe what I said is the best path forward."

"I can tell," Daniel says, his smile not fading at all. "Not that I'm going to back off on my plan, but I do wish you good luck."

He manages to make 'good luck' sound like a curse. "Nothing's better than having two good plans to choose from."

Daniel walks down to his office, and as he gives me his back, I can tell that despite his nice words, the man's dangerous. A predator. A wolf, just like me.

But he's right. *When* I win, it's going to be all the sweeter to have taken down a man as good as Daniel and not win by default.

Walking toward my office, I can't help but notice Ricky and Billy, two of Daniel's cousins or relations or whatever who work in building security, giving me some tough looks.

How transparent can those two be? They wear building security uniforms, but the nepotism of that is abhorrent because they're Daniel Stryker's errand boys through and through. They might wander the whole building, but everyone knows where their priorities lie. Which is what makes them dangerous. They're not the brightest, but they're loyal to a fault.

It's not the dog that you should watch but the dog keeper.

And I can read between the lines. Regardless of how professional Daniel might talk or act, this is a fight where only one of us is going to emerge the victor.

Getting back to my office, Helen's waiting for me, her purse already over her shoulder as it's time for her to head home for the evening. "Sir, unless there's anything else?"

I shake my head, stopping. "No. I'm going to stay late. Think I'll grab some coffee, but I'll get it myself."

"Coffee?" Helen asks, surprised. "Last time you did that, you gave me a ten-minute lecture on how it can't compare to a 'proper cuppa tea'."

"It doesn't, but I need the caffeine. Long night ahead. Please go home and enjoy your evening because we'll have some work to do tomorrow."

She smiles, looking excited, and though I don't tell her how the meeting went, I know she can read me well enough to know that I'm happy with the outcome.

I escort her to the elevator and see her out for the evening as I head to the executive-level breakroom. It's not my usual domain as Helen would typically get anything I need, but I can figure out the basics of the fancy machine.

A few minutes later, I have a cup of bitter bean brew that I've sweetened with a ridiculous amount of cream and sugar. It might as well be melted coffee ice cream in a mug, but the combination will hopefully serve me while I work.

I sip at the disgustingly sweet concoction as I walk down the hall back toward my office. I pause in my outer office, though. Helen is gone, her desk neat and tidy, but my door is cracked open. She would never leave my office unattended without closing the door.

From inside, I hear a murmuring voice. A feminine voice, and was that . . .

A giggle?

CHAPTER 4

ELLE

*I*t's crazy. It's stupid, and I know better.

But sure enough, that buzz is rushing through me. Anticipation, excitement, restlessness. And the whole elevator ride, I'm plotting. *Make my mark,* Tiffany said. But how?

That's the million-dollar question.

I could do something silly and annoying, like jam his photocopy machine?

Or leave him a note?

Hey, Mr. Sexy Ass Wolfe, you ignored my trying to hit on you so I'm going bold and brazen. Call me sometime. Anytime.

Or maybe he'll be in his office and I can accidentally knock something off his desk and try the swaying ass routine again? It's never failed me before, and I refuse to believe the ass I work so hard for has lost its powers of flirtation.

I eye the camera in the corner of the elevator, wondering if I could get in a few extra squats between the ground floor and the fifth. Deciding that it'd be weird if security is watching, I clench my pelvic muscles and butt instead. Nobody even has to know when you're doing Kegels. But all that serves to do is rush blood to my core, something I need no help with when the possibility of seeing Colton looms.

I have to corral an eye roll at how absurd this all sounds.

I mean, what chance does a nobody like me have with a hotshot like Colton?

He's sex in a suit, cocky arrogance in a blue Lotus as he pulls into the parking lot each day, and he's infuriatingly unaffected by me. Why the hell is that so sexy? It shouldn't be. Asshole douche is so *not* my type.

But somehow, Colton Wolfe is.

Or I imagine him to be.

But who does something like this? Even on a dare, this is my job we're talking about.

Tiffany's voice echoes in my ear, the devil on my shoulder doing her job as my dealer of adrenalin and unexpected thrills.

"Don't look nervous! You live for this shit. Walk right up there and tell that boy you think he is hotter than Carolina Reaper wing sauce and you want his bangers and mash." She licks her fingers like she's eating some especially messy wings, or maybe mashed potatoes. I'm not sure which is more worrisome.

"Ooh, I can't wait to hear about what you do. Pictures or it didn't happen. I trust you, but I need proof. Especially if you see his banger."

Hearing the bell ding on the elevator, my blood becomes alive, tingling and pounding as it rushes through my ears.

The executive floor is quiet and deserted, surprisingly so for just after five o'clock. *So much for the hard-working executives*, I think wryly.

I hear a shuffle on the plush carpet and look down the empty hallway.

Oh shit, there's Dad!

Before I can even decide to do so, I duck into a doorway and hide. I don't even know why. It's not like I'm doing anything wrong. I'm delivering a file, just like my boss instructed me to do. But with all the weird thoughts running through my head, I reverted to the teenager who was constantly trying to pull one over on Dad.

I press a hand to my chest, feeling my heart race and my breath coming too fast.

From afar, I hear Dad say, "C'mon, Ricky! We've got five miles to get through before dinner."

Dad's a runner, much to Ricky's not-delight. Ricky's more linebacker than pacer, but he makes do, and according to his own brags, he's getting better at keeping up with Dad.

Their footsteps get further away, and I chance a peek out of my hidey-hole. They're heading down the stairs, probably as a warm-up. Tiffany will be overjoyed because the stairwell pops out into the ground floor lobby. I can hear her moaning and groaning about how hot Dad's ass is already, which makes me dread the ride home.

Once I'm in the clear, I walk quickly into Colton's office.

The outer office is empty, a single nice but pretty standard desk standing like a sentry to the left of his door, everything neatly in its place.

"Damn, his secretary must be a former drill sergeant," I murmur as I look at the immaculate desk. The nameplate is polished gold and engraved in a fancy script. *Helen Riggs*.

With no one here to stop me, there's no turning back now. One, two . . .

The door opens with a soft click, and I step inside to reveal a beautiful office. Everything's classic, with three of the walls paneled in rich, dark wood, while the back wall's a floor to ceiling window overlooking the canyon. Brass trimmings and accents are everywhere. One section of the wall is a bookshelf, and every book is leather bound, perfectly aligned and immaculate.

And his desk . . . my God, you could throw a dinner party on Colton's desk and still have room for a huge platter of turkey in the middle. Even his chairs are exquisite, smelling of fine leather and gleaming arrogantly in the sunlight from the oil rubbed into each and every square inch of the material. On one corner is a rather modest-sized trophy, with a wide bowl that almost looks like a candy dish except for the wooden base and brass plate underneath. Moving closer, I can read the inscription. *All-Britain University Boxing Champion, 78 kg*.

Colton Wolfe really is a badass.

I can't help myself. I pick up the trophy, hoisting it over my head like I just won a boxing match myself.

Fuck, this thing's heavy.

I set it back down with a glance behind me. Still nobody around.

I should set the file folder down and get out of here, but I don't. Instead, I walk behind the desk and sit in the luxurious chair, pretending something quite different for a moment.

After setting the file on the center of the desk, I lean back in the chair, feeling it tilt supportively under my weight. After a brief moment, I go even further, putting my heeled feet up on Colton's desk.

I'm pushing it already. I know it, but fuck, it feels good. So much danger feels so good. I feel alive.

A frame on the desk catches my eye, and I sit upright to get a better look. It's a young girl, probably a teenager, and for a moment, I wonder if I somehow missed that Colton has a daughter. I search my brain for what I do know about him, which is admittedly a lot for someone who's never so much as looked at me.

I'm not ashamed of it. Google and I have had more than one late night search on the name Colton Wolfe. Sometimes to read what public information is out there, which is surprisingly little, and sometimes for a little photographic inspiration for my solo hands-on maneuvers.

But I've never read about a daughter.

I make a mental note to add that to my search this evening, because there will definitely be some action after sitting in his seat, smelling the combination of his cologne and leather, and imagining him bending me over his desk.

I look around the room, seeing a brass plate on one wall, and I feel drawn to it. I walk across the thick carpet, my footsteps silent. Reaching out, I see it's a hidden latch and pull it open to reveal a high-tech information center.

"Whoa."

Miranda would have a shitfit for a setup like this in our office. We've got Big Bertha, and she's a hell of a copy machine, but Colton's private setup is sleek and obviously top-notch technology.

A devious thought comes to mind, courtesy of my own waywardness, but I mentally blame it on Tiffany.

I could copy my ass. And leave a rather direct image of what Colton's missing on his desk. Anonymously, of course.

I'm not stupid. Well, at least not stupid enough to leave my name and number, as Tiffany suggested.

But the idea is gaining steam. One side of my brain's trying vehemently to talk myself out of it, while the other side cheers loudly about what a great idea it is.

One extra copy for Tiffany would be all the proof I'd need. And Colton would never know who it was.

It's very Cinderella-esque. Though my ass is better than any old glass slipper.

I eye the machine, which looks delicate, considering I'm thinking of sitting on it. With a thrill, I realize I'm wearing pretty scandalous underwear too. As if copying my ass isn't scandalous enough already.

I'm getting fired. This is stupid . . . and crazy . . . and a myriad of other adjectives that all end the same way. I'm so getting fired.

But I hike my skirt up anyway, giggling as I stand on my tiptoes and just barely wedge myself into the gap created by the lid of the machine and the wall.

I fumble for the buttons, pressing twice so that I get one for Colton and one as proof for Tiffany. Then, before I can second guess myself, I hit the big green button.

To my right, paper spits out remarkably fast. "Aaaand, that's my ass and a fair amount of hoo-ha too."

I consider grabbing the papers and making a run for it. I can still pretend this never happened.

But fate conspires against me. Or maybe there's some karmic bad luck to being a crazy bitch because the machine starts spitting out copies well beyond the two I requested.

"Oh, shit!" I exclaim. "No!"

But fate is a fickle bitch with an odd sense of humor because a slight breeze comes in through the window I hadn't even realized was open, blowing the stack of copies all over the room.

"Oh, my God! Oh, my God!" I mutter, trying to snatch them all. Out of the air, off the floor, and even off the desk, where I accidentally knock the picture of Colton's maybe-daughter to the floor.

I don't even take the time to wiggle my skirt back down because being ass in the wind is the least of my problems as the machine continues to spit out copies. I press madly on the buttons and even reach behind it to shut it off, praying that if I can just cut the power, the copies will stop coming.

It's then that I hear it.

With my naked ass up in the air as I bend over the copy machine that's still spitting out the obscene image of my most private parts that wallpaper the fancy room of my boss.

"What the bloody hell are you doing?"

I freeze, stopping my wiggling reach for the off button at the voice from behind me. The very deep, sexy, *British* voice.

Looking over my shoulder toward the door, I go pale.

"Well?" Colton demands.

His bark breaks my paralysis, and I hop off the machine. Unfortunately, my lack of grace catches up to me once again, and I stumble over my own feet. I try to catch myself, but my legs are as useless as a newborn colt's and I tumble to the ground in a half-naked heap.

Suddenly, there's a pissed off handsome face standing over me.

How the fuck does he look so hot when he's angry?

It's my last semi-pleasant thought before another screams loudly through my mind . . .

I'm getting fired.

And then . . .

Dad's going to be so pissed at me.

CHAPTER 5

COLTON

*T*he sight before me would be amusing, and perhaps a part of me is chuckling inside, if it wasn't so utterly brazen . . . and bizarre.

I'm nearly a hair's breadth from calling on security to have this woman promptly hauled off, but the ridiculous antics intrigue me enough to find out what prompted this outrageous venture.

Admittedly, her delectable ass might play a part in that decision to wait as well, I think as I pick up one of the dozens of copies of her round ass split down the middle by a shadow that appears to be a lace thong.

I shut the door behind me, closing us both into my private space. A threat to us both, but I'm decidedly in charge here.

"Holy shit," the blonde whispers from the floor, her legs dangerously askew.

I silently walk over and shut off the copy machine, and the whirring noise quiets, tragically ending the additions to the stack of copies in the tray.

I continue my trek, first closing the window and then sitting at my desk. I sip at my too-sweet coffee as if I haven't a care in the world. "Clean up your mess."

The order is cold, and I swear I detect the slightest shiver through the woman's body. I don't dare get close enough to help her up, knowing that would be a fool's errand and a sure-fire way to 'have your hand caught in the cookie jar'. An American phrasing I find rather amusing.

She huffs haughtily as she flips over, much like a tortoise who's stuck on its back. On all fours, it almost seems as though she sways her bare ass at me in one last attempt at . . . whatever game it is she's playing.

Seduction? If so, she is woefully clumsy and dependent on her rather pleasing looks. Or perhaps she has been sent to trap me in an unseemly situation.

Sabotage? Though she wasn't going through my desk or personal files as a corporate spy would do. I glance at the black screen of my computer.

Maybe there's another angle I haven't deduced yet. Best to stay wary.

I watch carefully as she stands, pointedly wiggling her skirt over her ass as she glares at me as though this whole thing is my fault. She scrambles around the room, picking up the copies.

Mindlessly, she stacks them neatly with every few additions, automatically facing them the same direction and aligning the edges as though they're significant. The unintentional action tells me something important about her. An attention to detail her current predicament contradicts.

As she works, she mutters to herself. "So fucking stupid, Elle. You're going to get fired, and for what?" She throws her voice high, obviously mimicking someone. "Make your mark." In her own sultry voice, she sneers, "Whatever the hell that means."

Her conversation of one only intrigues me more.

Having collected all the copies, save the one in my hand, she faces away from me, her back ramrod straight, and I know she's staring at the door and considering making a run for it.

With her not looking at me, I take the opportunity to glance from the copy I possess to the ass before me. Round, full globes that I could dent with my fingertips as I squeeze her, ones that would look quite lovely with a pink tint from a smack.

I clear my throat and my mind of inappropriate thoughts. "I could call security if you'd like. We have two officers on this floor at all times." I sound as if I couldn't care less. Truthfully, I'm much more interested in handling this . . . whatever this is . . . myself.

I notice her shoulders tense at the mention of security,

climbing a half-inch before she drops them heavily and turns around.

"No, sir. That won't be necessary. I apologize—"

I cut off her useless apology. "Sit," I say, gesturing to the chairs in front of my desk.

She freezes, and after a split second where I wait for her find her courage, I slam my hand on my desk, making everything bounce. The framed photo she reset on the corner falls facedown.

Her jump is a small victory. Her sitting down as requested is a larger one.

I peruse the photo in my hand like it's a work of art, letting her watch me visually critique her sexy buttocks.

She interrupts me, apologizing again, though this time I swear she's batting her lashes. "I'm so sorry, Mr. Wolfe. I got carried away. It won't happen again."

"Your name," I bark sharply, cutting her off.

"Elle Stryker," she says, just as sharp. She might as well be giving me her name, rank, and serial number.

My heart stops as the name rings a bell. I blink, noticing the faint resemblance. On the surface, they're nothing alike, him dark haired and her blonde, but there's something about the intelligence lurking in her blue eyes. "Stryker . . . Daniel is your father?"

"Yes," she answers automatically, but I can see the fear the admission causes.

But why fear? Because she's been captured being Daniel's insider, like his so-called bodyguards? Or fear that word of her inappropriateness will reach her father's ears? Or something else?

A hundred scenarios play through my head, one of which says that Daniel was in on this whole bizarre incident to cause some sort of scandal that'd weaken my position with the company and ruin my chances of heading HQ2.

It's pretty far-fetched, but the timing's tight. If Daniel's got a little core of familial operatives in the company . . .

Fury surges from my gut at the thought. Would he really stoop so low? I knew he was going to try to stop me somehow, but I thought he'd be honorable.

"Did Daniel put you up to this? Some off the wall attempt to try to smear me?" I demand. "Because if he did—"

"No!" Elle says bravely, raising her hand. She's scared, very scared, but in her voice, I hear honesty. She shakes her head vigorously. "He would never! And if he knew I'd done this . . . he'd kill me."

I open my lips to call her a liar but pause. She's convincing. Is she right? But why else would she be in my office, carousing like a half-naked tart after a night at the pub?

The sincerity in her body and in her face stays my words.

"Then why?" I ask.

She drops her gaze, her first true yield.

"Have you ever been dared to do something so crazy that you know you should say no, but there's a fire inside you begging you to do it even though you know it's ridiculous?" The words are a tumble of syllables across her pursed lips.

I arch an eyebrow, baffled, amused, and intrigued all at once. "A dare? So if someone were to dare you to jump off my balcony into the canyon behind us, Miss Stryker, would you?" I ask.

Normally, I'd be certain I knew the answer to such a ridiculous question. With this woman, I'm not at all sure that she wouldn't find a way to do it.

"No," Elle says quietly, her stock rising in my eyes by the word. Playful? Yes. Prone to foolishness? Obviously. But at least she knows how to comport herself when necessary. "Unless you're talking about base jumping, because then, I might do it. Though I'm scared of heights." She shrugs like that would mean nothing if she were actually dared.

And her stock skyrockets.

Intelligence and guts, with a side of crazy and planned maneuverings.

Fascinating. And terrifying if this is Daniel's daughter.

She's good, which means he's even better.

"So assuming I believe you, tell me about this dare," I prompt. I lean back in my chair and close my eyes as if she's going to tell me a bedtime story, but truthfully, I want to focus on her voice. See if there are any wavers in the lies or falters in the tale.

"My friend, Tiffany, and I work downstairs. We dare each other to do silly things to keep life interesting. Silly stuff, nothing unprofessional on the clock, and weird stuff only in our free time. It's just a thing we've always done. Well, she dared me to talk to you a few times because you're . . . well, you."

She pauses, and I crack one eye open to find her looking me up and down. Curious. I note the thick swallow and slight up tilt of her lips as I close my eyes again, waiting for her to resume.

When she stays quiet, I open both eyes.

"So instead of speaking to me, you wallpaper my office with . . ."

I pick up the paper again, and she snarls, "I did speak to you. 'Good morning, sir,' and I get a grunt. 'Nice suit,' and not so much as a thank you, and I dropped an entire file in front of you once and you virtually stepped over me on your way to the elevator." It's an accusation.

How could I have never noticed her? While I admit I'm not much of a morning person, have I really been so wrapped up in my own affairs that I've just walked by without seeing Elle? How could I never notice this stunningly beautiful creature?

I'm not unaware of my appeal and am no stranger to women chasing me for my looks or my money.

But the timing is suspect, so very underhandedly dubious.

"So with my unintentional ignorance of your interest, you and your friend decided the next logical step was . . . this?" I flash the image of her own ass her way before turning it back to my view.

"She dared me to 'make my mark' in a way of my choosing. Her ideas were crazy." Her bottom lip disappears behind her teeth for a flash.

"*Hers* were crazy? Do tell," I say, interested in what could be construed as crazier than this high-school antic.

With a sigh, Elle ticks off on her hands. "Leave my panties on your desk, leave an ass print on the wood, move everything one inch, and my favorite was drawing a mustache on the self-portrait she was sure you have, but since there wasn't one, I had to improvise. It didn't seem right to draw on that picture."

She points at the picture of a frizzy-haired girl I keep on my desk, a reminder of why I do what I do. "It's my sister, Elizabeth . . . Lizzie. She's home in London with my family."

Elle's eyes brighten, and I wonder who she thought Lizzie was to me.

I'm starting to believe this crazy story she's concocted, but

I'm not stupid. Just because she might have one reason to do this doesn't mean she doesn't have *more* than one. Or maybe she's a better liar than she seems to be.

I eye her thoughtfully and she meets my gaze unflinchingly.

I turn away first, forcing myself to think of something other than her sexiness in order to calm my thoughts. I decide to stalk her, like the Wolfe I am, and maybe see if I can use this situation to my advantage. I rise from my chair, pacing about the room and feeling her eyes track my every movement. She thinks she's watching me, but I'm observing her just as closely.

"Your father is a powerful man," I say, keeping my voice clipped and level, a schoolmaster at lecture. "So why are you working on the ground floor when I'm sure he could get you a job elsewhere?"

"He offered me one," Elle answers immediately, more confident than before. "I turned him down. I don't want any favors."

There's something to her tone, a distaste, perhaps, and I wonder if she is as unappreciative of her father's nepotism as I am.

Perhaps we have that in common—a desire to set our own course and lead our own successes and failures.

"Why not work for another company then?"

Elle smiles serenely, as if she expected the question. "There's earning my way and then there's blind stupidity. Fox is the best, I'm the best, and here, I'll learn to be even better. It worked for my father and it'll work for me, and best of all, he'll have a front-row seat to see me succeed."

Good answer. And in that self-confident smile, I get the sense that there's something more behind her than a mere mischievous little wood sprite. And something else . . . something more with her father.

I put pieces of the puzzle together. Daniel and his daughter have a good relationship, one where he wants her close by, but she still feels the need to prove herself to him and be independent of his reach. She's a bit wild and crazy but smart and methodical.

I grin, circling her, and I can sense her anxiety. Her breath catches, and her breasts, which have been lifting up and down in hypnotic, wave-like motions, stop, pressing out even more against her white blouse.

I swear . . . bugger me, but I think her nipples are hard right now. At the thought, my cock twitches. Bloody hell, I need to get laid. And quit staring at the photocopies of her ass.

It's time to stop this . . . for now. I need a bit of distance to decide how best to proceed here.

"You may leave, Miss Stryker. You'll hear from me soon."

Elle gets up to leave but pauses at the door, looking back at me with narrowed eyes. "What are you going to do?" Her suspicion is understandable, even admirable.

I lift an eyebrow. I've got so many options in front of me right now. I could fire her, but something is telling me not to. I could tell her father, but I don't want to do that either.

I could use this to my advantage.

"I don't know yet. You'll just have to wait and see."

SITTING DOWN BEHIND MY DESK, I PICK UP THE FINAL REMAINING copy of Elle's picture, looking at it but not truly seeing it even though it's gorgeous.

Even though the plain paper shows the generous curvy roundness of her sexy ass split by a swatch of lace, I see her eyes flashing with anger. I see her lips, plumped as she bit them, her nipples, hard against the cotton of her dress shirt, and her cheeks flushed in anger even as she's the one invading my private sanctuary.

I need to think strategically here, but every thought in my head is clouded. With a growl, I grab the paper and head to my private en suite. Locking the door behind me, I undo my belt and take my cock out. I'm rock hard, already resigned to the inevitability of what I'm about to do.

I grip myself firmly, angry at my own weakness. I grasp the photo, wrinkling the edges beneath my fingertips, and jack myself, up and down fast and hard as I picture her. Ass on my copier, bent over the same machine, sprawled out on the floor with her skirt shoved up around her waist, all tempting visions that tantalize me. I let my eyes trace the skinny strip of lace on the copy paper, wishing I could see just a bit more.

It doesn't take me long, less than a half dozen strokes to spurt long, thick ropes into the toilet as I grunt my release. I'm careful not to let a single droplet touch Elle's picture. I don't want it ruined.

Afterward, I wash my hands and return to my desk. I fold the picture up carefully, tucking it into my coat pocket.

With the edge off, I try to think through the unexpected happenings of today.

Daniel is going to come at this HQ2 fight with both barrels loaded like the strategic, battle-hardened business executive he is. He's bold, brash, and in your face. Rather like his daughter, I think. But where it is delightfully refreshing and intriguing in Elle, it's bothersome in Daniel when he's sitting on the opposite side of the table from me, the obstacle to my getting what I want.

While I'd considered that Daniel was using Elle as a means to get at me, if that's not the case, perhaps the better option is the reverse? To use Elle as leverage.

The question is how do I use that leverage? I could just expose her, drop a hand grenade on Daniel's day and reputation and secure the HQ2 project while he's picking up the pieces.

But that's not guaranteed, is rather unsportsmanlike in our professional competition of one-upmanship, and more importantly, it'd hurt Elle. I don't know why, exactly, but I don't want that.

In fact, I'd fancy seeing her again.

I mean, who wallpapers an executive's office with copies of their arse on a dare? It's wild, and I find myself intrigued, even wanting a little bit more of that.

Maybe there's a better way to leverage Elle Striker—for me, for her, and against Daniel.

CHAPTER 6

ELLE

Dear Universe,
      I am SO dead.
Signed,
Elle

I've always loved the bedtime story, *Little Red Riding Hood.* There's just something so dangerously exciting about the wolf pretending to be nice . . . before revealing he's anything but.

And that's exactly how I felt underneath Colton's gaze as he paced around the room, staring at me like I was a piece of fat, juicy steak. He was the Big Bad Wolfe, and I was Little Red Riding Hood, wondering if he was going to eat me up.

Or eat . . . something else. I couldn't stop looking at his mouth the whole time. I've never reacted that way to *any* man, but if he'd ordered me to prove it was me in those pictures, my clothes would have hit the floor before he could have said the 't' in skirt.

I'm not usually so wanton, am in fact rather discerning about who lies in my bed, metaphorically speaking, but Colton brings out some sex-hungry goddess in me. And I'm not entirely sure that's a good thing. Weakness, in any form, is not something I like to experience.

It was frightening, shivering in my seat, withering beneath his gaze, torn between desire and terror, the whole time literally counting the seconds until he exploded, screaming at me for daring to desecrate his office . . . before sending me home with a pink slip.

But he didn't.

Surprisingly, he was mostly calm, cool, and controlled . . . and oh, so sexy.

And I could've sworn when he looked at my ass on that paper, he got excited, his tailor-made dress pants looking extra tight in the front. But I'm not sure if that was just my imagination and wishful thinking.

Whatever the case, my need for adventure and thrills has finally landed me in hot water. Scalding, boiling hot, and I'm both the crazed stalker and the bunny in this ugly scenario.

What was I thinking?

You weren't, my traitorous brain answers.

For all the blissful buzz successfully completing a dare brings, the failure of one has never felt quite so acutely sharp.

The elevator, never the fastest of machines, seems to take even longer. When it finally dings and lets me out on the ground floor, Tiffany's already waiting at the doors, almost hopping back and forth in nervous excitement.

"Where have you been?" she whispers urgently. "It's been over thirty minutes since you went upstairs!"

"Let's go," I hiss, pushing her out the door and toward my car in the parking lot. I start Cammie up and gun it for the open road.

I glance in the rearview mirror, admitting to myself that I'm checking for Colton's blue Lotus. When the road behind us is empty, I quickly relay everything that happened, and Tiffany's jaw drops open further and further, first with delight and then horror.

"Close your mouth, Tiff, or you'll go catching flies. Or dicks," I say, tapping under her chin with my fingertips.

"Please say we're not fired. I *so* do not want to be slinging wings down at Hooters or something."

"Don't go dry cleaning those orange bootie shorts just yet," I reply, reminding Tiffany that between her freshman and sophomore years in college, she did 'sling wings' for money. "And I think *you're* safe, at least. I'm definitely not, though."

Tiff lets out a long, pent up breath before tugging on my arm. "Well, what happened then?"

Making the turn toward the highway, I shake my head. "I

don't know what happened. He grilled me for a few and then told me to leave. Said I'll have to wait and see?"

"Wait and see?" Tiff fumes as she roots around in her purse for her omnipresent emergency packet of peanut butter cheese crackers. She's a stress eater and always has a snack with her just in case the shit hits the fan, which it most definitely has. "What the hell does that mean?" she asks through a spray of orange crumbs.

Tiff offers me one of her crackers, a massive generosity on her part, so I take it, even though my stomach's too tied up in knots to really want food right now. "I don't know, but I don't like it. I think he's going to fire me, but I think he wants to fuck with my head some before he does. Honestly, I think I'm gonna be the one wearing orange shorts! Worse than that, though, Dad's gonna kill me!"

Tiffany stews for a second, her brain working through everything I've just told her as I take the exit for her apartment. "Okay, calm down, chica," Tiffany says, suddenly relaxing and waving away my worry. My hands tighten on the wheel in response, doing the opposite of what she says.

"I think this is actually a good sign. If he was going to fire you, he would've done so already. He would've called security and HR immediately and done it all right then, escorting you out in a blaze of shame and glory. That he didn't do that probably means that he's not going to. The question is . . . what is he going to do?"

Tiffany casually pops a peanut butter and cheese cracker sandwich in her mouth and munches loudly, swigging from her water bottle to make sure she doesn't have any orange flecks on her teeth. "He's a cocky, arrogant bastard who has you dead to rights. How's he going to use that?"

One does not disrespect Colton Wolfe like I did and get away with it, it appears.

Which means he's up to something, and it must be *worse* than getting fired. It just scares me what it could be, especially considering how interested he was in the fact that I'm Daniel Stryker's daughter.

I drop Tiffany off with a promise to let her know if anything happens to change things. As she goes inside, I hear her loud voice. "Ace, did you even move off the couch today?"

I cringe, thinking that she's got her own drama to deal with. Maybe she should give those orange shorts to Ace? I think I heard about a male version of Hooters once? Tallywackers, it was called, I think. Dad bods are all the rage, so maybe Ace could work there and do a little wing slinging of his own, far away from Tiffany's screeching.

THE NEXT DAY DAWNS BRIGHT AND SUNNY, THE ANTITHESIS OF MY mood. Sophie must've stayed away from my tossing and turning self, so at least I wake up without a hairball today. It's the only bright spot in my grumpiness.

Work brings coffee in quantities so massive that I'm running to pee every hour on the hour, which pisses Miranda off royally.

After lunch, she blows through and reminds Tiffany and me, "Back to work, girls." Like we weren't already busy, me with a copy job and Tiffany with the phone to her ear.

The afternoon drags out. Once the mailman comes by at two o'clock like he normally does and we prep the day's FedEx shipment for Arnold, there's precious little to do until five.

The boredom makes my nervousness even worse, because every time I hear the elevator ding or my phone beep with an internal call, I swear it's HR with a pink slip and a reminder to leave my parking lot access card on my desk when I go.

At about four o'clock, I see Betty Roberts, one of the HR supervisors, emerge from the elevator and my heart stops in my throat. *Oh, God, they picked now.*

"Hey, Tiffany?" Betty says, pulling out a piece of paper. Tiffany, who's playing this a lot cooler than I am, looks up. "Hey, we just got a call from the healthcare provider. Said they need to confirm your data, so could you fill this out for me, please?"

That little scare is nothing, though, when Ricky comes down forty-five minutes later. I've got my back turned to him, so when his hand claps down on my shoulder, I nearly jump over the reception desk in fear. "What the . . . Ricky!"

"Hey, glad you remembered my name," Ricky jokes, taking a step back. "Daniel wants you to head upstairs, wants to see you in his office."

"But I—"

"Tiff can handle the desk. Can't you?" he says, leaning over to look at Tiffany, who nods, but her brows are knotted together as she looks from me to Ricky. "Daniel said he sent a request to Miranda to borrow you for some work, so come on," Ricky says amiably, gesturing with his head for me to follow him.

Oh, fuck. I hadn't thought of this option. I've imagined Colton firing me, blackmailing me, seducing me . . . okay, well, that last one might not be so bad.

But never did I think of him narcing on me.

If he's told Dad, then Dad's going to go through the roof. He might fire me himself. More importantly, though, my secret of being a daredevil junkie's going to be exposed to my father . . . and that's one conversation I definitely don't want to have.

It's stupid, but he thinks I outgrew that craziness long ago, grew up to be a responsible, productive member of society and all that jazz.

And I am. Mostly.

I just like a little walk on the wild side every once in a while, and there's no harm in that . . . most of the time.

Dad's the straight and narrow type, though, and won't get that at all. I can already feel his disappointment in me, painful and heavy.

Miranda comes up, looking none too pleased to be pulled out of her office to help Tiffany. "Go on up, Elle. Tell your father hello." It's a slight jab, snarkiness that I'm only going upstairs by request because of my relationship with Executive Daniel Stryker, regardless of what official task Dad mentioned in his email request.

Even though I've already ruled her out, I mentally draw through Miranda's name on my list of potential dates for Dad with a thick, black permanent marker. No bitchiness allowed.

"Hey, Miranda," Ricky says, making big goo-goo eyes at her. "Anyone ever told you that you look just like a prime-time Shania Twain?"

What in the hell is Ricky talking about? I swear his tone sounds flirty, but that is the weirdest compliment I've ever heard, and I once actually had a guy tell me that my eyes were lickable.

Even eyeball licker had better game than Ricky.

Miranda blushes, flipping her hair and batting her heavily made up eyelashes. "Well, why, yes. Yes, they have. But not in years, you flatterer! Seems some people don't even know who she is or what good music should be."

She doesn't look at Tiffany or me, but it feels like she's talking about our recent discussions of Lizzo. For the record, I love her and her positivity. Tiffany is Team Cut a Bitch and prefers Cardi B and Nicki Minaj. I don't turn the station for any of them. But Shania? Nope, you can keep that man of yours and his boots.

"Nineties country is the best," Ricky says in all seriousness.

"Holy shit, you've got to be fucking kidding me," Tiffany mutters under her breath. "Prime Shania Twain, my ass!"

"I heard that!" Miranda says, her smile fading slightly. "Don't be mad our handsome Richard here's got a good eye." Miranda reaches out, patting Ricky's bicep in a way that says she's quite blatantly taking his measure, and I swear he flexes for her.

If I weren't embroiled in an HR-worthy situation of my own, I might be a little concerned about this scenario playing out in front of my very eyes.

"Oh, please."

"I just know a fine woman when I see one," Ricky says. He looks Miranda up and down, licking his lips slightly. "The good Lord knew he was making something special when he created you."

Miranda seems as if she's about to faint from Ricky's outrageousness, but Tiffany isn't amused.

"Someone kill me now," Tiffany mutters, fishing around on the desk to find a letter opener. "Here, just put it through my ear so that I don't have to listen to this any longer than necessary!"

Despite my being anxious, it takes everything in me not to laugh. "I don't think we need to go that far. Right, Ricky?"

"Sure, sure," Ricky says, laughing along while giving Miranda a wink. "Okay, let me walk Princess Stryker up, and I'll be back to see if I can still sweep you off your feet in a few, how's that sound?"

In the elevator, I look over at Ricky. "You know she's forty something, right?"

"And?" Ricky asks, not ashamed at all. "You might not see it since she's your boss, but Miranda's a total MILF. She's the sort of woman who can teach a man things about *things*."

I can't. Ricky and Miranda and sex all in one sentence. Just no. So I make a hardline play I already know the outcome of.

"You trying to learn things, Ricky? Here's the best two tips you need . . . one, when you think there's been enough foreplay and you're ready to move on, you're halfway there. And two, make best friends with her clit. Pet it, pat it, lick it, suck it, and then do it all again. You need to worship that little button and things will be A-Okay."

Ricky makes a strange sound, like he's choking on the words trying to get out of his throat. Finally, he manages to say, "Don't say shit like that, Elle."

I smile pleasantly, wearing my innocence like the sweetheart I'm not. "What? You were talking about having S-E-X with my boss. I think that warrants a bit of birds and bees talk. Wanna discuss the G-spot or prostates next?"

He rolls his eyes and the rest of the elevator ride is silent.

Except in my head, where once the distraction of giving Ricky shit is gone, my brain goes into hyperdrive imagining all sorts of worst-case scenarios about this meeting with Dad.

We get to the top floor, and I let Ricky escort me down to Dad's office.

My first thought as I step inside is that it's a half-step down from Colton's. Not that the view's any worse. They're almost equally arranged on the long hallway that makes up the fifth floor of the Fox Building, and they're equal in size.

But there's just a little difference in their choices. Dad's gone for more functional furniture, the opulent oak and brass replaced with the blacks, whites, and steels of a more modern aesthetic. All of it's high end. It's not like the decorator Dad hired went to IKEA, but still . . . it feels cold compared to the warmth of Colton's office.

"What's up, Dad?" I ask as I sit down nervously on the couch at his behest. At least it's soft leather. But that doesn't mean this is a warm and fuzzy 'check in with my baby girl' situation. No, I'm certain he's about to unleash an unholy ass chewing upon me. I just know it.

He closes his laptop and stands up, going around to the minifridge by the window and taking out two bottles of his latest obsession, some nasty tasting, healthy green juice. "Nothing much, honey. I just wanted to see you and figured you could use a juice break at the end of the day. How're you doing?"

I'm so surprised that I freeze, and Dad shakes the glass bottle in front of me before I remember to take it. "Uhm, fine, Dad. You know, busy but . . . fine, I guess."

I'm so confused. On one hand, I certainly don't want him to ream me out over this whole thing with Colton. I don't even want him to know about it. On the other hand, if he's really calling me up for afternoon juice chats, we need to have a serious discussion about boundaries and professionalism at work.

"Oh," Dad says, slightly disappointed, and I feel like I'm on the edge of a cliff, waiting for someone to shove me off.

Just yell at me already, I want to say.

But Dad's nonchalant as he says, "I know you're busy these days, but do you think you could squeeze me in for a cheese-burger down at Frankie's Burger Hut?"

Frankie's . . . it has been 'our place' for what seems like ever. And Frankie does make some damn good burgers. But more importantly, Dad and I have always shared Frankie's, never going alone or taking anyone else there, for some reason.

"Oh, uh . . . sure. How about lunch one day this week?" I offer.

Dad nods and takes a sip of his juice. How he manages to keep a straight face, I don't know because I can smell it from here, like freshly mown grass and pepper and something . . . bitter. *Blech.*

"How about you? How's everything?" I inch my toes off the cliff, tempting fate but wanting to get this show on the road.

"Well, I've got some potentially bad news there," he says sullenly.

Oh, shit.

"Uh . . . what?"

Dad fidgets with the label on his bottle, a nervous tic from a man who doesn't have them, which only makes more anxious. Good Lord, by the time he gets to yelling, I'm going to have an ugly case of the stress-induced shits.

"Remember how I've been telling you that I was pretty sure I had the HQ2 program sewn up? Looks like there may be a monkey wrench in the plan."

Phew . . . I mean, I'm not doing backflips that his long held goal of running his own HQ is facing a setback, but it sounds like he at least doesn't know about what I did in Colton Wolfe's office. "I . . . I'm sorry to hear that. I know you've really been putting in a lot of work on things. So did they go with another plan?"

"No . . . no, just a delay right now," Dad admits, smiling a little. "Guess I can thank my lucky stars for that. One of the other proposals was actually really good, and Mr. Fox wants to put a delay in the whole process so that he can hear more."

"Oh . . . whose plan?"

He looks up at me, and I can feel the answer even before he opens his mouth. "Colton Wolfe."

Karma . . . you really are a coldhearted bitch, you know that?

"I'm sorry," I immediately apologize before shutting my mouth.

"No, no, it's okay," Dad says. "But I could use a little help, honey. I know you work for Miranda, but Miranda works for Wolfe, so you're sort of in his chain of command. Can you do me a favor? If you hear anything, can you pass it along to your dear old dad?" He smiles as he says it, small crinkles popping beside his eyes, but he's definitely nowhere near the old man he's making himself out to be.

"Dad . . . are you sure? This doesn't sound like you," I ask, worried. I mean, I guess there's nothing wrong with it. We're all on the Fox team, but I've always seen him as Super Dad, and that includes a deep moral streak. This, though, seems like a gray area.

He leans toward me. "It's fine, honey. Look, Wolfe is probably plotting against me as we speak. It's only natural that I keep my eyes open. And I'm not asking you to go out of your way to do anything. I don't want you snooping around or doing anything shady. I'm just saying if there are any hijinks coming out of his office, you let me know. I just want the best proposal for the company to get the vote, and I truly believe that's my plan."

"Okay. I'll keep my ears open, and we'll hit up Frankie's soon?"

I realize that I think my dad just played me, at least a little bit. The check-in juice, the guilt-trip date, all to ask me to tell tales about whatever Colton Wolfe is planning. As if I have any clue about that.

No, my plan is to stay far, far away from Colton Wolfe so that I save my sanity and my job. Maybe if I stay out of his sight, I can stay out of his mind, and he'll just forget yesterday even happened.

"Sounds great, honey. I love you," Dad says, standing up. I follow suit, and he hugs me tight, still my Super Dad but a little more human, I realize.

Smiling, I set my unopened juice down and leave Dad's office. I head down the hallway toward the elevator, knowing Tiffany's gonna pump me for every morsel of the play-by-play of my conversation with Dad.

I'm almost there. I can see the buttons clearly against their metal plates when a distinctive British voice calls out to me.

"Miss Stryker? My office, please."

My heart jumps into my throat, and I stumble slightly as I turn to see Colton Wolfe leaning against his outer office door, his arms crossed over his chest. The smirk on his face is pure arrogance, a display of 'I know something you don't' that does not bode well for me.

Step into my parlor, said the spider to the fly.

But where the fly in the infamous poem initially refused to give in to the spider's welcome, I do not have that luxury because he's both my boss and holding all the cards. Even without false flattery, I go into the spider's parlor, hoping it's not the last time I'll be at Fox Industries.

CHAPTER 7

COLTON

*W*atching Elle swallow down her fear sends twin tingles down my spine. On one hand, I should feel guilty at what I'm about to do, using her this way. I should feel like a heel for scaring her.

On the other hand, watching her lips and throat work leaves me thinking about other, very unprofessional, things. I know I shouldn't, but Elle's so sexy that she's got me off my trolley a bit.

Which might be an issue, but it'll be a rather delightful one, I predict.

Things get even more amusing when she follows me into my office and I turn to watch her long, well-shaped legs cross as she sits down where I silently order her to with a pointed finger. She looks up at me with those big eyes, trying to show confidence and not her fear. I can admire the attempt.

"Mr. Wolfe?" she says, breaking the silence first. It's a small give, but one I'll take. I get the feeling that her every submission to my authority will be hard won, so I'll take an easy one with satisfaction.

I'm not going to torture her. Yet.

But that doesn't mean I can't devil her just a bit.

"Miss Stryker, you have been a major pain in my arse the last twenty-four hours," I declare without preamble, perching on the corner of my huge desk mainly to hide my crotch just in case. "Instead of working on a very important project, I've spent my valuable time thinking long and hard about what you did. It takes either stones or stupidity, and I'm still not sure which you have." I glare at her questioningly.

"Sir . . . if you're going to fire me, just get it over with without the speech. Put me out of my misery."

Elle's outburst surprises me. Oh, so my little daredevil has a bit of fire in her belly.

"It was a stupid thing to do. Actually, stupid doesn't even begin to describe it." Her confession is bitter but self-directed, and honestly, rather accurate.

I sit at my desk, contemplating her. She seems rather settled on the outcome she expects. "Hmm, well . . . it is a fireable offense, for certain. But if that were my plan, it would not have taken me all night to decide what to do with you."

It had actually taken me that long to play out each and every angle, measuring for maximum impact and conclusion. I had ultimately decided on my present course of action.

Daniel and I are adversaries in this race for HQ2, against each other but for the company's ultimate good. Evaluating everything I know about Daniel leads me to believe that he will be set off-kilter by having his dear daughter work with me, especially on this project.

There's a chance she could play me and serve as the insider spy for Daniel I'd originally thought she'd been, but I feel certain I can protect against that. And massaging this situation to my best benefit seems worth the risk.

And there's a small niggling seed that says I'm intrigued by the woman who could have the world handed to her on a silver platter but refuses it in favor of making her own way, the woman who does seemingly crazy things just for the adventurous high of it, the woman whose mere photo had me rock hard and coming fiercely in record time.

"And what, exactly, do you plan to do with me?"

I detect the faintest hint of heat in the words, like she's consciously saying them neutrally but unable to control the tightness in her throat.

"Move you up here, to be my dedicated assistant on the HQ2 project." It's a simple statement, but it causes all the air in the room to be sucked out.

"Excuse me?" Her glare could slice a lesser man.

"It's rather straightforward. You will be on my team, and that is not a request. The very placement will be a communication that you support my proposal, so to be transparent, I am using you for your last name."

"You want to use me against my own father? Against his proposal?" Her mouth gapes in fury. "And if I refuse?"

I am glad that she at least knows of the bids for HQ2 placement. Keeping Elle between Daniel and me is one thing, but it's not fair play to use her without her even knowing that there's a competition going on.

I shrug. "You won't. Your talents are many. I looked at your corporate file, and to be honest, you are wasted on Miranda's team. It seems your father is right that you should be at least a junior analyst, if not a more senior one if you'd gone into his department as he requested. This is an opportunity for you to move up as you wanted."

I don't give compliments lightly, but she doesn't so much as acknowledge the comment about her talents. "And if you weren't so bored and underutilized, perhaps you wouldn't feel the need to get up to such useless pursuits as yesterday's incident."

She repeats tightly through clenched teeth. "And if I refuse?"

"If we do not come to some sort of understanding, I will be forced to file charges with HR and have you terminated. The circumstances would, I'm sure, be rather embarrassing to your father."

"You're blackmailing me?" she snaps.

"No, I'm daring you." My lips quirk as I sense her attention perking up at the language. "You like dares, Elle."

I bait the trap, and I await her response eagerly.

"I . . . I don't *like* them," she weakly replies even as her hands clench on the arms of her chair. "I just—"

"Can't resist the rush that comes with them," I finish for her, making her nod gently. "But let's face it, Miss Stryker. Doing schoolgirl dares simply because your best mate challenges you must get rather boring after awhile. So I've decided I'm going to give you a refreshing new challenge."

"A . . . challenge?" she asks, swallowing again.

"Yes, a new challenge. Up the ante, if you will? I dare you to leave the reception desk and become my assistant. You'll be working *directly* underneath me."

I hear the tiniest gasp pass her lips at the phrasing, and I want to chase that breath into her body, taste it from her lips. It's the first real hint that she is as affected by me as I am by her. She'd said as much yesterday, but words can be selected for effect. This unconscious reaction is real. I can see the truth of it in her eyes.

"Why would you do this?" she finally asks. "You have an assistant. Helen, in case you forgot."

"And I appreciate her. But I'm already overworking her and need the help," I admit.

"You mean you need my last name." She seems resolved to my plan now, but not in the way I'd prefer.

"To-may-to, to-mah-to." I rise, walking toward the window. "Tell me, Elle. What reward did your friend offer you for yesterday's dare?"

She seems confused at the turn in the conversation, tilting her head. "She agreed to drinks, a mani-pedi, and because of the drama, my favorite cupcakes. Pampering, sugar, and alcohol to cure all that ails you," she jokes flatly.

"I see. So, drama aside, you two have fun with the silly little dares though, yes?" She nods slowly and I play my ace in the hole. "I find that I lack that type of lightheartedness in my life. Since coming to the States, I've been singularly focused on work, and that has served me well. But your incident highlighted just how boring I've become. It amused me."

Her eyes bug out. "Boring? You?" I shrug noncommittally. "You drive a Lotus, work as a top-level executive, and judging by your office, you probably live in a mansion with a pool and a butler. But I'm amusing?"

Her irreverence is refreshing, and I get the feeling she couldn't care less about my bank account or any fanciness my position and power afford.

"You're correct, but none of those things are . . . fun."

My brow furrows. "Or, well, they are, but I feel like there might be other types of fun I'm missing out on."

It's enough of a confession. I don't tell Elle about the conversations with Lizzie, my sister back home in London, where she good-naturedly nags me that my every update is all about work and she doesn't care about boring old dudes in suits. I don't tell Elle that the last three times I went out on the town, it was to the opera with tickets I won at a charity auction . . . and that I hate opera. I don't tell Elle that I don't have a single friend in the States to just catch a game or grab a pint with.

I haven't considered that I might be lonely, the one who stays late after everyone else goes home to friends and family. But that reality is glaring me in the face as I wait for Elle to agree to this plan.

Her silence stretches as we maintain eye contact, neither of us giving in this time. I wonder what she sees when she looks at me.

The late afternoon sun highlights her through the wall of windows. From here, she's even more beautiful. Long blonde hair that's pulled slightly up to show off the perfect swan's curve of a neck, shoulders . . . and I'll privately admit to my own little fetish, ears that look like an artist sculpted them.

The idea of taking one of those perfect shells of soft skin and tugging on it with my teeth as I sink my cock balls deep inside her has me hard as a rock again.

I pace back and forth along the windows in hopes of giving my stones some relief.

I want her to be drawn to me, curious to peek behind the veil of the intensely private British executive that I know the company sees me as. And she's a smart girl, knows this is a way out of the tediousness of a job she's overqualified for.

"I'll take your silence as you are caught between a rock and a hard place. And that maybe I'm taking the biscuit a bit with you. But regardless, this is an opportunity for you." I intentionally focus on what it could mean to her personally, not what it'll mean to me or her father, as a way of influencing her.

"And I have officially dared you to do it. So until you tell me to get on my bike, I'm going to assume you accept my . . . offer. When you come into work tomorrow, report to my office. Your first job will be to assist Helen with arranging a proper desk for you in this suite. All right?"

Elle blinks, still saying nothing, then tilts her head. "Mr. Wolfe . . . I have to admit I only understood about three-quarters of what you said. What's taking the biscuit? And why are you riding a bike?"

I laugh, smiling hugely because she didn't say no. "Just one of the skills you'll learn working for me. If I see you in the outer office tomorrow by nine o'clock, I guess we'll both know your answer. Choose wisely."

CHAPTER 8

ELLE

"*C*hug a lug, bitch. I need that tongue a' wagging pronto." Tiffany swallows her mouthful of wine before sticking her own tongue out, wiggling it rather obscenely in my direction.

"We're not that kind of friends, Tiff," I tease. But really, I'm trying to keep from discussing the topic at hand. The wine, my second glass, is working its magic, though, and it's getting hard to play coy.

I'll blame my so-slight buzz for what happens next. "He wants me underneath him."

Tiffany's glass nearly shatters as she slams it to the coffee table. Her feet find the floor as she stands up for the first time since we rolled into my apartment an hour ago. "What?"

I smirk, knowing I got her good. "Well, sorta. He offered me a job as his assistant."

Tiffany is dancing around the room, in grave danger of tripping over her own two feet and my dirty laundry as she sings seriously off-key. "He wants you, he wa-a-a-ants you. Elle's gonna get her some BBC!"

My eyes bug out. "What? What does BBC have to do with anything, and how much porn are you watching these days? Hitting on me and using Pornhub lingo?"

"Big *British* Cock," she says with a nod like that's obviously what that means. It so doesn't. "And I'm not coming on to you, though I might consider it if you give me another glass of wine." She drinks the last of it from her glass, raising it to ceiling in salute before pouring another. It's a good thing she's not driving home.

As she pours, she says under her breath, "He wants you to take his dick-tation. Bet he tea-bags and eats crumpets at the same time." She throws her head back, almost spilling her near-full wine as she closes her eyes and says louder in a fake English accent, "Oh, my, I'm arriving! Arriving now!"

It takes me two blinks to realize she's joking about *coming* and then I burst into laughter with her. We fall back on the couch, giggles erupting like a Coke and Mentos experiment is going off in our bellies.

"Quite splendid, indeed," I say through the snorts, my fake accent only slightly better than Tiffany's.

Eventually, we laugh ourselves out and the reality of the situation comes back to me heavily.

"What am I going to do?" I whine.

Tiffany's look of 'duh' makes me feel like I'm missing something. "Work for him."

I copy the look back because she's the one not seeing the big picture here. Before I can argue, she holds up a hand and lifts one perfectly sculpted brow, daring me to interrupt her. I wisely shut my mouth and give her the floor to speak.

"You're smart, he's hot, so give it a shot." She smiles messily. "I'm such a poet." More clear-eyed, she says, "I'll miss you and probably die of absolute boredom without you to make things interesting all day, but you need to grab this bull with both hands and hang on with all you've got."

"You think?" I say, knowing I've already decided. I'd decided before I even walked out of his office today, if I'm being truthful.

Tiffany takes a sip, feigning casualness. "Does Daddy know yet?"

I'm too deep in my own shit to give her any about the nick-name this time. "No, and he's going to kill me, or Colton, or both of us." It's a real fear, but more importantly, I confess, "I don't want to hurt him."

She pats my hand consolingly. "Don't you worry your pretty little head. I'll be Daddy's baby girl once you're busy with the Big Bad Wolfe. I'm sure Daddy will need all sorts of comforting and I'm pretty good at that."

She teasing, mostly. But then she goes one step too far. "After the wedding, do you want to call me Mother or Mom, you think?"

I kick out a foot, catching her in her middle, and she *oofs*. "Shut your filthy mouth about my dad, woman. Never gonna happen." She tilts her head, not meeting my eyes as if that makes her able to ignore my decree. "It had better not. Girl. Code."

She sighs, finally looking my way. "Fine. But how about if we trade tit-for-tat? You can break code and screw my brother, and in return, I get Daddy?"

I shake my head, grossed out. "No, I'm not fucking Ace. That ship sailed a long time ago. And you're not fucking my dad. New subject . . . what am I going to wear?"

Fashion might be the only thing to get Tiffany's attention off my dad, so I play that card intentionally.

She gasps, setting her drink down to stand. Grabbing at my hand, she half-drags me to my bedroom before shoving me onto my bed. Thankfully, my glass isn't quite as full as hers and I manage to not spill a drop.

Sophie jumps up, mewling and hissing her displeasure at being disturbed upon her throne, also known as my bed. I hiss back, knowing I'll pay for the disobedience later. There's definitely a hairball in my future.

I consider for a moment whether Tiffany's making a play for me as she eyes me thoughtfully. But she throws open my closet and digs in, pulling out skirts and tops.

If it'd been me, my room would've been a tornado of clothes in moments. Tiffany is methodical, though, lining up three tops that she eyes critically.

"Sexy, but not overtly so. You don't want to look like you got the promotion on your knees."

"On my ass, actually. I fell off the copy machine to the floor. It was a full *Hello Kitty* situation. Thank God I'd waxed recently." I cringe, knowing that waxing is uncomfortable as hell, but flashing full bush at Colton Wolfe would've been a million times more painful.

Tiffany smiles but remains focused. "Not chaste and matronly. You don't want to look like a virgin unless that's his kink." She looks at me like I'd have any idea. Actually, I shake my head, pretty sure that's not the way to his cock. Tiffany nods her agreement with my assessment. "But professional, of course."

"This one," she decides, holding up a grey button-up shirt. It's the softest cotton, which is why I bought it, but rather plain.

"Really?" I question. She's more of a fashionista than me, but that shirt screams bland and blah.

She throws it at me. "Just you wait and see. Trust me, put it on."

I pull off my comfy T-shirt and put on the grey one Tiff's selected, buttoning it up. In the mirror, I look a little Risky Business in just the shirt and socks. Well, maybe like a college girl's Halloween slut version of the outfit because my braless nipples are quite apparent through the thin cotton.

Hello, Headlights!

Tiffany pulls a deep plum skirt from my closet next. "And this." She instructs me to slip it on with a wave of her hand. I do as ordered while she digs around in my dresser. "Hose." She hands me a pair of thigh-highs, my favorite ones, actually, that are the same dark purple as the skirt, but silky sheer with small polka dots for some flair. "And last but not least, jewelry. Get it?"

She holds out a multi-strand necklace of faux pearls. "I am not wearing a pearl necklace to my first day on the job with Colton Wolfe." The argument is useless in the face of Tiffany's intelligence.

"I dare you to." Her brow quirks, knowing she's got me. "He might not even get the reference. It's probably called something else in London." I eye the necklace warily. "The queen's choker?" she postulates.

I still don't agree, but I carefully pull the hose up my legs. Tiffany hands me a pair of black heels, and I slip them on as I look in the mirror.

"Hair up, but leave a few ringlets loose. Professional makeup with a burgundy lip, something that goes with but doesn't match the skirt." Tiffany gathers my hair in her hand, holding it on top of my head mimicking a bun. "You'll have the sexy librarian look down pat, and something tells me that's the way into Colton Wolfe's . . . trousers."

"I'm not getting into his pants, Tiff."

She rolls her eyes. "Well, not till he gets in yours, of course. Ladies first. Always. It's a sign of a true gentleman."

"He's just using me to fuck with Dad. He told me as much, so don't go getting your hopes up that this is some Cinderella story." I sound sad about that, even to my own ears.

Tiffany's pity is loud and clear. "That's what he said. And it's probably even true. But it's not the *only* reason. Look at yourself, girl." She uses her grip on my hair to wiggle my head around, forcing me to look my reflection in the eye.

"I feel like a traitor," I say softly, not looking at Tiffany because I don't want to see her reaction.

She lets go of my hair, her mouth rounding. "Oh, honey, don't. No one is going to think that, least of all your dad." That she calls him that and not 'Daddy' shows me how seriously she's taking this right now. It must be requiring all of her brain power, considering how many glasses of wine she's put down.

She blinks, and the seriousness is gone in favor of something she knows will persuade me more than sweet platitudes.

"You're a daredevil on an adventure. Elle Stryker, Secret Agent, working side by side with the dashing, debonair Colton Wolfe while secretly helping her father. You're like one set of handcuffs and a nunchaku fight away from your own superhero action show, and I bet you could get Colton to help with the handcuff issue." She winks knowingly.

She's right. There's something about Colton that makes me want to know more—the way he dances between frosty formality and risqué entendre, the honest surprise at my confession that I'd been trying to get his attention, the bold declaration that he was going to use me. But what intrigues me the most was his quiet admission that he thinks he's boring and in need of fun. I don't share that with Tiffany, selfishly wanting to keep that tidbit to myself.

Mine! My precious! my inner Gollum screeches.

But this is a dangerous game I'm playing, one I'm woefully unprepared for. Everyone knows who my dad is, and as soon as word gets out about my new position, I'll be the topic of every water cooler conversation.

Fuck it, I think as I take the pearl necklace from Tiffany's hand. Might as well give them something easy to nitpick.

And she's right. I do look fucking fabulous. Sexy librarian, indeed.

Shush . . .

THE NEXT MORNING, MY GUTS HAVE TAKEN A FLYING LEAP OFF THE top of the building, leaving me a nervous mess.

Everything's going great until my phone rings.

"Tiff? What's up?" She never calls me in the morning, both of us too in a hurry to have time to gab.

A strange noise comes through the phone, and for a moment, I think she's being murdered and somehow managed to butt dial me for help.

"Are you okay? Do you need me to call 9-1-1 or come kick ass?" A horrible thought peeks out from the recesses in my mind and I grip the phone, whispering, "Did you kill Ace? Should I bring a shovel?"

Considering we live in the city and any deserted land is well outside the city limits, I hope it's not that. And mental note, I need to lay off the *I Almost Got Away With It* binge watching.

That same strange noise happens again.

"Early. I need you to come and get me early. It's an emergency, Elle. As soon as possible, please." I realize that sound is her growling angrily and sobbing uncontrollably at the same time.

"Are you okay? Is Ace okay?" I venture. "Wait, don't answer that. They might be listening." I don't know who they are, but if today is the first day of my Secret Agent spy show, I don't want to start it by causing my bestie to incriminate herself. "I'm on my way."

"Thanks." She must pull the phone from her ear because I hear her yell from a distance, "I am going to murder you in your sleep, Ace Young." And then the line goes dead.

At least I know he's still alive right now. When the police interrogate me later, I can tell them that's all I know.

I quickly get dressed, thankful I don't have time to second guess the outfit Tiffany pulled together for me. Not even the pearl necklace causes me to pause.

I'm not surprised when Tiff isn't outside as I pull up. She's probably wrapping Ace's body in rug or something. But like the loyal friend I am, I head to her door, which is noticeably absent of shitty loud rap music this time. I'm not sure if that's a good thing, though.

The door swings open before I can knock. Tiffany is perfectly pulled together as usual . . . from the neck up. Hair? Curled into loose waves. Makeup? Instagram ready.

It's from the shoulders down that is an utter clusterfuck of morning-after-frat-party-refugee chic.

"Is that a Rainbow Brite shirt? And where's the rest of your skirt?" Dumb questions, I guess, because she glares behind her, where Ace sits sullenly on the couch.

But seriously, her shirt is probably a girl's large at best, her belly button and several inches of abdomen exposed beneath the hem, and her skirt would be better described as a thick belt. I can't see her ass from this angle, but I bet if Ace looked up from the floor, he'd be getting more than an eyeful of his sister's assets.

Tiffany growls like an animal and Ace says, "I said I'm sorry." I get the feeling he's said it several times already. "I was trying to help."

"Your laundry," Tiffany replies crisply. "Clean the piss off the toilet, wash the dishes, and take out the trash. All of it. Capiche?"

"Yeah," is his sad answer.

"Before I get home." With that, Tiffany shoves me out the door. "Let's go, I have to go by the cleaners on the way to work, and then, I'll have to get dressed in your car. I'll probably flash truckers from here to the office when I take this joke of a skirt off. What was I thinking?" She gestures to the tiny scrap of fabric. "Why did you let me wear this thing in public? I thought we were friends. Friends don't let friends go out looking like hoes, Elle."

I wisely decide not to remind her that we quite often went out wearing the latest and greatest in slutty fashion in our younger days. Hence, why that skirt is in her closet in the first place.

She sits down in my passenger seat and I remind myself to get Cammie detailed. It's not that I don't love Tiff, but I'm well aware that her bare ass is resting on my leather seat right now, and that's just a little bit much, even for my bestie. I'm just grateful she's got underwear on . . . well, I assume she does.

I focus on the obvious. "Why are you wearing that? What did Ace do?"

"He claims he wanted to *help*." She does finger quotes around the word but one turns into a gun and she jokes at shooting herself. "Kill me now, because that boy took my laundry and washed it *all*. The dirties in my hamper? Maybe that would've been all right. But he took my work clothes too, the dry-clean only ones. Washed them all, and then to pour salt on the wound, dried them. I don't think I have a single respectable item left, hence my current attire."

"Holy shit," I gasp, wincing. Tiffany's always been a bit of a clothes hound, with a wardrobe that'd put mine to shame. But she's ridiculously organized about hers, usually only keeping special pieces and her current on-trend lineup. "I'm surprised he's still alive. I kinda assumed he wasn't when you called."

She holds her finger and thumb up, a skinny space separating them. "This close, I swear. If you'd been one second later."

She bangs her head on the headrest. "Turn right at the next light. The cleaners is on the left." I follow her directions and pull into the drive-thru line.

Tiffany requests her clothes from the passenger seat, glaring menacingly at the young guy when he stares at the long length of thigh she's showing. I can't help but laugh a little. "You can't blame him. I mean, you're a cough away from an 'is there some other way I could pay?' situation."

Her glare hits me full-force. "Now who's watching too much porn?"

And of course, that's when the guy steps out the door to hand over Tiffany's clothes. As if this morning could get any worse, he's now looking at us like we're a dream come true. No, scratch that . . . like a fantasy come true.

I have to get out and push the seat forward for him to hang the clothes in the back seat, and I swear to God, he sniffs the air as he leans down in front of me. And then he misses the hook twice because he's side-eyeing Tiffany in the front seat. I can't see his eyes, but I can tell because his head's angled all wrong.

"Thank you. Have a nice day." Polite words said with zero kindness and a full dose of get the fuck outta here seem to wake him up.

He steps back, having finally gotten the clothes secure. "Oh, I will. You ladies have a great day too." He tips an invisible hat and steps back so I can get in and close the door. But before I can put Cammie into drive, he leans down, putting his forearms on the open windowsill.

"My name's Joe. Would either of you ladies . . . or both of you . . . like to grab a drink tonight? I get off at six."

I blink. I guess I should give him some credit for shooting his shot, but to ask both of us out seems beyond the pale, so I'm not feeling that generous. "Nope."

I slip the shifter into first and gun the engine with my foot firmly on the brake. He takes the hint and moves back. A split second later, we're flying down the road, beelining for the highway.

I look over to Tiffany, seeing that she's still scowling and ruminating about Ace's misdeeds.

"Want me to go back? You could get to know Joe a bit better. I could dare you to go out with him, if you want?" I offer it seriously, but she knows damn well that I'm kidding. It's against rule one, and possibly rule two, though if things got that far between my bestie and the dry-cleaning guy, it'd be on her shoulders, not mine.

"Just drive," she says with a sigh, but there's a hint of a smile, so I'm taking the win.

The next stoplight, the last one before we hit the open road of rush-hour traffic, is a long one, so Tiffany unbuckles and works her way over the console and into the back seat. She absolutely flashes her ass to the driver of the car next to us, and the angry looking middle-aged woman honks and yells something that looks like 'what the fuck?' But the jacked-up truck in the far lane has a guy who looks like Tiff just made his day, judging by the width of his smile. He waves, and I shrug like whatcha gonna do?

Tiffany strips and gets dressed in more work-appropriate clothing while I drive on. As we merge onto the highway, Truck Driver honks his horn and waves again as he continues down the frontage road.

I laugh and look in the rearview mirror. "It seems you have another fan this morning, Miss Young."

She flips me the bird and smarts off. "Well, with Ace's help, at least you were too distracted to have what would've surely been an epic freak-out this morning. You're welcome." She tips her hat, copying Joe with a smirk.

"Thanks, you shouldn't have," I say dryly, but secretly, I think she's probably right because now that she mentions it, I can feel the butterflies.

No, bees. Actually, more like wasps, mean and aggressive, buzzing through my belly at the thought of walking into Fox this morning, bypassing my usual desk, and heading for the elevator. I imagine everyone's eyes on me as I walk down the hallway toward Colton's office, whispering behind their hands at Daniel's traitorous daughter.

This isn't the usual happy sensation when I'm about to crush a dare. Not anticipation. This is dread. Not excitement. This is fear.

"I can't do this." The blurt is unconscious but true. "I'm just going to go to my desk like usual and deal with any fallout. You said it yourself. Colton's not going to fire me. He'll have to explain why he didn't do something right away, and he won't do that."

I glance in the rearview mirror to see Tiffany watching me through guarded eyes. I don't like that. She's always pretty open and filter-less.

My mind keeps spinning. My mouth keeps running.

"Or he could just go to Dad, bypass anything official because he damn well knows that'd be worse to me. Shit. He's right, rock and hard place. I could hit him in his hard place with a rock, see if he'd like that."

"Snarky is not an attractive look on you," Tiff ventures, not commenting on my solo encore performance of last night's argument.

Her silence ironically reminds me why I'd decided to go along with this whole crazy idea in the first place.

I picture Colton staring out the window over the city, cutting a powerful silhouette but confessing to wanting a bit of excitement. I picture the heat in his eyes as he scanned the photocopy of my ass and the considerable bulge I know I saw in his slacks, no matter how much he tried to hide it.

"I'm doing it." This dare isn't done yet, but it will be. And suddenly, I can't wait.

CHAPTER 9

ELLE

*T*his is . . . *crazy.*

And isn't that why you like it? the devil on my shoulder asks.

He has Tiffany's voice. Yes, he. And yes, Tiffany's voice. It doesn't make sense, but I've long since grown used to it.

How am I going to pull this off? Walking down the corridor of the fifth floor, I realize that I've got thirty minutes, *tops*, before Dad knows what's happened.

At which point, I have no idea how to explain myself.

But I walk into Colton's outer office, where he's perched on the corner of an empty desk, chatting with Helen, who gives me a glance.

"Mr. Wolfe?"

"Hello, Miss Stryker. This way," Colton says, standing up and walking into his office. As I follow him, I can't help but admire the way his ass fills out his fresh suit pants, black today but not funereal. Instead, he looks powerful and magnetic, and when he looks back over his shoulder, he totally catches me checking him out. I can tell by the amused twitch of his lips. I can even smell him, his masculine cologne woodsy and smoky, a combination that makes me think of naked camping trips even though I've never been an outdoorsy girl. "I'm glad to see you this morning."

His tone is all business, no teasing banter and zero flirtation. To anyone listening in, it'd seem strictly professional. But I'm already better at reading him, seeing behind the cold and stoic façade. There are flames licking along my skin, lit by the heat of his gaze. I make a mental note to thank Tiffany again for the wardrobe assist last night because apparently, she did right by me.

"It took me a lot of thought, to be honest."

"Good," Colton says, smiling a little. "Being thoughtful and intentional about your career is always an admirable trait."

Scratch that, maybe I'm not so good at reading him because I can't tell if he's being sarcastic. He knows that my appearance here is a total give in to him, and it pisses me off that I've done it. It pisses me off even more that he's likely enjoying it. But I decide to take it at face value for now as he continues.

"There's going to be a lot demanded of you, and that means I want you all in, starting now. We'll begin with the rules."

"Rules?" I bristle automatically at the word, the cage it invokes.

Colton nods, taking a file folder off his desk and handing it to me. I'm pretty sure there's a flash of something in his expression, though. Curiosity, perhaps? His brows did jump ever so slightly. Cocky arrogance for sure in the smirky purse of his lips. Why are they both so attractive?

"You're no longer working a straight nine to five, where the most secretive thing you deal with is which floors like which flavor of doughnuts." He grins and gestures to the file. "Read it over, and if you want to discuss any of my rules, now is the time."

The list of rules inside the folder is pretty straightforward, I'm surprised to find. I guess I expected something a bit more salacious given our arrangement.

I'm moving to salary, with a nice bump in pay, and while it might be normal, one thing sticks out. "Don't share information outside of this team, Mr. Wolfe?"

"Let's be honest. Mr. Fox has built this company by often having teams compete against each other to fuel the creative juices, so to speak. If I have an advantage over another team, I don't want to give up that advantage. As I said before, your placement on my HQ2 team will send a message and I'm doing that intentionally. But I need to guard against your loyalties being divided. I will not have you working for me and helping your father on the sly. Am I understood?"

I nod and Colton continues. "I believe myself to be a good judge of character, and while you are rather unconventional . . ." His lips do that twitchy thing that I'm beginning to think means he's laughing on the inside. "You are morally just. I presume that has to come at least partially from good parenting and that Daniel will respect your loyalty to my team as well. If not, by signing this contract, you'll have a ready argument against disclosing anything private. This is to make it easier for me to trust you and easier for you to stay trustworthy."

He pauses, looking at me expectantly.

"Understood, sir."

His eyes flare wide, and bright sparks light in the deep blue so fast that if I hadn't been watching, I would've missed it. A dark, delicious knowledge twines around in my core. He likes my calling him sir. I'm not into anything too wild, shocking, considering my daredevil tendencies, but with Rule Two always in place, my sex life has been pretty . . . typical, I'd say.

But if he'd rather me call him sir than honey, I could be into that. I tuck the knowledge away for when it'll be most useful because every card I can stack in my deck against this man is going to be important.

"Any other questions?"

"So many . . ." I drawl out. "But for another time, Mr. Wolfe."

"Good. First things first. Arrange with Helen to have a desk brought in for you." He points to the corner of the room, by the window, at least.

"You intend to have your assistant work in your private office?" I say incredulously, hoping he hears just how outlandishly ridiculous that sounds. He might as well be telling everyone from the front door to Mr. Fox's office that I'm at his every beck and call. It won't take long for those water-cooler conversations to tack on that I'm doing so on my knees.

I mean, I would. Because Colton Wolfe is the kind of man you get down and worship appreciatively. God knew what he was doing when he molded this particular clay. But I don't need every Tom, Dick, and Henrietta knowing that.

Do we even have a Henrietta? Probably, but so not the point here, Elle!

He's going to ruin me, I realize.

I may be intelligent, adept, and willing to earn my way into the responsibilities I desire. But after this, I'll always have a shadow on my record, the question not whether I deserve my accolades, but rather how I earned them.

"It'll make it easier for us to work closely on the HQ2 project," he answers as if it's no big deal. But then he winks, and that's the real truth. He knows and he's doing it on purpose.

Before I can growl or argue or claw his eyes out for being so good looking and having me by my lady balls, he calls out, "Helen?"

Helen comes in, formally introducing herself. Of course, I've seen her around the company before, and she's professionally friendly. Still, she's kind of stiff, making me wonder if she's pissed about the whole situation.

Colton nods as if he's successfully set us up on a blind date from hell, though, and says he'll 'leave us to it' before disappearing.

To her credit, Helen helps me. I call down to facilities management, but they want her authorization before delivering furniture to Colton's office. I guess my new role hasn't made news down there yet, at least.

Not that that luxury will hold because I'm sure I don't imagine the knowing looks the two guys give me after they set me up by Colton's window.

I'm literally sitting there twiddling my thumbs and staring at the pretty view when Colton returns an hour later. Helen hadn't wanted my help without knowing what my role would be, and the desk was my only assignment from Colton.

Mission accomplished. Not nearly the buzz of a dare, but at least I got one thing done.

Colton returns with a grim smile. Actually, on second glance from my spot in his office, it's more of a predatory, feral teeth baring.

"Helen, Tom Givens won't be giving you any more trouble. But let me know if there's anything else."

Helen looks at Colton like he hung the moon and stars and every planetary mass in the universe. It'd be sickening, except I get the feeling he just did something major for her. And I'd be a bit jealous if she wasn't old enough to be his grandmother. I mean, Tiffany talks about DILFs, and I know MILFs are a thing, but surely, nobody's going for GMILFs. Least of all, Colton.

I shake my head, not wanting that image anywhere near my eyeballs. Real or imagined.

Colton enters his office, eyes flicking to the left immediately as if he's looking for me. I can't help but sit up straighter.

"Tom Givens is a douche canoe who wouldn't know his ass from his elbow if his assistant didn't do all his work. Whatever he did to Helen was shitty, and whatever you did to him was well-deserved."

Okay, so maybe that wasn't the most professional start to my day with Colton, but it's the truth and every clerical person in the building knows that Tom Givens can barely turn on his computer. He's a dinosaur in a post-meteorite world.

Colton's lips twitch, but his tone is ice cold with zero honey. "Tell me what you really think." It's barely an invitation, and strictly about Tom, unfortunately.

I shrug. "I did."

I don't bother fighting my smile when I see Helen lean back in her chair to gauge Colton's response to my outburst. She offers me a thumbs-up that I value like the rare approval it likely is. At least she's warming up.

But he closes the door to that one lifeline, shutting us in together. "Let's get to work, shall we?"

So formal. I don't know why it makes me want to pull out every ain't, gonna, and slang vocabulary I can just to fuck with him, but I swallow down that urge. I'm already pushing it this morning, and I do want to succeed with this new role. Especially since I'll likely be on my ass looking for a new job after the HQ2 project ends. Even Miranda's not going to touch me with a ten-foot pole after this.

The morning gets into swing, and I see the gossip about Colton come to life before my eyes. He's not the Big Bad Wolfe. He's the Terminator. I watch in barely suppressed awe while he handles two video calls, always turning the conversation to some advantage for the company regardless of the situation.

He clicks away on his computer, seemingly multi-tasking, but on what, I have no idea. He hasn't given me any assignments so I sit, prim and proper as a fucking lady, doing jack shit but watching him. It's almost like he's forgotten about me.

In everything, it's fascinating to observe him work. No wasted motion, no wasted words. It's a stark contrast to his opulent office, and I'm nearly startled out of my chair when my phone buzzes just before lunch.

Tiffany: *How's it going with Sir HotsALot?*

Me: *I don't know yet. Boring, if I'm honest. How bad's the gossip?*

Tiffany: *Bebop came sniffing around. Told him you were upstairs somewhere and he took off to hunt you down. Not sure he bought it, though. You need to tell Daddy before he finds out on his own.*

She's right. He doesn't deserve to be blindsided with this news by someone else. I owe him some brutal honesty, even if it kills me.

Me: *TY for covering me.*

I add a heart emoji and prayer hands before hitting *Send*.

Tiffany: *Of course. Oh, and boredom is not allowed. I dare you . . .*

I see those three dots pop up and my breath comes faster, waiting to see what she types. I don't even know what the dare is yet, but the anticipation and excitement are brewing.

Tiffany: *I dare you . . . to tell him to put your skills to better use. I can't wait to see if he takes the safe route and gives you some copies to make or if tells you get on your knees and suck him off. Proof's in the pudding what kind of man he is, and don't we all want to know? Wonder if he eats pineapples?*

I gasp as I read it and then glance up at Colton's throat clearing sharply.

"Miss Stryker, may I?"

He holds his hand out, and I get up, walking toward him. Uncertainly, I lay my hand on his, not sure at all that holding his hand is appropriate or why he wants to, but I do it anyway. His hand feels soft, strong against mine, an unexpected intimacy.

A smile blooms so slowly that I watch it grow . . . lips pressed firmly together, relaxing, tilting up, lips parting, and then the flash of white teeth. Oh, fuck, is that a dimple?

Colton squeezes my hand but reaches with his other. "I meant the phone, Miss Stryker."

I grasp it my chest, out of his reach, but he uses the hand he's still holding to pull me toward him.

"Company phone, company time, and I'm your boss. I believe I'm entitled to confirm that you're upholding the rules and not divulging team secrets already." There's not a doubt in my mind that he doesn't think that. He just wants to know what made me gasp, and instead of asking like a regular human being, he's making a power play.

Pisses me off. But under the anger is embarrassment.

I push through the blush I can feel on my face and shove my phone his way. Fine, if this is how he wants it, he can damn well see.

His brows rise as he reads Tiffany's last text. "First, explain pineapples to me. Is that an American idiom I'm unaware of?"

Oh, I thought I was blushing with embarrassment. But nope, this right here . . . this is embarrassment. I'm not shy about sex or anything, but this conversation is about to go seriously haywire.

I lick my lips, searching for the safest way to say this. "It's an old wives' tale. If you eat a lot of pineapple, it makes you sweeter." I gesture vaguely to his crotch, hoping he catches the drift.

"Sweeter?" he says, but his lips are twitching again.

Motherfucker. He's playing me again. Well, fine fucking dandy. Two can play this game. I lose the shyness and go straight for the jugular. I plaster a big, fake customer service smile on my face and explain crisply.

"If you eat pineapple, it'll make your jizz sweeter so women don't mind swallowing when you fuck their face and come down their throat. In return, if a woman eats it, her juices are tastier too. Encourages reciprocal oral sex. If there's nothing else, sir, perhaps I could get back to work? If you'd like to actually give me any? I could order fresh cut pineapple to be delivered to your home, if you'd like?"

That's it. He's going to call HR in 3, 2, 1 . . .

His face goes blank and then his brows lift in surprise before they slam back down and heat takes over. He growls, his voice deep and rough. "Yes, order me a pineapple, Miss Stryker."

Well hell, I didn't expect that reaction to my outburst. I nibble my lip, knowing it's a bad habit but feeling like I need to stop my mouth from running. I can feel the chaos churning through me. Or maybe that's desire, hot and wild?

"And as for the dare?" He's taunting me.

I stand straighter, smoothing my skirt with both hands now that he's let them go. "I would like to stay busy and be of use— on the HQ2 project," I add hastily and pointedly. "Put my skills and talents, as you so politely called them, to work."

Dare done.

And we both know it. There's a little extra fizz in the bubbles shooting through my veins right now, that familiar feeling of success and accomplishment, and he's looking at me with what seems to be pride in his smile.

"Very well. I'll send you a list of bullet points momentarily." He lifts his chin, gesturing for me to return to my desk.

I'll freely admit that I add an extra swoosh to my saunter across the room and that I take special delight in crossing my legs, knowing that though he's looking at his computer screen, he's all too aware of me.

Not just a dare done, but utter victory.

Ding.

My email chimes, and I look over his to-do list, but I feel his gaze and glance his way to find him eyeing my legs. *Oh, yeah, Big Bad Wolfe, two can play this game and I'm a fucking winner.* "Yes, sir. I'll get right on this," I virtually purr.

I swear I hear the tiniest, quietest groan as he goes back to work, and I take that as a sign that he's conceded this round. I get to work on the bulleted list.

The first item is actually to order a pineapple, and I jealously wonder who's going to be swallowing him down, but then Colton has me running from one thing to another. Whether it's going downstairs to retrieve a report, on my own computer doing research, sending emails, making copies, or more, it gives me time to think.

My computer clock ticks over to five o'clock, but Colton looks like he could go another eight hours fresh as a daisy except for his sexy, grizzled jawline.

Meanwhile, the only thing I want to do right now is get some Epsom salts and the big bucket under my sink and soak my feet. These heels are gorgeous and make my ass look fantastic, but they're more 'entrance' shoes. As in, make your entrance and then sit your ass down.

They'd look sweet up in the air while you're getting plowed, too, that devil on my shoulder says. Damn, Tiffany is such a horndog. Okay, maybe I am too, but I've been sniffing Colton's pheromones all day.

In so many ways, he reminds me of Dad. Driven, hard-working, professional, all traits I admire. In a lot of ways, working with him today has made me ashamed of my antics with Tiffany downstairs. How could I think I was doing a good job when people like Colton are up here making me look like the class clown in the back of the room?

But then isn't that one of the reasons he wanted me up here? To add a little bit of that crazy lightness to his day?

"Excuse me, Mr. Wolfe?" I ask as I set the latest report on his desk. "Will that be all?"

"Yes," Colton says, not even looking up from the papers he's reading. "Thank you."

Deflated, I go to my desk and collect my things. Great . . . I didn't do anything to note. Give me three weeks, and I'll be back on the front desk—if I'm lucky to last that long.

"Miss Stryker . . . I spoke too soon," Colton says, causing me to turn around. "What I meant was that your office work is done for the day."

"Sir?"

Colton flashes that full-dimple grin, the one that says he knows he's the shit and is also well aware that I know. "We're having dinner tonight. Go home, relax, and change if you'd like. I'll send a car around eight."

"What?" The shout is not pretty or dainty in the least. It'd be enough to get Helen in here in she hadn't already left for the day.

Colton's left eyebrow, dark and inky, lifts. "I dare you . . . to have dinner with me. Let's have some fun."

The words rush through me, leaving heat in their wake. He's got me and he damn well knows it.

"No car. If we're going out for fun, I dare you . . . to give me a ride in that gorgeous Lotus, or no deal." He knows I'm going with him regardless, but I can make some rules of my own.

"You like cars?" he asks, seeming surprised.

"I like speed and barely controlled horsepower under my foot, just waiting for me to let it run wild. You're lucky I'm not daring you to let me drive that machine, which I'm barely holding myself back from because I do know my own limits, especially those of my insurance. They'd shit a brick if I dented that monster. So Lotus at eight or I'm going back inside, putting on my least sexy pajamas, drinking a glass or two of wine, and watching *Friends* reruns."

"I'll take that dare. Eight, my Lotus, no not-sexy pajamas."

He holds out his hand for us to shake on it, but when I place mine in his, he turns our grip, placing a gentlemanly kiss on the back of my hand. It's old-fashioned and not especially intimate at all, but I can feel the brand of his lips on my skin.

"See you at eight . . . Elle."

I turn and leave, my mind in a daze. All day long, I've been Miss Stryker to him.

Now I'm Elle?

I float down the hall toward the elevator, only to run into interference in the form of Billy. He waves a finger in the air, telling me to turn around. I knew it was too good to be true. There's no way I was getting out of here today without this conversation with Dad, even though I'd hoped and wished and begged fate.

I steel my back and let Billy march me down the hall. It doesn't escape my notice that this is the opposite of yesterday when I'd come up to talk to Dad and then been dragged into Colton's office. Let's just hope there's not another dare in this conversation. I'm all for them, but at this point, I need to make sure I can keep everything straight.

Dad doesn't smile when I enter this time, nor does he offer me a gross green juice. Small favors, I guess.

Instead, I have that little girl sensation of shrinking as he looks at me with disappointment.

Billy closes the door, and though I've been locked up with the Big, Bad Wolfe all day, only now do I feel in danger. "What's up, Dad?" I say brightly, employing my nothing-to-see-here tactics. Hell, they worked when I was a teenager. Maybe they'll work now. I cross my fingers behind my back.

"What the hell, baby girl?" Dad thunders. Billy cringes, and I fall to the leather couch. Quieter, he bites out, "I asked you to let me know if you heard anything sketchy. I specifically said not to do anything shady or go above and beyond, and what do you do? Go and get yourself assigned as Wolfe's right hand for his HQ2 project?"

Dad plops to the other end of the couch, eyeing me like he can't imagine what fanciful shit is going through my brain.

"Did it occur to you that this assignment might have absolutely nothing to do with you?" I know I sound bitter and pissy, but seriously? How narcissistic can my dad be? "Or that maybe, just maybe, I might actually be of help to his project?"

"So you think it's a coincidence that Wolfe pulled my daughter out of the available clerical pool? You think this isn't all about me, about my HQ2 presentation, about his HQ2 proposal?" He shakes his head, incredulous.

I grit my teeth. "Of course it's not coincidence. He told me matter-of-factly that my last name on his project would irritate you and paint his project in a positive light comparatively. Not that it needs it, based on the tiny bit I've seen and what you've already said."

Dad scoffs, knowing I'm right. They've both got good proposals, and either one would be a good choice for Fox.

"I'm well aware that I'm a pawn in whatever dick-measuring pissing match you have going on with him. What I expected was for you to be able to handle that and win anyway. You don't need me and have been doing this longer than Colton. Just do your best, Dad. Isn't that what you'd tell me?"

I raise my brows, daring him to dispute me. "Remember when I tried out for volleyball in junior high? What'd you tell me then?"

He sighs, lost to the past for a moment. "That you couldn't control what Madison Kirkland did on the court, but you could control what you did and do your best and let the chips fall where they may. But she sprained her ankle before tryouts even happened, so that's not exactly the same thing."

Oh, shit. I forgot that part.

I look at Billy, who's damn near whistling Dixie as he scans the ceiling for God knows what. I had made the volleyball team as a starter that year, and Madison hadn't even tried out until the next year. Because that sprained ankle? It was an honest mistake, a real and true oops, but that might've been because Billy and Ricky were up to no good and Madison was an accidental casualty of the unsanctioned slip 'n slide we'd popped up on the football field. She'd had no hard feelings about the matter, especially when Billy carried her books and backpack to class every day for weeks afterward.

"Just do your best, Dad, and let me do mine. In the end, it certainly won't be me who has any real effect on the outcome unless you let this get to you. Trust me to be able to handle Colton and whatever game he's up to."

It's a plea for sanity. And that's just for the professional piece of this big clusterfuck. I haven't mentioned that we're going to dinner, nor am I going to, because I don't think that's relative to the situation at all. I'm not so green as to not consider that Colton might be manipulating me from every angle, but my gut—and other areas of my body and his—tell me that part of our arrangement is different.

"Colton? You're calling him Colton? I like that even less," Dad fumes dangerously.

I glare back just as dangerously. I learned it from him, after all. "Dad. Enough. You . . . work. I'll work." I wave my hands around like we're beleaguered elves trying to make the deadline on Christmas Eve. "And it'll be fine."

I stand. "If you'll excuse me, Tiff's waiting downstairs for a ride." I move to the door, but Billy doesn't budge from his path-blocking battle stance.

He glances over my head and must get silent permission from Dad because he opens the door. I stick my tongue out at him like we're kids again. I just can't help it with him and Ricky. We grew up together, but somehow, when we get together, it's like we never grew up at all.

He doesn't do it back, though he licks his lips like he wants to but is oh-too-mature for that shit now. He's not, so Dad must still be watching us.

"Tell Tiffany I said hello," Dad says offhandedly from behind me.

"Sure thing," I toss back, having zero intention of doing so.

CHAPTER 10

COLTON

*L*eaving my suit for a moment, I head into my bathroom, showering quickly. The shower is always a great place to review my day, and as I do, all I can think about is Elle.

From the first moment I saw her this morning, looking like any gentleman's vision of a professional, beautiful woman, to the way she kept up as I pushed her to do more and more, it was difficult today not to praise her.

She worked hard, and it was actually a boon for both me and Helen to have another pair of hands and set of eyes, but all day, Elle was distracting me. I'm sure I did a good job of hiding it, but every time she twisted in her desk, my eyes were glued to the way her breasts stretched the fabric of her blouse, the way the texture of her demure but sexy bra would imprint itself against the thin cotton. And the silky swish of her legs as she crossed and uncrossed them was nearly my undoing. I wanted to trace the polka dots on her hosiery like a connect-the-dot puzzle, seeing where they led.

By the time lunch came around, it was all I could do not to bend her over my desk and spank her bum pink before shagging her senseless in just those hose, the ridiculous heels, and that pearl necklace.

She even found time to gab a bit with her mate downstairs with a conversation that had initially befuddled me but then amused me quite a bit.

And that mouth! Not just the plump fullness of her lips but

the wildly inappropriate things she says. The discussion about pineapples and the filthy words on her tongue had damn near sent me running for the en suite again, not giving a single fuck whether she could hear me jacking off. Hell, maybe I'd even want her to hear . . . to watch . . . to help.

As much as I want her, I'm intrigued by her. She knows exactly what she's gotten herself into, or what her father and I have gotten her into, but she's not resting on her laurels, letting herself be used. No, she still wants to work, wants to be useful and learn, and I can admire and appreciate that.

I consider wanking off before dinner tonight, knowing it might be the prudent course of action after a day of blue balls. But I want to wait, want to see what adventures the evening holds. Not that I think I'll be getting off with Elle tonight, but a man can fantasize.

I get dressed, pulling a navy suit from my closet. I refuse to call the trousers pants. I've not been that Americanized just yet, but I do give in and skip the tie, leaving the top two buttons casually undone before pulling on the matching jacket. The suit's just right for the evening, slightly less formal than what I wear for work but still slim fitting and showing off my broad shoulders.

I sit in my Lotus, letting the purr of the engine work its magic before I pull out of the garage and into the street. The traffic is slightly lighter this late, but what little there is, I'm able to dodge as I eat up the road and the minutes until I can see Elle again.

Of course I checked on where Elle lives, and it surprised me when I traced the address from her file.

Her flat is in a reasonable, middle-class part of town. But that's just it. Daniel Stryker's an executive for Fox and the man dotes on his daughter, from what I hear.

So why is his daughter living in a little one-bedroom flat?

The only reason I can think of is that Elle's so fierce, so independent minded, that all she wants is to not accept her father's help. And that fascinates me, especially given my own family's tendencies to use their trust funds as fluffy cushions against being even as lowly as the upper class.

All thoughts of Elle's living situation evaporate as I pull into the carpark at her complex and see her standing outside, waiting on me. Any disappointment I might have at not seeing her personal space is washed away by her sheer beauty as she takes my breath away.

The 'little black dress' might be a bit cliché, but it's cliché because it works. Especially on a woman like Elle, whose curves become even more accentuated by the clingy hug of the fabric.

She's let her hair down too, still with those sexy curled strands framing her face, but now the rest of her blonde hair hangs loose and sexy down her back, perfect for burying my hands in as I hold her close while driving myself deep inside her.

She looks calm, cool, and collected, the quintessential bland socialite good girl. But she's nothing of the sort. She's reckless, wild, and clumsy, prone to outbursts of coarse language and brutal honesty. Surprisingly, I prefer her just the way she is. Her unexpectedness is refreshingly attractive.

In fact, it's hard not to just jump out of the car, snatch her up in my arms, and haul her upstairs for some wild and crazy, tear the clothes and damn the consequences rompery . . . because I think she'd be amenable to that. Instead, I do the responsible thing and park, getting out and going around to open the door for her.

"Good evening," I greet her, taking a moment to let my eyes wander over the long length of leg she shows getting in. She flashes me thigh-high stockings with no garters, my favorite, and in my trousers, I feel another twinge. I'm second guessing my decision to hold off on wanking one out.

Getting through dinner is going to be difficult.

"Hi," Elle says, buckling in as I get back in the driver's seat.

Silence descends, and I put the car into first and hit the road. The growl of the engine fills the space between us. It almost seems as if she wants me to be quiet so she can enjoy the motor running as we take off and gather speed.

"Did you get the figures crunched for the potential sites?" Elle asks, though her eyes are roving along the dash hungrily. I want her to look at me the way she's appreciating my car.

"No work tonight, Elle." Her eyes jump to me, and it's my turn to focus elsewhere, keeping my eyes on the road and the small amount of traffic. "I dare you . . . to not let work interfere with our fun tonight. Let's let it be just you and me."

"You're really getting into this dare thing, aren't you?" she challenges.

I tilt my head thoughtfully. "It seems to be the impetus for you to have fun, so I'm simply following suit."

She laughs, loud guffaws bursting from her. She points a finger my way, "First, stop talking like that. Repeat after me . . . YOLO."

I mime her exuberance, sounding out the word. "Yoe-loe." The road clears in front of me, and I glance over to see her watching me closely, a wide smile on her face. "What's that mean?" I ask.

"You Only Live Once. It's basically my motto. Live big, live loud, and with no regrets. Or at least if you have regrets, make it for things you've done, not for things you didn't have the balls to do."

I consider that. It's actually quite profound for what, on the surface, could amount to choices that might be mistaken as immature and unthoughtful. But she's not. She's just willing to be bold and daring. She's actually living, not just existing as so many people do.

"I like it," I decide. "YOLO!" I yell out, feeling a bit ridiculous, but perhaps that's the point. Nothing ventured, nothing gained.

She laughs along, yelling out with me, both of us wild and free as we repeat the motto several times, trying to outdo the other's volume.

"Where are we going?" she asks after we settle comfortably.

I spontaneously decide not to tell her even though we have reservations for eight thirty. "It's a surprise."

She clasps her hands, her eyes bright in the dim glow from the dashboard lights. "Yes! I love surprises."

I'm not the least bit surprised that this woman loves a good surprise.

We soon reach the restaurant, one of the best Japanese restaurants in the state. Yamashiro might not be the most famous nightspot, but what it does have is small, intimate tables and a delicious menu. Both are essential for what I want tonight.

After ordering our appetizers, I pour Elle some wine. "Japanese custom. You never pour your own drink unless alone."

"Then how do you get refills?" Elle asks, smiling as she pours my drink in return. "Ask?"

"That'd defeat the purpose!" I tease. "No, you're supposed to keep an eye on your partner's glass and refill it for them when it's empty. Builds camaraderie, you know."

"Sounds like a good way to get the other person hammered."

I chuckle, nodding. "You're on to my evil plan," I deadpan, pleased when she smiles. "So, is this your first time here?"

"Yeah . . . so be warned, I'm going to want to try everything."

She means the food, but my brain hears something much dirtier, though both ideas grab my attention. I find her openness inspiring, her lack of a rut refreshing.

I sip my sake, simply looking at her, and she stares back shamelessly. She gives in first, though it's with a tough question. "I feel like I'm at a major disadvantage here. You basically know all about me, and I know nothing about you other than that you have a sister named Lizzie who's important to you because you keep her picture on your desk. Tell me . . . things."

"What do you want to know?" I stall.

She's not fooled in the slightest. "Tell me three things, two truths and one lie, and I'll see if I can guess the lie."

"A game?" I shouldn't be taken aback, but I find that she surprises me at every turn. I think for a moment, blinking as I search through the file cabinets of my past in my mind. "I have a sister and a brother, but the most important person in my life is my Nan. I am *not* wondering what type of knickers you have on under that dress, or if there is a God listening to my prayers, perhaps there are none at all. I am the black sheep of my family, near banished to America."

Elle's eyes narrow, and she takes a large gulp of sake before sputtering slightly. "I don't think you quite get the gist of this game."

"No?" I ask. "Two truths, one lie."

"Well, yes. But that's rather deep. I meant like, my panties are red, my favorite band is Smashing Pumpkins, and my last boyfriend had a thing for toes. Silly stuff like that."

I hum, filing the information away. The red panties I might be able to confirm or deny, but it's more fodder for my fantasy again. Her favorite band is interesting but not ground-breaking information. And I prefer to not think about her past lovers lest my jealousy get a bitter hold on my mood.

"I think I prefer my way. I want to know more about you than superficial things, Elle." She blinks, looking confused as if no one has ever actually taken the time to know the Elle beneath the silly antics. "And I think you'd rather know the real me than know that I prefer boxer briefs, black, Calvin Klein."

She smirks slightly, and I know she's imagining me in nothing but my Calvins.

But she acquiesces. "Are you really the black sheep? Are you not close to your family?"

"We're . . . well, an ocean apart," I reply with a very false feeling smile. "Of course, I ring home when I can, and my sister visits as frequently as she can. I think you'd like her. Lizzie's a bit of a handful."

"How old is she?"

"Fourteen now. I know, I know, that's a big age gap. After me, my parents decided that two boys were enough until one Christmas party, a bit too much schnapps, a bit too much fun, and Bob's your uncle."

Elle nods, chuckling. "Sorry. I'm going to be laughing at some of your sayings for awhile, I guess. Do I sound that silly to you?"

"Not really," I reassure her. "Growing up, we watched so many American shows on the telly, and of course, most of the films in the cinema were Hollywood productions. Even on the BBC. Meanwhile you've had to make do with the occasional side character and *Masterpiece Theatre*."

Elle laughs, relaxing even more, and we cross the line from two foreigners to just two people learning about each other. Our appetizers arrive, and Elle lets me feed her a piece of tuna sashimi with my chopsticks, her pink lips wrapping around the succulent fish that's almost the exact same color and making my mouth go dry.

I don't think I've ever wanted to be a fish before, but right now, I wish my name were Charlie the Tuna, Chicken of the Sea, because I'm jealous as hell of the bite she just took.

"Mmm . . . Sophie's going to be so mad at me if she finds out," Elle says as she chews her bite thoughtfully. "She's my cat, and she's the real owner of my apartment. She's laid claim to everything, whether by claw or hairball."

"Sounds a lot like Mr. Scruggles," I tell her, thinking of my family's old cat. "He's at least twelve years old by now and fancies himself the right lord of the manor. Woe to those who dare to deny Mr. Scruggles anything he wishes. In fact, the only one of us who can control that Siamese terror is Lizzie."

Elle tilts her head, smiling. "You really love your little sister, don't you?"

"That obvious, huh?"

Elle nods. "What about your brother?"

A sour mood washes through me. "What's the word you used today? About Tom?" I rack my brain for a moment, searching for the odd term. "Douche canoe. That's it. My brother's a douche canoe. We're not close."

She laughs but hears the request to drop it. "What about you?"

"Just me and my dad," she answers automatically, though I see her slight freeze when talking about him. She has fierce loyalty to him, something I can appreciate.

Which is the problem. As Elle tells me about the way she grew up, with Daniel first mourning his shattered marriage before committing himself to the twin goals of becoming the world's best father as well as a powerful executive, I'm torn.

The man's had a lot of shite rained down on his head by the world. But the whole time, he's been an outstanding father when far too many others would have lost themselves in the nearest pint or even blamed their child.

Daniel didn't. Which just makes it harder in my mind to know that I'm using Elle to my advantage, to knock him off balance. I'd rather him be some over-the-top villainous type, allowing me to cast myself the hero in this battle. But perhaps we're both heroes in our rights? Or does the current situation, with Elle my assistant and my date, make me the villain?

Shit, that thought stings sharply.

"Colton?" Elle asks, making me shake my head. "You looked lost there for a sec."

"Sorry, this stuff is hot," I lie. "Maybe too much wasabi on the sushi."

We finish up dinner, and the whole time I want to pull her close and taste the last whispers of ginger ice cream off her lips. It's not until the valet closes the door that I lay a hand on her thigh. Even through the fabric of her dress and her stockings, it feels taboo in a way I can't place. "Can I tell you something?"

"Of course." The words are mere breaths, her eyes locked on my fingers.

"I'm a little torn," I admit. "Half of me wants to pull you into my arms and give you a good snogging. The other half of me wants to be more gentlemanly and take you home. And there's a third half who feels like a shite bloke for basically tricking you into coming out with me tonight."

Elle blushes and leans in. "You are a gentleman. I'm not quite sure what snogging is . . . but it sounds like I wouldn't mind it. And you really suck at math, which worries the fuck out of me, considering your job."

I lean into her, cupping the back of her head. I move slowly toward her, giving her ample time and space to stop me, but she leans in too. I have hint of a thought that the air between us is superheated, and then our lips touch, electricity crackling from her mouth to mine.

Her lips part as I tease along the seam with my tongue, demanding entrance, and she moans as I deepen the kiss. I explore her mouth while my hand kneads her thigh, both of us clamoring to get closer to the other.

I'm on the verge of pulling her into my lap and fucking her right here in my car . . .

HONK! Honk, honk, honk!

Startled, we break apart and I become aware that we're still sitting in front of Yamashiro. The valet holds up a finger, not his middle, unfortunately, telling the honking patron behind us to wait a moment. I roll the window down and give him an extra tip.

"Sorry about that. Got a bit carried away."

"No worries, dude. I'd get carried away by her any chance I could too." He grins like we're friends but has smarts enough to not lay so much as a glance at Elle, who's giggling and fixing her lipstick in the mirror.

I pull out of the drive of Yamashiro, not sure where I'm going next.

Home. Take her home and fuck her senseless, my cock chants.

My home, her home, it matters not, as long as there's a flat surface.

Can't wait that long, just pull over somewhere dark.

I wish I could say that my brain prevailed, but it's Elle who interrupts my body's woeful decision-making process.

"My turn now. You dared me for dinner, so I dare you . . ."

I chuckle. "No. That's not how this works. I do the daring."

Her glare is fiery and fierce again. I hate pissing her off, but fuck, is she stunning with that flush on her cheeks and the glint of defiance in her eyes. "It *is* how it works. You asked me to help you have fun, and this is how I do it. So I dare you . . ." She stalls for a moment, her fingertip tapping her lip in thought. "Let's play putt-putt!"

"What's a putt-putt?"

She's making that up, right? It's got to be the most nonsensical word, ever. "Putt-putt," I say, sounding it out again. It sounds like something a toddler would say on repeat while playing with a truck . . . putt-putt-putt-putt.

"It's like golf, but miniature, which makes it more fun." She nods as if her statement actually makes it so or makes any sense whatsoever.

"Small does not equal fun," I challenge.

Brazenly, she drops her gaze to my crotch where my dick stands up and tries to wave around like he's calling out, *Large and In Charge, Ma'am!*

"Noted. That's definitely true in some cases, but not all. Think like doll houses are fun, tiny foods are cute, and mini golf is going to change your life. Trust me, Colton."

Oddly, I do.

Which is how I find myself holding a cheap metal club and playing what I suspect is largely a child's game an hour later.

Neither of us is particularly good, and given the odd looks we're getting, we are majorly overdressed for this activity, but it is fun. We figure out how hard, or rather how gently, to hit the balls by the second hole, but my ball gets trapped in a whale's belly on the fourth. We have to answer a riddle to gain exit, but that only takes a couple of tries. The fifth, sixth, and seventh hole, I stand behind Elle under the guise of helping her line up her shot. I can say that my aim isn't much better than hers, but my cock enjoys nestling against her ass.

It should feel wrong. It feels right.

It should feel fast. It feels impossibly slow.

"On the ninth and last hole, Colton Wolfe has the point

advantage. This could be make-it or break-it for the English upstart."

Elle's voice is thrown low and dramatic, mimicking a sports-caster as I prepare for my winning shot. I spread my feet wide, adjusting my grip on the tiny club and looking left to aim before settling my eyes on the neon yellow ball in front of me.

My competitive nature is taking over, and I want to win, espe-cially with the score this close. But there's something else I want to win even more than bragging rights.

I relax and instead lean casually on the club. "So, what do I get if I win?"

Elle's lips purse as though she's fighting a smile. "Ooh, you're learning. Are we wagering here?"

"I dare you . . . if I win, you come home with me. If you win, I go home with you."

It's a bold move, but I didn't get to the position I'm in by making small steps. I think Elle, of all people, will appreciate the go-big or go-home American-style gamble.

She sucks in a breath, her breasts rising deliciously as they beg for my kisses, nibbles, and tongue.

"That's against the rules. Seriously, there are rules."

My brows drop down. "Why is this the first I'm hearing of this? There are rules to this dare game you enjoy?" I make it apparent that I think she's making things up on the fly, but she shakes her head.

"Tiffany and I have been doing this for a long time, and we've learned a few things, some the hard way. Rule one, nothing that'll hurt someone, ourselves included. Rule two, no sex. Rule three, nothing illegal." She pauses so that her words sink in. "Your dare violates rule two."

I hold up a finger. "Counter. The rules you have for your game with Tiffany do not have to be the rules for our game. They can be different, as long as we agree to them."

To neither of our surprise, she opens her mouth to argue. It's like it's a habit with her. But I hold up a staying hand.

"Also, I find it interesting that I merely dared for you to come home with me, or vice versa. You're the one who mentioned sex. What if I'd wanted you to organize my closet?"

It's a deadpan joke again, and I wonder if she'll respond

favorably because it feels like another bold move to make in the midst of her setting boundaries.

"Do you want me to organize your closet?" she retorts, crossing her arms. I think she's aiming for a stern look, but it only serves to press her tits up.

I chuckle. "Of course not. I have people for that." She throws her hands in the air, frustrated, but she's smiling, enjoying our banter. I am too. More seriously, I say, "I don't want you to do anything you don't want to do, Elle. I'm daring you to listen to your heart, listen to your body, and okay, maybe your mind a little bit, because I don't want you to regret anything. I dare you . . . to do what you want with me."

Fuck, that gleam in her eye is sexy as sin and I know I'm in trouble. I may have met my match with this woman, and I couldn't be more pleased about it.

"Dare accepted. Though how do you know I don't want you to come home and scrub my toilet?"

I press a hand to my heart and screw up my face in disgust. "If that's what you want with me, I guess I'll have to do it. But we both know you'll be staring at my ass the whole time."

She growls but laughs. "Shoot your shot, Wolfe."

I line up my aim again, double checking my form. Under my breath, I whisper, "Oh, I intend to."

I swing, and the ball sails toward the windmill. It looks like I have a real shot at a hole in one, and I'm already half-celebrating my win when the fan speeds up with the bit of non-mechanical wind in the air. My ball hits the blade at the last possible moment and bounces off.

"Ooh, he almost had it in but was re-jec-ted. Harsh, that one's gotta hurt." Elle's back to her sportscaster voice, but she lines up her own shot. She's also unsuccessful.

We both try again, and then again. Finally, my fourth shot goes in. Unless she makes hers and ties us, I've won.

She steps her feet as wide as her dress will allow her, gripping her club loosely in her hands. She looks to the windmill, judging her distance and aim, and adjusts one more time. From the angle where I stand, I can tell she's off, but it almost seems like she did that . . . on purpose?

She knocks the ball, and it rolls wide, nowhere near the windmill.

I'm on her in an instant, holding my club behind her back to cage her to me. "Did you let me win, Elle? Was that for pity or because what you really want, deep down, is to come home with me?"

Her teeth dent her bottom lip, and I kiss her gently to soothe the slight nervous tell. "No pressure. We're playing at playing here, but I would like to take you home with me."

"To organize your closet or clean your toilet?" she whispers with the corners of her mouth starting to tilt up.

I duck down, my lips oh, so close to that ear I want to suck and bite. I settle for nuzzling it. "No, to spread you out on my bed and trace every inch of your body with my tongue. To slip my fingers inside you and find what drives you wild. To slam into you hard and fierce as your tits bounce with every thrust of my cock into your sweet heaven. To hear my name on your lips as you come apart for me, shattering into pieces beneath me."

Her breath is a rapid staccato against my ear, and I revel in the tiny whimper I hear deep in her throat.

"You're still my boss. And there's this whole HQ2 thing with my dad." Her protests are weak, excuses running through her fingers like sand in the face of the desire enveloping us.

I can understand the argument. Hell, I could make it myself because I have just as much to lose here. She could report me to HR. She might still be a spy. I don't care in the slightest. I just care about getting inside her—body and mind.

"Both of those are true. I still want you, but only if that's what you want too, Elle. I dare you . . . to decide where we go from here."

CHAPTER 11

ELLE

*H*is eyes bore into mine, with no subterfuge, just raw desire. I can feel the same echoing through my blood.

Is this a dare I dare to accept?

So many thoughts run through my mind at the same time, a tornado of 'what-ifs' and 'then-whats' that make me dizzy as chaos reigns inside me. I'm not wrong that this could be the most dangerous dare I ever take, both professionally and personally.

Big risks, big rewards, I think.

Big dick, Devil-Tiffany interjects, reminding of the hard ridge of cock Colton pressed against me as he helped me aim my mini-golf shots. There's definitely nothing miniature about him.

I shouldn't make a decision like this based on dick, though, or at least not *solely* on dick, right? But fire is working its way through my veins, not just hot but bubbly and bright. If I do this, I know exactly what's going to happen, and I want that too.

Let the chips fall where they may.

He waits patiently, watching my every thought flash across my face. I'm not exactly known for my poker face, unless it's lying about a dare, so there's no telling what he sees.

Even as I think, I know what I'm going to do. I've been waiting for his attention for years and now I have it. It's uglier and more complex than I wish it were, but I'm not going to lose this opportunity any more than I'm going to sit around at work and let the big boys play while I watch.

That's not who I am, a sideline sitter. I'm a jump into the open waters of the dark ocean at midnight with no life vest kind of girl. Even if I can only doggie paddle, metaphorically speaking. *Cannonball!*

"Let's go," I say with a smile as I push on his chest. "But you'd better not disappoint. I'm gambling big here, Wolfe, so you'd better make it worth it."

I aim for lightheartedness, but there's a note of truth to the words. I'm risking a lot here, maybe even more than he is, given our roles at work and the complication my dad adds to the equation.

He lets me off the hook kindly, another point in his favor. "I'll make it so worth it, love."

"Love?" I question, one brow raised sharply. "Is that what you call your harem?"

He laughs loudly. "Harem? Do people even use that word anymore? And what makes you think I have a harem?"

That devil on my shoulder must be to blame for what pops out of my mouth. "Big dick energy."

Colton's mouth drops open for a moment, gaping like a fish, and I like that I've shocked him speechless. Especially when he starts shoving me out to the parking lot toward his Lotus. "Let's go."

Each block that passes as we wind our way deeper downtown ratchets up the tension between Colt and me.

His hand strokes up and down my leg, from knee to the edge of my thigh highs, leaving a trail of heated tingles. "Do you wear stockings often?"

"Why, do you like them?" I ask, trying not to whimper as his fingers move a little further between my thighs before stroking back down.

"Fucking love them," he grits out, and I store that away in my deck of cards to use in my favor. Colton's finger reaches my knee and then turns around, making the return trip to high on my thigh. "Any other surprises under here?"

"Hmm . . . play your cards right and you might find out," I promise him.

Colton's answering smile is full of hope. "I can't wait to see what you dare me to do."

It sounds like he means it, and I feel like we're in this

together. Adventures to a new land. Maybe I'll call it Elle-topia because Colton-topia is too much of a mouthful. I can't help the adolescent giggle that I hope he's a mouthful.

Though, I might dare him to clean the toilet just to torment him . . . and to check out that ass. Nah, on second thought, maybe I'll dare him to wiggle it for me Magic Mike style? Seems like that might be a bit more of a shock to his staid, stoic system.

And I want to shake him up a bit the way he does me.

Colton makes a left turn, pulling into a parking garage. "You live in Tristone Towers?" It's a stupid question, considering he waves at the guardhouse and the security arm rises as we approach.

But Tristone Towers is the crown jewel of downtown's residential district. The three slanted, triangular-shaped towers group together to make an even larger triangle, like a housing complex designed by a *Zelda* nerd.

Colton doesn't seem at all phased by the opulence around us, and I wonder again at his past beyond what little I've read. He said he's the black sheep of his family, but I can't imagine that's true with his success.

Colton pulls into a reserved spot, getting out and coming around to my side. He reaches in as though he's going to help me from the car like a gentleman, but at the last moment, his hand traces up my thigh once more. "You ready?"

I nod silently, my eyes laser locked on his hand before I look up. But I don't meet his eyes. Instead, my gaze stops at his waist and the very large bulge straining to break free of his slacks.

Holy shit! Mouthful? Definitely more than a mouthful. Can you get choked by cock? Because if so, I think I might gag on him.

As that particularly filthy thought shoots through my mind, I must make some noise because Colton moves his hand to cup my jaw. "Elle?" The tension in the single syllable is so sexy in its hesitancy. He's giving me an out, but that's not what I was thinking at all.

I'm standing on the edge, making that last instant decision. Do I jump and pray that I fly, risking that I might crash? Or do I play it safe and back away from the possibilities that lie 'out there' somewhere with no safety net?

It's not the dare this time sending butterflies through me. It's him. His very presence, dark and deliciously dangerous, along with the peeks behind the façade he wears to the kind and maybe even injured boy inside who wants to experience fun for the sheer joy of it.

I look up at him, still in his Lotus as he waits to help me out. "I dare you . . ." His breath catches excitedly. "I dare you to show me those Calvins."

Who said that?

Colton looks surprised, shocked, and then delighted, so it must have been me.

I'm on the verge of laughing it off as a joke, but as his head turns left then right, scanning the parking garage and noting that we're blessedly alone, I stay silent.

I'm not sure if people being around would make a difference to me now, though I'm not usually quite this adventurous in the bedroom. But I'm feeling more daring than ever, so I'm all in and praying he is too. I think it'll be good for him, in more ways than one.

"Here?" The pause is so readily obvious, a sure sign that I'm pushing him outside his comfort zone.

I nod, letting him decide, but I help him along by dropping my gaze hungrily. I'm not exactly a pro with lots of tongue tricks, but I've never had complaints about my oral skills, and I'd like to show him that blowjobs can be a footnote on my list of talents.

"Fuckin' hell," Colton groans. His accent suddenly got thicker, like he's forgotten to moderate it for being in America. "This is bonkers."

But his fingers deftly work at his belt and then the button slips free. The quiet teeth of the zipper sound loud from my proximity, and then I see the thick ridge of his fully erect cock covered by black cotton. I lean forward, nuzzling it against my cheek as I walk my fingers to the waistband of his boxer briefs.

I hold my breath as I pull the cotton down, revealing his hard length. There's a clear drop of precum on the tip, and I lick my lips, imagining how he tastes.

"Elle . . ." He's muttering deep and dark, barely words. I feel like all the power is in my hands, or well, in my mouth, and whether I choose to give him what we both desperately want.

I lap at his slit, groaning as his salty-sweet flavor covers my tongue. I kiss the crown and then envelop him in my mouth, taking him deeper and deeper with every bobbing movement of my head. I hum against him, feeling the vibrations in my palms where I grip his base.

He steps forward, blocking me in the car. If anyone came into the garage right now, they'd see him air humping his car, not knowing that my open mouth was right here in the passenger seat, gobbling him down.

He fucks my mouth, his intensity building as he gets impossibly harder in my mouth. "Fuck . . ." he grits out a moment before I feel his balls tighten up against my fist and then the first spurts of his cum splash across my tongue. I swallow him down, not wanting to miss a drop.

My legs scissor, and I know I'm soaked through with desire. I just blew my boss in the parking garage after our first date . . . was this a date? I should be freaking out right now, but the thought turns me on even more, giving me the same high that a successful dare does even though this dare was for him.

"Holy shit," Colton whispers softly, more emotion than I would've expected post-orgasm from a powerful man like him. "Let's go."

He takes his cock from my mouth, and I whimper like he's taking away my favorite candy. He quickly adjusts his underwear and half-ass fastens his pants, leaving the belt undone in favor of grabbing my arm to help me from the car.

He hustles me toward an elevator that seems unexpectedly fancy for a parking garage. But as the doors close and we rise just one floor up, the glass walls suddenly make sense. The view takes my breath away as we float higher and higher into the air, the entire town unveiling itself slowly as we climb toward the clouds.

"How do you leave your place with views like this?"

Colton chuckles and steps behind me, his hands resting on my hips as he lightly presses his body against me, almost the way he kept doing on the putt-putt course. I still can't believe I got him to do that, but I arch instinctively now the way I wanted to then. My ass presses back toward him, and my nipples harden in my bra as I lift my chest. "I've seen much prettier things tonight."

I know he wants to take me right here in the elevator, both of us riding a torrid tidal wave of sexual arousal that would steam up the glass walls of this great elevator. But he holds back, wanting to draw this out.

Because he's not on edge the same way I am. I'm hungry, needy, ready for this.

The elevator dings, opening up to reveal a sight even more opulent and stunning than the elevator ride. The far wall of the space is two floors tall, sloping with the slant of the building's roof downward to the doors to an outside balcony that rings half the building.

The inside's just as beautiful as the outside. Just as classically opulent as his office, everything's high quality, black marble and cherry wood, chocolate-brown leather and high-end electronics. It looks exactly how I'd expect, like a British bachelor pad.

"Nice place," I say with a wink. Nice is the understatement of the century.

Colton gestures to the couch, his lips twitching at my slight. "Have a seat."

I sit down, and Colton goes to the open kitchen area, where a cabinet door reveals a well-stocked liquor cabinet. "What's your poison?" he asks, already pouring himself a whiskey.

He's slowing us down, something I don't want. I want the unrestrained lust we were floating in moments ago, the mindless drive of our bodies toward one another, and the pleasure pinging from him to me and back again. I don't want to *think*. I want to *do*.

My blood rushes in my ears as I stand up, heading over to the kitchen to pluck the whiskey tumbler from Colt's fingers. "Whatever you're having," I purr, letting the liquid rush down my throat. It's smoky, deep, and rich . . . like him.

He takes the now-empty tumbler back, setting it on the counter behind him. His thumb comes up to trace my lip as he lowers his head toward mine. His tongue peeks out, licking at me, tasting the whiskey from my lips. Before he even truly kisses me again, he pulls back, eyes searching mine.

"So?" he questions me, but I don't know what about, nor can I pull together a reasonable thought right now.

Fuck him, get fucked by him. Missionary, doggie, sixty-nine, pretzel, cowgirl, prone bone, butter churner.

My brain is listing out sex positions like a *Cosmopolitan* writer who moonlights for *Penthouse* and consults for *Pornhub*.

"So?" I repeat cluelessly.

His grin is pure arrogant bastard. "The dare was to come home with me and do what you want with me. So, what do you want to do? Or was the scene in the car the sum total of your fantasies?"

Oh, if he only knew the filthy images flipping through my mind like a retro ViewMaster.

Click . . . bent over the counter. Click . . . spread eagle on his bed like he described earlier. Click . . . slick and soapy against the shower wall. Click . . . face down on his desk with him licking me from behind.

"Bedroom. Now." My voice is steady and certain, no doubt that I mean precisely what it sounds like.

Colton's jaw clenches, and he takes me by the hand, leading me to a staircase and upstairs to a huge bedroom suite. The space is blanketed by rich navy walls, giving it a warm, masculine feel, and it's easily bigger than my apartment.

His bed's just as big as the rest of the bedroom, a fluffy white comforter roughly the size of a tennis court stretched out over the thick mattress. Well, maybe it's not that big, but you could fit three or four people in there easily.

Maybe Colton has. I don't know.

The errant thought gives me a moment's pause, but no more. Especially when Colton steps in front of me, looking at my lips like he wants to consume me.

"I know I won, and the prize is for you to call the shots, but I'd like to offer a new dare if you're game."

My brow jumps, inviting him to tell me more. Anticipation, excitement, and restlessness begin their familiar buzz again.

"You tell me your boundaries, exactly how far you want to go tonight, and then let me get us there."

I purse my lips, not surprised at all that he wants control back. "Are you a control freak, sir?" I use the endearment intentionally, wanting to gauge his response. If I agree to this, I want to be specific in my rules.

"I do prefer to be in charge, but I'm certainly fine if you'd prefer to call the shots." He shrugs, and that answers enough.

"Okay," I say, thinking carefully about tonight but also the future, about what my choices now are going to mean at the office tomorrow. "No sex."

Colton flinches, disappointment shooting through his eyes, but he swallows thickly and nods. It's a test and he passed.

"I want to come. I want you to come. And I want to go home tonight. I won't pull up to the office tomorrow in your car like the whore people already think I am." He tries to argue that, but I stop him. "Focus on now. Can you do that? Because I am."

"How many times? For you, for me?" he clarifies, letting me know his focus is right where it should be.

I smile, knowing I've got him but also that it's going to be to both of our benefits. "Well, you're one up already," I tease. "Let's go with two for me and one for you. Make it even."

Colton nods. "Counter. *At least* two."

"Feeling pretty good about your own talents, are you?" But I smile my agreement. And the deal is struck.

"Hold still," Colton murmurs in my ear as he steps a slow circle around me, his eyes drinking in my figure through my dress. "I want to see you."

"I . . . I want to see you too," I tell him. "I've been undressing you with my eyes for ages."

"You will." Colton's voice is thick with want and hidden humor. I still can't believe he had no idea I was crushing on him as he strutted through the lobby. The clueless, hyper-focused man needed to be clubbed over the head—or flashed my naked ass, apparently—to get his attention. "For now . . . just hold still."

I do as he says, not moving as his fingers trail over my shoulders and down my arms, goosebumps pricking my skin right behind his touch. Coming back up my arms, he explores my back and neck with just his fingers but still setting my body on fire by the time he starts lowering my zipper.

My dress slithers down my body, leaving me in just my lingerie, stockings, and heels. "My God, you're stunning."

His bald admiration makes me flush with pride, and I lift my chest a little bit, preening for him under his gaze. Colton steps around me, looking me up and down as he slips his suit jacket off and undoes his tie. "I want to undress you."

Colton surprises me by shaking his head, grinning as he hands me his tie. "I have a different idea. Cover your eyes with my tie," Colton dares, leaning in again until I can feel the heat from his body though we're not touching . . . yet. "Then we're going to play X marks the spot."

A game? He's learning . . . fast, and I like it.

"I think you mean G spot? I've never heard of an X-spot, though if you want to find mine, I wouldn't mind a bit of a wild goose chase."

"Goose chase?" he echoes like a parrot.

I smile. "It's an expression. It means running after something that isn't there . . . like an X-spot."

He smiles, getting it. "Not a goose chase." The phrase still sounds like a foreign shaping of his tongue, like the expression amuses him. "X marks the spot. You will think of a spot but not tell me. I'll test to find out where the spot is, with my fingers, my lips, my tongue, touching you wherever I think it might be, with whatever I want. We play until I find the X."

"Or the G?" I barter.

"You're not a very good listener, are you?" he teases. "You're not supposed to tell me the place you're thinking of or it ruins the game."

"Just to be clear here, finding my G-spot is never, ever going to ruin a game. It's basically a touchdown, field goal, *score*, hole in one every time."

His lips do that twitchy thing again, like he's barely holding back from laughing at me.

I trace the tip of his tie over my skin and along the edges of my bra. "Okay, so other than the obvious worship and G-spot discovery—that's a hint, by the way—what do I get if I win?"

"Damn near anything you wish," Colton promises me. "Well? Are you up for it?"

Oh, it's on. Biting my lip, I place Colt's tie around my eyes, cutting off all light. At the last minute, I pull it back down, lifting one sculpted brow his way. "No feet. No shame, but that's definitely not my kink, and your feet have been in dirty socks all day. Not to mention whatever hazards were on that putt-putt course. Gross." I shudder exaggeratedly and curl my own toes, breaking the tension of the moment when Colton laughs out loud.

Sex, or not quite sex, doesn't have to be the Serious Thing people make it out to be. It can be fun, filled with heat and humor. Or at least that's my experience.

Having said my piece, I lift the fancy silk tie back up over my eyes, shutting out the light once again. I hear a shuffling of sound and I realize that he's shucked his clothes. I'm naked . . . well, nearly naked in my lingerie and stockings, with a nude Colton Wolfe, his tie blindfolding me as we prepare to play what I think might become my new favorite game.

He starts easy, his fingertips tracing my ears and his tongue licking a line along my collarbone. It relaxes me, and soon, I'm having fun, any trepidation forgotten.

But then Colt starts really playing. His fingers work at the clasp of my bra, sliding it down my arms before his mouth engulfs my right nipple and I surge upward in surprised need. He lets go too soon, driving me crazy. I can feel the air around me, heated but empty, and I try to figure out where he's standing.

To my left. No . . . to my right. I don't sense him there, either.

I feel a nudge along my hip, something blunter than a finger.

"Oh, my God, is that your toe? Did you stick your big toe on my hip?" I laugh as I say it, hearing how crazy it sounds a second after it leaves my lips.

His answering laugh only makes me blush beneath the blindfold. "If you think I can get my big toe up to your hip from here, you might be sorely disappointed in my lack of flexibility, Elle. I'm not exactly yoga-bendy."

I giggle. "You said bendy. That doesn't seem like a Colton Wolfe word."

"Touché."

"Yeah, that's more like it. Fancy and French."

This game is weird and silly, and I love that he came up with it. The serious and staid Colton Wolfe playing putt-putt and not just seducing me but being playful as he does so. I like it. A lot.

I take matters into my own hands, reaching out to find something long, thick, and incredibly hard lined up against my belly.

Colton hisses.

"So, not your big toe then?" I say coyly.

"You're forgetting the rules," he says gruffly as I stroke him from base to tip. "I'm the one finding the X."

I lick my lips, knowing he probably sees the flirtatious movement. My God, he's huge. I can feel the head of his cock pressing against my inner wrist even as I push down to his base, and as I jack him slowly, he hums in pleasure. "You didn't say anything about distracting you from your hunt, though. I play dirty. I'll provide the distraction, and you . . . you keep searching."

"Play dirty? I'll show you playing dirty."

It's the only warning I get before I'm swooped up into his arms and flung through the air. I have a split-second shock of freefall before I bounce on his tennis-court-sized bed. A second later, my legs are resting on his bare, broad shoulders and he's running his fingertips along my inner thighs.

"Oh, shit," I say huskily. I'm not even going to pretend he isn't rocking my world just by being between my thighs, and he hasn't even really touched me yet. "Do you want a clue about the X?" I ask, but there's a begging plea in my tone for him to get on with this.

Fuck, I need him, need this. No matter how crazy it might be, no matter how stupid I might feel tomorrow. Right now? I'd agree to give Tiffany carte blanche on dares for infinity if it'd get Colton to lick my clit. And to be clear? Tiffany can come up with some crazy shit. But I think Colton's tongue would be worth it.

"No more cheating. This is my game, Elle." A tease of punishment paints the edges of the words, and I have to consciously decide whether I want to see what that looks like from Colton or play nice.

His breath whispers across my core, hot through the satin, and I decide to shut right the hell up and let the man play his search and destroy game.

His tongue licks slowly along the right edge of my panties. "Is this the X?"

I bite my lip and shake my head, not trusting my sassy mouth.

"Here?" he asks, kissing the other edge. I shake again, more than just my head, damn near my whole body, screaming for him to go a little more central and he'd be *just* right. Like a goddamn Goldilocks bear's porridge.

He moves my panties to the side, exposing me to his gaze. Though I'm blindfolded, I can feel his eyes like a palpable caress. "So pretty, Elle. Look how wet you are. All this for me."

It's not remotely a question, and I'm not going to deny that every bit of my arousal is for him. Any denial would be a lie and he'd damn well know it, so why bother? I'm not ashamed of how turned on I am. I'd shout it from the rooftop if I thought it'd get me what I want.

His finger traces my slit first, circling my clit at the top, and I surge upward at the powerful sensation. I'm completely at his mercy, gone in my own goose chase for pleasure. But I hope there's an actual goose at the end.

What? My brain is so weird sometimes, but I forget about goose, geese, and every other flying bird when I fly apart under Colton's fingers and tongue.

I'll definitely be adding this to his list of talents, I think as he sucks on the nub of my clit, his fingers deftly and expertly shoving inside my wet heat to tap at my G-spot like he had a fucking map the whole time. Cheater! But I don't care as long as he keeps doing whatever magic he's doing.

"Oh, God, Colton. I'm going to come." Some women say it nice and polite, like they're complimenting their partners on doing a good job and to please continue. I growl it out like I've been possessed by a demon, threatening a beheading of both of his heads if he dares to stop.

Sharp tightness clenches my entire pelvis, my pussy clamping tight on his fingers and my hands fisting his hair so he can't get away. I buck and thrust, riding his mouth wildly as I fly through outer space. I don't even need the blindfold because my eyes are shut tight as I lose myself to pleasure.

A fierce quiver takes over my whole body, making me shake and shiver in release. "Wow," I think I hear Colton whisper. But maybe I'm wrong because suddenly, I'm falling in a blind tangle of limbs.

"Oh!" I yell out as I come to a rather abrupt and hard stop. I hear an *Oof* from below me and reach up to remove the blindfold.

Colton is sprawled out on the floor next to his bed on a fluffy rug, a big grin stretching his lips. He looks like the cat that got the cream, but I got the cat's tongue so he can be as smug as he wants because I'm still the winner here.

I'm half laid on top of him. "What happened?" I ask, looking around. The lights are dim, but I'm still adjusting to the brightness post-blindfold.

"I think I found the X," he brags. "And then you started shaking so hard, you knocked me over." He sounds rather pleased with himself so I decide to take him down a notch.

"That makes it one to one. Unless you concede that I win our battle?"

I don't want him to admit defeat. I want that second orgasm, and I want him to have another too. Okay, I want my second one a smidgen more than I care about his. I'll discuss my selfish lover tendencies with myself later, but right now, I want to do whatever he just did to me again.

Because that was not an orgasm. That was a freaking unicorn of rainbow-sprinkled epicness that I never knew existed.

"I want us both to win." He shifts on the floor, pulling me astride him.

And I get my first good look at a naked Colton Wolfe.

Holy hell, he's like a playground of delights—bumps and ridges I want to trace with my tongue, nooks and crannies I want to suck and kiss, and that thick cock peeking up from where it's nestled against my pussy. I'm used to appreciating his handsome face, with the chiseled jaw I want to nibble and high cheekbones I want to hold in my hands. But his body only makes him that much more handsome . . . and sexy as fuck.

I feel him throbbing, his cock trapped between us, and I rub myself up and down. There's only the thin slip of soaked-through satin stopping him from entering me, but I can tell he remembers the boundaries I set before we began playing and is being careful to uphold them.

That alone tells me something significant about Colton Wolfe. He may be a machine in the boardroom, a monster in the bedroom, and a black sheep of his family, but he's a good man underneath it all.

"Want me to ride you like this until we both come again? So close to fucking, but not . . . quite . . . there." I'm teasing him, but I'm teasing myself too, and we both groan at how good the friction between us feels.

"Fuck, Elle . . . yes, ride me." His fingers make divots in the flesh of my hips as he guides me. Faster and harder, I jerk against him, letting his crown bump at my clit with every thrust, sending pulses of pleasure through my body. "So wet, you're soaking me."

Any other time, I'd probably be embarrassed as hell by that, and maybe later, I will be. Right now, I'm thankful as fuck for every bit of juice I'm spreading along his length and the pre-cum from his cock, too, because it's only making this slip and slide of almost-sex that much better.

He reaches up, tangling his fingers in my hair and pulling my face to his. Forehead to forehead, he kisses me hard and hot, his tongue forcing its way into my mouth. Conquering, claiming, devouring. And then he nibbles my earlobe, groaning like it tastes good. I think he has a thing for them, and when his whispers go forceful, I think maybe I do too.

"Come on me, Elle. Enjoy how good I can make you feel and know it'll be even better when I get inside you."

Fancy promises, but damned if the promise of another go with Colton doesn't do it for me.

I cry out his name, bucking and riding him like a mechanical bull I once rode at a shitty bar in college. Forward and back, never losing contact as I pulse over him, hanging onto his shoulders for leverage and dear life as my body spasms and jerks.

His arms wrap around my waist, fully encircling me and holding me immobile as he takes over, using me to take what he needs. He thrusts fast and hard against the soaked satin, so close to where we both want him to be. And with a grunt of release, I feel him cover me in his cum.

I sprawl over him, giving zero fucks that we are messy as hell and I'm only making it worse. Sex is not a neat and tidy affair unless you're doing it wrong, and prissy folks who think it should be need to get over themselves. Or maybe just have sex so good that they don't care about sweat, saliva, and cum on every available inch of skin. I laugh at my own random thoughts.

My legs rest outside his, my arms noodles against the fluffy rug, and my head in the nook where his shoulder meets his neck. "Wow is right," I say, copying his earlier sentiments. Well, the sentiment I thought I heard him say, but real or imagined, it's the damn truth.

He chuckles beneath me, jostling me. "That good?"

"Don't be fishing for compliments, Wolfe. You know it was."

"Fishing for compliments? You Americans do love an animal idiom, don't you? Goose hunting, compliment fishing, and I've heard others." He hums as though he's thinking, which is impressive because my brain is still coated in rainbow-sprinkled fog. "Oh, 'elephant in the room', which made me literally look around, and 'hold your horses' instead of 'wait, please', and 'wouldn't hurt a fly', which seems rather ridiculous because why wouldn't you kill a fly?"

At that one, I do find the energy to laugh. I lift up, blinking to clear my eyes. "Just don't be a one-trick pony." I'm baiting him, and he grins.

"Think I've already proven that's not the case, haven't I?"

"Touché," I admit.

He throws my earlier words back at me too. "Oh, fancy and French, Miss Stryker."

We both laugh at that. Two sex-exhausted, animal idiom-loving, fun-seeking people who definitely should not be together. But I can't imagine a more ridiculously amazing way to spend the evening.

It's been a wild night, but there's one thing I know.

Dare done.

In so many ways, with the insertion of games and fun, laughter and seduction, we made the dare for a night out our bitch.

I just hope we don't pay the price tomorrow.

CHAPTER 12

COLTON

I have a morning meeting the next day, leaving Elle to arrive on her own. Not that I think she can't handle that, and honestly, a separate arrival might even be the safer course of action, but I feel a twinge that perhaps I'm throwing her to the wolves.

What is it with the animal idioms in America?

Though tossing Elle to this Wolfe would be fine and dandy with me, I think as I smack my lips.

"Everything good?" The waitress has mistaken my taste for Elle as delight for the passable eggs and bacon breakfast. I'd hoped the fruit salad would be better, but it's all honeydew and cantaloupe, my least favorite and in this quantity, virtually gag-inducing.

"It's fine," I say generously. It's not her fault the food is mediocre at best. Nor did I choose this establishment.

No, my meeting location was the call of the man across the table from me.

"Any questions or concerns I could clear up, Mr. Wolfe? We'd really like to collaborate with Fox. We can really help streamline processes for you, and that'll have a really positive outcome on the bottom-line figures."

The man sitting across from me is wearing an off-the-rack suit that has not been tailored in the least, though it is freshly dry cleaned. His hair is swept to the side in an attempt to cover the increasing amount of pink skin visible through the thin strands.

He uses corporate babble as if the words actually mean something beyond being trendy catchphrases. And most annoyingly, he says 'really' approximately every fifth word . . . for the entirety of his presentation. *Really*.

"I don't believe so, Michael." But then I think again. "Tell me how you got on my schedule."

I'm not some elitist prick who thinks my time is simply too valuable to deal with the day-in and day-out of operations. They are my main purview, actually. But for me to meet with what equates to a cold-call salesman is not the best use of my time by any means.

"Of course. I met with Mr. Givens, and he seemed really keen on the potential impacts we could have by partnering together. He really helped grease the way for me with your assistant, who was really hesitant at first. But Mr. Givens assured her that I could really help Fox. And bing, bang, boom . . . here we are."

Michael emphasizes his speech with finger guns, an American gesture if ever there were one.

Tom Givens. I had that discussion with him about his behavior only yesterday, so for this meeting to have already been on my calendar, it can't be retaliation, though that's my first thought. Instead, perhaps it's a telling sign that Elle's assessment was correct. Tom is a dinosaur douche canoe who's unable to perform his job to even mediocre standards. Because this meeting has been a complete and utter waste of my morning, without even a good cup of coffee to show for it.

"Indeed, here we are." Michael's salesman smile melts at my dry delivery. "Please feel free to send your proposal to Helen. She is rather adept at knowing where my attentions are best spent." The compliment to my assistant is in direct rebuttal to his complaint about her. "Good day, Michael."

I don't bother offering a handshake, not after I saw him lick the bacon grease off his fingers, but I do give the waitress a fifty-dollar bill as I pass her. "Thank you, Miss."

She calls out after me, "Have a nice day!"

The trip to the office is quick, but not fast enough for my racing heart. I'm excited to go to work, not for the usual reasons but for Elle. I know she's there, waiting in my office. No, not waiting . . . working. She'll be busy this morning, just like I've been. But surely, she's as anxious to see me as I am to see her?

I hadn't wanted her to go last night, but I'd understood her reasons. Still, I'd kissed her senseless before putting her into the car I called to return her home. Which was her request, even though I'd offered to take her home in my Lotus.

"This has been perfect. Let me run off like Cinderella before the clock strikes midnight. It can be our fairy tale." She grins as she says it, light laughter in her eyes.

"It's two in the morning, Elle. Let me take you home. I won't even get out of the car if you don't want me to." My argument hadn't been enough.

"I dare you . . . to order me a car, Colton." Her raised brow had said this was a test and I'd damn sure better pass it. She set the rules at the beginning of the evening, and if I didn't uphold them, she'd know that I played dirty. And not in the good way.

So I'd relented. Letting her ride away in that car had nearly been my undoing, though. I knew my Lotus could chase her down and catch her by the first stoplight, but I hadn't, wanting to prove that she could trust me.

And now, after a few hours' sleep and a useless meeting, I'm ready to see her.

"Good morning, Mr. Wolfe."

The voice calls out rather loudly as I approach the elevator, and I follow the sound to see one of the front desk workers eyeing me carefully.

Realization dawns. "Good morning . . ." I should use her last name, but I find that I can't find it in the filing cabinet of my mind, which only serves to prove Elle's point of my obliviousness. "Tiffany," I finish lamely.

"Young." At my look of confusion, she clarifies, though the disappointment in the set of her mouth is obvious. "Tiffany Young. I work for you. Well, not like other people do, but I'm in your leg of the org chart. It'd be nice to know you at least look at my name before signing off on Miranda's annual evaluation."

She's a ball buster, just like Elle. Though Elle has said that Tiffany is the devil on her shoulder, I suspect it's a bit symbiotic. Equal opportunity devils spreading trouble, merriment, and wild, crazy fun wherever they go.

"Yes, Miss Young." I use her name as if I remembered it myself and am all too familiar with her annual review. "Good morning." I add a charming smile, expecting it work as it always does, but she simply scowls.

"Don't play her."

She says it so quickly I almost think I imagined it, but the bold way she meets my eyes tells me she both said it and meant it. She's protective of Elle, something I can understand and support.

"I have no intention of doing so," I promise solemnly.

I turn, walking briskly toward the elevator, presuming the conversation is over. Tiffany is under no such compunction.

She appears at my elbow, holding a file folder which seems to be a cover story.

Her voice is low, her eyes dark. "To be clear, that wasn't a request. I will gut you like a second-rate fish from the market and spread your entrails across the seven seas as shark chum and deny ever having this conversation if she so much as sheds a single tear over you."

I force my mouth to close from its shocked gape. "That was rather . . . graphic and thought out. Been waiting long to use that?"

"Busted." A smile. "But that doesn't make it less true." Another scowl. Her face is like a menu of emotions, bare and unfiltered.

The elevator doors open and I step inside. Tiffany puts her V'd fingers to her eyes and then flips them around to me, mouthing, "I'm watching you."

As the doors close, I can't help but chuckle. That is definitely not a scene I would've ever had before Elle. No one but her—or her friend, apparently—would dare talk to Colton Wolfe that way.

Upstairs, I bid Helen a good morning and enter my office with high hopes of seeing Elle, only to find the room empty even with the additional furniture of Elle's workstation jammed up against the east wall.

Seems the girl really does have a presence.

And without her here, my gut drops in fear. She didn't bail after last night, did she?

"Helen, where's Elle?" I consciously keep my voice steady.

"Oh, she ran down to make some copies for me, work on the

Harrigan project since she wasn't sure what you needed this morning on the HQ2. She'll be back shortly."

My heart starts beating again.

Of course, she's just working. Not bailing on me, not running after one night of magic.

"That's fine, of course," I tell Helen, who's already moved on. No, she never stops moving, always working hard to keep up with my busy schedule. "You were right about that Michael chap, and I told him as much. Useless waste of my time."

I can't see her, but I hear the pleased smirk in her answer. "Mmm-hmm."

I get to work, sitting at my desk and clicking my way through my morning emails. Just as Helen predicted, Elle is back shortly. It's like she's brought the sun back with her.

Somehow, she's even sexier than yesterday in a cerulean skirt that's a little tight, a dark sweater with a V-neck that doesn't cut down low enough for my unprofessional side's taste but that accentuates her curves, and . . .

"I didn't know you wore glasses."

Elle smiles, plucking the frames off and setting them on her desk. "I don't really need to except when I'm doing a lot of paperwork. Helps avoid eyestrain headaches."

I smile, taking another moment to look her over in her outfit. She's accentuated her cheeks with just a touch of blush, and her lips . . . well, I know of only one place I want to see them right now, and that's fastened around my dick. She's having none of that.

"Good morning, Mr. Wolfe."

Back to professionalism. I would've expected nothing less from her.

"Good morning, Miss Stryker. I trust you slept well and are ready to get to work?"

"Yes, sir." The slightest smirk graces her lips, teasing me.

"List for the day is in your email now. Let me know if you run into any issues."

And so it goes for hours. I work, she works, and I find some comfort at just her presence in the room.

"Can you create a pie chart of the potential profit margins for year one of HQ2 under my proposal? The first year is always skinny financially with the upfront investment, so I want to make it look good without being misleading. I want it polished but honest."

She dips her chin, acknowledging the request, and spins to her computer.

I watch for a moment. We're being productive, and I like having someone at my side through the grunt work, but we're not necessarily having any fun.

"Miss Stryker?" I wait for her eyes to meet mine. "Open up."

I hold up a grape from the barely touched lunch still sitting on my desk, a grilled panini sandwich and a tastier-than-breakfast fruit cup.

One of Elle's brows arches high and the other drops, giving me a 'seriously?' look.

"I dare you . . . open up."

Her victory is written on her face. "I think I've created a monster. You're really getting into this." And then she drops her mouth open, her tongue sticking out and giving me much filthier thoughts than tossing a grape for her to catch.

I growl at the sexy sight but continue with the light fun. I close one eye to aim, giving the grape a few practice arcs before letting loose. It's a little wide as it flies through the air, but Elle leans forward, catching it perfectly. She smiles and chews it openmouthed, no attention to manners. Somehow, I prefer this to a well-mannered Elle.

Around the mouthful, she roars. "And the crowd goes wild . . . ahhhh!"

It breaks the nose-to-the-grindstone feel, and from there, we work and we play.

Luckily, the door is closed or Helen would probably think I've lost my mind.

I prefer to think that perhaps I've found it.

"I dare you . . . to send me a silly selfie." I maybe would've preferred a sexy selfie, but I rather enjoy the delight on her face when she sees my goofy smile on her phone and saves it as my contact photo.

"I dare you . . . to do the chicken dance. And again with the American animal idioms."

She does it, even singing the song quietly.

And that's when things get a little riskier.

We promised to keep things professional at work, and we are

working hard between dares, but professionalism seems like a rule to be rebelled against.

"I dare you . . . to sit in my lap for sixty seconds."

"Mr. Wolfe . . ." she warns. But then Elle glances at the door, double checking that it's secure, and a sly grin takes over her expression. I'm pushing her big time, but I can see the gears in her head turning. She blinks, somehow making her eyes look wide and innocent as an angel when I know she's anything but, and then she reaches under her skirt. She fiddles around for a moment and then slips her panties out.

"If I'm sitting in your lap, I'm going to drive you crazy too." She stuffs the panties into my hand, and I'm only able to resist the urge to sniff them by putting them securely in my pocket to indulge in later. Then she turns oh, so slowly, knowing damn well what she's doing, and inch by inch, she lowers her ass to my lap.

I lay one hand on her thigh and the other cups her ass. And we sit, staring into each other's eyes.

I read once that eye contact becomes awkward after ten seconds for most people because it implies a level of intimacy they're unaccustomed to.

But our gazes never waver. Her blue eyes are shot through with flecks of gold and full of mischief and pure, unadulterated happiness. I wonder if she sees as much in my eyes as I do hers.

Ten seconds. Thirty seconds. Forty-five seconds. Sixty seconds. And still she sits, and still I don't want her to move.

There's a noise outside the door, and Elle jumps up, but when the door doesn't open, she stills and calms. Her bright eyes pin me in place too.

"I dare you . . . to *not* touch me or yourself for the next twenty-four hours."

"What? That's not . . ." I pause, realizing what that smirk means. "What do you have up your sleeve?"

The innocent angel act reappears. "Why, nothing, sir. Just what I said, hands to yourself but not *yourself*."

I'm intrigued by what she might be up to, so I agree, all the while imagining my hands behind my head as Elle sucks me, rides me, doing all the work, so to speak.

She claps and scampers off toward her desk. She grabs a pen

and then meets my eye boldly . . . and drops it to the floor. "Oops, how clumsy of me. I'll get it."

She bends at the waist, putting her curvy ass on display as she picks the pen up. Still upside down, she looks back at me, and I tilt my head to force my eyes to hers. It's agonizingly difficult to break my enjoyment of her assets.

It hits me just how difficult of a dare she's presented because I think she's going to taunt me at every turn.

I can't wait.

She sashays back to her desk and sits down, the swish of her stockings as she crosses her legs driving me mad. And then she sighs lightly and uncrosses them before crossing them with the other leg on top.

I am so fucked. I look at my watch, setting a mental timer for twenty-four hours even though I have zero expectations of making it the full time.

Elle's a godsend again . . . or maybe sent by the devil because she takes advantage of her dare to tease me mercilessly for the rest of the day as we work.

I click away at my computer, comparing strategies and locations by dollar sign, by potential, and by tax benefits and making some decent headway on my goals for the day. Surprisingly, though we do goof off, I get quite a bit done. It seems I can have fun and be productive. Who knew?

Elle did.

"Oh, my," Elle says, drawing my attention. She deliberately swirls a finger through the whipped cream of the Frappuccino she grabbed on a mid-afternoon break. She meets my eyes before sucking it clean, moaning lewdly the whole time. "Mmm."

"You're a naughty fucking lass, you know that?" I finally complain, trying to stop myself from just flogging the bishop under my desk. "You're doing this on purpose."

"Of course . . . but that's what makes dares so much fun," Elle says. "The challenge and the conquest."

"We'll see who gets conquered," I mutter, forcing myself to look down at the spreadsheets on my desk. Elle's throaty chuckle sends another tingle down my spine, and by the end of the day, I'm hanging onto the dare by a whisker.

My poor dangly bits are aching, and I need to wank so badly

to the point I'm worried I'm going to need an ice pack just to be able to eat dinner.

"Mr. Wolfe?" Elle says, catching my attention.

"Yes, Miss Stryker?"

Elle gets up, giving me another show of legs and hips and swaying breasts before laying a final file folder in front of me, bending down and showing me the deep, cream-colored valley between her breasts.

"I finished my work for the day. I hope you're . . . satisfied?"

I growl, unable to look away as she gives her shoulders a little shimmy and my balls start aching again. "You know damn well that I'm not satisfied."

"Well, sir, I'm sorry about that," she purrs, sounding not the least bit sorry at all. "I'll see you tomorrow."

She'd told me throughout the day that she had plans with Tiffany tonight. I'd asked her to skip and come to my place again, even dared her to do so, but she'd refused, saying she wouldn't break the date with her friend because Tiffany 'needs' her. I can respect that, even if I am disappointed at not seeing her tonight.

"If you need help, call me," I order, glancing at the clock on my computer. Six oh five . . . nineteen hours and fifty-five minutes until I can let off this pressure inside me.

If I can make it that long without busting a penis artery.

Elle leaves, giving me a satisfied smile at the door before opening it up. A minute later, my mobile dings, and I look to see it's a message from her.

Thank you. For . . . a lot.

There's so much in her five words that I'm not sure how to reply. I know she enjoyed teasing me, and even more the fact that while I am her 'boss', she had so much power in the office today.

At the same time, she wants freedom and support on her quest to prove herself. That's something I can understand first-hand. Though she hasn't had to run halfway across the globe to have a shot at her freedom the way I have.

CHAPTER 13

ELLE

I know I can't see it. I mean, his office is on the other side of the building from the parking lot. Still, I can almost feel Colton's eyes on me as I climb into my car, and it makes me grin.

"Come on!" Tiffany calls from the passenger seat. "I need some retail therapy and a full disclosure on all things Colton Wolfe. Like does he really eat you all up like the big, bad wolf? And does he say, 'I'm arriving!' when he comes? I need to know these things."

I cut my eyes to her sharply. "What makes you think I have any idea? I've only worked for the man for two days, Tiffany."

Her grin is knowing. "Me thinketh the lady doth protest-eth too much-eth." Her butchering of Shakespeare makes her sound like she has a lisp, but I get her point.

"I'm not protesting," I argue uselessly. Tiffany can read me like a book. She's always been able to, and right now, she's got those eagle eyes locked on me, scanning for any small tell. I'm not good enough at bluffing, not with her, at least, so I might as well get this over with.

"Fine . . . yes and no."

It takes her a solid three seconds of blank-faced blinks to replay her questions and then my answers, but once it hits her, she starts shimmy dancing in her seat. Her arms flail around, and she's kicking my floorboards like they've done her wrong.

"Ohmygod! Elle! Yes! Ahh!"

I laugh but can't help sniping, "Hey, watch the car! Be nice to Cammie."

Tiffany rubs the dashboard. "So sorry, Cammie girl, but did you hear? Your momma got laid." Her whisper is to my car, but her eyes and grin are all for me.

I shake my head at her craziness, trying to decide just how much I want to tell her, but ultimately, I know she'll get everything out of me.

I can at least make her wait, I think evilly.

"Whatever," I answer, dropping my baby into first and pulling out. I carefully avoid really opening her up until we're out of the parking lot and onto the private street that wraps around the hill the Fox headquarters is built on, but thankfully, Tiffany stays silent for a bit. She knows that these thirty seconds are mine.

I punch it, all three hundred and seventy-two horsepower leaping at my command, jerking the car forward and leaving a short streak of tire rubber behind us. For thirty seconds, it's just me, my car, and the road, and life becomes very simple.

Finally, I see the stop sign up ahead and slow it down, following the law as I hit my signal and turn left to take us back toward downtown.

"You know they're going to figure out who keeps laying rubber on the road, Miss Fast N' Furious?" Tiffany says, even though she's grinning. "And no, despite your saying it all the time, I'm not playing Thelma to your damn Louise."

"And *you* know I've never even gotten a speeding ticket in my life," I point out. "There are only two times I break the law—that road, and when someone pushes me to do something stupid." I give her a side-eye.

She balks, offended. "I don't dare you to do illegal things. That's rule three."

I shake my head. "Skinny dipping in a pond on private property, which required trespassing? Ring any bells? Or how about the time you dared me to dine and ditch? Wrong, girl . . . so wrong."

She smiles sadly. "I felt so bad about that one. Did I ever tell you that I went back and paid the waitress, even gave her a big tip as an apology for being stupid kids?"

My mouth falls open. "One, we weren't kids. We were nineteen and damn well knew better. Two, I went back and paid too, even gave her twenty bucks on our ten-dollar tab."

We meet eyes, both surprised that we didn't know the other had gone back. And then we burst out laughing. "Guess that waitress didn't mind the dine and dash so much after all. She made bank on us!" Tiffany manages to gasp out between laughs. "But still, we don't do illegal stuff."

"Rule three is nothing *too* illegal. But yeah, as we get older, that's a moving target. I'm not willing to risk jail time for a thrill."

"Me neither. But handcuffs? Those are a different story. One you'd best get to telling about Mr. Wolfe unless you want to have this conversation in the middle of Macy's."

"Definitely not."

"All right then, spill. Is he feeding you the D?" She asks this as though she might be asking about the weather, like it's no big deal to be fucking your boss.

It is a big deal. A very big deal. And a very big D, too, but that's beside the point. Mostly.

But first, "What makes you think we've been intimate?"

She giggles and feigns a fancy old-lady pearl-clutcher accent. "Been intimate? Oh, my heavens!" In her usual voice, she charges right on through me. "What's got you so formal? It's sex, Elle, not trade negotiations."

I shrug, and she continues the charge, full steam ahead.

"Did he tell you we talked this morning?" At my head shake, she smirks. "Girl, your new boss came into work today with that look a man gets after one thing only, then he proceeded to actually smile, even when I threatened him. What magic did you work on him?"

"Just a little somethin'-somethin' I like to call *moi*." It would sound self-aggrandizing if I weren't so obviously being sarcastic as fuck. "Wait, you threatened him? Colton Wolfe—your boss, my boss, and the one who manages our boss? You threatened him? Have you lost your mind?"

She plants her palm over her chest. "Do you think I don't have your back, regardless of whose dick you're getting? You could be screwing the president of the company, the mayor, or a mob boss who would kill me with zero hesitation, but I'm your girl. Ride or die, bitch. I've got you and am perfectly willing to threaten to chop damn near anyone to bits for you."

"You threatened to chop Colton to bits?" I say blankly, still in shock.

She growls like a rabid raccoon when the trash man takes his stash away, her teeth flashing predatorially. "Well, I threatened to turn him into shark chum and spread him across the seven seas if you so much as shed a single tear."

I blink, her words hitting home. "That is so . . . so . . . sweet! Oh, honey! Thank you!"

Okay, so I might be a bit hysterical, but I swear I'm going to tear up over how awesome my best friend is. And how creative and violent, but mostly how sweet.

At the next stop light, I awkwardly reach across the console to grab her up in a big hug. "I love you too, girl."

Tiffany's aw-shucks look does nothing to disguise the happiness in her eyes. "You've got me, babe, and I've got you. I know you'd do the same for me. Though I'd appreciate it if you didn't threaten Daddy when I finally get in his pants, 'kay?"

Ugh. All lovey-dovey friendship thoughts vaporize into thin air.

"You are not getting in my dad's pants, and eww. Just no."

My face is so screwed up in disgust that I'm probably going to need a wrinkle-reducer mask tonight, but Tiffany just smiles like she knows something I don't know.

Shit. "You haven't, right? Wait . . . I don't want to know." I shake my head to stop the images from forming. I do not want to see that in any way, shape, form, or fashion. There's not enough eye bleach to make it go away if it materializes. "Yes, I do. Tell me the truth, bitch."

"No, I haven't been in Daddy's pants."

I let free a relieved sigh.

"Yet."

Damn it.

"But speaking of Daddy, what's his take on the whole Colton sitch? Did he go all growly possessive? 'No daughter of mine . . .' Or was he all disappointed dad? 'Baby, you can't . . .' " She goes in and out of mimicking my dad's voice.

"He's furious, of course. He told me Colton was using me to get at him . . . as if that's some great newsflash I was unaware of." I roll my eyes, knowing Dad still sees me as his little girl sometimes. "I told him that it would all be fine, for him to work and me to work, and if we all do our best, the best proposal will win."

Tiffany thinks on that silently for a moment. "That's true. Or at least it would be if it were just work, but there's more going on and you know it."

"I know that." I point at myself and then her. "And you know that, but my dad doesn't need to know that. I've never told him about my sex life before, so why should this be any different?"

Tiffany points at me sharply, our fingers crossing in between us like a sword fight of fingers. "A-ha, so you admit that Colton is your sex life? Gotcha!"

I laugh. "I said we didn't have sex. I didn't say we didn't do other things, otherwise how would I know that he doesn't say 'I'm arriving' when he comes?"

And at that stupid joke again, we both crack up.

"Let's get to the mall, girl. We have so much to do and so much to talk about still. Sorry, not sorry, Macy's."

Tiffany pulls a piece of pink paper out of her purse. "I made a list of everything I need to replace the stuff Ace destroyed, plus I need a dress for the company dinner."

"The company dinner. Oh, God, that's this weekend!" I slap my hand over my mouth, glad that Cammie is responsive enough to hold steady with one hand.

"You did not forget." At my look of horror, Tiffany's eyes pop wide. "How could you forget?"

Fire burns in my belly. "Well, I've had a lot on my plate, you know?"

My brain's dropping into warp speed now. Mr. Fox invites the entire company to his estate twice a year, once for a winter holiday party and the other for a spring celebration. It's an opportunity to see and be seen, get to know people all over the company, and to have an elegant night at a fancy mansion.

I didn't grow up poor by any stretch. Dad always made plenty, and I never wanted for anything, but Mr. Fox is a different kind of wealthy, and to get to party at his house is a treat. Last year, he had an open bar of top shelf liquor, caviar appetizers, and a full spread of toiletries in the bathroom. I never knew that I would be so impressed with disposable toothbrushes in a guest bathroom, but damn, that did it for me. So much so that I added a few to a drawer at my place, though Tiffany has been the only one to use them so far.

Maybe Colton will use one if he ever sleeps over?

"Earth to Elle. Come in, Elle." Tiffany is snapping in front of my face and the car behind me is honking. I blink, realizing the light is green.

"Shit, sorry!" I wave, hoping the driver behind me sees the apology. "I totally forgot. This has the potential to be literal hell. I have this image of Dad holding one hand and Colton holding the other and them pulling me like a Gumby until I rip apart."

Tiffany is quiet for a minute, letting me pull into the mall parking lot and find a spot far away from other cars. It's not that I can't park in the regular spots, but Cammie is antisocial and wants her space. I don't mind the extra steps to the door because then she stays door-ding free. And yes, my car has parking preferences, and no, I'm not crazy. Much.

"Seriously, babe. Are you okay with everything? You said you have a lot on your plate, and that's true, but is it too much? Are you caving under the pressure? Freaking out from the stress?" She's talking fast, worried about me.

"I'm . . ." I search my soul. "Remarkably okay. I mean, there is the whole Gumby thing because it is a lot. I don't know how it's all going to play out, either, but that's never bothered me before. I thrive on chaos. You know that."

"Just be careful, Elle." Tiffany is unusually serious.

"I know your dad always has your best interests at heart, even if he's overbearing about it sometimes. Colton's still an unknown, though. I know he told you up front that he's using you, but honestly, that makes me suspicious as hell. It's like he's a magician telling you to look right here, and meanwhile, his other hand is doing all sorts of shady shit, and not in the good slight of hand way. Just . . . be careful."

And now I'm gonna cry again because my bestie is the best in the whole wide world.

"Thanks, Tiff. I will be. I know it's only been a couple of days, but I feel like I'm getting to know Colton. He is trying to get at Dad, I know that, but I think this is more than that. For both of us."

It's on the tip of my tongue to tell her about his wanting some fun in his life and about our dares, but I don't. That feels like it's private, just mine and Colton's.

Instead, we head into the mall to tackle Tiffany's pink list.

"What all do you need?" I ask, already touching a soft cashmere sweater. The grey would look amazing on Tiffany, and I start looking for her size.

"I did a fresh capsule wardrobe plan. Going to stick to basics black, white, and pale grey, with blush pink, burgundy, and teal accent pieces. I need skirts, jeans, tops, and probably a sweater so the A/C doesn't turn me into a meatsicle. Plus, a versatile dress for the dinner."

If I didn't follow Tiffany on Instagram and Pinterest, I wouldn't have understood a word she just said. But I do, so I do understand.

As chaotic as my closet is, Tiffany's is equally neat and tidy, which is why Ace's destruction was so hard on her. Tiffany could pack for two weeks in Europe in ten minutes, travel with only a carry-on suitcase, and look chic as hell the whole time. My closet? I could dress for a costume party, a cocktail party, the office, the gym, a date, and pull out the sweater I wore to the first day of tenth grade. I've got it all, and then some. And it's all shoved in there with zero rhyme or reason. Why not have a hot dog costume next to my favorite band T-shirt? I never know when I'll need either. And yes, I have worn that hot dog costume within the last year and *not* on Halloween. Long story, and of course, it was a dare.

But shopping is something we do well, so we make good progress in a short time.

"I dare you . . . to try this one on!" I hold up a pale pink dress with silver sequin flowers.

Tiffany's nose scrunches cutely. "For what? That is awful!"

I wiggle the dress, and the sequins make a swishy sound against each other. "For the dinner. It's even in your color palette."

"Not even if I was pre-partying and drunk on liquor I bought myself would I wear that to Mr. Fox's fancy dinner. But because you dared me, I'll try it on."

"And pose for pictures!"

She rolls her eyes and repeats after me, "And pose for pictures."

The fitting room has a large, sectioned mirror showing Tiffany every angle of the dress. It really is atrocious, which only makes the pictures that much better as Tiffany reenacts every bridal moment of 'it's The One' about the dress as though it's fine couture.

"You suck. My turn," she says as she sorts her stack of clothes into nopes and yeses, leaving the nopes on the rack in the fitting room lobby.

She surprises me, picking a navy-blue lace number that's actually gorgeous. I expected her to find the ugliest dress she could get her hands on and then dare me to pose crazily, maybe even send pics to Colton. But as I shimmy into the sheath and Tiffany helps with the zipper, I catch a glimpse of myself in the mirror.

"It's beautiful," I whisper.

"I dare you to wear it to the dinner."

Tiffany's whispering too, like neither of us wants to break the spell the dress has us under. It's not even all that fancy, not a wedding gown or a red-carpet-worthy dress, but it fits me perfectly, highlighting my every curve while being modestly knee length. Though the last several inches of length are all lace.

I shake my head. "I don't need a dinner dress. You know I've already got things I can wear." Even as I argue, I don't stop admiring myself, turning slightly to see the back, which is daringly low-cut and also made reasonable with a lace overlay.

"Uh-uh, I already dared you. You wouldn't back out on that, would you? Chicken."

I press my lips together. This isn't the usual wild and silly dares we do. This is Tiffany daring me to head into a corporate function looking like walking sex. Not in a slutty way, but in a classy, elegant way. I've never felt elegantly sexy before, but I do now.

I want Colton to see me in this. I want him to see me schmooze and small talk all night with friends and coworkers and not be able to keep his eyes off me.

And there are those old friends, anticipation and excitement, buzzing in my belly.

I nod to Tiffany in the mirror. Dare accepted. She smiles back soft and sweet, as if she knows this is different too. Like maybe that's why she dared me to do it.

"Okay, now let's find me a dress for the dinner. One that will make Daddy's tongue loll out but won't get me fired for looking like a stripper."

I growl and smack her ass, the pop loud in the empty fitting room. "For the millionth time, you are not fucking my dad, girl. But yeah, let's find you a dress too."

CHAPTER 14

COLTON

*L*ast night was godawful. Alone and hard, I considered that Elle wouldn't actually know if I took matters into my own hands. But I would know, and that would kill the fun of the game. So I refrained, no matter how hard it was . . . and I do mean my cock.

Which is sore and already half-hard at the thought of seeing its tempting torturer upstairs at the office.

I bolt for the elevator but remember to throw a chin lift to Miss Young. Her raised brow is sharp, as if she's seeing into my soul and finding me lacking. I wonder if she truly is the devil that Elle touts her to be. I'm not saying I believe that, exactly, but I wouldn't say I disbelieve it, either.

The doors are just about to close when a hand shoots through, and they open once again to reveal Daniel Stryker, of all people. Coincidence or planned ambush?

I don't believe in coincidences that are this well-timed and fortuitous. He's up to something, and only the next moments will tell what move he's making now. I provoked him by hiring Elle, so it's only polite manners to allow him the next play. And it will tell me where he's at mentally, professionally, and personally.

He steps inside, followed closely by his two hulking shadows who take up positions behind us. The space suddenly feels inordinately smaller. It's not just the actual square footage we each take up but the fury radiating in waves off all four of us that fills the box.

"Elle's working for you." Clipped and cold, he doesn't ask but states the fact. He doesn't even deign to look me in the eye, instead looking at my reflection in the polished wall of the lift.

"Yes. I felt her talents would be better used here." *All business,* I remind myself.

A lesser man, one who was truly only using Elle to prod her father, would throw more barbed weapons. Perhaps about how his daughter's pussy clamped on my tongue as she came crying out my name.

I am not a lesser man, or at least I'm not now that I've had a taste not just of her pussy but of her mind and chaotically good spirit. And what Elle and I do privately is not for public consumption, least of all by her father. It's ours, mine and Elle's alone.

"I see. I felt the same way," Daniel says, our eyes locked hard in a battle of wills in the reflection. "She never accepted my offer, though."

I turn to Daniel, giving him the full heat of my stare and the hard words he needs to hear. "She is an amazing woman." A flinch of a tell ticks in his jaw. A small victory, but a considerable one, nevertheless. "I can respect that she wants to be known for her own work and mind, free of any familial benefits or charity. She's not the innocent you believe her to be."

A pair of growls erupts from Billy and Ricky, and I risk a side-eye glance their way. But as I suspected, they're leashed, which makes them not the threat. They act on Daniel's behalf so it's his reaction that matters.

I explain myself as if I had only one meaning, not the double-entendre they heard, though I'm choosing my words carefully and purposefully. "She knew straight away that my requesting her reassignment to my office was a power play against you. She's smart, even strategic, when given the chance to be." The accusation is obvious and sharp.

"I am using her against you, quite well, I might add." My lips purse, but I'm unsuccessful at holding back the cocky smirk. "But I dare say, she's using me too. To prove herself . . . to the company, to herself, and I'm sure even to you. She's not just her daddy's little girl any longer."

I do let every salacious thought into my tone for my last zing, knowing that Daniel's fear is that I'll corrupt his little girl. I won't divulge that perhaps she's the one perverting me, turning me from a cold, clinical corpse of a man to something warmer, and dare I say, more fun?

My words make Daniel turn to face me fully. And I see the truth of who he is, not the driven, ambitious, office-perching executive, but rather the protective papa bear who will devour anything and anyone who threatens its young.

It's my last thought before he moves, quicker than I would've expected a man two decades older than me to be. He fists my lapels in his hands, pulling me nose to nose with him.

Interesting. I would've thought he'd have his pit bulls do his dirty work, but I'm rather delighted that he's gone so far as to do it himself. It actually bumps him up a few notches in my estimation.

"I swear to fucking God, Wolfe . . . if you hurt or take advantage of my daughter, they're going to ship you back to London in a fucking box. Understand me?" The words are spat into my face with a sneer.

I have no doubt that he would quite literally kill me, maybe not by his own hand, but perhaps so. His daughter is his weak point, but also his greatest strength, as it so often goes. He does what he does for her, and he will literally do anything for Elle.

If I'm honest with myself, I find it a rather beautiful type of love, to be willing to go that far for someone.

Using a nifty little trick from my boxing days, I break his grip on my lapels and push him back in one sweeping move. I hold up a hand to stop his coming back at me again, sensing that Billy and Ricky are on edge and wanting to jump into the fray.

"Stop before this escalates to foolish levels. Daniel, I have no ill intentions toward Elle. I plan on kicking your arse professionally. May the best man win."

The lift dings for the fifth floor before Daniel can reply, the doors opening and revealing two people waiting. Unwilling to make a scene in front of others, Daniel and I exit with Billy and Ricky hot on our heels. We strut down the hallway like royalty, two princes making a play for the crown. Power crackles in the deafening silence between us.

Just as we pass his office, Daniel stops and turns back to me. Framed by menacing glares from his security, Daniel's is equally robust and hate-filled.

"Remember, Wolfe. Shipping's cheaper than plane tickets."

Having gotten the last word, he goes into his office, and I head down to my suite, shaking my head. It's such an obvious weakness . . . but a man who's been cornered, especially both personally and professionally, will most definitely attack viciously. He's off balance, just as I wanted, but I hadn't planned on being this intimately involved with Elle myself.

My great plan may be twisting and morphing, making me equally off kilter. I'll have to play each of the angles carefully or the whole house of cards may come crashing down around me, leaving me the loser in the race to HQ2 and alone without my fun she-devil.

"Whoa . . . you look like your breakfast came with a side of UFC," Helen says as I enter the outer office. "Everything okay?"

"Hmm?" I ask, looking down and seeing my lapels out of place and feeling my hair a bit mussed. "Oh, nothing to worry about. Good morning, Helen."

I make a quick decision to not tell Elle about her father's ambush and threat. I know that she would take it as a lack of faith from the most important man in her life, and I find that I want to protect her from that pain. Working to please a harsh critic can be motivating, at least at first. But it can also be a self-fulfilling prophecy, leading to failure or at least the sense of it, regardless of actual success.

I double-check my lapels once more and straighten my tie as I choose to release the anger of this morning's arrival. Once I'm sure not a single tell remains, only then do I open the door to my office.

"Elle." The barest of greetings, but just her name on my lips is enough to make me feel like all the stress of the last few minutes is worth it. That she's worth it.

"Good morning, sir," she says. If Helen was paying any atten-tion, it'd sound like a perfectly reasonable and professional greet-ing. But I know her well enough to hear the beaming grin even before I lay eyes on her. "I hope you had a great night and are ready to get to work this morning? I know I am."

I can't help but grin at the instant reminder of just how much I want her. Not just my cock, especially knowing I have hours left on our latest no-touch dare, but maybe even other parts of me too.

I'm suddenly really looking forward to today. I don't bother stopping my answering smile from stretching my lips. "Slept like a baby, actually." The lie is smooth but she smirks knowingly.

Twenty-four hours have never seemed so long or so fun.

FASTER THAN I WOULD'VE IMAGINED, THE DAY PASSES. THOUGH ELLE and I make significant headway on improving the details of my proposal, we have an amusing time while doing so.

Elle keeps up her sexy teasing in anticipation of the end of the twenty-four hours. And we add more dares too.

We get silly, using the space by the long wall of windows as a catwalk. Elle does her best model strut, and I use my phone to snap picture after picture, telling her to 'hit me with your best shot', an American phrase I heard on the telly as a child.

I don't mention that I have very filthy plans for the photos. At least not until she dares me to play model as well, taking pictures of her own. Then, the tease is too tempting, and I wonder aloud why she would end our twenty-four hours with pictures of me when she can have the real thing. The resulting smile is full of heat and barely bridled lust that has me adjusting myself in my slacks. She snaps a picture of that too.

After this morning, I take an additional angle on our game of dares too, daring Elle to tell me things she might not otherwise offer. She seems to enjoy the idea and does the same to me.

Her favorite childhood memory? Christmas morning when she was thirteen because she got her first cellphone from Daniel. Mine? Sleepovers alone at Nan's home, complete with English breakfast mornings, just the two of us.

Her most embarrassing moment? Giving a speech in high school and being hit with a sudden case of nervous belly gurgles so loud the whole class heard them.

"They called me Nervous N-Elle-y for months after, never letting me forget it. And every single time I made a move toward the bathroom, just to pee, mind you, everyone would hold their bellies and yell to get out of my way. The girls would exit as soon as I came in, holding their noses like I let loose a lethal nuke of fart gas."

She laughs as she says it, but I can read in her eyes that it had bothered her back then. It makes me want to track down each and every one of those shit stain kids and teach them a lesson.

Her greatest fear? Not being good enough.

"Elle, you are already good enough, and you'll only get better from here because you're willing to work hard and take risks."

Her shrug says that she's heard that before and doesn't really believe it, which I find hard to reconcile with the powerhouse in front of me.

She redirects the conversation, asking me the same question. "Not being good enough."

Though the answer is the same, there are layers of meaning beneath mine, ones I'm not prepared to delve into today when we're supposed to be having fun.

"Don't make fun of me," Elle charges, her nails digging into my lapel where her father grabbed me not so long ago. Like father, like daughter, it seems.

"I'm not. I swear it."

I'm being honest, which paints her answer in perhaps a more truthful light as well, because from the outside looking in, we're both successful in our own ways, but I still fear not being good enough.

My phone rings straight through, not going to Helen's line as a gatekeeper. Only a select few people can do that, so I answer quickly.

"Colton Wolfe speaking."

"Colton? Can you come to my office, please?"

There are few voices that command instant respect and attention from me, but Allan Fox's is one. Standing up, I'm already grabbing my jacket to slip it on. "Of course, sir. I'll be right there."

Elle's eyebrow raises in question and I explain. "Been called to Allan Fox's office." Impossibly, her brows arch even higher. "I don't know. Could be good news or bad news."

I walk down the hall with haste, ready to meet my reward or my doom but praying it's the former. It's late enough that his assistant has already left for the day, so I knock once on Mr. Fox's door and he calls out,

"Come in."

I take one last breath for steadiness and open the door to see a mishmash of years surrounding the man at the desk in the middle of the far wall. There are golf trophies next to magazine covers with Mr. Fox's face on them, the abstract art over the bar is an original piece Mrs. Fox painted for her husband, and the overwhelming theme is eclectic, or even eccentric, billionaire. A lifetime of items he's accumulated during his tenure at the helm.

"Allan?"

"Yes, Colton. Come in, please. Have a seat." He gestures to one of the leather seats in front of his desk. "I wanted to talk to you about your proposal."

My chest pains with the breath I suddenly realize I'm still holding, but I don't dare let it go now. Did I win the race already? Has Daniel? I don't consider that anyone else has. I know who the front-runners are. I know who my competition is.

"Yes, sir. I'm happy to share further details or address any concerns you may have."

Allan waves his hand dismissively and my heart tries to sink, but I buoy it, not giving up just yet.

"No, it's more than that, you see. I've had off-table discussions with most of the board, and I think we all know that it's down to you and Daniel. Those two proposals are by far our best options, though going global is a large undertaking. One I hope you're prepared for . . . if the board votes your way." There's a glint in his eye that almost makes it seem like he's telling me more than he's saying.

"I appreciate the vote of confidence that the board feels my proposal has merit. I truly believe a global presence would move Fox into the next phase of growth."

"Yes, well . . . the board is rather champing at the bit to make the decision final with the shareholder report coming up. An announcement of a secondary headquarters would boost share prices considerably at a particularly convenient time. So . . ."

We're both tossing about corporate babble, the dance as old as time between reigning king and up and coming prince. Once, it was for the monarchy. Now, it's in a corporate arena.

"Yes?" I try to hurry his big reveal along, having zero patience for the dramatics.

"I'm sending you to London and Daniel to Tennessee for in-depth, hands-on investigations on your proposed sites. I want it all . . . seller's willingness to negotiate, tax breaks and laws that would benefit or limit Fox, and a projection of one, five, and ten-year situations if we go with that site."

What he's saying hits me like a ton of bricks . . . that fell from a crane . . . sitting on top of a building . . . with me down in a hole. That much weight, responsibility, and pressure stack on my chest at once.

"Of course. I'd be happy to travel to London and get a deeper insight into my proposal for the board's consideration." Shockingly, my voice sounds energized, not panicked.

Because inside? I'm, to borrow a phrase from Elle, freaking the fuck out.

"Good, good. I knew you'd be up for the challenge. But make no mistake, Daniel is too." Allan dips his chin, eyes narrowing as if he's evaluating me down to the very depths of my soul. "You'll both be announcing your go-teams at tomorrow night's dinner, if you can be ready?"

The question hangs, and I realize that Daniel has already had this conversation with Allan today. Daniel already knows that we're competing head to head, and he has at least an hour's advantage on preparation.

"I can certainly be ready to make that announcement tomorrow. When are you thinking we should depart for our site visits? It will take a bit to arrange everything on London's end—"

"Monday." Allan's jaw is set in stone, his lips lifted ever so slightly as if he's hungry for my answer.

A test, then, to see how well I think on my feet and adapt? Or to see if I bend and break under pressure?

Good thing I'm quite adept at dodging and juking, I think, proud of my usage of American football slang. See? Even with that, I am constantly learning, integrating, growing. Exactly how I want to lead at the helm of Fox.

I offer a congenial smile, not letting him see even the slightest bit of ruffled feathers at his proclamation.

"Hmm, it is a tight timeline, a team announcement in twenty-four hours and a departure just over forty-eight hours from now, give or take a few hours here or there." The summary is to emphasize exactly what pure madness they're asking of me, that I know it and he knows it. "Tight, but certainly doable."

Lines bloom on Allan's face as he smiles smugly. "Knew you could handle it, Colton. You've always been one to enjoy the pressure of a good challenge, and Daniel's got one in mind for you. But I think you'll rise to it."

It feels like he's telling me a secret, but I'm well aware of how skilled and intelligent Daniel is, and right now, just how on edge he is as well.

He leans forward and offers me a hand across his desk. I shake his firmly. "Thank you for the vote of confidence, sir. I won't let you or Fox down."

"Remember, eight thirty tomorrow night. And when you come by, can you spare a few minutes for my missus? She always loves when you come by and call these things garden parties in that accent. Gives her a kick."

His smile is warm and genuine now, forecasting exactly how in love he is with his wife. They are two peas in a pod, all fancy and upper crust chic on the outside but real and as humble as can be on the inside.

"Of course, sir," I reply, thinking of Allan's wife. She's funny and a good balance to the old man. Giving her a few jollies by simply calling her husband's corporate dinners 'garden parties' would be a pleasure.

I head back down the hallway, excited to share the news with Elle, but my office is empty. I look at my watch and realize it's after six.

She must've gone home already. I know her day of work was over, and she has to take Tiffany home, but my office feels empty without her. Actually, more than just my office. My gut feels alone without her here. I'm disappointed at not being able to share the leap of progress we just made on the HQ2 proposal.

But I shake it off, not willing to be distracted as I head to my desk. I have waited so long for an opportunity like this. It's everything I've been working for my whole life, and I won't fuck it up now over a bit of fun with Elle, because that's all it is. Right? A dig at Daniel, a way to lighten my days, a way for her to show off her skills a little too.

That's all. It has to be.

I don't have time for anything more. Especially not when I have a long night of work ahead of me, a proposal to win, and if all goes according to plan, a new HQ2 to run as Regional President.

Focus, Colton. Eyes on the prize, man.

CHAPTER 15

ELLE

"*C*ome on, girl, we gotta go!" I holler, leaning on the horn. I'm encased in Cammie, with her air conditioning blowing so fiercely that my hair looks like I'm in the middle of filming a White Snake video, so Tiffany can't hear me. But I yell again, all the same. "Come on, come on, come on!"

My fingers are tapping out a rhythm on the steering wheel as I wait impatiently. It's not White Snake on the radio. I only know who they are because Dad went through a hair band phase when he was young and liked to torture me with 80s rock ballads, but rather Lizzo, because I know it'll irk Tiffany.

"Feeling good as hell," I sing, agreeing with the lyrics because right now, they're true. If only Tiffany would move her ass.

When she doesn't appear, I get out and stomp my way to the front door, my flip-flops slapping with every step. Not everyone can make flip-flops sound angry, but I'm one of the rare breeds who can. It probably helps that I'm looking fit for *People of Walmart* in sweatpants, a tank top, a bare face, and wild hair, but picking up Tiffany is only stop one in our day. We've got mani-pedis this morning, blowouts this afternoon, and then we're hitting my place for makeup and to get dressed for Mr. Fox's dinner tonight.

I knock on the door, praying that it's not Ace causing Tiffany any more headaches, but when she opens it, I'm startled by what I see. "What the . . . you look like She-Hulk! No, scratch that . . . because this is not a good look at all."

I point at her face and grimace. "You look like . . . Shrek! What the hell, Tiffany?"

It's pretty appropriate. Tiffany's hair is pulled into a loose ponytail and the front part is held back by a large headband to keep it out of the green goop she's got smeared all over her face.

As if that's not bad enough, she's not even dressed! She's still in her black silk bathrobe, which normally makes her look ready to unleash sexy ass kickings, but right now, it just looks all kinds of wrong with her face covered in moldy swamp mud.

"Oh, shut up and come in!" Tiffany's tone is sharp, her bite letting me know that her goopy face is the least of our problems for today. "I woke up this morning with a breakout. Hence the avocado mask."

She pulls a Vanna White, making a circle around her face with one hand. "We've got a half-hour before our mani-pedis, and I trust that you and Cammie will get us there on time."

Sensing the danger in the air, I baby-step through the minefield. "Anything else you need to do to get ready? How can I help?"

I step inside, carefully avoiding the mess of pizza boxes, beer cans, and trash that have seemingly grown in a semicircle around the couch. The cause is clear as Ace sits slumped on the cushions, a game controller in his hands while the sound of video-game battle fills the room from the too-loud television. It's a small favor that it's not rap music this time.

"Watch out for Kevin. He's a crotch sniffer and will get right up in your business, so keep your legs closed."

"Uhm, excuse me . . . what?" I look around for one of Ace's friends, ready to enact the concept of 'touch me and die.'

"Him. Can you do something with that?" Her finger points toward Ace, and I cringe, knowing there's not a whole lot anyone can do with that. But then I see what she's actually pointing at when Ace leans forward.

"Is that . . ."

My question is cut off by a series of deep, mournful howls. "Is that . . . Kevin?"

Kevin is apparently Ace's . . . basset hound? He's simultaneously the cutest thing in existence and the ugliest dog ever. His mournful eyes droop nearly as low as his jowly cheeks, and his ears hang even lower than that, which makes it seem like he's melting before your very eyes. Even from here, I can see that his belly is far too big and round for his short little legs. He's like a goblin dog.

It's a gift, I guess, making you want to snuggle him while feeling so bad for his sad appearance.

Any sweet sentiments disappear when he hops off the couch to glare at me from under those heavy lids and howls again. Loudly, like he just cornered a squirrel named Elle for dinner. And definitely loud enough to be heard over Ace's video game.

"Kevin! No!" Tiffany snaps at the dog, "Hush before the neighbors call the landlord . . . again." The last part seems to be directed at Ace more than the dog, but Ace barely looks up from mashing on the buttons. "Ace, make him be quiet and leave Elle alone!"

I smartly don't point out that Tiffany is being louder than either the dog or the video game at this point. I might as well be whistling Dixie over here like Billy does, trying to stay out of the line of Tiffany's fire and Kevin's teeth.

"Can't you get him? I'm trying to get the insurgents!"

"Insurgents . . . I'll give you some damn insurgents," Tiffany growls. "If your sorry ass doesn't get up . . ."

"Get over here, Kev!" Ace growls in frustration before whistling. Kevin turns and bounds over to the couch, surprisingly nimble in jumping up onto the cushion. He gives me one last huff of annoyance before flopping over on his back, his head hanging off the side and his ears and jowls flapping upside down. He whines softly, demanding a scratch to his exposed belly, and Ace reaches over and pats him. "Good boy."

I think Tiffany's head is going to explode when Ace praises the dog, and I can't help but giggle. Which is a grave mistake because Tiffany whirls, glaring at me now. I was so close to not being hit with any of the flinging anger or glops of avocado, and I had to go and ruin it because a boy and his dog were being cute for a second.

"Oh, come on," I try to reassure her. "I'm fine. Kevin's fine. Let's just get ready. Clock's ticking."

The reminder is just what she needs to light a fire under her ass. She huffs but hustles down the hall, green goo and all.

Tiffany's bedroom is all organization. We just went shopping, but I would bet that those clothes have already been washed, dried, folded, and hung up. Every stitch of her new capsule wardrobe is probably ready to roll when needed. Without opening a drawer, I know that the right-hand ones contain bras, undies, and socks—in that order so that she can go drawer to drawer, tits to toes, to get dressed. Her closet is small but sorted by article of clothing and then by color, so if you need a white button-up, you can go to the long-sleeve area and then the white section, and poof . . . there you go.

It drives me nuts. There's no spontaneity, no craziness, no chaos. Blah, blah, and blah. But it's probably what makes us such good friends. She's the Yin to my Yang.

I flop on her bed, knowing she'll fix any wrinkles I leave before we go. "Ace is a pain in the ass, but Kevin's kinda cute. When did Ace get him?"

"He got him back a few days ago. Our cousin Shana took him before Ace left, but Ace felt like he needed his buddy again. Went and got him without even asking me." She's ramping up, so I settle in for the long haul and give up on being on time for our appointment.

"Then when I came home last night, Ace had invited his friends over to have a LAN party in my living room! Again, without even asking me! I left for a bit to grab dinner, and when I got back, they were all drunk and being so loud I could hear them in the hallway. I thought someone had actually broken in because they were yelling 'get him, take him down!' They were being so rowdy, I had to threaten to call the cops before my neighbors did. They hauled ass, leaving that mess you see in there behind. Ace hasn't apologized and damn sure hasn't cleaned up after his frat-boy bro-out."

Her voice has lost the angry edge, and instead, she sounds sad and scared. "He's still playing, barely stopped to wave bye to his friends. I'm not even sure if he's even gone to sleep since yesterday. I really want to help Ace get out of this rut he's in, but he's testing me, Elle. This isn't healthy, for either of us."

She flops down next to me, burying her face in her hands and then flinching back when she remembers that her face is covered in now-semi-dry glop. "Come on, go get that washed off and we'll get you some pampering so you feel better," I promise her. "And some food. Tacos? Sushi? Anything you want."

Tiffany heads to her attached bath, and a moment later, the

water turns on. I always tease her that she needs a little crazy in her life, and that's where I come in, but the amount of crazy Ace is bringing to the table is just too much. Even for a wild child like me, and definitely for a controlled non-chaos girl like Tiffany.

"Hey, why'd Ace name his dog Kevin, anyway? It seems weird. Like a people name, not a dog one." From the living room, I hear Kevin bay again when I say his name.

Tiffany laughs just a little, and though I'm not sure why, I take the win. "His name wasn't always Kevin. I think he got that from Home Alone, but Ace would never admit that. Kevin's name was Rick when he first got him. Right up until Rick got out one day, and Ace had to walk up and down the street, calling out, 'Rick, Rick, *Rick!*' and some neighborhood kids heard him and started teasing him about calling out for dick. Told him if he was that hard up, he should fist his own dick."

She laughs and then choking sounds come from the bathroom.

"You okay, girl?"

A loud snort and then giggles. "Yeah, just waterboarded myself a little bit when I laughed." It's quiet for a second, and though I can't see her, it seems like she's lost a bit to the past, maybe to a time when she wasn't on the verge of killing Ace.

"So Ace changed Rick's name to Kevin. Why he didn't go with Rover or Buster, I don't know. A dog needs a dog name."

I flop back on the bed again. "Nah, that's a Kevin if ever I saw one. He's too pitiful looking to be a Buster. But now that you mention it, I'm gonna save the Rick-Dick thing for Ricky. It'll be a good one to put him in his place at just the right time."

Tiffany reappears, looking better without the green goop and a bit of pink to her cheeks. She heads to her dresser, and yep, bras in the top drawer. "Red or pink?" She doesn't wait for me to decide, dropping her robe and slipping the pink one on. She pulls her boobs into the cups so she looks even perkier than usual. "Okay. Let's change the subject. So . . . you talk with Daddy?"

I swallow thickly. "Damn, straight to the jugular. Warn a girl first, maybe even a little warmup. Foreplay is good, you know?"

I let the 'Daddy' thing slide. It's getting to be a bad habit, but I've just got other things on my mind right now.

Tiffany snaps her fingers at me, telling me to quit stalling and get to chatting.

"Yes and no. We had the whole chat session in his office when he found out, but he blew off our lunch at Frankie's. I mean, he said he was busy, and I know he is, but that's not why he cancelled. He's too mad to sit across the table and share fries with me." I fidget with a string on the comforter and Tiffany slaps my hand.

"Stop that. It was expensive. And stop that." She points at my face. "Quit being all morose and pouty and tell your dad that you're a grown ass woman who can do *what* she wants and *who* she wants, *when* and *where* she wants."

She pulls on the matching pink panties and heads toward her closet, showing me that I was right about it too. Perfectly organized with all the new swag she bought.

"Easier said than done," I say, still pouting. "And I'm not doing Colton Wolfe."

It's not really a lie. I haven't fucked him . . . yet. But I want to, and he wants me. I know he made good on our dare too. It was obvious in the hungry way his eyes followed me around the office yesterday. I had been good, too, holding off until late at night, well after the twenty-four hours were up, in case he called me. I would've been down for a bootie call. Hell, I'd half been expecting one. But my phone hadn't rung, and before bed, I pulled out Maximus, my favorite vibrator, and came saying Colton's name.

That seems like a separate issue from the one with my dad, though. Or at least I want it to be. Personal and professional are getting so tangled up.

Tiffany's freshly waxed brows arch. "I'm not stupid, Elle. But if you're not ready to talk about that, it's fine. Here's what I want to know . . . Do you like working for Colton? With him on this HQ2 thing?"

I sigh and meet her eyes, hoping she can see the truth, even the bit I'm not ready to divulge just yet. "I do. All joking aside, I like it. He pushes me hard, but he respects my work. I feel like I'm finally doing something bigger, like this is worthwhile and my input is valuable. I feel like I can fly when we're kicking ass together."

"Then tell Daddy that," Tiffany says as if it's that easy.

"You're like, the world's greatest daughter and one kickass bitch. I'm proud to call you my best friend, and I'll be even prouder to call you my stepdaughter one day."

I throw a pillow at her, and then another when she ducks too fast. The second hits her squarely in her face. "*Stop!* No, just no."

She winks, and I realize that she was just pushing my buttons. Mostly. But I really should've called her out on the Daddy thing about three times ago.

She sets the pillows back on her bed, knife-hand chopping them so they're perfectly puffed. "Let your dad respect that. Give him a *chance* to respect that."

"Okay . . . okay," I reply, sighing. "Come on, we're probably going to miss our appointments. And if they take us late, we'll have to tip double."

Tiffany holds up her purse. "My treat since it was Ace's fault we're late. Again."

We make it safely down the hallway, but as we pass the kitchen, we're ambushed by Kevin, who jumps onto Tiffany's leg, sniffing at her crotch. "Kevin! No!"

She gets the hound off before he becomes a 'leg hound', but Kevin isn't done playing, latching onto the garment bag over Tiffany's arm and shaking his head. "*Rowf!*"

"Oh, my God, are you kidding?" Tiffany's voice has an edge of hysteria to it now. "Kevin! Let go!"

The dog is strong though, yanking backward like this is a game of tug of war and he's already planned the steak dinner he's going to feast on as the winner. Tiffany nearly gets jerked off her feet, but she's fighting for the garment bag with all she's got because it's protecting her dress for Mr. Fox's dinner.

I catch her by the waist, pulling as hard as I can as she gets her balance, the two of us against Kevin. Two against one should put the odds in our favor, but there's no telling when you're battle-locked in a tug of war over a dress . . . against a dog.

"*Ace*, get this dog off my dress!" Tiffany shrieks. "He won't listen to me and he's gonna wreck it! Kevin, no! *Kevin!*"

Her repetition of the dog's human-like name would make me laugh, but not now when there's so much at stake. Though I do have a sudden and serious lack of sympathy at Ace's being made fun of for calling out 'Dick' or 'Rick' or whatever asinine name he came up with for this monster of a melting-faced dog when he answers his sister.

"Hold on, I'm in a serious match!" Ace snaps, spamming the buttons by the sound of it. "Boom, bitches!"

Kevin shakes his head again, his hunting dog instincts I guess making him clamp down even harder as he twists and snaps his head back and forth.

Suddenly, with an ugly, zipper-like sound, the garment bag tears . . . and I can see that it's not just the bag that's torn. The skirt on Tiffany's dress is nearly ripped in half, the dress ruined.

"Holy fuck!" I gasp as Tiffany screams bloody murder. If her neighbors don't call the cops now, they need a better Community Watchdog organization.

Kevin, sensing his impending doom, runs off into the kitchen.

"Tiffany—" Ace's voice is shocked, his eyes horror-filled. But it's way too little, way too late.

"I'm going to kill you!" Tiffany screams, bursting into tears.

I pull Tiffany out of the house before she can make good on her promise, glaring at Ace with one eye, watching Tiffany's breakdown with the other, and somehow staying alert for any nosy neighbors or police showing up to find out what the hell's going on. It's like the eyes in the back of your head that magically appear when you're a mom. I'm nowhere near motherhood, but I'm going to take care of my bestie, no matter what.

The whole time, Tiff's crying, holding the ruined remnants of her dress like it's the body of a loved one. I get it, she really wanted to look good at the party, and this dress was a chunk of her wardrobe budget. The budget she didn't have but had to find because of Ace's last careless mistake. He's just racking them up, and they're all at Tiffany's expense.

"Ace . . ." I call to him from the doorway, pausing while pushing Tiffany out. He looks up, and I can see there's something going on in his head, something Tiffany isn't seeing or hasn't told me, but that doesn't matter right now. "What you're doing to Tiff . . . it's real shitty. I don't know what's going on with you, but the pity party's over. You need to sort your life out, now. I thought you were a better brother than this."

I let my eyes trace over him, the paused video game, the trash he's strewn all over his sister's apartment, and then down the hall where Tiffany is standing, still in shock.

I walk out before Ace can reply, guiding Tiffany toward my car. She's on the verge of a breakdown, and I'm going to have to get drastic here.

"What am I gonna do?" she weeps, looking down at the shredded dress. "I'm gonna have to miss, and—"

"And you're close enough to my size that you can wear one of mine," I remind her. "I mean, you've got bigger boobs, but we can still share clothes. It'll be fine, honey. You know I've got you covered for anything from a hoe-down to a red-carpet gala, with a stopover at a kink club or a masquerade ball in between. Benefits of never tossing clothes away."

I'm in full-on neener-neener mode, but she doesn't care. Yet. "In fact, I dare you . . . to let me pick your dress from my closet."

She laughs and snot bubbles out one of her nostrils. "Ew . . ." she moans, grabbing at the glovebox for a napkin.

"Do not get your snot on Cammie. Though, maybe we could make Ace give her a full wash and detail. Wax, even. Hell, maybe we can just wax Ace as punishment. Press those hot wax strips on his chest and let her *rip*! We could even film it for Instagram. Serves him right."

Tiffany smiles the smallest, saddest smile ever. "Okay, I'll borrow a dress." She avoids the topic of Ace altogether, and I let her for now, but she's going to have to do something about him.

"All right, then. Let's haul ass and see if we can still wedge in our mani-pedis without their gossiping about us the whole time."

Tiffany acts like she's filing her nails and chewing gum. "Rude."

She does a pretty spot-on imitation, not that it's ever been about us. We're always on time and ready for Wine and Whine. Until today. Today, we're *those* customers.

May the nail techs forgive us.

CHAPTER 16

ELLE

The Fox Manor is one of those places that a lot of people list on their Instagrams with hashtags like #LifeGoals or #BucketList. I mean, I get it, I really do. Allan Fox's estate really is that, a legit estate. Built a hundred and fifty years ago by a shipping magnate and situated on fifteen acres of forested meadowlands, it's a call back to an earlier time.

When the original family died off, their shipping empire long forgotten in the march of technology, Mr. Fox bought it as a near dilapidated wreck. Since then, he's renovated the place from the ground up, giving it a modern facelift while keeping the old-fashioned gothic architecture. The forest has been tamed back, the gardens redone, and the inside has been updated while still keeping the vintage, turn of the century feel.

I hesitate a beat too long when the valet holds out his hand. My car might not be the fancy European classics that usually grace Mr. Fox's circle drive, but Cammie's my baby and I'm protective of her.

"Be careful with her, please." The valet smiles politely, though I'm sure he thinks I've lost my mind, and I force my hand to open, letting the keys fall into his hand.

As we approach the door, I realize that maybe it's not just letting go of Cammie that's making me nervous. Behind those doors are my dad and my boss, two men who want very different things from me and are important to me for very different reasons.

My feet stop, and Tiffany tries to pull me along. "What's wrong?"

"Just . . . Dad and Colton . . . and I don't know what to do." I'm stumbling over my words, but my brain is even more of a mess.

Tiffany looks from me to the door twice before a smile takes her face. I know what she's going to say, and maybe I even want her to. Need her to.

"I dare you . . . to go in there with the clanging brass balls I know you have and don't let either of them jerk you around. Be big, bold, and *you* with no apologies. Oh, and I dare you tell the waiter that the hors d'oeuvres are utterly orgasmic and beg for him to bring you another taste."

It works. I crack a smile and swat at her hand. "God, you are the worst." She smiles at me, hearing what I truly mean, but I tell her anyway. "And the best."

Her shrug is casual. "I know."

Putting on my bravest face, I follow Tiffany into the foyer to the estate. Entering, we're both impressed when we see Miranda looking sexy in a slinky red number that makes my dress look positively casual when I'd worried about being overdressed. Miranda just needs Roger Rabbit to complete the illusion.

"Ladies!" Miranda says, smiling hugely as she comes tottering over on five-inch heels. Is she manhunting tonight or something? If so, good for her, I guess. She deserves a little happiness, and maybe some steaminess, in her life after losing her husband. Though I worry that she's hunting at a work function.

What's that saying? Don't shit where you eat.

Then again, I'm the last person who should offer that advice, considering I'm not sticking to the intention of it in the least by messing around with Colton.

"Hi, Miranda," I say cautiously. She seems exceptionally excited to see us, me in particular, considering I defected to the fifth floor.

She wraps her arms around me, pulling me in tight for a hug though I remain stiff-armed. I mouth at Tiffany, "What's happening?" But she shrugs, eyes wide.

"I miss you so much. Tiffany doesn't have anyone to cause trouble with. I thought I'd like that, but it's *so boring*." Her huff of boredom sounds like a sorority girl in a long line at Starbucks and smells like fruity champagne.

"That's because New Girl is about as interesting as plain rice cakes," Tiffany grumbles.

My head spins. "You hired someone to replace me?"

Miranda pushes at my shoulder like I told a funny joke. "Of course we did. You're all big time upstairs. Megan is perfectly nice. She's just still settling in."

She takes a sip of her champagne and looks around, eyes wide in wonder, and I again consider that she might be a tad bit tipsy already. "But enough on work, okay? Even if I'm surrounded by coworkers, that don't mean we have to talk shop, right? I mean . . . look at this place."

I'll give it to Allan Fox. When he renovated his estate, he did it right. The back garden's beautiful, the early evening lit up with tastefully hidden lights and a well laid out drink table.

"We've got a band," Tiffany notices as music floats over the grounds. "Terrible choice in music."

"What?" Miranda asks, humming to herself. "*Hazy Shade of Winter* rocks."

"Yeah . . . when it's actually done as rock and not jazz," Tiffany says before clearing her throat and elbowing me. "Incoming."

It's all the warning I get before I feel Ricky and Billy at my back. Billy puts an arm around my shoulders before placing a chaste kiss to my cheek, and Ricky pretty much drools over Miranda. "Hey, cuz, ain't seen much of you lately. What's been shakin'?"

"Just your dicks when you use the men's room," Tiffany shoots back. "So not much."

"Miranda, ignore them and their unfounded taunts," Ricky says, eyes roaming up and down Miranda's curves. "Instead, please tell me you've got an empty spot on your dance card for me."

I've never seen Miranda flirt, but she seems to be jumping right in the deep end and swimming just fine. She runs a red fingertip along her lip, drawing Ricky's eyes right where she wants them as she tilts her chin ever so slightly. She's a coy seductress. Who would've guessed?

"Maybe I do."

Ricky holds out his hand, dipping down in almost a bow, and she places her hand in his. They merge onto the dance floor, leaving the three of us standing there, gaping open-mouthed.

"What just happened?" I whisper.

Billy chuckles. "Ricky's always good with the ladies, and he's got the hots for Miranda bad. He's been waiting on her to be ready."

Huh, who'd have thought my cousin could be so . . . nice?

"Ah, Elle. Pardon me for being cheeky, but you do look rather smashing tonight." The dark voice comes from behind me, sending a shiver down my spine because only one man speaks like that.

I turn to meet his gaze but instead find his eyes slowly working their way up from my ass. "Colton." It's a greeting and a warning all rolled up in one. Billy is standing right here, after all, along with everyone else we work with.

He looks smashing himself, if I do borrow his lingo. He's got on a blue suit, a bit lighter than he wears to the office, perhaps, and his pocket square and tie are navy blue. We look rather matched, which gives me a zing of a thrill until Tiffany points it out and Billy frowns.

"You do look coordinated. Intentional, Wolfey?" Billy's sneer is as threatening as ever, but Colton looks entirely unruffled.

"Just a coincidence." My attempt at reassuring Billy is wasted, though.

"Mr. Stryker, while I appreciate relaxing certain behavior standards in favor of the festivities, *Wolfey's* taking it a bit far, if you don't mind," Colton interrupts, his voice polite and even cheery, but there's steel behind his smile.

Great, just great. Colton's not backing down, but Billy's not either. And while a battle of wits is a total mismatch, Billy's smart enough to know when he's being challenged. Colton, though, isn't going to swing first, but I'm worried that when or if he does, it's going to be on like Donkey Kong . . . and I don't want that.

A waiter interrupts the guys' staredown, and I take the golden opportunity to make good on Tiffany's crazy dare. "Oh, thank you! These puff pastries are utterly orgasmic. Mmm-hmm. Can you bring me some more? What's in them again?"

I shove an entire pastry ball into my mouth as two pairs of eyes turn to me. The waiter and Tiffany were already looking at me, him because he's a bit choked at my over-the-top perfor-mance and Tiffany because she knew the show I was going to put on. But Colton and Billy are staring at me now too. Colton with a knowing smirk and Billy in horror.

The waiter recovers enough to answer, though it's stumbled and mumbled. "Uhm, the pastries are stuffed with . . . sausage . . . and cream . . . cheese."

Okay, that's even worse. Or maybe better, because now I can't help but laugh. Unfortunately, I nearly choke on the mouthful and Tiffany has to pat me on the back. She's a little rough, and I spit the snack into a napkin.

"It's okay, girl. Sometimes, you gotta work past the gag reflex and swallow, swallow, swallow, but it takes time. It's okay to spit if you need to."

She says it faux sympathetically, but we all know exactly what she's talking about.

Billy's chest is rumbling, but it's not a purr. It's more of an animalistic growl, and when he straightens his jacket, it's a little too forceful, and I think I hear a seam give way.

"Excuse me for a moment."

He spins on his heel and stalks away. I estimate that I have approximately two to three minutes before he's back with Dad.

Tiffany gives a quiet golf clap. "Well done, Miss Stryker. Don't forget part one of the dare." And with that reminder, she's off, leaving me alone with Colton.

His lips do that twitchy thing where I think he's trying to hold back a laugh. "Well done, indeed." He copies Tiff's words, but where she made me smile with the praise, Colton makes me want to preen a bit. "I missed you yesterday evening. I had hoped you'd be in my office after my meeting so we could complete our twenty-four hours with a bang."

"Do you mean that literally?"

Instead of answering, he grabs two flutes of champagne and offers me one. He clinks his to mine. "Here's to exciting times, Miss Stryker."

We both sip, eyes looking over the rims so that we don't lose sight of one another. "Did you wait the entire time then?"

This is important—a testament to his willingness to play, the truthfulness of his word.

He hums. "Unfortunately, I had to wait significantly longer than the time assigned. I had some work to do and wasn't able to take matters into my own hands until later at home. Alone, which was not nearly as satisfying as what I'd hoped the evening would hold."

"My evening was lackluster and battery-operated as well." I speak quietly behind my glass. No one is listening, and I don't think anyone can read my lips, but it feels naughty to be discussing our night of masturbation at a work party. Actually, it doesn't just feel wrong. It is wrong. And doesn't that make those butterflies in my gut dance around like they're doing the Macarena?

The rest of his words hit me. "What were you working on so late? We had everything on the list completed."

His smirk worries me, the light in his eyes scary. "You'll see. I have a surprise for you, one I think you're going to enjoy."

It takes me a full two rounds of breath to realize he means something work related because my sex-hungry brain went right back to surprises like him tying me to his bed. I don't get a chance to ask for clarity, though, because I'm interrupted by Dad, of all people.

"Elle! My goodness, look at you! Billy, thanks for finding Elle. I was caught up chatting with Mr. Fox. Colton, it's good to see you."

Dad's dropping Mr. Fox's name like bait, hoping to trigger Colton, but Colton offers his hand and Dad shakes, the two of them squeezing maybe a little hard in a test of manhood, but not overly so. They at least look like they're going to get along, which is good for me. My head's getting ping-ponged so much since arriving that I'm going to have a migraine, and Tiff doesn't know how to drive a stick.

Still, even through the muted throb behind my temples, I notice that Dad looks handsome himself in a black suit with a floral tie for the seasonal theme of the party. I'm not the only one who notices, either, as Tiffany reappears from somewhere.

"Daniel, good to see you!" At least she doesn't call him Daddy to his face.

"You too, Tiffany." He kisses the air beside her cheek in greeting, perfectly reasonably, but a warning gong goes off in my head. "You're keeping this one in line, aren't you?" Dad's eyes cut to me. He's teasing like I'm some wild child, but I'm done with it.

Big, brass balls, Tiffany said. *Don't let them push you around.*

"You shouldn't be sending the goon squad after me," I chide him after Billy excuses himself to find Ricky. "I would have found you, and Colton's been a perfect gentleman. This isn't the homecoming dance in high school."

The reminder is sharp. That dance had been all I'd talked about for weeks, and within an hour of arrival, Billy and Ricky had scared off my date. I'd spent my first real dance, my first real date, sitting sad and alone on the gym bleachers. And it'd been Dad's fault for siccing the boys on me. He'd apologized, but apparently, that scab hasn't fully healed for either of us.

"Elle . . . excuse me, Colton, may I speak with my daughter alone?" Dad asks.

"Of course, Daniel. Elle, it was nice to see you this evening. Enjoy yourselves."

"I don't like this. Not one bit."

Once upon a time, Dad's biting proclamation would've had me backing down. We're the home team, the two of us against the world. But these growing pains were always going to happen, maybe not like this, where there's a competitive edge, but I was always going to have to stand my ground with him. Repeatedly, if necessary, until he sees that I'm fine on my own two feet.

"Dad, it's fine. I am fine. Other than my father stomping around and pissing off my new boss. If I worked anywhere else, would you walk up to my boss and start shit with him? No, you wouldn't. I get that this is different because of the HQ2 thing, but I need you to look at me. Really look at me."

I hold my arms out a bit, and Dad glares at me like he doesn't get it. "You look beautiful, baby girl. Which is another thing . . . I don't like the way Wolfe is looking at you."

I put a hand on Dad's arm. "Dad, I get it. I'm not your little girl anymore and that's scary. But it's okay. I can handle this project, I can handle Colton Wolfe, and most importantly, I can handle myself. If you'll let me. You taught me well. Now it's time for you to gloat over how good of a job you did raising me."

We're a veritable nine o'clock drama show on NBC, all up in our feels and on the verge of tears when Dad finally looks at me.

"Shit. I'm botching this up, aren't I?" I nod, and he sighs heavily. He covers my hand with his, though I know he wants to hug me. I appreciate that he's holding back because of the professional surroundings we're in because I know it's killing him. "I am proud of you, and I do believe you. It's just hard for a dad to let go of his little girl. Especially when . . ." He stops himself, though I know he was about to say something else cutting about Colton. It's progress and I'll take it.

"Thanks, Dad."

Guess Tiffany was right. I do have big, brass balls after all. That actually went pretty well, and hope blooms in my belly that maybe I can do it all. Work on Colton's HQ2 project, have a little fun with the dares with him, make Dad proud, and ultimately, who wins the HQ2 race will be out of my hands. We can all just do our best and let the chips fall where they will.

Inside, I'm doing a giddy dance of accomplishment accompanied by a choir singing, 'Get it, girl!' and I barely refrain from letting the music raise my hands in celebration. It's a good thing, too, because the actual music the party band is playing ends.

"Dinner is ready. If you'll please make your way to a seat. We encourage you to mix it up too. Please don't sit with your own department, if possible." Mrs. Fox is holding a microphone on the stage, inviting us all to sit at the numerous round tables spread throughout the garden.

Dad takes my hand and leads me to a table. "At least we're not in the same department, so I can sit with my daughter, right?"

It's an olive branch, one I take gladly as I sit beside him.

Tiffany reappears, taking the seat on the other side of Dad. "May I?"

"Of course, you're always welcome, Tiffany." Dad even stands slightly, pulling her chair out for her. He's such a gentleman. I really need to find him someone. Other than my best friend, who's making goo-goo eyes at him right now.

"Thank you so much, Daniel. Such manners, a kindness sadly lacking in so many these days."

I swallow the groan, knowing I literally just told my dad that I'm an adult and to back off and now wanting to pinch my nose and say 'gross' like I'm ten again.

The rest of the table fills up and introductions are made. I'm honestly surprised when Colton doesn't come to sit with me, but with Mrs. Fox's decree of not sitting with your own department, it makes sense. And I'm honestly glad to not feel like Gumby for a little while with Dad and Colton pulling on either side of me. Though maybe it won't be like that anymore with Dad realizing that I'm okay, even if this is awkward with us on opposing sides of the HQ2 thing.

The waiters begin bringing around salads. A hand reaches over my left shoulder, setting down my salad. But then a throat clears from beside me and I turn. "Ma'am?"

Oh, God. It's the waiter from the hors d'oeuvres dare. My eyes go wide, and he looks down to the small bread plate in his hand that holds three more pastry puffs. "You asked for more of these?"

"Oh, uh . . . yes. Thank you." He sets the plate down on the table, and I force down the laugh, not daring to look at Tiffany because I know she'll make me break.

"If there's *anything* else, please let me know. I'm Jeff, by the way." His demeanor is completely professional, his eyes locked on my cleavage.

"Thanks, Jeff. That's it, though. These are just so good." I pop one in my mouth as a way of ending the conversation, and he walks off to continue salad service.

When I do manage to look around the table, every eye is on me. Once I swallow, thankfully not spitting this time, I try to explain. "These were just so good and I was only able to get one during the cocktail hour. Wasn't that nice of Jeff?" The other people at the table nod politely, and finally, I chance a glance at Tiffany. Yep, she's grinning wide and biting back laughter too.

Bitch. Good thing I love her. If only she'd stop chatting up my dad.

"Everyone, if I may?" Mr. Fox says from the stage, interrupting my train of thought and thankfully pulling everyone's attention as I stuff another pastry in my mouth. Dare aside, they really are that good.

"Please continue with your dinner, but I wanted to say a few things tonight."

Mr. Fox goes on to rave about how we're a family at Fox, all working together for one goal and a bunch of other rah-rah pep rally speak. But he truly means it, so it comes off as genuine, not false at all.

"In closing, as everyone knows, the HQ2 project has been the cornerstone of our growth plans for the past year, and we've had several excellent proposals."

The entire room goes still. Is he going to announce which plan they've chosen? Next to me, Dad sits taller, sets his napkin on the table, and brushes off his lapels.

What's happening? Did Dad's plan get selected?

Emotions roil through me—excitement for Dad, sadness for Colton, and even disappointment for myself at having only gotten out of the clerical pool for a week. Megan had better get out of my chair if I'm getting shipped back downstairs to Miranda's team.

"We've narrowed it down to two plans that hold the most promise, Daniel Stryker's and Colton Wolfe's." Mr. Fox begins the round of applause and the room follows suit.

"I've asked them both to take teams to their prospective locations, and tonight, they'll be announcing those teams. Daniel?"

Dad gets up from his seat, eyes on Mr. Fox as he makes his way to the band stage. He takes the microphone and holds court over the room.

"Thank you, Allan. I'm honored that the Tennessee location is being considered and thrilled to take a research team for a more in-depth analysis. I thought hard about this, about what skills I'd need on the ground and who best to fill those shoes . . ." Dad goes on to list a team of six members, from legal to manufacturing, engineering to his assistant. It's a big crew, but it's a big undertaking.

Dad finishes his speech, and everyone claps politely, chatter breaking out at the tables. I hear someone whisper not-too-quietly that they hope they're on Colton's team. "Can you imagine a week in London with him?"

I frown, the shot of jealousy hot in my veins.

Colton takes the stage next. "Thank you as well, Allan. As I'm sure you understand, I feel that a global presence is the best way to proceed with our HQ2, and though it might seem obvious, I assure you that I considered the globe over before deciding that London would be best for Fox. It's a big request to have employees drop everything and travel abroad on such short notice, especially when everyone is so chock-a-block with their own work. Travel can be rather costly for the company, too." The dig against my dad is subtle but there. "So I've taken a slightly different approach from Daniel." Or not so subtle.

I sigh, thinking that I only thought I was making headway in their battle. Dad's sitting beside me again, his speech done, and he places his hand on mine reassuringly. He's not offended by Colton's speech in the least.

"As to my team. First, I'd like to thank Helen Riggs. She is the whip cracker who keeps my office running, and as such, I'd like her to remain here in my stead to keep everything tip top. I wouldn't trust the day-to-day to anyone else, but in her capable hands, I have no doubt it'll be in good care." People clap for Helen, and I start to feel a pit in my stomach.

"And as there is a significant time difference between London and HQ, I think that having the full-scale court won't be necessary. I can work during the London day, and as I wrap up, I can tag-team off to the US group, allowing for round-the-clock progress. For the US group, I'd like to invite Gary England from legal. Can't go wrong with a bloke named England for this particular project, can I?"

People clap as Gary waves. "And Debra Stevens from engineering." Debra is no-nonsense, a former Marine who's well-known for her efficiency. She receives a round of applause as well.

"And last but not least, I will need someone who can be at the ready to handle anything and put up with me." He flashes his charming smile, and everyone laughs at the self-deprecation. "A jack of all trades, if you will, who can coordinate between me and the US group. Someone up for the challenge this daring endeavor requires . . ."

Oh, God. Oh, no. He can't. I can't.

"I'd like to invite Elle Stryker to visit the proposed site in London. Pack your bags, Miss Stryker. We leave on Monday."

"What!" Dad hisses, and suddenly, everyone's looking at me. I hold it together while their eyes are on me, but Dad looks like he's turning purple next to me. He wants to say something, to demand that Colton not take me, but he can't.

Colton's hemmed him in, and Dad knows it. Tiffany, on the

other hand, is applauding like mad, whistling like a baseball fan in the stands until my face is flushed with embarrassment.

Mr. Fox takes the microphone back, saying something else, but I can't hear him. I just hear the whispers around the room about what type of help I'll be. The sneered implication of why Colton selected me and only me is obvious, and what's worse is that I can't even deny it.

Colton goes back to his table, far enough away that I can't see what he's saying to the group of people who greet him with smiles as he sits down. But I don't miss the smirk he throws my way. Even from across the room, I know this was his surprise, and the dare to not argue about this and to actually go with him is loud and clear.

"Absolutely not," Dad growls. "No fucking way."

"What a great opportunity," Tiffany counters, on my side even against Dad.

I blink and my brain starts functioning again. "Dad, Colton named me to his team, which is what I'm working on with him. It only makes sense for me to go. You're taking your assistant too."

Logic pings off him like Nerf darts, though, leaving no trace of a mark of reason.

"You'll politely decline and work with the US team here," Dad says, his voice firm but low. "Elle, you're not going anywhere with Colton Wolfe. And that's final."

So much for the progress we made earlier. Dad's back to treating me like I'm a kid again. And though it might seem like I'm being ornery just to needle him, I'm truly not. This is a great opportunity.

For some daring fun in London with Colton!

I hush the devil that's sending fizzy champagne bubbles to both my brain and my lady bits and force myself to focus.

HQ2. London. My chance to shine professionally.

CHAPTER 17

COLTON

*T*hat went well, better than expected, judging by the congratulatory handshake Allan gave me as I left the stage. And the triumph tastes sweet. It's preliminary, one step of many to come, but I'm going to celebrate the progress.

And I made sure I was looking directly at Daniel Stryker as I dropped the bomb that I was hand-selecting his daughter, and only his daughter, to accompany me to London.

He looked ready to lose his cool, even more than when he confronted me in the lift.

And he couldn't do a damn thing about it. For him to protest now . . . well, that's just bad form. It'd paint him in a bad light, as an overprotective father and a poor sport, while also torpedoing Elle's career at the company, something he doesn't want to do, either.

I fully expect him to have another play here, something to counter me, but I think he'll play it close to the chest so he can keep it mum. Most likely leveraging Elle herself.

Leaving the garden party, my phone buzzes in my pocket. I pull it out and see Elle's name.

Elle: *You should've asked me first.*

Me: *This way seemed more fun, more daring, I suppose.*

She doesn't answer for a moment, and I climb behind the wheel of my Lotus. I wonder if maybe Daniel has already made his play and I've come out on the losing side. At least with Elle. The jury is still out on the proposals.

The drive home is quick, but upstairs, it's quiet, too quiet, really. Like my office when she was downstairs, my penthouse seemed a lot fuller when she was here with me.

Elle: *Dad's furious. I'm furious.*

Me: *Which is more important to you? Your wishes or your father's?*

Elle: *Both.*

Me: *I won't apologize for giving you an opportunity to grow. Neither Gary nor Debra knew about being assigned to my team, yet neither of them is texting me pouty messages.*

Elle: *GIF of a shovel digging a deeper hole.*

Me: *Be at the office at ten in the morning if you're going. We have a lot to do. If not, I'll inform Ms. Carter of your return to her group.*

It's a line in the sand for us both.

If we proceed, I need her fully committed because this trip is going to be revealing, as well as decidedly important to my potential future at Fox. I need to know that she can be discreet and help me frame this option in the best light, without shying away from the reality of my life in London. And she needs to make the decision to put her own needs and desires, both personal and professional, over her father's demands.

If she elects to take the easy path and bow out, I will have my answer about our fun as well as our potential work partnership. Elle will eventually have another opportunity. She's too intelligent not to, but it won't be at the expense of my own dream.

I would truly hate to leave her behind. She's already become less of a novelty and more of a fixture in my mind, an injection of freshness to my days. But the choice is hers to make.

Having gotten ready for bed while we texted, I shut off the light, not really knowing if she's going to come or not. For all I know, she's going to march in and tell me she's going to obey Daddy Dearest's commands.

I'll be disappointed if she does. Hell, I'm disappointed that she's not next to me right now. I cup my cock, still unsatisfied even after last night's wank. It, like me, wants the real thing . . . Elle, not the fantasy of her I imagined as I fisted myself after her teasing and tormenting.

I almost text her again. If we can't figure out the work stuff, perhaps we could focus on the dares? I could dare her to come over, maybe sway her mind while I sway her body?

My cock jumps hopefully at the idea, but my mind overrides

my baser impulses. Elle needs time tonight to make this decision. And while I could probably get her to agree to just about anything while holding her on the edge of an orgasm, I want her to decide clear-headed. She needs to know that she's capable of standing tall and handling all of this—her father and me, and most importantly, herself.

I'M JUST GETTING MY SUNDAY STARTED THE NEXT DAY WHEN MY phone beeps, and I look up from my desk, rubbing at my eyes. I must have been gathering wool. It's nearly nine forty-five, and I've already been at work for over an hour. But my phone's still dinging as if I have a video call coming in.

"Whoever you are, I hope you . . . Lizzie?"

"Wotcher, Coltie!" Lizzie says, grinning. "How's it hanging, as the Yanks say?"

Her accent immediately takes me home. Here, in the US, everyone thinks I have an accent, but the truth is, I've lost some of it from talking to Americans every day. But Lizzie sounds like home. I tease her, wanting her riled up because it makes her accent even thicker. With everything going on, I want to wrap up in the dropped consonants and let the soft elegance wash over me.

"You don't need to know, and it's Sunday morning," I reply with a yawn. "Please tell me you forgot the time difference and aren't just calling to torture me?"

Lizzie giggles, shaking her head. "You're getting old, Coltie. Sunday morning? You used to just be getting home at that time, and by the look of things, I haven't woken you. Are you at work already? Don't you take the weekends off?"

"Hmph. I am not old, and yes, I'm at work. Americans don't take off. You can even get fresh-baked cupcakes here in the middle of the night, from a bakery ATM. It's madness."

Lizzie laughs, and behind her, I can see she's sitting in her bed at home, probably enjoying a weekend without school. "That sounds lovely. I think I'd fancy a cupcake right about now." She shakes her head. "Anyway . . . good news, I got top marks on my exams!"

"That's great! I've got good news too . . . but it's a surprise."

Lizzie pouts, her good cheer evaporating. "Ah, that's rubbish! I get enough surprises with Mum going on and on about her stupid charity galas and what her friends' daughters are up to."

I laugh lightly as though she's joking, but she won't meet my eyes, even through the screen. "Lizzie, you okay?"

She falls back against her pillow, sighing heavily and rolling her eyes. "I'm fine. Eddie's just being a right cunt, and there are some stupid boys saying . . . what's that slang you taught me? Oh, yeah, smack talking." Even the silly American phrase seems to brighten her mood slightly.

"Eddie's always going to be Eddie. Nothing you or I can do about him." I roll my eyes the same way Lizzie did because it's the god's honest truth. Our brother is a douche canoe. I consider teaching Lizzie that word too, but I'm not sure enough of the exact definition other than it's an insult, but it makes me laugh. Perhaps I'll save it for when I actually get to London, a vocabulary lesson surprise.

"But the neighborhood boys are different. That shouldn't happen, Lizzie. Tell Mom or the school. Or if it's that bad, send Nan to talk to their parents. I bet they'd behave straight away if Nan pinched their ears and dragged them home to Mummy."

She laughs, but I make a mental note to check on these boys while I'm home. I might be thousands of miles away, but a big brother always protects his little sister.

Lizzie suddenly sits up, grabbing her computer and bringing her face close enough to the camera that I get a clear view up her nose. "Hey, Coltie? Who's that?"

Lizzie's pointing behind me, and I turn, nearly jumping out of my skin when I see Elle standing in my doorway. "Oh, uh . . . my assistant," I tell Lizzie quickly. "Hard at work, you know."

"She's cute."

I feel heat prickling at my neck, and I shake my head. "Yes, well, I should get back to work, Lizzie. I'll call you soon, yes?"

"Okay, okay. Ta, Coltie! Ta, Assistant!"

Lizzie rings off with a smirk, and I put my phone down, inwardly groaning. I don't know how much Elle just heard, but Lizzie's going to be primed for matchmaking when we arrive in London. I'll have to set her straight right away.

"Mr. Wolfe," Elle says in greeting. There's no one here to over-hear her calling me by my first name, no one to question the inti-macy of that, so her formality screams 'I'm still mad.'

"Decided I would dress casual today. If the company won't do casual Fridays, then casual Sundays are a must."

She's daring me with her eyes to reprimand her, but I reward her instead, letting my eyes drip slow as molasses from her head to her toes. She's wearing a T-shirt with some sort of line drawing of a cat, black jeans, and fashionable trainers. With her hair pulled up and her glasses on, she looks like she would be right at home on any college campus or any of the dozen coffee bars within a stone's throw of here.

"That's fine. I went casual as well." I'm looking for common ground, but Elle snorts.

"That is not casual." She points at me derisively, and I get up from my chair, walking to the front of my desk with my arms outstretched so she can get the full effect.

I perch on the edge of my desk, running the backs of my hands down my polo shirt before slipping them into the pockets of my chinos. "Not a suit, not formal attire, not athletic gear, not pajamas, though I don't wear those, as you know." Elle hisses, her eyes narrowing. "Ergo, casual. My shirt's not even properly tucked in."

Her eyes drop to my waist, as I knew they would, where the front of my shirt is simply tucked behind my belt. "You have on a belt."

"Ah, a belt implies that the outfit is no longer casual. I see, my mistake." I unbuckle the expensive leather, pulling it from the loops with a swoosh. "Now then, casual."

This banter is not what I expected, not at all. I expected anger or excitement, perhaps resignation. But even this mildly adver-sarial disagreement is fun. Elle seems to agree because even as she nips and bites verbally, her lips are quirking adorably.

I think we need to address the elephant in the room, though.

"To be honest, I'm glad you're here at all, regardless of your attire. Though you look lovely. A little nagging voice in my head last night said you wouldn't show."

"I figured I owed you an answer one way or another in person," Elle tells me, sitting on the edge of her desk. I wonder if she's intentionally mirroring me, putting us on equal ground, or if she did it naturally, instinctually. She has so many layers I want to delve into and decipher and help her develop. "And I'll admit, you really fucked up my sleep last night. I'm running on about three hours' shut-eye and two espressos right now."

"Let me guess . . . one part of you knows that this is a great opportunity, a chance for you to get in on the ground floor of a project that could quickly vault your career if things go right. And as though that's not enough, there's also the promise that we can continue exploring what we've already started."

Elle shifts, her hips wiggling from side to side a little at my comment.

"To be clear, those do not have to go hand-in-hand. Either can be exclusive of the other if that's your wish. Though I find I'm rather enjoying our blend of work and play."

I purposefully cup my cock, rearranging myself, and Elle's eyes track the movement hungrily.

She is still mad, but she's also still as needy as I am to address the fire we built but never put out properly.

"Perhaps. But my father—"

"And there's the other part. The daughter, who her father wants to remain his little girl, safe and secure by his side, protected from the big, bad Wolfe."

Elle nods. "His first words were that he flat out forbade me from going. I'm honestly glad that my passport's locked in my fire safe at home. He looked like he could have broken into my place and stolen it otherwise."

I smile, enjoying that Daniel is on edge, not just because of the HQ2 proposals, as I'd originally intended, but because I think the growing pains between father and daughter might be good for them too. Good for all of us.

"So, you know what your dad wants you to do. You know what I want you to do. The only question is . . . what do you want to do? And do you have the guts to follow through with any of those options?"

I'm calling into question her boldness, something I know she prides herself on but something she's currently wavering on.

"I won't dare you on this. You need to decide."

She looks disappointed, as if she was hoping she could fall

back on me or Tiffany daring her to go. But I won't allow her to throw that at me if everything implodes. We're either going together because she wants to accompany me, or I'm going alone because she's chosen not to go.

She wants to say yes. I can see it in her face, in her body language . . . she wants to go with me. She wants what I promise her, namely, her freedom.

"Tell you what," I interrupt her loud thoughts. "Don't think about Daniel today. In fact, don't even give me an answer until we're done with today's work. Just think about how much you could learn, how great an opportunity this is, and even how much fun you'll have."

I close the distance between us, pressing myself between her knees. She gasps, her thighs clenching, not to keep me away but to hold me in place against her. The breathy sound of her gasp hitches when she realizes that I'm hard, aching for her. "Colton . . . the office . . ."

"Is empty. It's just us for now."

Slowly, giving her time to stop me, I lower my lips toward her. But she doesn't stop me. In fact, she licks her lips in preparation, and that's all the permission I need to kiss her. I cup her jaw, sipping at her gently until she opens for me.

She arches, trying to deepen the kiss, but I stay right on the edge of polite snogging, stoking her fire. After a moment, I pull back, tracing her kiss-plumped lip with my thumb.

"Shall we get to work?"

Her smile is full of ice and poison. "You don't fight fair, Mr. Wolfe."

"Nor do you, Miss Stryker." With the starting gun still smoking, we're off in a race against the clock.

Most of the day is grunt work, setting up the details for our trip. We start off with booking tickets to Heathrow, business class, of course. There's no way I'm sitting in economy for twelve hours, and I'm not going to put Elle through that, either.

"Should we book for extra baggage?" Elle asks at one point. "I mean, a week of suits plus casual clothing is going to mean laundry. I might have to get Tiffany to plan out my outfits so I can be efficient. She's a pro, where I'd pack everything I own, just in case."

"This is a business trip, not a fashion show," I remind her, tapping my chin as I consider other options. "One and one is fine. If you need anything beyond what you pack, I'll put it on my credit card."

Elle looks up, surprised. "What?"

"I said, I'll take care of it if we're going somewhere and you need appropriate clothes," I repeat. "And maybe, just for fun, I'll take you to AP for a shopping spree." I wink, but I'm not kidding in the least.

"AP?"

"Agent Provocateur," I say, smirking. "I bet they have a few pieces you'd look . . . smashing in. I could dare you to give me a fashion show right there in the dressing rooms."

With the afternoon sun coming in the windows, I can see the flutter of her racing heartbeat in the exposed line of her neck. I think she's rather excited by the idea, as am I.

"We'll see, but I feel like you're counting your chickens before they hatch. I haven't even said I'm for sure going."

While that is technically true, we've booked two seats on the flight, a two-bedroom suite at the hotel, and she's planning her wardrobe as we speak. She's going. She's just not ready to admit it.

"Touché. And hatched or not, why, exactly, would one need to count chickens?"

Elle's laughter is raucous. "I have no idea. It's just an expression."

"Another delightfully odd one. I'm sure you'll find some of the slang in London to be amusing as well. I've lost the habit of some of it, but hearing Lizzie always makes me smile. I suspect you'll need translations as much I do here sometimes."

I'm still talking as if she's going, and she doesn't correct me this time, but that she hasn't said it straight out is beginning to make me nervous. I assumed Daniel would balk and Elle would have some reservations, but I honestly expected her to be certain by now. Truthfully, I wouldn't have been surprised if she'd sassily told her father where to stuff it with his overbearing protectiveness. I have a feeling it will come to that before he backs off and lets her alone.

The looming question, though, makes me long for surety, for

her to be as invested in this as I am. But she is right about one thing. I don't fight fair, and there's one thing I can offer her that Daniel can't. Well, actually, there are several—a career not based on nepotism, freedom to be her daring self, and world travel. But I have one other thing in mind.

"I'd say we've had quite a productive day, wouldn't you?" Elle looks up and nods agreeably. "Just one thing we haven't done today."

She pushes her glasses up, tangling them in her hair as she narrows her gaze. "And what's that?"

Smart girl. She can hear the change in my tone, the dark desires creeping into what has been our professional conversation.

"We made a dare of twenty-fours of abstinence, and it seemed we both held to the letter of the dare, down to the slowly ticking hands of the clock. However, you did not sound particularly satisfied by your . . . what did you call it? Lackluster and battery-operated evening? That seems a shame after we teased and taunted each other so mercilessly."

Elle may be torn about what to do about her father and this trip to London, but she has no reservations about our fun. At least I have her there, for now.

Her lips purse, fighting the smirk. "I did tease you quite a bit, didn't I? Perhaps I should drop another pen? Pick it up slowly with my ass in the air? Guess you finally noticed."

She's planting images in my head, erotic and seductive ones, with the scalpel-like precision of a surgeon. But she's not the only one who's been paying attention to what's arousing.

"That would be a sight to behold. But I have another idea."

I wait, letting the dramatic pause add flair to her anticipation. "Come here, Elle."

She's out of her chair in a second, coming around behind my desk where I've turned my chair. I spread my legs, manspreading, I've heard it called, and she steps between them as though she's going to sit on my lap again.

"Na-ah-ah. On your knees."

I see the hesitation, her mind whirring so loudly I can almost hear her thoughts. With narrowed eyes that communicate that she's still not committed to this course of action, she follows the order, dropping to her knees.

"Good girl." Her brow arches sardonically, warning me. I lean forward, getting in her space the way she's in mine. "I want to be crystal clear. This has nothing to do with work or with London. This is just you and me, like before. Agreed?"

She seems relieved, her shoulders dropping from their scrunched position and the line of her lips relaxing. I can't resist giving her a smacking kiss, my hand wrapped around the back of her neck. She calms even more.

"Okay. What did you have in mind, sir?"

There she is. My daring girl.

"A dare, of course. Helen will be here at three to coordinate her workload for the week, and you know she's a stickler for punctuality. I thought we could make good use of the fifteen minutes until she arrives."

"I'm guessing I already know what you'd consider a 'good use of our time' given our current positions?" She's grinning, and I can see the hum of energy flowing through her as she wiggles like a happy puppy about to get a biscuit.

I smirk back. "Well, I did have some options I thought you might take under advisement." Corporate babble has never sounded so weirdly sexy as it does right now. I even consider making a joke about mergers, but she jumps in before I get the chance.

"I dare you . . ." Her fingertip goes to my chest, pushing me back in my chair. "To take your dick out, right here in your office. I'm going to suck you off. I know that's what you want, but I'm not going to make it that easy for you."

I hoped she wouldn't. My fingers are already deftly undoing the button of my pants, though I give a sly glance to the door. It's closed but not locked.

"Fourteen minutes, Elle."

I undo the zipper as well, shoving everything down and pulling my already hard cock out. Precum leaks from the crown, running a single clear rivulet down my shaft. Elle groans hungrily, and it's taking all I have to not lift my hips toward her mouth.

"Want to hear the rest of it?" She bites her lip, knowing she's driving me mad and loving every second of it.

Tick tock. The clock is moving too fast, and her mouth isn't full of dick yet.

"I'm going to suck you down my throat, and you are not going to do a damn thing. Hands behind your head, hips still. You're going to sit there and let me service you, sir."

Another drop of precum oozes from my tip, and victory is already written on her face. "If you can make it until two fifty-eight without coming, I'll be still and you can fuck my face and come down my throat. But either way, you're done by three."

I hiss, already on the edge. There's no way I'll make it, but the idea is sexy as fuck.

"Agreed?" Elle bats her eyelashes at me like she's got all the time in the world.

"Yes, yes . . . please." I know I'm begging like a weakling, but she's driving me bonkers. My fingers are already interlaced behind my head, my neck craned to have to the best view.

But her fingers go to the waistband of her jeans, undoing the button and unzipping the zipper. "You didn't think you were the only one going to get off, did you?"

Fuck it, I think. I could just lay her over my desk and slide into her heat right now. We'd both come in record time, I predict. But her brow arches haughtily, a silent reprimand, and I stay still like a fucking good boy.

As I watch closely, her hand disappears and begins moving inside her jeans. "Fuck, Elle."

She smirks, an evil seductive temptress destroying me without even touching me. But finally, blessedly, she does. Her mouth kisses my crown, sucking the precum that's pouring forth, and she moans in delight as my flavor coats her tongue.

She swallows me halfway on the next stroke, and a jolt shoots from my spine through my hips. Though I manage to stay still, I can't stop my mouth. "That's it, love. Take all of me. Suck my cock and rub that pretty pussy. Are you wet for me?"

In answer, she takes her hand out of her jeans and pushes her fingers into my mouth. I suck them clean, savoring her flavor. I whimper when she takes them away, shoving them back into her snug jeans.

She's bobbing over me with haste now, messily and loudly sucking me down deep. Her eyes cut to the clock and she pulls off. "Two fifty-eight. Do it."

Not needing to be told twice, I grab her head, guiding her as she takes me back into her mouth. I use my hands to hold her still, fucking her mouth as I watch her carefully. My cock disappears down to the root as she takes me deep into her throat.

"Fuckin' hell, Elle. Make yourself come because I'm going to come down your throat."

She cries out around me, falling over the edge, and her thighs quiver beneath her. The vibration of her pleasured sounds pulses in her throat, milking my orgasm from me. I hold her against me, buried as deep in her as I can get, and she swallows every drop.

The clock on the wall ticks over the hour. Perfect timing.

Elle wipes the corners of her lips daintily as if we're at fucking tea with the queen, which makes me smile. Sexy minx and mannered lady, with a healthy dose of crazy daredevil added for spice. She's so fucking perfect.

"Best get back to your desk. Helen will be here any second." As she turns, buttoning her jeans, I swat at her ass.

Her head whips around. "Mr. Wolfe. That is inappropriate at the office. If that happens again, I'll have to talk to HR." Teasing heat shines in her eyes as she scolds me, and I can't help but laugh.

I tuck myself away too, soft and spent. "Maybe we'll both have to chat with HR. I was just sitting here, minding my own business and being still, when my assistant just gave me a jobby out of nowhere."

"Shh," she hisses. "It's three o'clock, and you know who might hear you."

As if her words conjured Helen, I hear papers rustling outside the door. A moment later, the knock is loud, as though Helen doesn't want to interrupt anything. I wonder if she suspects something? But Elle and I have been discreet at the office, just silliness, mostly. The sexy teases have been behind closed doors.

I quickly double-check that both Elle and I are righted and at our respective desks and call out, "Come in."

Helen comes in like a woman on a mission. "Good afternoon, Mr. Wolfe, Elle. Shall we get to debriefing on the week's bullet points? I trust Elle has made the travel arrangements?"

"She's finishing them up now, actually. Why don't we step back to your office so she can focus on that and we can go over your week?" Helen nods and spins, immediately heading for her desk.

Our travel plans are already made, though there are several

more items I'd like research on before we make the final proposal. "Elle, can you pull the most recent tax laws, please, including anything currently proposed and expected to pass? I know I looked at them before, but I want to really dig into the potential benefits and pitfalls there."

I leave Elle to that assignment, hoping she'll also spend some brain power deciding whether to accompany me, and go into the outer office, helping Helen with the handover of the duties she'll be overseeing here. Thankfully, she's already up to speed on most of them, having been my right-hand woman for so long. But we do a run-through of everything so that we're on the same page, with aligned expectations.

"What if something hits the fan?" Helen asks. "Afternoon here is past bedtime for you in London, and if there's no time—"

"Helen, you're as keen as any executive here. So go with your gut and send me an email with your decision on any issues. I'll back you. It's not like I'm unreachable, either. I'm going to London, not the moon. I'll call in daily to get updates, both from you and from Gary and Debra. I'm not abandoning you, but I do trust you in my stead."

It's simple and truthful, but Helen's touched by my endorsement. From that moment on, we fly through the rest of our work, Helen trusting her instincts and brains more and more. By the time four thirty rolls around, I feel fully confident in her, and equally important, Helen feels confident in herself.

"Go home," I tell Helen finally. "Have a good dinner, a nice bottle of wine, and relax. Because tomorrow's going to be your debut on the big stage."

"Sounds good . . . and thanks, Colton," she says, grabbing her purse and disappearing. I give her a minute to get to the elevator before going back into my main office, where Elle's gnawing at the tip of a pen, looking confused.

"Have you made your decision?" I ask without preamble, assuming what's got her nose wrinkled so adorably. "We're wheels up tomorrow, Elle."

"I . . . I just don't know," Elle says, tossing her pen on her desk. "Colton, I need you to understand something, to truly get what it is you're asking of me. It's been Dad and me for so long. Mom left us, walked out and said fuck you to the two of us, and we were destroyed for a while. Ever since, he's done everything he can for me. He doesn't want me to get hurt or let me out of his sight. He doesn't want to lose all he has left."

I grit my teeth, both understanding and not. I don't have family like this. As I told Elle, I'm the black sheep of my family, so this parental protective streak feels foreign to me. But I can see that it's coming from a place of love. Truth is, I don't hate Daniel. In almost any other situation, I'd consider him a mate and be happy to share a pint with him down at the pub. It's just that he's between me and my dream, and now, between Elle and what I think her dream is.

There's a time for every baby bird to leave the nest.

"A caged bird stands on the grave of dreams." I'm sad for her, angry for her. I can see her wings being clipped before my very eyes.

"What?"

"It's from a Maya Angelou poem I read as a boy. Your dad loves you and has created a beautiful life for you, but no matter how golden, it is still a cage. I won't begrudge you if you'd rather live comfortably there. I can even understand the appeal. But I'm standing here with the key to your future, the cage door open, and yet, you're too afraid to fly."

She flinches, the smallest tightening of her jaw, when I say she's afraid. Daring girl doesn't much care for that.

"But what if I'm already flying? Have you ever seen a hummingbird eating? They look like they're floating in midair. Like magic. But they're working their asses off, flapping their wings like mad. We just can't see it. Maybe I'm flying and you don't want to see it."

"Perhaps." I don't want to admit that she's right, but she may have a point.

"You say I'm caged, but what you're offering isn't freedom. It's just a different cage. One of your making instead of Dad's."

I swallow thickly, unprepared for the depth this whole situation has taken. I meant for this to be fun, an adventure for us both. Yes, with the boon of pissing off Daniel and increasing my odds of realizing my own dreams.

But somewhere along the way, it became about the battle for Elle's dreams and her heart.

Whether she gives that to me or not, I truly want her to recognize the power she wields in making her own dreams come true.

"Come on," I tell her, reaching over and taking her hand. "I have an idea, a dare."

CHAPTER 18

ELLE

"You've got to be kidding me."

"What?" Colton asks, following my eyes. "I've seen this place from the highway dozens of times. Before, I never gave it much thought. Now, it seems like fun."

He doesn't have to say that he means he never considered doing something this outrageous before I came into his life. I hear that underlying truth loud and clear.

My eyes are currently fixed at the top of a crane towering over us, the blinking light at the top mocking me and probably warning low-flying aircraft to stay away. Around us, miniature golfers do their thing, go-karts scream around a track, and off to the side, neon lights advertise an arcade with something called a 'Tilt-A-Hurl', but the pride of Fun Land towers over us. This is not the same family friendly putt-putt place I took him to. This is a three AM, crack-high crazy idea of an amusement park for adrenalin junkies.

"Colton, that damn thing's half a mile in the air!" I protest, my stomach sinking as someone leaps from the crane, their screams the only way I can track their progress through the darkening sky. I keep waiting for the sound of a human body bouncing off the asphalt surrounding us, but instead, laughter soon rings out . . . whether that's relief or just insanity, I'm not quite sure.

"It's 125 feet," Colton corrects me, pointing at the sign advertising the 'Leap of Faith' bungee jump. He takes my hand, giving it a squeeze. "You said you were afraid of heights but that you'd base jump if given the chance. And if a dare were involved, of course. I thought you'd like the challenge of this. Seems appropriate, don't you think?"

"Maybe, but I suddenly have a very strong desire not to place my life in the hands of what's basically a giant rubber band," I reply.

"Come here." Colton leads me over to a picnic table, the smell of cheap pizza and churros wafting like perfume from the garbage can full of greasy paper plates and leftovers nearby. Sitting me down, he straddles the bench, turning me to face him, his knees outside mine.

Colton leans forward, kissing me firmly. His confidence is heady and addictive, his lips soft and seeking. We certainly have kissed before. I mean, I've pretty much tasted most of his body by now, but this kiss somehow feels more intimate than what we did this afternoon. Like he's silently and generously lending me strength in my moment of doubt and nerves.

When he pulls back, he's smiling, satisfaction written in the set of his mouth as he traces the pulse in my neck with his thumb. He tilts his head, and I think he's coming back for more. Instead, he asks me a question.

"Have you ever heard of flipism?"

I'm already mentally kissing him, so it takes me a heartbeat, maybe two, to register what he said. "Is that where you flip people off? Or when someone's flippant?"

His lips do that twitching thing, but this time it feels like he's full-out laughing at me so I push at his chest. "Shut up and just tell me. Don't make it like some high school vocabulary pop-quiz I didn't study for. Asshole."

He laughs for real at that, holding up both hands to show he meant no disrespect. I huff and dramatically cross my arms anyway, not letting him off the hook that easily.

But he knows I'm playing and runs his palms down my arms. I relax automatically, letting him have my hands back, and he intertwines our fingers.

"Flipism is the art of the coin toss. You know how you assign one option to heads and one to tails, but there's that moment when the coin is in the air, and deep inside, you know what you want it to land on. Or sometimes, it takes the coin actually landing and you feel that seed of disappointment or relief in the result. That moment of intuition about what you really want, the revelation of your true preference . . . that's the foundation of flipism."

"That sounds like a lot of really fancy talk for a coin toss." I laugh at the absurdity, but there's that tiny little bit of me that likes the ease and lack of responsibility in the decision-making process. Though I don't think Dad would take 'I flipped a coin' as an adult decision-making process. "So you want me to flip a coin about going to London?"

His eyes cut to the right, toward the big crane of death. "Not exactly. I was thinking you could be the coin. Stand at the top and I think you'll know. Do you want to stay, not go to London, and keep your life the way it is? Do you want to jump and go to London? See what happens."

His eyes come back to mine, deeper thoughts there than I think either of us expected with this whole mess, and certainly some heavy talk for an amusement park where some kid just hurled loudly in the trash can. Not the one by us, thankfully, but the one by the go-karts. Too many circles, I guess.

I blink, trying to ignore the retches because I'm a sympathy puker, and focus on Colton's words. "I think if you stand there, if you jump, in that moment in the wind, you will know your preference. And then you just have to follow through, brave girl. Fly, or if you are fluttering away like a hummingbird, choose to be an eagle and soar. Rather American, yeah?"

He looks pleased at himself for making his pep talk end on a Go-America note. I mean, how are you supposed to be all 'nah, think I'll skip' on that? It'd be downright unpatriotic.

"This isn't even about all *that*." I gesture, his face encompassing all the stuff he just dropped on me. "I'm just scared because it's so damn high. Fear of heights is a perfectly reasonable mode of self-preservation."

"How about if I go first? I'm going to London. I'm all-in here . . . in more ways than one. I'll jump as a show of good faith and wait for you right there." He points at the ground below the crane.

"You would do that?" I ask, shocked that anyone would be that nice . . . or that suicidal. Even Tiffany wouldn't do that, not even on a dare. Well, maybe then, but the stakes would have to be major. Something like Louboutins if she jumped.

Colton waits patiently, giving me the space to decide for myself. I realize this isn't even the hard decision. I'm just figuring out if I want to stand up on the crane and see what the coin in my belly tells me. At a minimum, I can do that. Jumping? I'll have to wait and see on that.

"Okay," I say, taking the mental plunge. "Let's do this."

Colton grins and runs off to get the tickets before I can change my mind, coming back and taking me by the hand.

"Okay, I'll go first, and then you can go."

He doesn't add the 'if you want to', but I hear it loud and clear, anyway.

The elevator's slow, and I can't even look out the wire mesh of the cage as we rise higher into the air. It's ridiculous. I didn't have a problem with Colton's great glass elevator to his penthouse, but the feeling of the breeze lifting the little wisps of hair at the back of my neck has me trembling like an autumn leaf.

"Hey," Colton says, pulling me in front of him and wrapping his arms around me. "You've got this." I won't admit, not to him and not even to myself, that the cocoon of his arms soothes me, making the itchy, twitchy feelings along my spine calm.

The walkway sways with our footsteps, and I'm gripping the dual metal rails with both hands as the attendant outfits me with my harness. "Hey," he says, his breath stinking with cheap cigarettes that he probably smokes in between jumps, "It'll be great. Time of your life."

His utterly monotone voice and dry delivery makes it sound like he's being sarcastic, but I think he just doesn't care that I'm about to jump out of my skin again. He must do this dozens of times per day. I'm just another body to him. Which makes me think of something else . . .

"Where's the safety certificate for this thing? How many days since the last incident?" I picture a dry-erase board with a big, fat zero on it because they've probably already lost at least two people today. I'll be the third, barely an afterthought on the news tonight when they report the *Faulty Bungee Massacre at Fun Land* story.

"Are you like, with the feds or something?" the attendant asks, suddenly interested. That feels like an even worse sign.

"It'll be fine," Colton assures both me and the attendant. The guy shrugs and turns to us, the question of who's up in his eyes. "I'll go first. Elle, I'll wait for you on the ground, okay?"

I nod, my lips dry and my tongue unable to work up any spit to moisten them. Finally, I grunt a sound that I think might mean 'yes', and Colton kisses me once more. It's over too quickly, making it feel like a goodbye. Shit, maybe he's gonna be victim number three.

The attendant finishes getting us both into harnesses, cinching us up tight before clicking me onto a round pole. "You'll wait here. But I'll keep an eye on you, make sure you're good." To Colton, he says, "Let's fly, man." Colton's carabiner attaches to a safety line that runs down to the drop zone.

He begins doing some kind of safety talk and lists out options for how to fall off the platform. Apparently, backward is easy because you can't see it coming, but stepping off sideways is a popular option too. "Any questions?" Colton shakes his head. "Three, two, one . . ."

Colton shouts and swan dives backward out into the darkness. I scream in fright, watching the light on his harness drop for what seems like forever before he reverses, bouncing higher and bringing to me the sound of his laughter. "Fuckin' right!"

Colton laughs all the way down as the attendant lowers him to the cushion below, pausing while the ground staff unhooks him. As if the cushion would do a damn bit of good if I'm falling from 125 feet up. The line's reeled back up, and I get hooked in when suddenly, the radio at the attendant's hip squawks.

"Well, will you?"

It's Colton's voice, and I knit my brows together as the attendant holds the radio out. "Will I what?"

"Will you be flying to London with me?"

As I stare out into the darkness in front of me, I don't have an answer, and the attendant shoves the radio back on his belt. For the first time, he seems keenly interested in what's happening here. "He a good guy?"

"Huh?"

The attendant looks at me like I'm stupid. "The British dude . . . he a good guy or an asshole?"

A tiny laugh breaks through. "Maybe a little bit of both?"

The attendant nods sagely. "I can see the appeal of that, plus, you know, London. If I were a chick and a nice guy-slash-asshole asked me to London, I'd go. Long as he's not a real asshole, just the regular garden variety dumbass type."

I'm a bit dumbfounded. The guy barely said a word at first and now he's offering relationship advice like *Cosmopolitan*.

"Come on, you're up."

I face forward, looking out over Fun Land and the bit of town beyond. From up here, I can almost imagine I'm just standing on top of a medium-sized building . . . except for the weight of the harness on my shoulders and around my thighs.

Do it. Don't do it. Stay. Go.

I take a deep breath and close my eyes. I'm going to do this, but I don't have to look. "Aaaahhh!" I scream, jumping into the possibilities of London and Colton.

For a long time, what seems like a year, at least, nothing happens. I can feel the wind whistling past me and it takes my breath away. I'm just about to scream again in fear as I splatter on the ground like a messy pancake when suddenly, I'm sent flying upward again.

My eyes pop open, and I'm in the air, my arms and legs waving everywhere as the tension lightens, and suddenly, I'm floating . . . free . . . no weight on my shoulders, nothing but what I've done, the courage that brought me here.

And Colton.

How did he know I'd do this? How did he know I'd like it? Right now, I feel like I want them to wind me back up to the top so I can do it again. But maybe there's something just as thrilling half a world away.

I start laughing, giggling as I drop down again, bobbing up and down like a yo-yo.

"I'm coming with you!" I scream in between laughs, letting the words buoy me as I'm slowly lowered to the ground where Colton waits for me, grinning proudly.

"WHERE TO NOW? WE DO HAVE *SUCH* AN EARLY MORNING AHEAD OF us." Colton thinks he's being clever and subtle. He's not in the least.

"Yeah, you're right. Super early. Guess you'd better take me home." His disappointment is written all over his face, like a boy who lost the championship game. Okay, maybe not quite that bad, but I'm a damn good trophy.

Not that he's lost me in the least.

"I need to grab the bag Tiffany packed for me and make sure she's all set before we go to your place."

His head whips to me so fast I think he'll get whiplash. Though if he didn't from that freefall, I guess he won't now, either. "What?"

I repeat slower. "Tiffany. She's at my apartment. Part of my prep work today was getting her to go over and work her capsule wardrobe magic on my closet. She's probably got me packed into one tiny suitcase with a list of outfit options, complete with helpful photos, if I know her. And I do. Plus, she's having some difficulties with her brother, a bit of roommate-itis, so staying at my place for the week and taking care of Sophie will probably be a lifesaver for them both. Just a little break before one of them kills the other one, because I won't be here to provide snacks and shovels . . . or an alibi."

Okay, maybe I didn't say all of that particularly slow, after all, because Colton is still processing like a lagging computer. I can almost hear the dial-up *bing-bong-bing-bong.*

"You didn't know if you were going, but you already arranged for Miss Young to prepare your things and care for your cat in your absence?"

I shrug. "Plan for the worst, hope for the best."

"Indeed," he agrees as he pushes the pedal closer to the floor. I snug back in the seat with the increased acceleration and realize I'm going to miss Cammie. God, I hope Tiffany doesn't crash her. I told her she could drive my car this week, too, which is a bigger lend than either my apartment, my closet, or my cat. Cammie is a notch above it all, and I pray Tiffany doesn't fuck it up.

Even though it's my place, I knock before I go in. Tiffany's been here all afternoon, and there's no telling what she's gotten into, and there are some definite possibilities I don't want to walk into.

Like this one.

"Hey, Tiff," I start, but she's screaming.

"Oh, my God, Elle! Mr. Wolfe! I mean, Colton! I . . . just . . .

hang on." And she ducks under the blanket she was only half-covered with when we came in.

Before she hid, we could see her as clear as day—a shiny mask in her twisted-up hair, spots of pimple zapper cream on her face, free-titting it in one of my baggy tank tops, and shoveling ice cream into her mouth as she messily cries over some Hallmark movie.

"Good movie?" he asks dryly, his brow rising in question to me even as he talks to the lump on my couch that is Tiffany.

She makes some sound of displeasure that's muffled by the blanket, or maybe her hand. Sophie echoes it, meowing her displeasure at having her catnap interrupted, but then she spies the ice cream precariously sitting on the couch and decides to mosey on over like I won't notice.

Fur mom guilt at leaving her for a week stabs at my heart, and I don't scold her for stealing treats she knows she's not supposed to have. I go blind and let her enjoy, choosing to devil Tiffany instead.

"Guess what we did tonight?"

That's enough of a dangling carrot. She pops back out, thankfully covered her headlighting nips with the blanket at least. "Fuck like rabbits? How was the BBC?"

I hiss, and Colton seems to choke on his own spit. "That's not what that is! Quit saying that! And no. We went bungee jumping!"

It's a bit of a squeal, and my neighbors will probably be glad I'm going to be gone for several days.

"Bitch! You did *not* do that without me!" Tiffany's jaw is set in stone, giving her a sharp, mean edge. I figured she wouldn't want to do something that crazy, but maybe I was wrong?

"Sorry, but we did. It was a coin toss thing." I look to Colton, who's smiling cautiously. "But we bought the video of the jump, so you can laugh at me screaming like a banshee as many times as you want."

She considers my offer. "Forgiven. But first round's on you next time."

I'm getting off easy, so I agree quickly and get out of the line of fire. "I'm gonna grab my bag so we can go, 'kay?"

Tiffany nods, and I disappear down the short hall to my bedroom. I don't bother double-checking anything in the suitcase waiting for me. Tiffany will have packed me better than I would myself. But I pause when I hear Tiffany and Colton talking.

"This is a big deal to her. I know I already did the whole threatening thing, but let me say again . . . don't hurt her or I will *truly* kill you."

I hug the soft scarf she pulled for me to wear on the plane to my chest. *Aww, she is the sweetest and loves me so much.*

"I have no intention of hurting her." Colton's promise rings true, warming me from the tips of my hair to my toes, but Tiffany's not so easy.

"Not meaning to and doing it are two separate things. I don't care whether you mean to or not. If you hurt her, I will hurt you. And that's before Daniel gets ahold of you. She's got a lot on the line here, and yeah, you do, too. But not like she does. Don't fuck her over to get ahead of her dad. She deserves better than that."

"She deserves everything."

I can't take anymore. I loudly come out of the bedroom, lugging my suitcase to interrupt their Elle-love fest.

"Ready?" Colton asks. If he had on a tie, he'd be adjusting it nervously, but instead, he clears his throat . . . twice.

Seems the big, bad Wolfe is afraid of my bestie.

Good.

As we leave, Tiffany hugs me and whispers in my ear, "I dare you . . . be reckless with your heart, be bold with your body, and be that badass bitch in the boardroom. Show him what you've got, girl. Show them all."

"I will."

And the jitters start up, but they don't have anything to do with the dare from Tiffany. They have everything to do with the man taking my suitcase in his hand and waiting so patiently for me to say goodbye.

CHAPTER 19

COLTON

*T*he alarm goes off way too early, especially after a night of virtually zero sleep. I'd had too much on my mind and Elle in my arms to get any real rest.

After grabbing her things, Elle had stayed over and even agreed to sleep in my bed. After I dared her to, of course. I'd figured one thing would lead to another and had been looking forward to finally getting inside her.

But after the adrenalin of the bungee jump had worn off and she'd asked me approximately seven hundred and thirty-two questions about London, Elle had drifted off into a dead sleep, squashing my hopes for a pre-trip shag as she tossed and turned. Even asleep, she's active as can be.

And now, I'm keeping her busy as a beaver—another idiom that made me laugh particularly hard when I'd learned that 'beaver' was American slang for pussy. Though it's not Elle's fanny I'm occupying. It's her mind, because I don't want any last-minute second thoughts.

"The car's waiting downstairs. Let's go." I don't ask her if she's ready on purpose because I don't think either of us is really ready for this, but it's happening. "Go, go, go." I shoo her out the door, promising to buy anything she needs if Tiffany forgot it, but Elle seems certain that won't be the case.

The drive is quiet, though I try to ask Elle a few questions. Even work-related inquiries get short, distracted answers. I will the driver to go faster. For the love of the Queen Mother, let us just get to the airport and on the plane. Once that happens, I'll breathe easier, knowing that Elle won't back out on me.

The security line moves quickly, and Elle and I step up to the conveyor belt together. I wiggle my toes in my socks, hating the way being nearly barefoot in public makes me feel vulnerable. I heave Elle's suitcase onto the belt, and it disappears into the scanner, mine following closely behind.

Elle steps into the body scan machine and follows the directions of the TSA agent. Well, *almost*. He tells her to lift her hands over her head, but she places them behind her head, elbows wide, almost as if she's preparing to get frisked. I wonder if she's ever been stopped by the police and what crazy story she might have about it. After the machine beeps, she steps through, and I do the same, though I place my arms correctly the first time, experienced at the both the US and UK airport procedures.

"Ma'am, is this your bag?"

Elle turns to the agent and nods, her eyes a mix of nerves and confusion.

"I'll need to check the contents. Something flagged on x-ray. This way, please." Elle shoves her feet into her trainers, not bothering to tie them, and steps to the side. The agent has her bag hoisted onto a table, and the few people around are looking over curiously.

The agent unzips Elle's suitcase, lifting the perfectly organized clothing and looking through it. Seems Elle was right about Tiffany. Toward the bottom of the bag, she pulls something out. Even from here, I can see the smile threatening the professional blank look on the agent's face.

"Ma'am? Is this yours?"

"Oh. My. God." Elle virtually screams it, and more eyes turn her way, where the agent is holding up a hot pink vibrator with a bunny-ear clit stimulator that's wobbling back and forth. "She did not put that in my suitcase. No, no, no."

Elle's shaking her head like she can make the scene go away. And barring that, she looks as if she's wishing she could melt into the floor and disappear.

There are snickers of laughter, and I see a couple of teenagers in line pull out their phones, aiming them at Elle. I try to go over to her, but the agent closest to me shakes his head and holds up a staying hand.

"She? Are you saying you didn't pack your bag yourself? Do you have any reason to believe there could be any contraband inside?"

Elle growls. "Can you put that thing away? My best friend packed my bag because she's better at it than I am. I guess she thought I'd need a little stress relief. Right now, I don't think I'll ever be able to look at that thing again and not see it waving around in your hand in the middle of the airport." Elle's hands are waving around much more than the agent's but she's made her point. Though it's with a beet-red face. "Confiscate it if you need to. Just let me get the hell outta here so I can go die of embarrassment alone. Please."

The agent seems wholly unperturbed by the whole thing, as if this is just a normal Monday morning for her. Hell, maybe it is.

"No need for that, ma'am. Just have to remove the batteries for flight. I'd recommend that you pack them securely in your purse instead of in the device."

"Device? Oh, God." Elle's sweating with mortification, and people mostly look to be feeling bad for her at this point. The agent lays the vibrator back on top of the still perfectly situated clothes and hands Elle the batteries.

She rezips and taps the suitcase as she hands it to Elle. "If it helps, that's not even the first one today, and not even in the top one hundred of size. No need to have shame in your game. Though I once pulled out a double-ended dildo the size of my arm." The agent holds up her arm, showing Elle, and everyone who's eavesdropping—which is *everyone*—just how big the dildo was. A pained shudder goes through all of us. "Have a great trip."

Elle rolls her suitcase over to me and holds her palm up right in front of my face. "Do. Not. Say. A. Word." I smirk, fighting the laughter down. "It's five o'clock somewhere, right? After that, I need a drink." And with that decree, she stomps off, shoes still untied and face still a bit pink.

So fuckin' cute, she is. And naughty.

It's barely ten in the morning, but if she's drinking, I'm drinking. I grab us two scotch on the rocks as she collapses onto a leather barstool. When I return, she's got her phone pressed to her ear.

All hints of embarrassment are gone, replaced by fiery fury. "Yes, I am. I'm already at the airport."

She's quiet, listening intently with a straight back. She might as well be mid-meeting at the office for all the 'yes sir' she's giving off. When I set the tumbler down, she mouths 'thank you' as she picks it up and then swallows the whole thing in one go. Impressive. And worrisome.

"Yes, Dad. We did talk about this. And you acted like your word was law and ignored me when I disagreed. You'll be working in Tennessee. I'll be working in London. I'll see you back home next week when the proposals are done."

Her lips press together and her eyes cut to me. It doesn't take a rocket scientist to figure out that he's saying something about me. I sip at my scotch slowly, watching Elle intently and admittedly trying to hear what Daniel's saying.

"I don't think so. You don't need that, Dad. It's . . ." She pauses as if she's searching for a word but then sags. "Inappropriate."

Interesting. Dangerous.

I wonder where Daniel's keen mind has taken their conversation and can barely wait for her to hang up so that I can ask. As he takes his conversational turn, Elle nibbles at her lip, a habit I haven't seen her do much. At least not with this type of nervous energy.

Much like Daniel's, my mind is churning. My proposal, his proposal, Elle, London, and though I hate to admit it, a significant portion of my brain is busy replaying how good Elle felt in my arms last night.

"I'll talk to you later, Dad. We're boarding the plane." I raise a brow at her lie, and she shrugs at me like 'what else can I do?'

"Yeah, I love you too."

And with that, she hangs up. Her sigh is heavy and breathy, her head thrown back as she prays for patience to keep from killing a man. I feel damn lucky that she's not currently contemplating my murder.

When her head returns to its normal position, she narrows her eyes. "Guess you want to pump me for information too?"

So that's Daniel's game. I'm not surprised. It was my first

thought, after all. That Elle was a spy, and then that he would use her access to sabotage my proposal. But I can see the toll it's taking on her, the fray around the edges as she dances between her father and me, gripping at her own integrity with scrabbling hands and morals. That she is fighting us both speaks to the woman Daniel raised, the good person Elle is.

And I make a decision. One I pray I don't come to regret.

I don't ask about Daniel. Not about the phone call, not about his questions, and not even about his proposal.

"Actually, I do have a question."

Her eyes look tired, resigned, as if she already knows exactly what to expect from me. "Do you want to grab a bite before we leave? And some snacks from one of the shops here? It'll be better than anything on the plane."

"What?" she asks, confused.

"Food. What do you want?" I say, my mouth tilted up in an encouraging smile. I look around us. "At least we're not stuck with breakfast only, unless you want breakfast? That's fine too. I've developed an affinity for breakfast tacos, actually. Did you know they're delicious cold, straight out of the refrigerator in the middle of the night?"

"What are you talking about?" she repeats. "Don't you want to know what my dad was asking me? And cold tacos are disgusting."

"Nope," I say, sounding utterly American. I'll have to remember to demonstrate that word for Lizzie for a laugh. "I heard you loud and clear, and I happen to agree. He's working on his proposal. We're working on mine. May the best man win. I happen to think that'll be me, both because I'm me" —I run my hand down my chest— "and because I believe my proposal is better for Fox. Truly."

She blinks. "Cocky bastard."

"Thank you." I choose to take it as a compliment. "So, breakfast tacos or are you feeling a burger mood? I'm going to suggest we skip the sushi. Something about airport sushi sounds like a bad idea before getting locked onto a speeding bullet of an airplane with a tiny washroom."

"Was that a poop joke? The upright Brit makes a crass poop joke? Will wonders never cease?" Elle laughs, and I feel like a fucking champion for taking away the reservations lurking in her eyes.

We wander up and down the terminal in search of sustenance, but sadly, there are no tacos to be found.

"I dare you . . ." Elle says suddenly, stopping my search. She's smiling big, as if she likes the idea she just came up with. I can't wait. "Follow my lead."

I don't have a chance to ask a single question before she gasps dramatically and says too loudly, "We're gonna miss it! Come on!"

And then she takes off running down the concourse, zigging and zagging around passengers, her suitcase remarkably rolling smoothly behind her. I have no idea what she's doing, but I'm a man who can follow orders when need be, so I follow her lead and run after her.

"Pardon me . . . excuse me . . . pardon . . ." I say to the people we're running around as I try to catch up with Elle.

People are looking at us, some jumping out of the way, and someone yells out, "You can make it." The support for this weird and unknown destination is sweet and unexpected.

Elle runs up to an empty desk, nearly body slamming into it as her feet stop but the rest of her doesn't. "No! We missed it!" She's crying to the ceiling, hands spread wide in theatrical agony as if the flight we missed—er . . . didn't miss—is a devastating blow.

Arriving two steps behind her, I gather her in my arms, running my palm along her hair. "It's okay, love. We'll get the next one. I'll get you there, I promise."

Still, I have no idea what's going on, but the dramatics and pretend play are wildly fun. This feels different from the other dares we've done, more playful and public. Like the other dares have had some ulterior motive—getting to know each other while having fun being the primary. This is us against everyone else, and even if it's not real, there's something here that is.

"I believe you, honey. Well, if we're stuck here, at least feed me tacos and tell me I'm pretty."

She says it like a telly show I saw once where a character said to 'slap her ass and call her Sally'. I didn't understand that at all as a boy, maybe even less now, but Elle I understand just fine.

"Come on, pretty girl. Let's get you fed."

She laughs, and I can already see more ideas blossoming. She's using them as a distraction from her father. I know that as sure as I know that we're not going to find tacos before our flight leaves. But I'll keep searching for whatever food she wants, and she'll keep searching for a way to rebel against her dad. For now, it's working.

CHAPTER 20

COLTON

The flight is surprisingly empty. I mean, there are people scattered here and there, but the business class section at the front has only us and two other people, a man in a suit who's already steadfastly focused on his laptop and an older woman who's already snoring. The flight attendant hasn't even done her pre-flight safety speech yet.

I sit next to Elle, enjoying her excitement as she looks out the window. She watches the ground crew bustling around and then watches the ground disappear far below us as we find our cruising altitude high in the sky.

Her blonde ponytail whips back and forth as she tells me to look out the window. When she looks out again, I don't do as she asked. The better view is right next to me.

Elle looks beautiful. Stunning, really, even dressed for travel in fashionable trainers, leggings that make her ass look positively grabbable, and a soft top that hugs her curves and drapes tantalizingly over her breasts. It's perfectly proper, but that doesn't stop my mind from wanting to spread the V-neck wide and lift her tits out to feast upon.

I can't help myself. I take her hand, interlocking our fingers. I can feel the softness of her thigh against the back of my hand, begging me to move higher . . . higher.

The flight attendant stops beside us, offering drinks. Elle starts to say something, but I interrupt her. "Nothing for now, thank you."

The flight attendant's perfectly sculpted brows don't even move. I'm sure she's seen way worse than a slightly rude and pretentious flyer. Elle, on the other hand, looks ready to slice and dice me when the cart continues on its way.

"Excuse you. I wanted a water bottle. I have a per diem and I intend to use every last penny of it, Mr. Wolfe."

"There's a one-liter bottle in your bag. I bought it at the airport shop for you, remember? And besides, I have something else in mind now that we're alone for a while."

"Alone?" she scoffs, looking around. "We're on an airplane with tons of other people."

I don't turn around but estimate anyway. "There are two others in business class with us, and maybe sixty others in coach. Poor sods, their knees are going to be pained after this long of a flight."

Elle fakes a British accent, making fun of me. "Poor, unfortunate souls. They should've splurged and gotten the comfy seats like I did." She places a hand to her chest and slathers the entire thing in 'entitled brat' tones. "You sound like a bougie ass." Back to her own sass for that dig.

Frowning, I explain. "That's not what I meant at all. I meant that there are fewer witnesses, and now the flight attendant will be at the back of the plane for a bit."

There's that light in her eyes. "Witnesses? For what?"

I lean in close, getting intimately in her space, even though no one will overhear me. "Have you ever heard of the mile-high club?"

Her eyes widen, knowing exactly where I'm going with this. "Yes, and I won't be joining today. Our first time will not be at thirty-seven thousand feet or whatever the captain said."

I can taste the victory already, though. "First time? So you've already thought about it? Thought about a second and third time too, haven't you?" Her smirk is answer enough, so I press on.

"And now, you're thinking that doing something a little crazy, a bit unexpected might be just right for our first time. It does seem rather suited for us, don't you think? Your sneaking into the lavatory but leaving it unlocked, the race of your pulse as I come in and lock the door behind me. Our eyes locked in the mirror as I spread your shirt wide and pull your luscious tits out, fondling them in the mirror while you watch. You'd feel my cock against your ass and reach back to cup me, driving me wild. I'd push your trousers and knickers down . . . are you wearing panties today, Elle?"

It's a test to see how hooked she is. When she silently nods, her breath hitched, I know this is happening. But the lead up is so delicious that I continue our verbal foreplay. I let go of her hand, flipping mine so that my palm rests high on her thigh, almost to the crease where it joins her body.

"You'd spread these lovely legs for me, letting me test your wetness. You'd be soaked for me, so hungry and ready for my cock." My pinkie finger glances over the seam of her leggings, and I groan deeply at the heat I can feel there. Elle matches my groan.

"You'd have to be so quiet, not making a sound as I play with your clit and slip my fingers inside you, stretching you to take me. But it'd be so hard to hold those cries of pleasure back as I made you come all over my hand. Then I'd press my cock against you, letting you coat me in your cream before I fill you up. Right there, pressed against the vanity, your eyes and mouth open wide in pleasure as I fuck you for the first time at thirty-seven thousand feet until we both come."

She shudders against my hand, where I'm openly cupping her now. "And then we'll return to our seats, smelling like sex, with no one the wiser."

Her eyes are clouded with lust and need, and I consider just rubbing her off right here. That's another fantasy altogether, making her come in public, even though there's no one around. But I want inside her too badly.

I know that she's using me and the dares to rebel against her father, to feel free and alive. In a way, I'm using her as a distraction from the hell that we'll face when we get off this plane, the one I haven't told her about yet. But even in the face of those pressures, the truth is . . . I just want her. Not because of her dad or the proposals, not because my family is awful and I'm nervous about subjecting Elle to their particular brand of manipulation.

But because she's amazing and lovely and makes me feel alive.

So I do it. The one thing I know will push her over the edge of sanity and reason. Because I'm already there, in this world of her creation where rules don't apply, consequences don't happen, and we can be free.

"I dare you . . . go to the lavatory and wait for me, Elle."

Her head lolls back and she rolls it to look at me. "I kinda hate you right now." Her body says she's lying.

I kiss her hard, pushing my tongue into her mouth, and she meets me stroke for stroke with her own. Her hips lift against my hand too. Fucking hell, maybe I will just get her off here, swallowing any sounds she makes, because she's primed on the edge.

She pushes against my chest, and I break the kiss with a growl. "Excuse me, sir. Be right back." She works her way out of her seat, shoving her ass in front of my face.

Holy shit, I can smell her arousal and my mouth salivates to taste her. My cock tells my mouth to wait its fucking turn because the only thing getting a taste of her right now is hard as a fucking rock between my legs.

She doesn't look back as she walks the few steps up the aisle to the lavatory. I consider for a split second that she might be leaving me high and dry, going in there to get herself off, but I don't hear the tell-tale click of the lock and my cock surges in my trousers.

I force myself to count to thirty and then adjust myself before getting up to follow. Walking is painful, but I manage without limping or coming in my pants like a teenager.

"Colt—" she says as I sneak into the washroom, but I cut her off, kissing her quickly and claiming her body with my hands. She melts against me, pushing into my kiss as my touch unlocks any remaining doubts inside her.

"Remember, quiet," I whisper in her ear before nibbling on the delicious lobe. She whimpers, her soft breasts flattened against my hard chest, but I can feel the hard tips of her nipples. She runs her hands up my chest and around my neck, holding me close as she pulls herself up to my ear this time.

"Just do it. Just fuck me already. I dare you." The words are needy moans, and she tells me how much she means it when she spins in place, a very tight fit in the small space, and pushes her ass back toward me.

She pushes at her leggings, lowering them and her knickers at the same time until the full lushness of her ass greets me. If there were room, I'd bow down and kiss her, eat her pussy out from behind. But there's no space, no time for that right now. But I can grab her cheeks, so I do. Cupping the flesh in my greedy hands, I knead her.

"Going without you, Mr. Wolfe." Her right hand leaves its balancing perch on the sink and drops between her thighs. I can't see her hand in the mirror, but I can tell she's rubbing her clit and it lights a fire inside me.

"Fuck, Elle. Wait for me, damn it."

I grab a condom out of my wallet and then let my trousers and boxers fall. One quick stroke of my cock and then I'm rolling the condom on. Elle is bucking against her fingers, her luscious ass bumping against me and not helping matters in the least. But at last, I'm sheathed and lined up as she arches for me.

"You ready?" I ask her. In the mirror, her cheeks are stained pink, her eyes at half-mast with pleasure, and her bottom lip puffy from where she's biting it to stay quiet. Her nod is sure, her body certain of its answer.

I don't dally. No, I slam into her in one forceful thrust, bottoming out as she goes tight as a wire. Every muscle clenches, and I can feel her pussy clamping down on my cock. Her free hand claws at the mirror over the sink, and her mouth opens in a silent scream. Actually, not so silent.

I cover her mouth with my palm, growling in her ear to be quiet. She nods and kisses my palm, so I keep it there.

We don't have time for sweet and tender, slow and leisurely, and I don't think either of us even wants that right now, anyway. This moment has been building between us, and like a match to kerosene, we ignite instantly.

Trying to be quiet, I pound her, our bodies pumping together with hard, violent thrusts that thrill every nerve inside our bodies. My hips ache I'm fucking her so hard, but Elle takes it, begging me silently for more.

"Take your tits out for me. Let me see you." One hand stays on the mirror for leverage, the other leaving her clit to work the wide V-neck of her shirt off her shoulders and then lift her breasts out of her bra. The bra acts as a shelf, setting her tits up in a sexy frame that lets me see her pearled-up nipples. They bounce hypnotizingly with every thrust of my cock into her sweet pussy. "Beautiful girl."

Her hand drifts back to grip my hair, nearly pulling it out at the roots, but I don't give a single fuck as long as I can stay inside her. The reach back makes her body bow, letting me in even deeper, and we both reach the edge of what we can take.

"Come for me, Elle. Come all over my cock. Right now." The words are spat from between my gritted teeth, barely formed whispers.

She whimpers and lets go of her death grip on my hair to press my palm against her own mouth tighter. She's crying against the flesh, knowing she's being too loud but unable to stop it as I feel her pulse around me. Her quivering walls milk my cock, pulling every bit of cum from me as my balls pull up tight.

She droops, exhausted and spent, and I hold on to the condom as I pull out of her. "Oh, my God, that was . . ."

I arch a brow at her in the mirror, waiting for her to find the words, but she shakes her head. "I can't even find adjectives. You fucked my vocabulary out of my head."

I tie off the condom, tossing it in the trash and handing Elle a couple of paper towels to clean up. "Might I suggest fantastic, amazing, incredible, brilliant?"

Elle smirks, throwing the messy towels in the trash. I like that it's not awkward or fake, either of us pretending that sex is this neat and tidy thing. Hell, I'm rinsing my meat and two veg in the sink while she watches, for fuck's sake.

"You have a pretty high opinion of yourself, it seems." The tease is light and bantering.

I dry off, slipping back into my boxers and trousers as Elle rights her own clothes. I place a smacking kiss on her mouth, murmuring against her lips. "I was talking about you, love."

She blushes, looking pleased as punch with herself. And with me.

"How long have we been in here? What degree of walk of shame are we talking about out there?"

"There's a scale?" I inquire, thinking that perhaps I missed this bit of Americana.

"Oh, yeah." Elle nods definitively. "One to five, one being the worst. Five is just an awkward 'I'll call you' when you both know that's not going to happen. Maybe that's bumped to a four if the sex was bad too. A one is full-blown morning after, in your party dress from the night before, walking through the frat house as the entire pledge group offers to make you breakfast and complements your singing ability."

She shrugs as if it's no big deal. "I was a little loud in my drunken state, apparently. I might've yelled *yeehaw* at one point? Tiffany and I went to a country bar a few times."

She looks as though she's evaluating what she might or might not have done on this apparently not-all-that-hypothetical story that illustrates a level-one walk of shame.

Part of me wants to laugh at the outrageousness. Part of me wants to travel back in time and destroy any man who ever had sex with her or heard her having sex. The Neanderthal urge is a weird, foreign thing for me. I'm usually more casual, or at least I have been in my own relationships. Which haven't ever been anything serious. But there's some jealousy in my core, a greediness in my gut. I want to know her stories. I want to be *in* her stories. All of them.

"Well, I think we're safe. Probably not more than ten minutes in here, and no one seemed the wiser when I came in."

"Ten minutes? I've played seven minutes in heaven that weren't remotely this good. Maybe your high opinion of yourself . . . and me . . . is warranted, after all."

I like this. The playful lightness she brings to every situation. Even sex in an airplane lavatory.

"I'll go first, make sure the coast is clear. You follow in a couple, okay?"

Elle nods, and I make my escape. As I suspected, no one even looks this way as I sit back down. Elle slips in a few minutes later, her ponytail a little tighter and her skin glowing.

"How's everyone doing?" The flight attendant has made her way back to the front of the plane and is standing at my side. I nod politely, and she holds out two water bottles. I take them, slightly confused, and then she pulls two wet wipes and two tiny bags of pretzels from her pocket. "These flights do get rather long and boring, don't they? We have about eight hours to go, so stay hydrated."

Elle goes stiff next to me, so I jump in to defer any weirdness. "Thank you. We are feeling peckish, I guess. And a good nap is probably a good idea."

"Would you like a blanket?" Her face is perfectly impassive, not a sign of anything untoward, but it's quite obvious that our field trip to the lavatory didn't go wholly unnoticed.

"No, thank you. I think we're fine now."

The flight attendant nods and walks off. I look to Elle, not sure where this is going to rank on her scale now, but instead of mortification, she's fighting back giggles.

"Oh, we are so busted."

I find that I don't care in the slightest.

CHAPTER 21

COLTON

"Welcome home," the officer on duty says as he hands me back my passport. "No place quite like it, eh?"

There isn't . . . and that's why my hands shake as I tuck my passport away. This is the beginning of a new phase for me, a sign of success to return to the fold of home a changed man. No, an improved man.

I've missed the rolling countryside, the bustle of downtown, and my family. Or at least some of them. I can't wait to hug Lizzie and Nan, at least.

But bringing Elle here means I'm letting her see more of me than she's ever known. She's going to see the good, the bad, and the ugly, as they say. I only hope that I haven't misjudged her and that she can handle it.

Elle emerges from the immigration office with her bags, taking a deep breath as she breathes in the air. "Ah, London." Then her nose crinkles in disgust. "It kinda smells like car exhaust."

I chuckle. "Well, we are at the airport. Maybe try again once we're a bit further out."

She agrees and follows me out of the airport proper. I've been here dozens of times before and know exactly where I'm going, so I'm keeping a quick clip. Elle, however, is dawdling behind me, looking around at everything.

"Have you traveled much?" I ask, trying to hurry her along a bit. While I want her to enjoy and see everything, we do have work to do.

"Some, but nothing like this. Dad would take me on work trips sometimes, and we went on vacations. But never outside the US. Oh, except for the time we went to Cancun." The thought of Elle lounging on a sandy beach in a tiny bikini is an appealing one. Perhaps we'll go there someday.

"I'm the opposite, I suppose. I've been all over Europe but went to the US for the first time to interview with Fox."

We make our way to the VIP area and see a black-suited man holding up a sign with my name. "I'm Colton Wolfe."

He dips his chin in polite greeting, introducing himself as Oliver before he takes Elle's suitcase, leading us to a black Rolls Royce Ghost. All business, he has us situated in the back and merges into traffic with ease.

From her new vantage point, Elle oohs and ahhs quite literally as the city is revealed to us. "What's that?"

Oliver's eyes meet mine in the rearview mirror, silently asking if I'd like to answer or if he should. I blink, and he delves into what amounts to a city tour for Elle on the way to the hotel.

I appreciate his care and involvement with Elle for the moment as nerves begin to snarl in my mind, making me useless as a tour guide.

I haven't seen Mum, Dad, or Nan in years, and especially not Eddie. Only Lizzie, and even then, it's been a while.

Of course, I've kept in contact with everyone, each in their own way. Nan and Lizzie I call, Mum less frequently. Dad and Eddie are more the rare and family business-only email types, which is probably best, especially with Eddie. We've had enough rows that I don't need to start a new one every time I see his face.

And that's the problem. This won't be an easy reunion, especially since it will be coupled with my introducing Elle to the thermite grenade that is my family.

Oliver stops the car smoothly in front of The Rosewood. It's one of London's most luxurious hotels, situated in High Holburn. Elle's head is leaned back, looking from the arched entryway up the columned second story to the tall tower. "Wow," she breathes.

"This way, ma'am." Oliver helps Elle out, and I tell him that I've got it from here. He will be on-call for us for the entirety of the week, so he hands me a sleek black card with his number, instructing me to call anytime, day or night, for anything at all.

We head through the archway and into a beautiful courtyard. Elle's hand grips my bicep where she's got her hand laced through my arm like we're the prince and princess. To think, a few hours ago, we were fucking in the washroom.

I can't help but smile at the contrast. She is truly versatile, and while at first glance, she might seem a rather simple woman with simple desires, I'm finding her to be complex and deep. Even if she can gasp with child-like wonder at a beautifully artistic marble staircase.

The suite has her running around like a child again, holding up feather pillows on the couch and shoving an entire macaron in her mouth in one go before flopping onto one of the beds. Crumbs fall out a little as she says, "I'm in heaven. Actual heaven."

"Not sure what a naughty girl like you is going there," I joke dryly.

Her middle finger pops up along with her head. "Well, being naughty got me here, and that's basically the same thing." She looks around again, her eyes wide.

She kicks her feet crazily in the air and then sits up as if it never happened, tucking them underneath her. Her eyes are crystal clear, pinning me in her gaze.

"Okay, spill it."

I flinch, but only on the inside. My face shows zero reaction to her words, but perhaps that's a tell itself? "What do you mean? You're ready to get to work?" I pray that's what she's getting at.

"Yes, work. But first, what's the deal here? I know good and well that this is the suite you had me book, but I had no idea it was this swanky. *This*" —she gestures around the room— "is most definitely not included in Mr. Fox's per diem for this trip. Neither is the Oliver-in-waiting-Rolls. So, what's up? Tell me that and then we'll talk work."

Ah, but they are one and the same, though I'm not prepared to tell her that piece of the puzzle just yet. But I can start with small steps to the horror that awaits.

"I thought you'd enjoy a bit of posh. Seems I was correct, given your dance around the room."

She points at me as I sit down beside her on the bed. "That wasn't a dance. And you're avoiding the question."

Smart girl. Ball busting girl.

A bit of careful truth seems prudent. "Much as your father keeps track of you, my family is likely already aware that I'm in London. They'll want to see me, and I want to see *some* of them."

"Lizzie?" she guesses correctly.

"Yes, and Nan. I'll admit that much as you wish to show Daniel that you are independent, I wish to show my family that I'm successful."

"Black sheep. You weren't kidding?" Her voice is soft, more sensitive than most would be to a poor little rich boy.

I grit my teeth, wishing I didn't have to tell her the truth of my family. "My family follows the theory of not needing 'the spare'. I have an older brother, the golden child, and am therefore an unnecessary addition."

Her arms go around my neck, pulling my head to her shoulder. It's a tragic truth that the simple yet genuine affection melts something inside me.

She doesn't disagree with me or tell me that surely, I'm mistaken. No, she just accepts my word and comforts me through it without meaningless platitudes.

"So they've got eyes and ears all over and you want them to hear how rich and successful you are, hence, the fancy car and fancy hotel."

"Something like that. Does that make me superficial? All these trappings are shallow, but . . ."

"Is it their language?" At my raised brows, she explains. "Like, are they people who would see you happy and equate that with success? Or are they people who are only going to see success in dollars and cents? Or is there something else? What's their language?"

"Money. At least, that's true for my parents."

She's perceptive, and I wonder if she's applied the same insights to herself. It's a gamble to ask, but I do anyway. "What about Daniel? Are you speaking his language?"

Her lips purse and she quiets. "Actually, I think I am, though he'd never admit it. Dad's always wanted to keep me in a bubble, but he's this forceful powerhouse and set that example for me my whole life. For me to truly be an adult in his eyes, I think I'm going to have to piss him off royally by giving him a taste of his own medicine. It's gonna hurt us both a lot, and it's going to be so damn hard. But in the long run, he's not going to let me go without a fight, and he won't respect me unless I fight for my independence." She smiles sadly, and I think she just realized all that herself.

She shakes her head. "Enough about me. Tell me the rest of it about your family. Are we going to meet them while we're here?"

There's more, so much more.

That my dad takes being an asshole to a whole new level of boorishness. That my mom lets him walk all over her. That my brother is a douche canoe. That I want to steal Lizzie away and let her stay in the States with me so that she has a fair shot at normalcy away from my father. That Nan is getting older, and losing her is probably the scariest thing I can think of.

I don't say any of that.

"Yes, we will, but I think we've had enough share and tell for now. And after the long flight, we probably should catch a few winks so that we're fresh. We've got work and family stuff looming, and being jet lagged won't do us any favors."

"Show and tell," Elle says, correcting me. She kicks her trainers off, flopping back on the bed again. Her arms are spread wide, taking up most of the space, but I lie down beside her. "Cat nap times two, coming up. Good night, Colton . . . or good morning . . . whatever."

I chuckle at the cat nap, thinking it's another idiom, but after everything else, I just let it pass without comment. Elle seems lost to her thoughts and will hopefully get some rest. I don't think I'll sleep a wink until I see my family.

Half dozing, Elle says, "Hey, did you see the lady downstairs glaring at my sneakers?" She brings one hand to her nose, turning it up snootily. "Apparently, my shoes do not meet *de riguer* standards for the Rosewood. Pretty sure that means I don't, either."

"Definitely not," I agree. My eyes are closed so I don't see the pillow coming, but it hits me square in the face with a *whomp*. "I meant it as a compliment," I say, trying to explain and bat away her follow-up swings.

I give up on defensive maneuvers and tackle her, the pillow smashed between us and her arms pinned at her side. "I bet she's never played putt-putt, never bungee jumped, never shagged in an airplane. I bet most people haven't done half the things you've done. So who gives a fuck about your shoes? I know I don't."

She smiles like I just gave her the sweetest compliment. Or like she's proud of all the crazy dares she's done, so I give her one more.

"I dare you . . . to have a kip, a nap," I say in both English and American, translating before she even asks. "Boring, I know, but needed."

She lifts her head, and I think she might be about to headbutt me since nothing about Elle would surprise me at this point, but instead, she presses a soft kiss to my lips. I take that as her acceptance of my dare.

Just like on the plane, she's softly snoring within minutes, and I lie awake next to her, both of us still in our traveling clothes. My mind plays over strategies and outcomes, procedures, and possibilities of meeting my family and getting my proposal through to the finish line.

Time to put up or shut up, Colton.

CHAPTER 22

COLTON

"*J*ust a quick visit to the fam, right? We've got work to do, Boss." Elle's teasing today is a bright spot of fun in the nerves tensing my spine.

"Yes. Just what we need to do." There's more I should say, but I don't. Not yet. I want to pretend just a bit longer.

After a few oohs and ahhs, Elle falls silent. I can feel her eyes on me, but I continue looking out the window of the Ghost.

I suppose it must be clear, the expression on my face. I see so many things that are familiar. There's the Tesco's I'd stop by after boxing practice, and the chippy shop I'd frequent for lunch on the go. Even just the street signs, the people on the sidewalks, and of course, the pubs, all bring back memories. They all feel like home.

Oliver makes a turn, and I see one change that pierces my heart . . . the gym's gone. Sure, it was old, a dilapidated brick and concrete box built with public funds and barely kept together, but I loved that place.

The roof leaked when it rained, and it was a sweltering sweatbox in summer and a dank, half-frozen icebox in winter.

But it was real. It was a place where money meant nothing, social class meant even less, and the only way to prove yourself was through blood, sweat, and skill.

"Do you know what happened to the boxing club that was there?"

Oliver's eyes look to the corner where the club once stood

before turning back to focus on the road. "It closed a few years ago. It was a bit of a kerfuffle, but then some minted hen tossed a coin at it, and Bob's your uncle, the jammy bastards got a fresh place. It's north of the High Street."

Elle laughs and then leans over to whisper in my ear. "What the fuck did he just say? I know he's speaking English, but I got lost after 'it closed' and didn't understand a word."

I lean into her ear, not because I need to but because I'll take any opportunity to nibble them. "My best idea? Nan bought the boys a new club."

She pulls away before I get my taste, her eyes wide and jaw dropped. "As in, *funded* a boxing gym? Minted, indeed."

My lips quirk, amused that she understood a bit more than she let on.

My attention turns to the land rolling past us as we find our way closer to home. By the time we make the last turn toward the compound, my heart is racing. Elle holds my hand, and I trace a line along her skin with my thumb, not in affection but in distraction. It gives me the smallest grounding to something beyond home, beyond London, beyond . . . my family.

The twin hedges that line the lane come to a halt, and we can see my ancestral home for the first time. Elle is transfixed, and I wonder what her first impression will be. Will she be impressed or disgusted by the obscene showiness? Will she think it charming and posh and dance around like at the Rosewood, or will she shrink under the weight of history and high society rules?

"This makes Allan Fox's estate look like my place," Elle says as the asphalt ends and the tires start to crunch on the crushed marble that makes up the rest of the park lane. "And I've always been amazingly uncomfortable with Mr. Fox's whole shebang. I mean, how many forks do you need for one meal? I can tell you . . . one. Just lick it clean between the salad and the steak." She's rambling nervously, neck craned as she looks around. "You sure this isn't a royal palace or something?"

There's no walking this back. Allan Fox measures his estate, a very fine house in all respects, in acres. The Wolfe compound is measured in square miles, although a good portion of it is a working farm. And that's just the main property of the family home. There are others—vacation homes, country homes, city apartments. All of which make Mr. Fox's home, and even my US penthouse apartment, look dinky in comparison.

I try to see through Elle's eyes, imagining seeing it for the first time and not growing up here with it seeming normal. The house truly is impressive, and I feel a weight in my chest as we approach the front of the main wing.

A true country estate for the landed gentry, the three floors of Victorian splendor stand in a solid, slightly imposing façade, austerely ornate and lined with windows that make me feel watched even as the car stops.

Elle is nearly silent as she gets out, though I think I can hear her heart beating as fast as mine. It's for an entirely different reason, however. She gawks at the manicured gardens stretching off to the left and right of us, searching for the source of the sound of the horses in the stable.

The front door opens, and a servant descends the stairs toward us.

"Master Colton."

The man who greets me is a long-familiar face, and while there's significantly more gray in his perfectly coiffed, conservative haircut, he looks exactly the same as he did when I was just a boy running around the family estate. Even his suit and cravat look the same.

"Alfred!" I greet him, grinning foolishly. "You are a sight for sore eyes. Bloody good to see you!"

I don't think I'd realized how much I'd missed him until he was standing right in front of me. There's a part of me that would love to pull the older man into a back-slapping embrace. However I know Alfred, I know the way he was raised and trained, and instead, I offer my hand, shaking his warmly.

"Quite lovely to see you as well." The words are formal, but the affection feels good. I think he's missed me as well. "And your guest?"

"Oh, of course. This is Elle Stryker, a coworker . . . and friend." I know I stumble over finding a label for Elle, but it seems like something I should discuss with her before tossing out anything more . . . significant.

Elle offers her hand, and Alfred shakes hers as well. "Alfred Duncan, ma'am."

She smiles, looking from me to Alfred. "Do you really have a butler named Alfred? Are you sure your last name isn't Pennyworth?"

Alfred chuckles. "Quite sure, ma'am. And technically, I'm not a butler but a house assistant."

"Oh, my apologies." Elle's hand covers her mouth. "I didn't mean to offend."

Alfred dips his chin deeply, not offended in the least. "Master Colton, can I show you in?"

"Coltie! Wotcher!"

The cry echoes from the front steps of the house as a manic ball of rugby shorts, trainers, T-shirt, and blondish hair comes pelting out the front door and down the steps. Lizzie launches herself to hit the grass before flinging herself into my arms.

"Lizzie!" I yell, swinging her around me in a huge circle. A fresh wave of emotion floods through me as I feel the tickle of my sister's hair under my chin, of her wiry arms locked around my neck.

It's been too long. Far, far too long.

"I'd say surprise, but I'm certain everyone knew of my arrival before the plane even touched ground."

Lizzie rolls her eyes, huffing heavily. "You know it. Like the bloody MI6 around here." She elbows Alfred, who offers only his polite 'of course, Miss' smile before he steps back to direct Oliver.

I trust that Alfred will have Oliver squared away with parking and a scrummy snack in no time.

For the first time, Lizzie notices Elle, who's looking on with a mixture of amusement. "Hi, there . . ." Lizzie's stilted greeting says she's searching her mind for something, and with a raised brow, she settles on . . . "Assistant."

Lizzie steps closer to me, putting herself between Elle and me and effectively giving Elle her back. "Coltie, what's with the fit bird?"

I move so that we're back in a circle, placing a hand on Elle's lower back. "Lizzie, this is Elle Stryker. Elle, this is my sister, Lizzie."

Lizzie's eyes are sharp, not missing the intimate touch. "Ah, taking after Father after all, Coltie? Getting off with the closest tart?"

The venom in the words surprises me. "Lizzie, don't be rude. Elle is my assistant and my friend."

Lizzie doesn't pout. She's too well-trained at Mother's elbow to do that, but I can feel the sulk. "Sorry, Elle. Just miss my brother. It'd be nice to have him to myself, you know?"

Elle's smile is kind. "Of course. I hope he'll have time to really hang out with you while we're here."

Lizzie scents blood in the water, and like a shark, she attacks. "Why are you here, Coltie? And does Nan know?"

Before I dodge those questions, I hear Nan herself bellowing in the gardens.

"Get out, you old cocker! Get out of my gardens!"

I run for it, wanting to make sure Nan is okay, with Elle and Lizzie hot on my heels.

Nan is a lady through and through, proper and posh at all times. Well, at least when she's in public. Privately, I've seen her a bit knackered, singing an old dirge off-key, while holding court over an empty ballroom. But these are things we don't speak of. Suffice it to say, yelling is not her style by a long mile. But her voice calls out again.

"No. I've already told you. Bugger off."

Around the east end of the house, we find her in her garden. If I weren't so worried, I'd probably shed a tear at seeing her in the flesh, but I can't take time to take in her dark hair, dyed but again one of the things we don't discuss in polite company, startling blue eyes, and arms that used to rock me to sleep as a boy.

None of those things matter, considering she's holding up a dirty spade, threatening an even older man with it as though she could decapitate him at any second.

As we get closer, I can see that it's Geoffrey Blackwire, a sour old wanker who used to work for the family. I understood he retired, but it's not uncommon for lifers to be allowed a space on the estate. If I recall, his grandson lives with him as well. Will, I think his name is. He's Lizzie's age, give or take a year or two.

But right now, Geoffrey's sneering at Nan as though he doesn't know who the fuck he's talking to, to borrow an American phrase. Another flits through my mind. *I'll kill the motherfucker.*

"What is going on here?" I boom. A side effect of being in the US, where everything is loud and aggressive. There's no finesse and delicateness there like there is in the UK, but as Geoffrey jumps nearly out of his skin, I'm finding it a rather useful tool in my arsenal. Perhaps not as much as Nan's spade, but sufficient enough to turn his attention to me.

"You." Geoffrey's entire face pinches together as if he's sucked a lemon. "What are you doing home?"

I certainly don't answer to him, but when Nan drops the spade and runs to me with open arms, I hug her and answer as she asks the same thing. "Home for business, and wanted to see you, of course."

Nan beams. Geoffrey sniffs as though something smells dank. Lizzie smiles. And Elle . . . watches it all play out like a show on the telly.

Geoffrey tries to interrogate me again, but Nan has had enough now. "Geoffrey Blackwire, you hear me proper . . . get out of my garden and don't touch my roses or I'll have you in a row house on your arse." She points, and though he grumbles, Geoffrey does comply this time. Nan tsks. "That man is going to destroy my hard work."

To be clear, Nan's rose garden is her favorite place in the world. She reads books about roses, strolls the rows of blooming flowers, and even goes so far as to prune them on occasion. With gloves on, of course. She would never deign to actually touch the soil to plant them, but she oversees the gardeners and has a tight-knit relationship with each of them.

"He's messing with the roses again?" Lizzie asks, letting me know this isn't the first time this has happened.

Nan sighs, anger replaced by sadness. "Poor sod, so forgetful these days. Thinks the garden's his, tells me about planting it himself. To be fair, he did plant a bit. But he comes to cut flowers for his bedroom several times a day, having forgotten that he's done it already twice before tea."

With that drama handled, for now, at least, Nan seems to see Elle for the first time. "And who might you be, love?"

Lizzie jumps in. "Coltie's got himself a sweetie. He works with her."

She's sacrificed me like the fatted calf on my own return. Nan's eyes are sharp. "Are you, now? Colton's sweetie. Well, isn't that the bee's knees?"

"Elle Stryker, this is my grandmother, Dorothy. Nan, this is Elle." I swallow, but the damage is already done, so I drive the final nail in the coffin with a confirmation. "My girlfriend."

I feel Elle tense, and I know we're going to have a conversation about this later tonight. But perhaps I can talk her down with apologies for my presumptiveness on my knees. Or by letting her offer a dare of her choice.

Elle fumbles, trying to be polite through her shock. She fetches a pretty poor curtsy, her foot slipping on the grass as she does and causing me to catch her.

"Hello, madam. It's a pleasure."

Nan waves Elle off. "Bollocks, Elle! I'm far to old to faff around with all that bowing and curtsying codswallop. I'm not Queen Lizzy. Call me Nan as Coltie does and come over here so I can get a good look at what he's got himself into."

Nan looks Elle up and down boldly, having no reason or care to be subtle. "Lovely child. You must be a special lass to have captured my Coltie's heart." Under her breath, she mutters, "Better than the harlots his brother brings home, for sure."

"What?" I exclaim. "What's Eddie doing now?"

Lizzie rolls her eyes again, something that's apparently a habit now. "What isn't he doing? Or more like, who isn't he doing? He's shagged half of London by now, I'd bet."

"Hush, Lizzie," Nan scolds, but I can see the truth in her eyes. Lizzie's right, and Eddie's even more of a git than I'd thought. "Have you seen any of them yet?"

Them. We are a family divided, always have been. On one side, Nan sits with Lizzie and me. On the other, Dad and Eddie hold court as though their shit smells like Nan's roses. And somewhere floating in the middle is Mum, pulled this way and that by whichever way the tide is going.

"Not yet. I didn't call first, didn't want to give them warning that I was coming. You know Dad would've had Mum coached and worked up over what a tosser I am."

Elle's touch on my arm is so soft but meaningful. She doesn't know the storm we're walking into, but she's supporting me. I adjust my mental image of the battlefield, adding her to my team with Nan and Lizzie.

"I don't know what rubbish has gotten into that daughter of mine."

Nan's bite is unexpected. She's usually a bit more genteel with her turn of phrase, but perhaps she's as fed up with Mum as she is with Mr. Blackwire.

"She's allowed that prat, Eddie, to make this entire family miserable and treated you so badly, it made you leave not just your home, but the entire country." Nan looks at me sadly, as if apologizing for all the years of hell I went through. "I don't know where I went wrong with Mary. She was such a happy girl when she was young. There are times I wonder if she traded in her brains for her fanny when she got married to your father."

"Nan!" Lizzie says, aghast. I know while she can hardly tolerate Eddie, Lizzie still gets along to some degree with our mother. "Mum is doing her best. It's not all on her."

"Her best is not enough. Not when she lets your father run feral all over the country. And Eddie is even worse, his father exponentially degraded."

Bollocks. I'm not sure what to say. I hate Eddie with the very fibers of my being, but he is Nan's grandchild, and Mum is her daughter. I wonder how much I've missed if it's gotten so severe as to warrant Nan's ugliness. Or maybe it's Nan herself. Perhaps she's gone off her rocker a bit? Or at the minimum, permanently damaged her mouth's filter?

Alfred reappears, interrupting Nan's rant. "Master and Lady Wolfe have arrived and are prepared for guests now. They are waiting in the parlor and request your presence."

All formality. All business. We are family. That should mean something other than this coldness. But though my heart wishes it were different, I'm well-versed in this song and dance.

"Let's get this over with."

CHAPTER 23

ELLE

*T*he hallway stretches on, dark oak paneling and maroon walls pressing in on me as Alfred leads us through the gigantic mansion. We pass a set of stone stairs, surrounded by stained glass windows that let multicolored light pour in.

Our feet don't make a sound on the plush rugs as Colton and I follow Alfred. Lizzie is in front of us, offering Nan a stabilizing elbow. Though she's leaning on Lizzie, Nan is strong, with a presence about her, an edge to her regality. I get the feeling she'd verbally fillet you with a smile, all the while sipping brandy with her pinkie out.

"How are you holding up?" Colton whispers out the side of his mouth as his hand clenches my waist stiffly.

I step closer to his side, keeping my voice low too. "Overwhelmed. Interested. And I hate to say it because I know this is your family, but a little bit entertained. It's like getting thrown into the middle of a Downtown Abbey scene, though that might be the accents, mostly. But the family drama, fights in the garden, the estranged son's return . . . it's definitely not what I thought meeting your family would be like."

Mindlessly, Colton corrects me. "It's Downton Abbey."

I shrug. "I know, but it's habit to say it wrong because it drives Tiff nuts. Sometimes it's the little things that say 'friendship,' you know?"

Colton's smile is tight, false. "The family drama hasn't even begun, I'm afraid. I do apologize for dropping a clanger and calling you my girlfriend without discussing it first."

I search my mind, heart, and poll those butterflies in my belly, but I find not a bit of offense. Instead, I find iridescent happiness.

"It's fine. I know we're doing more than the 'fun' you proposed, but we don't need to worry about that now. Focus on your family, and I'll follow your lead. It's what a good girlfriend and a good assistant would do."

I wink big and fake, hoping to make him laugh or at least smile. All I get is that twitch at the corners of his lips before they press together again.

"I need to give you a dare, an important one."

His nerves make me nervous, and I pray to whatever ancestor is haunting this hallway that Colton's not about to ask me for my knickers before meeting his parents. Because I'll fucking do it and then be a complete goob in front of them. Well, I'll probably embarrass myself regardless, but at least if I piss myself, there will be a layer of cotton absorbency before I wet the rug.

"Okay."

"Whatever you see here, whatever you hear here . . . it has to stay between us. Not your father, not Tiffany, not the people at the office. Just us. I will divulge what I need to, when I need to, but I need this life to be separate from that one. I dare you . . . to keep my secrets."

I stop in the hallway, letting Alfred and crew turn a corner to give us a bit more privacy, though they don't seem to have been listening to our conversation as they discussed Lizzie's latest marks at school. Turning to Colton fully, I search his face. It almost seems as though he's embarrassed by the privilege of his life, dreading for anyone to glimpse behind the curtain he's created as Colton Wolfe, Fox executive.

"You don't have to dare me for that. Or order me as your assistant. I can respect that you want to be your own man, not whoever *this* was supposed to make you." I gesture around the hallway lined with antique oil paintings, marble busts, and closed oak doors that lead to any myriad of rooms.

"Thank you, Elle." Colton places a chaste kiss to my lips and leads me to follow Alfred again.

Just past the corner, double doors stand open, and Alfred waits to the right of them. With a sweeping arm, he invites us

into the room. He booms, "Master Colton and Miss Elle Stryker."
I jump and then instantly feel like a dork, but the old guy's
surprisingly got a voice like a wrestling match announcer, and I
am definitely not ready to rumble.

When Alfred had said the Wolfes were waiting in the parlor,
I'd envisioned a frilly, fancy room where ladies sip tea and nibble
finger sandwiches. Something frou-frou and white. But this is
nothing like that image.

The room is cavernous. That's the only thought that comes to
mind as I look around the space, with its vaulted ceilings,
paneled walls, and ornate furnishings. The back wall is occupied
by five towering windows, bookended with heavy drapery and
capped with stained glass that matches the ones over the stairs.
Light floods the room and the thickly carpeted floor in identical
beams separated by shadows from the stone columns between
the glass. If I didn't know this was their family home, I'd think I
had walked into a centuries-old church for all the history around
me, from the floor to the ceiling and windows to walls.

"Jeez, and I thought your office was fancy," I whisper once we
step inside.

A man clears his throat, and I look at the two people I haven't
met before. The man is obviously Colton's father. He looks so
similar through the shoulders and chest, although his face is
narrower, giving him a pinched, harsh expression. He's wearing
khaki, his white shirt nearly blinding in the gaps of his khaki
vest. If I had to guess, I'd say he's been horseback riding today.
Either that or jodhpurs are making a comeback with the British
elite. I suppose either is possible, for all I know.

Colton's mother has clearly lent her perfect face to her son
and daughter, with the same piercing eyes and sculpted cheekbones. Around her neck is a beautiful multi-strand string of
pearls, antiques, by the look of them, with a small brooch of some
type in the middle. Her dress is simple and elegant, slim to her
wrists and swirling out in an A-line to her knees. She looks
equally aristocratic, though her smile is considerably warmer
than her husband's cold indifference.

"Colton, such a lovely surprise!" Colton's mother says,
coming forward to embrace him. "How much I've missed you.
It's been so long!"

"Mother," Colton says, his voice thick. "I've missed you too."

The two embrace, and I can see that whatever family issues they might have, he and his mother love each other very much.

"You should have visited sooner." The slight scold is softened by her picking invisible lint off his shoulder, as if she can't bear to not touch him but doesn't know how to do so without an excuse. "I've been so worried about you."

Do they not just throw an arm over each other's shoulder? Or if that's too much, maybe just do the entwined elbow thing?

The thought makes me think of Dad and our movie nights. It's nothing for us to snuggle up on the couch and share the same popcorn bowl. I never gave it a second thought, but perhaps I should've been more thankful for it.

"I know, Mum," Colton says, smiling a little. "But no reason to worry. I'm fine, just glad to be home."

"Colton." His father's greeting is flat, cold if I had to pick a word, and somehow drops the temperature in the room ten degrees in an instant. Either Colton's father isn't the warmest of people or perhaps he isn't all that happy to see his younger son. At least, he's not stepping forward to embrace him.

Colton is as equally stiff with a nod. "Father."

Well, that explains a lot of the tension and friction, and probably why Colton came to the States. Hell, I'd fly across an ocean to get away from this much ice as well. The rest of us are all frozen in place too, watching the icebergs of men threaten each other with frosty glares.

"What have we here?" Colton's father asks, giving up the staredown to look at me. It doesn't feel like he lost or gave up, though, but rather that he's attacking from a new vantage point.

And I'm suddenly facing the British Inquisition, the fly pinned under the magnifying glass of Colton's parents.

"This is Elle Stryker, my girlfriend and coworker. Elle, this is my father and mother, Edwin and Mary Wolfe."

The label as his girlfriend is still fresh and bright, sending a thrill up my spine.

Mary looks ecstatic at the announcement. "Darling! I suspected when Mother and Lizzie looked so giddy, but . . . really?"

Colton reaches over, and I take his hand, nodding. "Yes, Mrs. Wolfe. Uhm . . . yeah. Really. It's nice to meet you." At least this time, I don't try to curtsy, though I still feel like I should.

"Well, welcome, dear," Mary says, giving me a warm look. She steps forward, her hands going to my shoulders as she leans in to kiss the air beside my cheek. "My word, Elle, you're trembling! Are you okay?"

"I'm sorry. I'm nervous. I just wasn't expecting . . . this is so much, and I . . . gah."

I'm flustered and likely acting a fool, but Mary takes it all in stride, laughing softly. "Relax, Elle. While we Brits might be famous for our stiff upper lips, we're not monsters. I'm not going to eat you alive. What porkies have you been telling this poor girl about us, Colton?"

Colton isn't smiling, though, glancing past his mother to Edwin. "The truth."

"What's that supposed to mean?" Edwin asks, his face pinching even more. "Do you have something to say, boy?"

"I've merely told Elle some of the history of the family," Colton replies. "I'm not going to feed her bog roll and call it candy floss."

Before Edwin can cut back at his son, Mary steps forward, putting her petite body between them. "Come now, there's so much to catch up on. Alfred, could you serve tea while we wait for Eddie? He's supposed to arrive home soon, and I know he'd like to see you, Colton. You boys were always so close."

Colton snorts. "Mum, you know that's not true. So does everyone else here, so there's no need for airs."

Mary flushes, shrinking a bit, and I feel bad for her. Right up until she says, "Well, I guess that's true. It was more competitiveness than closeness. You were always trying to live up to your older brother, weren't you?" She smiles again, like everything is sweet and totally fine, but I can tell by the tight set of Colton's jaw that it's anything but.

Alfred jostles the teacups he's setting down on the large table in the room. Something tells me his steady hands did it intentionally to break the tension in the room and draw everyone's attention to tea service. He's a genius because it works.

The table is larger than most people's actual dining tables, holding ten people easily with plenty of elbow room. Inside, I giggle about my total lack of a dining table at all. My apartment has a bar top between the kitchen and living room that's always served me just fine. Hell, most of the time, I eat on my couch while watching television, so this seems beyond fancy.

And it's not even the actual dining room.

Edwin and Mary sit at opposite ends of the table, boxing us in like two nobles holding court. Nan sits next to Mary, Lizzie plopping down beside her, and Colton holds out a chair for me before sitting at his father's side. Everyone is quiet as Alfred moves around the table, setting steaming tea before each of us.

This is not like the tea parties I had as a girl, where Dad would cut peanut butter and jelly sandwiches into triangles and we'd sip Kool-Aid from plastic cups. Grape, of course, because it looked the most like tea but was deliciously sweet.

But this isn't idle chats and silly gossip about my dolls.

This feels like serious business.

Confession time. I don't like tea. Give me coffee, black as my soul or sweet and creamy. Either is just fine. Hot chocolate, hell yeah. But tea tastes like dirt water, as far I'm concerned. I hadn't really considered that coming to London and meeting the Wolfes would require me to drink it down like it's delicious angel tears. My mouth is already filling with too much spit and I have to force myself to swallow it down.

I hold myself still but watch Lizzie. She's young, so surely, she'll drink hers as sweet as possible. Maybe I can follow her lead on how to fix mine so I don't make a fool of myself . . . again.

I've got a small pour of milk and an unhealthy amount of sugar in my cup, stirring it gently just like Lizzie. She picks hers up to sip, but I'm saved by Alfred's booming wrestling announcer voice.

"Master Eddie and . . . companion." Even though Alfred maintains his professional tone, I can hear a hint of disdain. It's a fine line he's walking, precisely appropriate but almost . . . catty. It makes me want to sit down with him to see what he really thinks of everything that's going on around here. Over a glass of scotch, maybe. Anything but tea.

Eddie Wolfe doesn't walk in so much as he struts in like peacock, and I get my first real look at the eldest Wolfe son.

As I do a quick study of his features, I'd say that where Colton gets his face from his mother, Eddie is nearly the spitting image of Edwin, right down to the pinched face and hawk-like nose that nearly cuts the air in front of him.

Where Colton is walking sex in a suit, attractive almost to the point of being pretty, Edwin is . . . not. He's dressed well in designer gear and looks to be quite fit, but he's not a head turner.

Still, considering he has a girl on his arm, he obviously doesn't have to look very hard to find female companionship . . . although honestly, as the girl totters and giggles her way into the room, her fake breasts in danger of popping out of her low-cut top and her vag nearly visible at the hem of her skirt, I wonder just what the girl is interested in . . . Eddie or his bank account.

"Later, we'll head up to Soho. You'd like that, wouldn't you?" The baby talk tone is weird to say the least, but the girl's hanging on Eddie's arm like a desperate little puppy. She's straight up fawning over him. "I've heard of this new club, and you know I can get us in—"

"Eddie." Edwin's bark is sharp, cutting Eddie's not-at-all humble brag right off.

Eddie just grins, though, his eyes slowly leaving the girl to turn to Edwin. "Father." The greeting is only a single word, but even I can feel the casualness that seems in direct conflict with everything around us and everything I've learned about the Wolfe family. Eddie doesn't even look at the other end of the table when he says, "Mum."

"Hello, Eddie," Colton says, his voice strained but polite as he stands up. "It's nice to see you."

"Coltie!" His performance is a virtual mime of surprise that fools no one. When no one responds favorably, he gives up and comes around the table. "Oh, stop with the faffing. Come here, old chap! Give your brother a hug!"

There's something in the way he says it, like he's commanding a minion instead of a brother. It pricks at my nerves, and to me, he just sounds condescending.

Colton approaches his brother warily, hugging him and holding back any response as Eddie cinches him in tight and starts pounding on his back a little too hard to just be excitement. It looks and feels like a big brother picking on his sibling, something they've done a thousand times before in their lives, and even though Colton's the same size as Eddie now, the pantomime goes on. Edwin and Mary even smile, as though this is a normal, sweet greeting, and I'm suddenly very thankful I'm an only child. At least I never had to put up with aggression in the guise of affection.

When he's done, Eddie claps his hands and shouts, "Alfred! Forget the tea, we need wine! And make it the good stuff. Not the piss rubbish Nan drinks. It's time to celebrate!"

Nan hisses, her teacup clattering to its saucer. "You wouldn't know piss rubbish if your tart of the day were pissing in your face and calling it gold."

I choke on my tea, and not because it's gross tasting, though it is. But uhm, did little old sweet Nan just make a joke about Eddie getting a golden shower? Surely . . . not? And eww times a thousand. When I look at her, trying to keep my brows from crawling up into my hairline, she looks innocent as can be. But there's something in her eyes that says she isn't the daft old woman she lets everyone think she is. A keen intellect is hiding inside her.

"Mum," Mary whispers, sounding scandalized but patting her mother's hand. "I'm sure he was just being cheeky. Don't be crude in front of guests."

Eddie smirks, having gotten away with abusing Colton and insulting Nan. And that's all before he's sat down.

He steps to Edwin's side, pulling a chair out. His 'friend,' who seems to think this is some sort of comedy performance for her benefit, goes to sit down, obviously assuming Eddie is being a gentleman for her.

She learns the hard way, crashing to the carpeted floor with a squawk that makes her sound a lot like a startled chicken. I gape at the poor thing as Eddie sits down, not even offering the girl a hand up or even a glance to acknowledge that she's on her ass on the floor.

Admittedly, I've been in a bit of the same situation rather recently with the whole debacle in Colton's office. The one-upmanship I can offer on Eddie's girl is that at least I had on panties. She *very* clearly does not. And I'm not the only one who notices. Colton looks away immediately, being a gentleman. Edwin sneers down at the poor thing, somehow both ogling her openly and judging her all at once.

I know he's Colton's father, but the only thing I can think is . . . disgusting pig. And I can see where Eddie gets his 'charm'.

Lizzie goes to help, but the girl shrugs her off. Pulling together what dignity she has left, she smooths her hair and what little dress she's wearing as she gets up and pulls out a seat to sit next to Eddie.

"Smooth, as always," Colton says, staring daggers at his brother.

"Alfred!" Eddie bellows, seemingly oblivious to how he's acting or perhaps not giving a damn, "hurry up, you're taking too bloody long. I'm much too sober for this." Eddie leans back in his seat, finally realizing that a guest is at the table. He eyes me with a flirty smirk I'm sure he practiced in the mirror, even though his girl is right next to him. "Well, now, who is this yummy biscuit?"

I glance at Edwin and Mary, expecting that even if they favor Eddie that they'd have some sort of line . . . but Mary just looks cowed while Edwin is almost amused by his eldest child's boorish behavior.

Meanwhile, the only thing keeping me in my seat is Colton's hand on my thigh, gentle and supportive. Though I'm supposed to be the one helping him through this mess, for the moment, I'll take the silent order to play nice. Otherwise, I'm going to end up in a jail somewhere, and they'll probably only serve tea to drink. I'll die of dehydration, and Eddie's definitely not worth that.

"Elle Stryker," I grit though clenched teeth. I've been called a lot of names by jackasses in my day, but 'yummy biscuit' feels like one of the most demeaning. That might have more to do with Eddie than the actual turn of phrase, though. He makes me feel like I need a shower to wash off the oiliness of his gaze.

"Elle is Colton's sweetheart," Mary adds. "Isn't that wonderful? They just arrived."

"Well, now." Eddie's leer somehow becomes even worse. Even from across the table, it feels too intimate. "Perhaps I should call bagsy on the piece of American pie my little brother's brought home?"

I glare at Eddie, having been insulted and hit on by better men than him. "What's bagsy mean?"

I don't even look to Colton as I ask, but he answers my question. "Like 'dibs' in America." Colton stands, both palms flattening on the table as he leans across toward Eddie. "Quit being a prat. Respect Elle. She's my girlfriend."

Eddie's shrug is careless, but Colton sits down. At least I

won't be bailing him out of jail either. Eddie really brings out the worst in everyone.

"A right tart," Eddie's girl says as she laughs, her voice rising piercingly until she breaks and ends up snorting like a pig.

And here I thought I actually should pity the girl. But it's every woman for herself when she's throwing me under the bus and then laughing like a jackass on meth.

"Seriously?" I don't mean the word to come out, or at least to be audible, but it slips out and she hears me. The whole table hears me.

"What's that, Yank?" the girl asks, maybe getting that her comment wasn't appreciated. The only good news is that I know for a fact that she's not concealing a weapon. I've seen up and down her dress, and there's nothing there other than exposed body parts. Though her acrylic nails might be deadly weapons.

Maybe she can give Eddie a hand job later and Bobbitt him? It'd serve him right, I suspect.

I backpedal my thoughts, though, playing the part of the well-mannered woman my dad raised me to be. Though the sweetness is all saccharine. "I was saying, we haven't been properly introduced. You know my name, but I don't know yours."

"It won't matter tomorrow," Nan says, sipping her tea.

Eddie proves her point, saying flippantly, "Oh, this is Amelia."

She squawks again. "Ava!"

Eddie shrugs, and Nan looks rather pleased with herself for being correct.

Alfred appears with a bottle of wine and stands at Edwin's side, waiting to be acknowledged. When Edwin nods, Alfred uncorks the wine and dramatically pours a small dash in a wine glass.

Edwin swirls it around, putting on quite the show as conversation stops, waiting for him. He sniffs and then takes a sip, swishing it around like it's mouthwash. I'm not a wine connoisseur, but I've had my fair share of vino. Maybe more than my fair share, if I'm being entirely truthful. What I've never done is hollow my cheeks like I'm giving a blow job and make squishing sounds in my mouth that make it look like I'm a spitter, not a swallower.

Finally, Edwin swallows, and without looking at Alfred, he deems it acceptable. "It'll do."

Alfred pours a glass for Edwin, then for Eddie. Ava takes one as well. Colton declines, and while I'd rather have wine than tea any day, I decline as well, following his lead. Lizzie and Mary decline as well, but Nan accepts with another biting remark. "If he's drinking the good stuff, then by Queen Victoria, I am too."

Nan means it. She picks up the glass, and faster than I can say 'bottoms up', it's empty and she's setting it back on the table. I'm reminded of the Japanese dinner with Colton because, as though he expected it, Alfred is standing at the ready to refill it.

"Nan, don't get knackered before we've even had a proper dinner." Edwin's scold is met by a glare so cold, it could send snow to the equator.

"Mind your own," Nan says, gesturing to Edwin's wine glass with her own. "So, what brings you to hell, Coltie? Though I'm certainly glad you're here."

Nan is on a roll. I think I might love her a little bit. I'm also still worried she might be a smidge crazy. Or maybe more? What's bigger than a smidge?

A long-ago memory of a home-ec class I once took comes back to me. Smidge, pinch, dash . . . smallest to largest. Nan is definitely a dash mad. At least. I bet she could hang with any dare Tiffany or I could give her, and that's a grand compliment in my book.

"Yes, Coltie. You practically ran out in the middle of the night. I never even figured out why you were going over the pond." Eddie's smug self-satisfaction says he knows exactly why.

"I'm here on business," Colton says evenly, avoiding Eddie's baiting dig. "I'm doing quite well in the States, serving as a board member for Fox Industries."

Let's be real. Colton is not 'doing quite well.' He's the fucking rock star of the company. *Sorry, Dad!*

Edwin, however, seems less than impressed. "You've got a management position in the family business all ready for you, and you sod off to go make money for someone else's company in the States? Disappointing."

I feel Colton's fingers tense on my forearm and know he's about to blow, so I step up to the plate to save him. "Excuse me, Mr. Wolfe. But what is the family business?"

"Agriculture, mostly," Mary says, smiling wanly. "The family name has stood for quality fresh meats in the UK for centuries. Business began with just one man who raised livestock and walked farm to farm to sell eggs each day. Over time, it grew from his one-man operation to the company we have now." She sounds almost nostalgic, sentimental about the growth.

"Don't waste your breath trying to get Colton back in the family business. We all know why he left." Eddie leans forward, getting closer to watch Colton's reaction. "He couldn't handle being second-best."

"That's right, love!" Ava says, batting her eyelashes. "He just couldn't measure up to a dish like you!"

She starts laughing and snorting like a pig again, and I can't help but cringe.

Even Edwin seems turned off by Ava's gross misconduct, though he excuses his son's. "Right, right, enough of this tripe," Edwin growls. "What actually brings you back home, Colton? You say you're doing so well in the States, yet here you sit."

The accusation hangs heavily, mostly because Edwin all but throws it in his son's face. Eddie, of course, is quick to see that and press the advantage. "Exactly, Dad. Colton, you abandoned your family without a word, and you come back unannounced with an American girl and some story of heralded success. I think it's all bollocks."

"Eddie!" Lizzie protests, but apparently, being the youngest child means being ignored in this household.

"No, he's quite right," Edwin says. "I've barely gotten much more than a formal Christmas card from you in years, you barely speak to your mother or your grandmother . . . so I don't buy that this is simply a family visit. Let's be honest, shall we, Colton? You want something, and I demand to know what!"

"Dad!" Lizzie appeals again, working her way up the food chain.

"Hush, Elizabeth!" Mary admonishes her daughter. "Your father is speaking!"

"Well?" Edwin demands. "Speak, boy! Or has your time overseas turned you soft?"

I feel Colt's fingers tighten, and I'm worried that he's about to unleash on his father when instead, he leans back, crossing his ankle over his knee and laughing.

"You know, this all used to bother me. And honestly, I did go off because I didn't want to put up with the lot of you, nor did I have to." His voice is hard as steel, though he's casual and loose as he talks to his dad. When he turns to the other end of the table, the warmth returns. "However, I came home for many reasons. First, because I miss *some* of my family."

"Colton—" Mary starts, her eyes soft.

"It's all right," Colton says, tapping his fingers together. I've seen that hand gesture before . . . in the office. Every time he's figured out something important, he runs it through his mind one last time before sharing it. Whatever's about to happen is Colton's true play of this whole charade with his Dad and brother.

I wonder what it could be.

Colton's set at Fox, but maybe he does want to jump back into the family business? Or maybe this is a coup and he's going to take it out from underneath them? Or maybe he's come to rescue his sister, and Nan and Mary too?

Whatever it is, Colton's about to drop a bomb on Edwin and Eddie. After only knowing them for an hour, I'm pretty damn excited to see them get their comeuppance. Hell, I could dance a gleeful jig on the table, even without a dare, I'm so eager to hear it.

"Father, Eddie . . . you may not have been keeping up with me and my endeavors in the States, but rest assured, I have stayed well informed of yours. I've watched from afar as you've cocked up half a dozen nitwitted business ideas, and its only sheer luck you haven't lost the entire estate. Well, luck and restricted access. Eddie, you're an utter prat. Father, you're a disgrace."

Edwin and Eddie are both blustering, yelling at Colton, but he soldiers on, talking to his dad as though about the weather while shanking him left and right. Badass to the bone, and prepared as though he's been dreaming of this moment for quite some time.

"You bully and badger Mum, you treat Nan like rubbish, you've let Eddie run amok, and you practically ignore your only daughter, other than to perhaps scheme which of your Eaton mates you're going to marry her off to."

"I will not—"

Colton runs roughshod over Lizzie's interruption too. "I came back because I'm taking *my* land," Colton thunders. "Fox is looking to build a new HQ, and I'm going to be the man to lead it. This visit was simply a polite formality to check on my kin and to put you on notice that I will be here, watching closely and stepping in every time you get out of line. I've been absent, but no more."

There's a moment of shocked silence, each of us processing what that means to us.

My brain is pretty much on a repeat of . . . *what the actual fuck, what the actual fuck*? There's a tiny question of 'can he do that?' mixed in, but then my brain goes right back to 'what the fuck?'

I mean, I know we're here to do the scouting on the London property for HQ2, but I thought this was just a family visit because work brought him so close to home. There's nothing in any of the paperwork I've seen that said the proposed site is Colton's land. That changes . . . *everything*.

It's his land . . . there's no negotiation. It's his land . . . the price is at his discretion. It's his land . . . he can set this deal up so that it's irrefutable as the best option for Fox. It's his land . . . Dad is so fucked. It's his land . . . and he didn't tell me.

Eddie suddenly bursts out laughing. "*Your* land?"

"That's right," Colton says. "The estate Grandfather promised me in his will."

Edwin stands up, so red I would be worried about his blood pressure if a small ugly part of me wasn't wishing he'd drop dead right about now and save us all the trouble. Not really, of course . . . but maybe a little.

"That land, you say? Tell me, Colton, since your grandfather died when you were still in nappies, who do you think controls the trust that owns that land?"

He pauses dramatically, the feral grin growing wider and uglier by the second. "That's right, boy. It might be your land in some old codger's will, but it's my land until the day I pass. And even then, it won't be going to you so you can lease it or sell it to some American pissants. It'll go to my son. My only son."

And with that, he looks to Eddie, who's smiling like he's been handed the keys to the kingdom just for being born and breathing oxygen.

CHAPTER 24

COLTON

There's yelling and arguing, there's negotiation and discussion, and then there's the verbal weapons of mass destruction my father and Eddie unleash on me. To be fair, I do the same to them. Everyone else listens as we bicker with sharp barbs, bringing up everything from childhood wrongs to business mismanagement.

Mum's head initially ping-pongs as she tries to soothe the anger flowing like lava between her menfolk, but eventually, she wilts under the weight of so much hostility and her head falls, her eyes locked on the napkin in her lap.

Nan and Lizzie seem shocked at first, but their delight at someone finally standing up to Father is a buoying lift that keeps me going. They have had to keep their mouths shut for far too long in the name of manners and power dynamics, and if I'm the one to take him on, then so be it.

He has no hold on me. Not anymore. I have finally outgrown him. I don't need to prove myself to him. I don't need to impress him. Perhaps I thought I did when I began this journey and wanted to throw my success in his face as revenge, but listening to him rant brings home one lesson loud and clear. He is as weak as his power over me is. My desire for his approval, his affection, his love is naught but the past.

There is power in the freedom.

Mid-bluster, Father's vein bulging dangerously, I simply get up. Elle startles, probably thinking I'm going to amp this up to a more physical altercation, but I pull her chair out. Helping her up, I take her hand and walk to the doorway.

"This is pointless. You can't stop this from happening. This is a mere formality, a nicety because we are family. You've made it quite clear that you don't consider me family, however, so perhaps we will continue this as professionals only. I'll be in touch."

I don't let him respond, walking out before he can have the last word. But from behind me, I hear Eddie whining. "Father, you said it would be mine. What is going on? Do something."

A victorious smile takes my face. I might not need Father's approval, but it sure does feel good to throw a wrench in their plans, their very existence.

Alfred escorts us out, opening the front door for us. "Oliver has been well cared for while waiting for you, Master Colton." Lower, he whispers. "You do know how to rouse a ruckus, don't you, sir?" His pride and glee are a resounding job-well-done, and it feels more important than my father's.

Right as we step outside, Lizzie runs up. "Coltie! Fuckin' hell, you handed Father his arse! Bloody brilliant." Thankfully, the front door is far enough away from the parlor that no one besides us can hear her. No one would care about her course language, but the sentiment would be considered near-blasphemy. And Lizzie is still a child, still subjected to Father's whims and whimsies, unfortunately.

I take her hands. "Lizzie, watch yourself. It's one thing for *me* to piss Father off, quite another for you. Please just keep calm and carry on. I'll be in touch soon." I kiss her forehead, and she nods, giddy excitement still shining bright in her eyes. I hope she can keep it in check long enough for this to be handled with Father.

Oliver pulls down the long drive, and I can't help but stare out the window into the coming darkness. Even without the light of day, I know the rolling green hills like the back of my hands, each scar and line a story. Of my boxing fights, of my ancestors' fights for the land and for a living.

Elle breaks into my thoughts as she addresses our driver. "Oliver, you're about to hear things that you're *not* gonna hear. You feel me? Like some driver-passenger confidentiality thing, 'kay?"

His eyes meet mine in the mirror as he answers Elle. "Yes, ma'am."

She's not done. "And I'm about to basically go bat-shit crazy. I don't want you to judge all Americans by what I'm about to do. Understand?"

"Bat. Shit. Crazy?" he mouths, confusion written in his knitted brows. But he holds the car steady, joining traffic with experienced ease.

"I've found that Americans have a fondness for idioms based on animals. Just say yes. It's safer for you that way." I try to reassure him with a smile, but his quiet 'yes' is more question than affirmation.

"Good. We understand each other." Elle's summarization couldn't be less true. Oliver has no idea what she's talking about. But I do.

I try to prepare myself for a verbal battle that feels more important than the one I just had with my father. I'm not ready when she smacks my arm over and over, two-handed catfight style with her hair flipping back and forth as she flails.

"What the fuck was that, Wolfe? You're such a bloody bastard! I could smack the ever-loving shit out of you right now! You've got some explaining to do, mister, so get to it before I . . . ugh!"

Her voice has gone on a journey from screech to hysterical high-pitch squeal and back down to a growly snarl as she pushes at my chest. With the seat behind me, I don't move in the slightest, which seems to piss her off even more.

The whole production is hilarious and makes me want to smile. Wisely, I purse my lips and don't do so.

"I'm sorry, Elle." An apology seems like the best place to start, but she amps right back up.

"You should be!" She's smacking me again. This time, I gather her hands in mine and kiss her.

She fights it for one long heartbeat and then she kisses me back, hard and fierce. It's not passionate. It's punishment. "You scared the shit out of me, Wolfe."

"Why are you calling me 'Wolfe'?" I ask, my lips still pressed against hers.

She smacks me once more, with her lips, not her hands, and

answers with a smile. "I don't know, because I'm mad at you, I guess." But she seems less so than a moment ago.

"You said 'bloody'. I think I'm rubbing off on you a bit." A dangerous observation, but it goes over well with her smile growing slightly. "You ready to hear it now? Or do you need to smack me a bit more?"

She sits back, crossing her arms over chest as she orders, "Let's hear it."

"Ages ago, my family invested very heavily in land and got right jammy when they got a contract to supply the Army and Navy with rations. In fact, later on, our bully beef and condensed milk were the Tommies' favorite rations in the trenches, compared to the Maconochie."

"The what . . . never mind. I take it the basic gist is that your family got richer?" She rolls her hand at the wrist, telling me to get on with it.

"Yes . . . the Depression put a crimp in that, but come World War II, we were right back making rations for our boys and the Yanks, too. The Estate has an airfield nearby, and during the war, it was a base for American planes and their escorts. The whole time they were in England, they enjoyed our family's products. And we just kept growing from there . . . bigger and bigger."

"And you gave it all up?" Elle asks suspiciously. "Why?"

"I figured that would be obvious to you, of all people. Your father could hand you a position easily, same as I could take up an executive level position in our family offices. Father and Eddie have certainly chosen that path, and it's done them no favors. They squander their days playing at being businessmen, all the while mismanaging trusts, wasting money on sports teams they know nothing about, and throwing about their perceived power like gormless twats."

My distaste for their lifestyles is bitter on my tongue. "I want to earn it myself. Otherwise, it's meaningless."

Elle swallows thickly. "Well, shit, I had a good temper tantrum worked up here and you just squashed it by being all . . ." She waves her hands around at me, luckily at the air and not making contact this time. "Good and upstanding." She sounds almost . . . disappointed?

I'm so confused. "I'm . . . sorry?" Apology seems the safest again, even though it didn't quite work before.

"It's fine," she huffs, rolling her eyes in a move that reminds me of Lizzie. "Tell me the rest . . . the HQ2 part."

"It struck me as soon as I heard about the proposal race," I admit.

She interrupts with a hiss of accusation. "So you've known all along and didn't say a word?" I nod slowly and she sneers in victory. "Just wanted to make sure you knew I'd caught that. Continue."

I let her get away with the catty snark. It's warranted, given all I've thrown at her in the last day. Especially since I suspect this conversation, while about work, is with Elle, my girlfriend. Not Elle, my assistant.

"The Estate's mostly empty, bordered on one side by a large road that leads to the parkway, is less than five miles from a small airport that would be excellent service for shipping, and is close to the trains as well. I know the property like the back of my hand. It has everything HQ2 needs. And I do believe in the rest of it. I think we need an HQ2 overseas to grow."

"But how . . . Jesus, Colton, there's so many hoops to jump through on this, just on the corporate side," Elle says.

And there's my smart assistant.

"We need to get back to the hotel and call Gary and Debra to fill them in. Especially Gary. You need to fill him in on the family trust angle so he can research the legality of that and give you some advice there. Even if it's off the record for you and not for Fox."

I know she's right, but I've kept this side of my life—my family—a secret from the people at Fox for so long. They all know I come from wealth. That privileged upbringing is impossible to hide, but the degree of pedigree is another thing altogether. One I won't be able to keep secret anymore. Not if I'm going to make this work for the HQ2 site, and I have every intention of doing so.

"Agreed. Think I can dare him to maintain secrecy as well?" It's wishful thinking at best. Gary is discreet, for certain, but this will be gossip around the water coolers on every floor of Fox within hours. "I might need to discuss this with Allan first so he's not blindsided."

Elle gapes at me. "Mr. Fox doesn't know either?" At my

cringe, she shakes her head, nearly whopping me with her hair again. "Stupid man. Stupid, sexy, smart man."

I don't dare mention that two of her descriptors are the literal opposites of one another. I just let her look at me critically, knowing I deserve it. And also knowing that she's already on my side. That alone feels like a win. Or at least the beginning of one.

"What about your family? Business aside, or maybe in addition to, what's the deal? Because that was harsh. And I say that as someone who knows helicopter, overinvolved, overprotective, high-expectation parents."

I chuckle at her description of Daniel. With a fresh dose of my family, he's not seeming nearly so bad to either of us, I'd wager.

"You saw the basics. Father's an ass who favors Eddie regardless of what he does. Or more likely, doesn't do, because he flits about with no destination. He's an oxygen thief that lives on a trust fund. He's the reason I took up boxing as a boy."

So many memories assault me at once, the physical pain echoing fresh, and out of habit, I clench my jaw in preparation for the punch landing.

Elle sees it and lays a comforting hand on my thigh. "Out with it. I said I'll keep your secrets and I will. But I think you need to get this out. For work, for us, but mostly, just for you. Think of it like ripping a Band-Aid off. Spill it all at once, scream at the loss of skin, and then you can scab it over."

Gross imagery, but perhaps she's right. I've buried this down for too long. And though this thing with Elle is still rather new, I know that deep down, I can trust her. I would've laughed at that idea weeks ago, and in fact, I did think she was wholly untrustworthy and Daniel's spy. But even just her behavior today has alleviated so much of my doubt—what little bit that had remained after our dates, our intimacy on the plane, our time together.

And so I do something I swore I never would. I tell her everything.

"He and his mates would bully me, hitting and kicking me once I was down. They nicked any money I carried and often my books, too. I'd come home a mess, and Mum would demand to know what happened, but when I'd say it was Eddie, Father would step in. He claimed I was telling porkies or that I had started it and was sour that I'd been bested. And Mum chose to believe him over me, standing right there in front of her with bruises and scrapes and even split lips. It went on like that until I got bigger and started standing up for myself. Took out a couple of Eddie's cronies, and then I started training. It wasn't until I started beating up Eddie that Father had any real concern with us. I busted Eddie's nose once."

I look to Elle, gauging her reaction. I expect her to be horrified at the violence, both Eddie's and mine. She looks to be on the verge of fuming actual smoke out of her ears, though.

"I'm going to bust his nose again. Oliver, turn the fucking car around."

I love that she wants to defend me. It's somehow sweet and sexy at the same time, putting tiny stitches over wounds from long ago. I shake my head at Oliver's questioning eyes, though.

"It's fine, it was a long time ago." Elle snorts, her head working a circle around on top of her neck. It's the most attitude I've seen from her, and she's already shown quite a bit. But she falls back into my story as I keep talking. "Nan always had my back. She's the one who put me in boxing, and I know she watches out for Lizzie too. Nan's a spitfire, even now. Though it's getting harder for her to get around, she's still as sharp as a tack."

"She's something else, that's for sure. Your whole family is . . . wow."

The dry delivery says it all. They are . . . something else.

"YES, GARY. THE PROPERTY IS IN TRUST, AND WHILE I'VE HAD MY first meeting with the family, I'd like to know the actual language of the trust. I want specifics on their power over the land. I don't want any surprises."

His follow-up questions are spot-on and professional, not giving any inkling that he's brimming with the gossip I just shared with him. I have to hope that's a good sign, but I cross my fingers anyway.

"Mr. Fox is aware of the progression of the situation and on board with our next steps. I'll be in touch tomorrow for the latest update."

I hang up the phone, glad for the time difference that will let

Gary start his day with an outlined mission of teasing out every detail of the trust. Hopefully, he finds me some good news.

"All set?" Elle asks, coming out of her bedroom in a fluffy robe with wet hair.

She's given me privacy while I made phone calls to Allan and then to Gary. Debra's work plan hasn't changed, so I was able to let her just continue on with her research. Allan had taken the news in stride, better than I'd expected, to be honest, even suggesting that he expected me to have ties to properties in London, whether direct or indirect, and that my proposed site was tied up in my family's trust was no different than it being with any other seller. In fact, he'd alluded to it even being preferable because family can be easier to deal with than corporate giants who are selling off large plots of prime real estate. I didn't correct him that he didn't know my family.

"Yes. It's done. It'll be all over the office in moments, I'm sure." I lean back on the couch, running my fingers through my hair. I've made the same movement at least a dozen times as I paced about.

"If it's any consolation, Tiffany didn't know anything. I talked to her before I got in the shower because if I didn't give her the London update, she probably would've been on the next plane here to pull it out of me."

I blink slowly, my jaw tightening of its own accord.

"You can stop that question before it even makes it to air, Colton Wolfe. I didn't tell her anything other than how beautiful London is, how amazing the hotel is, and that I joined the mile-high club. That part didn't seem confidential. She said Dad is in Tennessee, but I didn't want any more info than that because it didn't seem right. Oh, and Sophie almost killed her sleeping on her chest. Apparently, my cat's a slut and will straddle anybody who lies down in my bed."

"Thank you for not saying anything else." It's all I can offer because I did have that split second of doubt. Not in Elle, per se, but just in people in general. I've found them to be backhanded and selfish far too often, and distrust is my gut instinct.

She comes over and sits beside me on the couch, her legs curled underneath her. "Of course I didn't say anything. I said I wouldn't and I didn't."

The reassurance shouldn't be necessary, but it soothes me,

anyway. Elle weaves her fingers into my hair, pulling me to her, and I go happily, my cheek resting on her breast.

"Today sucked ass." The declaration makes me chuckle, and I nod. "What do you need? A hot bath, a strong drink, a long nap, a good fuck? What do you need to feel better, to wash all that suckage away?"

She's a fucking angel. It's the only explanation for a woman who would go through what we went through today, right at my side while I went to battle against my own father, and then offer kindness.

I nuzzle her breast, knowing the truth. "Fuck, Elle." It's both answer and exclamation, and she takes it as both.

"You wanna fuck me hard and rough? Get out all that aggression with a good pounding? Or do you want to lie back and let me fuck you? I can drain all that tension out and you won't even have to move."

"Fuckin' hell, the way you talk to me. I love it." I pull her into my lap, her knees on either side of my hips. Her robe falls open, revealing that she's nude underneath, and I can't help but grind up against her.

I cup her tits, squeezing them too hard, but she arches into my touch anyway, so I reward her with my tongue, tracing a circle around her nipple before pulling it into my mouth. Her cry is sharp, her nails sharper as she holds my head to her, demanding more.

I surge upward, standing, and she wraps her legs around me. I carry her to my bedroom, the only one we'll be using tonight. The only one we'll be using for the whole trip.

I let her slide down my body and lick the sweet curve of the shell of her ear. "I want to shove you face down on the bed, fuck you raw from behind until you think you can't take it anymore, and then I want to feel your velvet walls grip me tight as I come inside you."

"Okay." Elle's breathy and easy agreement sends all my blood south, and my already-hard cock turns to steel. She drops her robe and spins, climbing onto the bed. The image of her crawling on her knees, her ass and already wet pussy on display for me, is the sexiest thing I've ever seen.

I rip my clothes off, giving zero fucks to where they land as I throw them. I have the good graces to trace my hands up her legs, from her ankles to the backs of her thighs, before spreading her ass, but that's all the foreplay I can muster as I push her flat to the bed and straddle her.

I grip her hair gently, turning her to me, but it's not for a kiss. "I dare you . . . to take all of me, Elle." I hope it's enough of a challenge before I unleash on her. I hope she understands it won't always be like this, but after today, I need this, need inside her too badly.

"Just fuck me already, Colton."

Fuckin' ball buster, she is. I love it.

I slam inside her, bottoming out in one stroke. I feel her thighs clench together, trying to keep me from riding her so deep, but I spread her ass further and slip in again. I watch my cock disappear into her pussy, coming out shining with her honey.

My hands wrap around her waist, pinning her to the bed, and I fuck her. Hard and rough, deep and powerful, I thrust into her again and again. Her cries of pleasure urge me on, though I'm so lost to my own pleasure that I'm barely giving any thought to hers.

Right selfish bastard, but I can't do anything else but ride her.

Her walls clamp down on me, that tell-tale sign that she's close to coming even if I haven't touched her clit, haven't stroked her G-spot.

"Come, Elle. I need you to come. Please." I'm an utter arse, but some small part of me knows that if she comes, it'll make my rough treatment of her less damning.

She moans low and loud, almost as animalistic as my own grunts, and then groans, "Now."

The first few quivers of her pussy around my cock are all it takes. Bright white heat jolts down my spine, and I come hard, filling her with rope after rope of cum. She pulses around me, our bodies and our voices in symphony together.

As it ends, I collapse over her, keeping the bulk of my weight off her but needing to explain. To apologize. To say something.

"Next time, I'll take my time with you, worship every inch of your skin with my tongue, my fingers. Whatever you want."

She's boneless and still panting. "I fucking want more of whatever we just did."

Surprised, I sit up, angling to see the blissed-out smile on her face. I just rutted into her like a beast and she's raring for another go.

"You're . . . wow." I know that she described my family the same way earlier, but I think she's the truly spectacular one here.

"And then we can do the soft and slow worshiping thing. Just give me ten minutes and one of those ten-dollar water bottles and I'll be ready to roll."

Though some might disagree, I'm not a stupid man. I get up and get the lady a water bottle and don't mention that they're fifteen dollars.

CHAPTER 25

ELLE

*T*he sound of birds reaches my ears, and I sigh, snuggling up in the soft feather bed and humming happily. Jet lag be damned, being put to sleep with a triple string of toe-curling orgasms will knock anyone out for a good eight hours.

Soft kisses tickle the back of my neck, and I hum, chuckling throatily when I feel familiar teeth nibbling on my ear. "You know if you keep that up, you're going to gnaw them off."

"Can't have that. They're too perfect," Colton says, holding me loosely. I turn over and look up into his handsome face, the eyes that promise me so much and deliver so much more. He leans down and gives me another soft kiss before pulling back, grinning. "Okay, morning kiss delivered, but it is time for our friend, Aquafresh."

I giggle and follow him into the bathroom, where we quickly wash up, Colton shaving while I scrub my face and give my mouth a rinse of Listerine. "So, what's up first?"

"Brekkie," Colton says through a foamy toothpaste smile.

I look at Tiffany's list and pick a simple teal skirt and grey blouse outfit. It makes me feel a bit dressier, and with the previous glares at my tennis shoes, I figure I should aim for a bit nicer than casual work wear. I try to hurry but have to swat Colton's hands away so I can pull my skirt on, only to have him push it up to cop another feel.

"We've got work to do, Mr. Wolfe. And an uphill battle at best. Come on."

He gives in with a groan that has a bit of a whine in it, but we do make it downstairs. The hotel restaurant is a five-star, white-glove service deal, way fancier than my usual pre-work grab-and-go. The maître d' seats us, placing a napkin in my lap, which feels absurdly intimate.

Colton waits until the suited man is barely two steps away before saying, "He won't bite, Elle. I promise."

I smirk a bit at my own reaction, but seriously, I'm not used to strangers getting that close to my business, especially with their noses turned up as though I smell even though I just showered. I bury my own nose in the leather-bound menu, attempting to hide my blush.

"I dare you . . . to let me order for you."

That's an easy dare to take, though I worry they're going to bring me something weird. But I figure I can try a bite of just about anything. "Okay, as long as there's coffee."

Colton orders me a 'fry up' which doesn't give me a lot of context clues, but when they serve me, it's a plate piled with things that do not seem to go together at all.

"Okay, bacon and eggs I get, even sausage, but what's with the rest of this?"

"Bangers and bacon, eggs and fried bread, beans and toma-toes. The perfect start to every day."

Colton digs in, and I follow his example, though baked beans feel like bar-b-que food to me, not breakfast.

"It's good," I agree. Mostly about the bread, if I'm honest. I'm not a no-carb girl by any stretch, and this bread is delicious. I hold up a slice. "What makes this so good?"

"Butter, lots of it. And it's real, fresh butter, not like you have at American grocery stores, but straight from the farm."

I bite into another slice, preferring it to the beans. "As much as I could sit here and play tourist all day, I feel like we need to get a game plan laid out. What are you thinking?"

Colton sips at his tea, thinking. "Gary's looking at the trust legalese, meeting with my own attorney here in London. Debra is looking at site renovations. I think we need to focus on corporate tax breaks and UK headquarter benefits, really sell the final result of this deal. I know there will be some hoops to jump through to get to that point, but it's an angle we need to work so we can highlight it for the board."

We discuss the various stages of the process, from initial contracts to full build out with daily operations. It's . . . a lot, a huge undertaking, by any measure. But the bulk of that will be true regardless of the chosen location for the HQ2, so we try to flesh out the ways that London is the preferable choice.

The conversation goes on well past breakfast as we move back up to the suite, where we spread out, turning the dining table into a makeshift conference table. Colton and I each work on our laptops, and I point out the corporate law he requested that I pull.

"This is going to be an issue. We'll have to get some approvals pre-built to ensure we maximize the tax break. Otherwise, our first-year costs are going to be exorbitant. But if we can get the council to pass an exception, especially since it's a previously zoned commercial site, we should be fine."

Colton leans over me, one hand on the table and one on the back of my chair. The cage of his arms feels good, but his praise feels even better.

I like that he can see me as a sloppy, sweaty post-sex mess and then turn right around and appreciate my brain. "Good catch, Elle. I think that's doable. Bringing a company like Fox across the pond would be a boon—for tax base, employment, and shipping. Can you follow up on positive impacts an HQ2 would have? It'd be something we can present to the council as well as Fox."

"Yes sir, Mr. Wolfe." I'm just as turned on by his all-business persona as I am his Mr. Sexy Times Guy. He winks at me, hearing the tease in my almost professional, but not quite, tone.

"Get to it, Miss Stryker."

That smirk on his full lips is damn near my undoing, but I rally and focus on work.

Colton's phone rings, breaking our heads-down work session, and I realize that several hours have passed. He glances at the screen and his jaw goes tight. "It's Mum. I have to take this."

He paces around as he talks, and though he's basically in the same room with me, I try to give him some modicum of privacy. I can hear snippets of his side of the conversation, though.

"Yes, Mum. I understand, but he's . . ." Colton cuts off, and apparently, Mary has no problem interrupting her son. *She should've interrupted Edwin and Eddie yesterday*, I think snidely.

"That would be lovely. I'm sure she would enjoy it."

My ears perk up at that, especially when Colton pivots to look at me apologetically. *Shit, I'm going down*. I can feel it.

"Yes, she'll be there shortly."

He hangs up and sighs, looking at the ceiling as he runs his fingers through his hair, gripping at the strands.

"How bad is it? Just give it to me straight. They hate me, right? They've called you home to forbid you from seeing the American trollop? Oh, shit, did they realize I took the silver teaspoon from my place setting? I swear, I'll give it back if they won't press charges."

My lip trembles and Colton's eyes go wide. "You stole a teaspoon?"

I straighten my back and frown in disappointment. "Of course I didn't steal a teaspoon. I'm crazy, not stupid. Or a klepto. But now you're not so freaked about your mom. What'd she say?"

I'd hope the irreverence would help him chill, but Colton's grin has zero happiness in it. No, it's a cold, professional teeth baring that makes him look like someone said, 'Say cheese or the kid gets it.'

"She's invited you for tea, but I'm not certain you should go."

I blink. "Okay, tea doesn't sound bad. Other than the tea itself, which is gross. But I can sit with her for a bit like yesterday. Maybe Nan and Lizzie can come too?"

He licks his lips, and I can feel the hesitancy. "I'm missing something, aren't I?"

"She invited you to tea with her friends. She likely wants to show you off as my American sweetie. This is a divide and conquer mission, probably at Father's instruction, and they intend to conquer . . . us."

"Oh, shit. This is bad."

"You haven't understood the worst of it. I can handle Father, but you have to tea with . . . what's the American expression? Ah, *ladies who lunch*. Mum's friends' only care in the world is their station, the gossip about others, and appearances. I'm getting the better end in this bargain, and I'm going to be working alone all day."

I am so fucked. And the worst part? I have to drink another cup of dirt water.

"So, HAVE YOU HEARD ABOUT THE NEW FLAT HE'S RENTING?" A woman says behind a disapproving frown as she sips her tea. "Absolutely atrocious! And in the . . . well . . . *up-and-coming* side of town."

The way she says 'up-and-coming' sounds like she's being too polite to say ghetto. Or as though she can't stand the taste of the word.

"Oh, my!" the woman to my left stage whispers. I've already forgotten her name, too struck by the absolute frozen stillness of her forehead. I vaguely wonder how much Botox that takes because she's got to be pushing seventy and is completely expressionless. "It does serve him right after the way he ran amok on Patrice. The poor dear."

Her lips don't seem capable of smiling or frowning, but I still get the sense that she feels no real sympathy for Patrice, whoever she is.

The ladies gathered around the table hum agreeably, and I have to choke back a sip of tea. I've been holding on to being polite for the past half hour by the skin of my teeth, giving bland smiles as I listen to the gathering play social ladder scramble.

"Mary, dear, you mentioned your middle child has returned from the US? How is he doing there? Probably losing his mind with the change in culture."

I think this lady's name is Francis, if I remember correctly. And honestly, I'm using the term 'lady' pretty loosely. Oh, she's dressed as a lady, cut from the same cloth as the rest of the harpies gathered around the table, right down to the antique diamond earrings and matching bracelets, sipping tea and nibbling tiny sandwiches with impeccable manners, but there's nothing ladylike about this piranha.

Obliviously, Mary beams. "Yes, he is. Back home for a visit, though I hope to keep him a bit longer. But he's doing well in the States, brought home his sweetie, Elle."

She's already introduced me, and I've already made it through the firing squad line-up of judging eyes that are an odd combination of Mean Girls meets Golden Girls. But those same clear and sharp eyes turn back to me once again.

"Nabbed yourself a fine one, eh?" Francis asks me. "Must be quite the fortune for a girl like *you*. You're just his assistant, correct?"

My mouth drops open. It's not the words so much as her obvious belief that Colton is somehow above me simply because of his bank account and station.

I swear I hear Margaret, one of the other 'ladies', quietly joke, "Ah, well, now we know what he sees in her."

I close my mouth, my teeth clacking against each other harshly. I clear my throat and force myself to swallow down the vitriol I want to blast these women with. It would feel so good to just flambé them like a pig over a spit roast, but that would only prove their point.

That I'm less than, their un-equal. Rude, crude, and American to boot.

And as much as I hate to admit it, Colton might need his mother's help on this business deal with his dad. Pissing her off, embarrassing her in front of her snobby friends, would sabotage that.

But I'm my dad's daughter, and I've seen him play this game before. I've seen him win this game before. The best way, the only way to come out the victor, is to play their game better than they do.

I turn back to Francis slowly, letting the dramatic effect intensify and knowing that each of them is waiting with bated breath to be proven right about me. Even Francis's lips are tilted up in anticipation.

"I do feel fortunate to be with Colton. He is such an amazing man who appreciates intelligence and independence. He sees me as an equal, a partner . . . though perhaps that's a rather American ideal you would be unfamiliar with?"

I smile sweetly, as though I'm merely educating her on a minor cultural difference. "He values my mind and ideas, actually wants to listen to them and share his own with me. We talk and have fun, spending time together doing absolutely nothing but enjoying each other's company. That is quite rare, wouldn't you think?"

Francis's tiny smile is falling, and I go in for the kill. She's made some assumptions about me, but I've made some about her, too, after listening to them snipe, snipe, snipe about everyone and everything while simultaneously offering humble brags about their wealth, their station, and even their children and grandchildren.

"Sadly, some couples are rather exhausted with one another after a short period of time, or the women are relegated to being seen and not heard."

I shake my head sadly, feigning disbelief that someone would settle for so little. "I certainly wouldn't trade my education, my outspokenness, nor Colton's interest in me for sitting around like an old biddy with nothing better to do than make myself feel better by downing others. That would be so distasteful, an utter waste of my days."

Mary flounders, trying to smooth things over. "Oh, Elle, dear. Let's not make a scene. Of course Colton appreciates such American openness, but we do prefer a less direct . . ."

The damage is done.

Her friends are sneering at me, and Mary looks heavily disappointed as she realizes it. There's no salvaging this tea or this potential connection with Mary. If I've killed Colton's chances, then I might as well go out with a bang.

I turn to Margaret, the woman who thinks my only redeeming skill might be blow jobs.

"And yes, Colton does enjoy my mouth." *Blink. Blink.* I let them remember Margaret's catty peanut gallery comment. "It's not shameful or embarrassing to have a happy, healthy sex life."

Ooh, the sharp hiss as I dare to say the word 'sex' over proper white tablecloth tea is loud enough to gather the attention of the surrounding tables. But fuck it, I'm on a roll.

I take my napkin from my lap, dabbing at the corners of my mouth with a quirked brow to emphasize my point. "Excuse me. I think I'll find better company. At a local *up-and-coming* pub."

I turn to Mary, one last sliver of regret in my belly. Her back is ramrod straight, her eyes frosty, in such contrast to yesterday when she was wilting beneath Edwin and Colton's fight. I don't know what type of 'breeding' or 'training' went into making her the way she is. And yes, I'm well aware that it sounds as though I'm talking about a dog, not a person. But I have no interest in becoming whatever it is she is. And thankfully, Colton doesn't want me to be.

They're already talking about me as I walk away.

"Well, I never . . ."

"That little upstart . . ."

"What did you expect . . ."

It takes all I have to not turn around. There's simply no point. I can't change their entire outlook on the world, about what is valuable.

Outside, the sun is shining, completely oblivious to the storm brewing in my day.

What had begun on a high note, working with Colton and hoping that I would be able to smooth over the roughness with his family, has turned sour, like an off-key note sung too loudly.

Oliver offers to drive me back to the hotel, but right now, I prefer walking because it gives me an opportunity to stomp off a little bit of my anger.

Within a few blocks, the anger cools into disappointment.

I'd been excited, in a way, even though Colton had warned me. I'd wanted to make friends with Mary. But I'd never had a chance.

Intentional or not, she invited me there as a freak show—*look at the silly American*—to show me off for her friends' judgement and entertainment. I was set up to be the display of the day and expected to sit there like a quiet mouse while they pointed, snickered, and insulted me.

She'd sat there complicit while they talked poorly about Colton leaving the UK, about his not helping the family business, and while they judged him lacking at every turn.

I mean, how could they seriously find fault in Colton, of all people? Sure, he's not perfect. No one is. But his flaws were not the ones they were blathering about. But Mary's silence had implied agreement.

And though it makes me mad, it mostly makes me . . . sad. I understand why he spent so long trying to prove himself, but he was set up to fail that mission from the get-go too. He's the spare. Hard to believe they see it that way, especially having met Eddie, but last night and today prove Colton's point in a way I never would've imagined.

I find myself wandering along a stretch of road lined by a mix of flat-front houses, the garden windows so close to the walk that I could almost touch them. Slowly, the residences give way to small businesses, storefronts with worn signs and displays that tempt me to come inside. For a chocolate, a beer, or a souvenir. I realize I'm getting close to the hotel and think a soak in the huge marble tub to wash away the slimy feeling on my skin from that tea sounds perfect.

Ahead, I see a fluff of hair that looks familiar, though I think I'm imagining things at first. "Lizzie! Lizzie!"

Several heads turn my way at the shout, one of them exactly who I think it is. But Lizzie looks like she wishes she didn't have to talk to me. Another one of Colton's family who doesn't seem to like me. I'd thought Lizzie and I had gotten on okay, though.

I catch up to her and realize there are tear tracks down her cheeks. She's not trying to avoid me. She's trying not to be seen like this.

"Oh, my gosh, what's wrong?" I dig around in my bag, finding a pack of tissues, and mentally thank my dad for teaching me to be a prepared traveler. Nothing like having to get out of your airplane seat to blow your nose when the cabin pressure changes. I'm glad to have them available now as Lizzie takes one, breaking into fresh tears.

"I'm sorry, Elle. I'm fine. Just a bit . . ." The attempt at a lie fades off. She's clearly not fine, though she's trying to keep a British-style stiff upper lip.

"Come on, let's grab something to drink. We can sit down and you can tell me all about it." I can tell she's about to say no, so I throw in a bone. "Not like I'll be here to tell tales, anyway."

It works. Teenage girls are the same the world over, and I was once one, so I know how they work.

"What do you mean?"

I roll my eyes, knowing it's a habit she has and will relate to. "Oh, I had tea with your mother and her friends just now. It got ugly. I might've hair-flipped out after calling their existence a distasteful waste of time."

Lizzie's hands smack over her mouth, but then she pushes at my arm. "You did not!"

I nod. "I did."

And that's enough. With a promise to tell her everything, she comes with me to the hotel. We find a cushy couch in an empty corner of the lobby and curl up. "Okay, I told you my day. Now, tell me yours."

Lizzie bites her lip, and I think she's not going to at first. But slowly, the story comes out. "Will Blackwire is such an utter dolt. We used to be friends when he first moved in with his grandfather, and Mum always says he has a crush on me. But I don't give a fuck. There's a proper way to behave and an improper way. He's a bully, pure and simple."

She goes on to tell me about his mouthing at her, increasingly misguided attempts at flirting, for sure, but in crude, rude ways that no girl or woman wants to hear. Never in the history of time has a catcall of 'Look at that fat arse! Sit it on my face!' worked, and I don't know why guys, at any age or any spot on the globe, think it would. Especially when it's followed up with attempts to grab said arse despite Lizzie's protests.

"You know what? You're right. There's a proper way to behave and an improper. I think you've just been choosing the wrong option, just like Will."

Lizzie looks mad as a hornet—and yes, I hear the American animal idiom even without Colton pointing it out—until I explain exactly what I mean.

CHAPTER 26

COLTON

he day has been productive but absolutely dreadful without Elle here to add a bit of light and fun to the work. But I've conferenced with Roger, my London attorney, and Gary, bless his soul, for the middle of the night call, and we've worked out most of the details of the trust.

It seems I am correct that Grandfather left the property to a trust in my name. My father has been steward of the trust since I was a boy, but it should be a simple matter to resolve that and take control of the property myself now that I'm of age and in good standing.

Regardless of what he told Eddie, that property is mine. And I will see Fox HQ2 successful there. However, there are many steps until that's a reality.

Mostly, the licensing and zoning of the land, as Elle mentioned. It will take a council vote to return the land to its previous rights, allowing Fox's operations, but considering it's only been decommissioned for fifty years, it shouldn't be too much of a hassle.

After the long day of work, I decide to reward myself with a drink downstairs in the bar, thinking I can catch Elle as she comes back from tea with Mum.

I hope she wasn't too hard on her, though I'm not sure if I mean Elle giving Mum a hard time or the reverse. It could go either way. Especially with Mum's friends. And Elle's mouth.

In the lobby, I see Elle walking outside, her teal skirt over her lush arse immediately drawing my eye. At first, I'm confused why she's leaving, but then I see Lizzie at her side, still in her school uniform.

Lizzie should be home by now. After school activities might keep her for a bit, but it's getting late.

Right before I go over to find out what's going on, I see Elle place her hands on Lizzie's shoulders. Face to face, Lizzie nods along with whatever serious business Elle's saying. It piques my interest, and I don't interrupt . . . yet.

They walk outside, and I follow a moment later, admittedly a bit stalkerish but hoping curiosity won't kill the cat. I chuckle to myself at the Americanism and turn the corner after Lizzie and Elle.

In the quick minute it took me to catch up to them, all hell has broken loose. Or it's on the verge of it, at least, because there's a snot of a boy standing way too close, almost in Lizzie's personal space. And she's a girl who doesn't have much of one, happily hugging friends. Her school bag is on the ground at her feet and her head is hanging low, giving her a forlorn look.

I can't hear him, not yet, but the leering look on his face speaks clearly. As do the smarmy looks on his mates.

I run over, damning the traffic as I cross the street and get close. But suddenly, an arm grabs at me, pulling me into a doorway.

"What the hell, Colton? You're going to ruin it for her! Shh!"

Elle is scolding me, but Lizzie's being damn-near mauled visually by this creep. She told me there were neighborhood boys giving her a hard time, and I wanted to follow up on it but didn't have an opportunity yesterday while arguing with our father. I hate that it's like this, that she's going through something, but I won't shy away from the opportunity to fix this for my sister.

"Let me go. I have to help Lizzie. Don't you see what's about to happen?"

For a small thing, Elle's got a death grip on my arm, her nails digging deeply into the flesh there. "Yes, I see. But I don't think you do. Just watch."

The boy steps forward even more, one hand coming up to twist a lock of Lizzie's hair around his finger. I see her eyes glance sideways, toward the guy's friends, and then to the other side, to Elle and me. With her free hand, the one that's not holding me back by brute strength, Elle flashes a thumbs-up at Lizzie.

Wait, something's up, I realize.

Lizzie's head was down, but there's a brightness in her eyes. She's . . . faking?

"Come on, Liz. Just one little smooch. You won't want no other boy after you've had me." Braggy bastard sounds like believes his own press as his mates agree with a chorus of 'yeah, Lizzie' and 'c'mon, bird.'

"Will, I've told you no at least a dozen times and you never seem to listen. You don't hear me or don't want to."

Will? It hits me . . . that douche canoe is Will Blackwire, the gardener's grandson. Lizzie's tormentor lives on our own fucking property. I'll have him thrown out on his arse by nightfall.

"Don't play hard to get, Lizzie. We're happening and everyone knows it. That's why no other boys ask you out. They know that fat gash is mine, and one day, you'll know it too."

I hiss in fury and Elle literally growls beside me. "She's fourteen fucking years old, you creepy pervert. How old is that guy, anyway?"

Somehow, we're both holding each other back at this point. "He's got to be sixteen, maybe seventeen by now. What's happening? Tell me something's happening or I'm going to go kill him right fuckin' now."

"Will, if my fat gash is supposedly yours, does that make your dick and bollocks mine?"

Will's lewd grin makes him look like he's glad Lizzie's finally catching on to his plan. "Of course, anytime you want." He throws his arm around her shoulders and grabs his crotch lewdly, like he's ready to go, and he's standing close enough to Lizzie that his hand has to brush against her belly.

"Then listen up, because I want you to hear this. You demanded a kiss. You ordered me to go on a date. The answer is, the answer always will be . . . NO!"

And with that, Lizzie pulls a knee up quick and fast, slamming into Will's groin. I hate the fucker, and even I cringe a bit in sympathy as he folds in half and cries out.

Lizzie's not done. She leans over and grabs his ear like Nan used to do to us. "I'm done being nice. Come near me again and

I'll knee you even harder. I'll make it so that your wanker won't even stand at attention first thing in the morning." Holding Will's head up, Lizzie waves her pinkie finger around and makes a sad face.

While Will writhes, his legs crossed and his cries turning to whimpers, Lizzie bends down and calmly picks up her school bag. "Anyone else want to ask me out?"

They all shake their heads no pretty quickly, and I'm so fucking proud of my baby sister.

Lizzie turns and struts toward the doorway where Elle and I are waiting. She high-fives Elle, and I can see that whatever just happened solidified something between them. Something really good and full of powerful strength. My badass girl teaching my sister to be just as kickass, literally. "Did you see me, Colton? Did you see me take down Will?" She whispers it, but it's still loud enough that I can hear the overlay of pride.

"I did, Lizzie. I saw you take him down like a badass. Seems you learned some self-defense skills even without my teaching you how to box." Lizzie looks at Elle, who's literally whistling like she had nothing to do with this. I suspect she had everything to do with it. "I guess I have you to thank for this?"

Elle smiles, stopping her tuneless song. "Maybe? Depends on how mad you are."

"That was bloody brilliant, other than the time warp that made that one quick conversation seem like an eternity to a pissy big brother."

"In that case, yeah. I told Lizzie to stop being proper and to be right. Even if that meant fucking up his shit. Oops." She covers her mouth like she's going to teach Lizzie new curses, but that ship has long since sailed.

"Well then, great job." I kiss the tip of Elle's nose and then Lizzie's forehead. "And great job to you too, Sis."

Elle leans into me a little as I throw my arm around her shoulder. Similarly to what Will did, but oh, so very, very different because Elle obviously welcomes my touch.

"I hope you feel the same way after I tell you about what happened at tea. I was definitely right, but I was wholly improper. I might have told them we have a healthy sex life and that you like my blow jobs. Though not in quite those words, but close enough."

"You what?" I say, shocked to the core.

Lizzie laughs. "Serves 'em right."

I wait a quick moment and Elle explains about tea. My mother . . . I'd expected some sort of awfulness, but not what she put Elle through. Maybe it's the American rubbing off on me, because while I know I should be horrified at Elle's crass language at tea, I mostly find it . . . amusing and daring.

CHAPTER 27

ELLE

*T*wo days pass, and Colton and I spend every hour working hard, sprinkling in dares to keep us energized. Though as of yesterday, the dares have morphed into things like 'I dare you . . . to take a five-minute break' because we've been working nonstop. We did at least kiss like teenagers on a make-out date for the five minutes, but going further had to wait as the timer dinged and we got back to the grind. And not the good kind. Well, work's good, but not the sexy kind of grinding.

The phone calls to Gary and Debra back home are progressions of Colton's plans but nothing new. Just bullet points on a list checked off. Necessary but not a huge victory.

We haven't heard from Edwin or Mary, and Eddie apparently has gone on a bender with Ava, according to Nan and Lizzie, who stopped by for quick spot of tea yesterday. It was a much more pleasant experience than tea with Mary and her cronies. And Lizzie also joyfully reported that Will hasn't so much as looked her way since she nailed him.

At this point, I've been in London for several days and have barely seen beyond the hotel windows. It looks like a beautiful city, and I would love to see more of Colton's haunts, but with the clock ticking, there's just no time.

There's one person in my life who has no concept of time, though, or at least not as it applies to her. She's all-access, all the time.

Tiffany.

"Oh, my gosh, girl! It is so good to hear your voice!" I scream it, even though she can see me through our laptop screens. The time difference means I'm eating lunch and she's settling down in my bed. "Show me Sophie so I can talk to her."

Tiffany raises her brow but does as I say, shoving her screen in front of a sleeping Sophie. "Hey, baby girl. Is Auntie Tiffany taking good care of you? I'll be home soon for snuggles and treats."

And yes, it's all in baby talk. There's no shame between Sophie and me.

Sophie raises her head from her paws and walks over to plop in Tiffany's lap before lying right back down. "She just turned her back on me! Laid in your lap and gave me her back. Grr, I think you stole my cat, Tiff. Hope she gets along with Kevin because when I get home, she'll probably want to go with you."

I'm salty about it. I've raised Sophie since she was just a tiny kitten, but the fickle beast is picking her current food-giver over me.

"Sorry!" Tiffany's apology doesn't sound sincere at all, and she's scratching behind Sophie's ear. Sophie's tongue lolls out, proving her switcheroo loyalty. In baby talk of her own, she whispers to Sophie, "I'm not sorry at all, Miss Sophie-Tophie-Pants."

"I can hear you. And what did you call my cat?"

"That's between me and your pussy. Wait . . . I didn't mean it like that." Her brows raise, waiting for me to break, which I do.

I laugh hard, and Tiffany does too. And it feels like there's no time difference, no mileage difference between us. We're the same as we always have been.

Except I'm not, and she knows it.

"All right, bitch, tell me all about that BBC. How many times, how many ways, and have you gotten Big Ben tattooed on your ass yet?" Her smirk feels like home.

"No tattoos. Been too busy to get out and find a decent artist." I'm not getting a tattoo, no way, no how, but if I told her that, it'd be a dare faster than Tiffany could say 'dare you'. "Colton and I have been working so hard on this deal. There's a lot of research and paperwork to fill out, and he's gone to meet with a council member this afternoon to get a feel for the process of rezoning the property."

Tiffany rolls her hand at the wrist, telling me to get on with it. "That's not what I'm asking and you damn well know it. Work, work, work, yada, yada, yada. Tell me about you . . . and him . . . personally. Slowly, with lots and lots of details."

I bite my lip, thinking of the promise I made. I won't say anything about his secrets, but I can tell the parts of it that aren't something Colton wants held quiet.

"I met his family. He introduced me as his girlfriend."

Boom. Mic drop.

"What?" Tiffany screeches so loudly that even Sophie looks pissed, getting up and hopping out of frame.

I nod. "I know. I haven't said much, but there's something between us. I mean, other than just sex."

The admission feels significant. He brought me into his world, and I'm bringing him into mine. Not just for friendly threats and casual sex, but telling Tiffany this is serious is step one in Colton being mine on my side of the globe. And in me being his.

"Are you okay with that? I mean, where's your head? Where's your heart? This isn't just because of the BBC, is it?" Tiffany's face is close to the camera, searching mine pixel by pixel as if she can read my mind through the screen.

"More than okay. There's a lot you don't know about him, a lot I'm still learning too. But this is . . . something. He's more than just the big, bad Wolfe."

"And you're sure this isn't about the HQ2 thing, about getting one over on Daddy?"

I make a sour face. "Ugh, puh-lease stop with the Daddy shit right now. And no . . . I mean, yeah, I'm sure it's not about that. We don't even talk about that, just us and the London proposal."

Tiffany nibbles her lip. "And after the site is chosen? What if it's London? What if it's Tennessee? Then what?"

"I don't know. I haven't gotten that far yet. Still flying by the seat of my pants here like usual, you know?"

But she brings up a good point. If we succeed, Colton will be moving to London, and Dad and Tiffany—my family—will be in the States. If Dad succeeds, he'll be in Tennessee, and Tiffany and Colton will be in California. Or maybe they'll all scatter—London, Tennessee, and California.

And where will I land?

LAUREN LANDISH

"I feel like this might be my fault a bit. I told you to be reckless, be bold, and I know that's like waving a red cape in front of a bull. Toro, Toro." She flips the blanket around a bit, miming a cape, though she's no matador. And my blanket's not even red. It's yellow. "You're already halfway to reckless anyway, but this might be a bit much, even for you."

She might be right. But I can't think about that right now. One thing at a time, that single touch to the surface of the puddle that is my life, and then I can see where the ripples lead me.

"It's gonna be fine, Tiff. This isn't your fault, but that means you also don't get credit either when it all goes right."

"The hell I don't," she balks. "If this goes to shit, that's on you. But if you end up becoming Mrs. Elle Wolfe, I want a fucking dedication credit in the wedding program for bringing you two together."

"You are crazy, girl. I love you."

"Love you too. Miss you like crazy, though. Too bad Sophie doesn't."

I stick my tongue out at her and hang up, laughing but feeling something deep and questioning start to take root. I really do tend to just put one foot in front of the other, trusting that I'll end up somewhere amazing that's right where I was meant to be. But this situation calls for a bit more finesse than that and a hell of a lot more planning and direction.

My next call isn't nearly as easy, and Tiffany's existential questions about what I'm doing were anything but straightforward.

"Hey, Dad! How's Memphis?"

"Elle, baby girl! Hell, I've been missing you. How are you?" He doesn't answer my question, but I don't think he's avoiding it, rather just doing his dad thing . . . focusing on me.

"I'm good. London is beautiful." What little I've seen, that's true. "Though Colton and I have been working hard so I haven't seen much."

"How is the proposal coming?" Dad's voice is tight, like he's fighting the words. But is he trying to hold them back or not wanting to seem too worried about our progress? I'm not sure.

"Dad, I don't think we should talk about that. You do you, and I'm doing me. I want to make sure that whatever happens, we're good after this."

He sighs, looking off screen at something in his hotel room. "I know, baby girl. I'm stuck here because I truly want this for myself, but there's that dad side of me that wants to see you succeed too. I hate that we can't have both. I don't want you speaking out of turn, but this is what we do . . . talk about our days, what's happening, funny stories. And I know the proposal is what you're doing."

He throws his hands in the air like he doesn't know what to do with them, or me, or this whole mess. "I don't want to ignore the hard work you're putting in, but I don't know how to ask about you without it seeming like I'm hitting you up for insider trading secrets on Wolfe. I just . . . I'm trying, baby girl. And not doing too good of a job of it."

"Dad . . ." I laugh, so relieved I can feel it down to my toes. And though I'm not usually a crier, there's a bit of a sting behind my eyes because I can see the honesty in his eyes, even through the screen.

He's not over it, but he's making some peace with my working with Colton and being in London. I was right. Standing up to him hurt like hell, but I think it was the only way to get us to a new level.

"Help an old man out. What am I supposed to say here?"

"I think you just said it. We're fine, Dad. And I am doing well, learning a lot, no matter what happens."

Dad's teasing banter is back with the awkwardness dissipating. "Oh, I know what's happening there. Don't be disappointed, baby girl, but I'm winning this race. Memphis all the way!"

"Team London, old man!"

It sounds like we're cheering on our favorite sports team, not cheering for a corporate decision that's going to determine so much of our lives in the next few years. But I'm glad to have my dad back, for us to be back to some semblance of normalcy.

I realize just how special that is after spending time with Colton's family. Dad didn't apologize for going a bit caveman and trying to keep me from going on this trip, but he doesn't need to. I know where that's coming from, and it's a place of love. I can feel his heart, can hear it in his hopes that I somehow succeed even if that'll kill his own success.

"Hey, Dad?"

"Yeah?"

"I love you."

"I love you too, baby girl. Did I tell you about the cute little apartment complex I found down the street from the new head-quarters? It'll be perfect for you when we move here."

I roll my eyes and can't help but laugh. My dad's the best, even at his worst.

CHAPTER 28

COLTON

*O*liver turns the wheel of the Ghost onto a gravel drive. It's not smooth and maintained like my parents' home, and the overall effect is bumpy and rough, especially surrounded by the overgrown trees. Though the green lushness speaks to what it once was, what it could be again . . . if I have my way.

It's been years since I've been here, but pulling up to the main house makes memories assail me.

"Papa, let's go fishing! Before the rains come and we can't catch anything."

"Yes, yes. Come along, Coltie. Grab your fishing rod or you won't be catching nowt."

I grab my rod and my tackle box, scrambling around Papa like a gnat as he walks steadfastly toward the manicured trees, unperturbed by my rambunctiousness as he waves to the gardener.

I look to the right, knowing that through that copse of trees is a large pond where my grandfather taught me to fish. Dad hadn't been quite correct that my grandfather had passed while I was still in nappies. In fact, he'd been off by a few years. Not that he would've ever changed a nappy himself, so he wouldn't know.

But I'd been six when the best man I knew had left us. He taught me not just fishing but hard work. Not only with his mind, when I'd run toy cars along the run in his office, listening in while he made business calls, but with his hands, helping the stable workers care for the horses.

"They know who cares for them. If you only appear for the show,

they'll never give you their best ride. Daily care and attention, you working for them . . . that's how you earn their respect, how you get them to work for you too."

He'd been a bright spot for far too short of a time, and standing in front of his home, the home I'm claiming, feels like I'm finally doing right by him.

"Colton? You okay?"

Elle's quiet question pulls me from the past, and when I look at her, I see the future I could have. Right here at the Estate.

If Fox chooses my proposal.

I nod several times, letting the rattles shake away the cobwebs of the memories in my mind. "Yes, of course. Just a lot to think about. Let me show you around."

I help her out of the car, keeping her hand and tucking it to my elbow.

"This was my grandfather's estate. The house will need a full renovation, but that's nothing to do with Fox. It can be whatever we want, modern and sleek, rustic and old-world, or anywhere in between. The kitchen, living areas, and main bedroom should probably be first after making sure the bones are safe." I look at the house critically. "Definitely need tradespeople to certify the foundation, redo the roof, and check the plumbing, electric, and gas. Then we can get started on the fun stuff."

Elle pulls at me, her eyes wide as I turn back to look at her. "We?"

I blink, hearing what I said again. "I . . . I . . . I shouldn't have assumed. I'm sorry, but I thought you'd come with me." My words trail off as I see the play of emotions on Elle's face.

I cup her cheeks in my palms. "What is it, love? What's going through that head of yours, because I can see there's something dancing in the chaos there?"

Her smile is soft but pushes her cheeks against my palms. "It's all hitting me, I guess. Dad's talking about apartments for me in Tennessee, and you're talking about moving me to London. It's a lot when two weeks ago, my biggest concern was whether or not Miranda was going to be in a bad mood or a good mood and my mission of the day was to dare Tiffany to do something crazy."

My hands fall to my sides. "You're lumping me in with your father. I'm sorry if it seems like I'm trying to pull you one way and push you another, without regard for what you actually want. I thought this was . . ." I gesture around to the Estate, able to picture it so clearly.

Elle and me having breakfast on the veranda. Me with tea and her with coffee.

Heading across the property to Fox HQ2 to work for the day, slipping away for dares at every opportunity, whether we should or not.

Coming home to our home in the evening. Falling into bed and into each other, only to do it all again the next day.

"I'm not 'lumping you in with him', and don't say that like it's a bad thing. He means well and is trying to take care of me because he loves me—"

"I love you too."

The words burst from my mouth unintentionally, but no less true for their spontaneity. Silence stretches between us, save for a lone bird calling somewhere in the distance.

"What?"

I gather Elle into my arms, her hands on my chest, but she's not pushing me away. I'm going for it, for her. I'm going to be this daring, brave man she's taught me to be. It might've been with silly, small challenges, but the lessons I've learned at her side have taught me one thing. Fortune favors the bold.

Indeed, she was wasting away working for Miranda mere weeks ago, but by following her own wild instincts and desire for a touch of danger, she's landed somewhere I'd like to think is far more favourable. In my heart.

So I jump off the platform, just like she did.

"I love you, Elle Stryker. I know it's utter craziness and ridiculously fast, and I'll wait if that's what you want. But I love you. So . . . yeah, I love you." I think maybe the more I say it, the less shocked she'll be? Like I can acclimate her to it by overdose.

She's biting her lip so hard it's turned white and I can't read her eyes, which terrifies the fuck out of me. "Are you done? Got it all out?" she asks, still not giving me a hint where she's at.

I nod, standing tall to face her firing squad but not letting go. In fact, I hold her a bit tighter, preparing for her to knee me like she taught Lizzie and possibly even make a run for it.

"I love you too."

My arms sag, and my whole body droops. "What?"

She smiles now, and I finally feel my heart start beating again.

"It is fast, and my dad's going to absolutely murder you, so there's that. Fair warning."

She shrugs like her dad putting me six feet under is no biggie, a minor inconvenience at best. "But in case you haven't noticed, I'm not exactly a think-things-through kinda girl. So yeah, I love you too."

I smile as I realize what she's saying. She loves me. And not because I'm some rich bastard or a hot-shot executive or because of my family name. In fact, it might be in spite of those things, because Elle could give a rat's ass about any of that. The animal thing makes me laugh out loud, and she eyes me with one raised brow.

"One, you should see yourself right now. Big, bad Wolfe? More like cute, dopey dog. And two, it's rude to laugh when someone says they love you. Really rude, Wolfe."

Oh, shit, she's calling me by my last name only. Reverse, reverse! I hold her tight, pinning her hands so she doesn't start smacking me again. "I'm just happy. You make me so bloody happy, Elle."

"Well, okay then. Show me around." She gestures to the Estate surrounding us. "Oh, by the way, if Dad wins this whole HQ2 bid thing, we're moving to Memphis. He found me . . . I mean *us*" —she winks exaggeratedly— "a cute little place nearby. Should be perfect, don'tcha think?"

I'm not a stupid man, and I know she's throwing darts to see if she can get a bullseye and hit me where it hurts.

"He's not going to win this, and you know it as well as I do. We've worked too hard and it's too perfect. But if, and that's a huge if, he does, I'll find us a place in Memphis. Where is that, anyway, other than in Tennessee?"

She laughs like I'm an utter dolt. I'm faking. I obviously know where Memphis is and am more than familiar with the basics of Daniel's proposal since he made it to the whole board. But I know I'm right. London is the better choice. There's no doubt.

As long as I can get the trust and zoning squared away.

"Come on, the council rep will be here any minute, and I want to show you around first."

And I do. I take her into the house, not gloating at all, or at least not out loud, as she talks about kitchen appliances and wanting an actual dining room table. Who knew that was a big deal? We walk the property a bit, and I show her the pond with so many fond memories. She listens as I talk about my papa as though it was yesterday when it was so very long ago and for far too short.

Then I have Oliver drive us down the side of the property to the site I have in mind for the actual Fox HQ2. Getting out, I see the council rep has already arrived.

"Baron Berkman, so lovely to see you. Thank you for coming out to the Estate, and Fox Industries' new secondary headquarters." I say it as though it's a foregone conclusion, planting the notion in his mind.

We shake hands, politely and professionally. "Very good to see you, Colton. I hear it's been quite some time since you've been home?"

"It has. But I'm here now, and ready to bring some brilliant things home to roost. Can I show you around, tell you what I envision?"

Baron Berkman nods, and we spend the next hour poring over the blueprints Debra sent me, discussing the actual build-out itself. As we move on to the economic benefits a Fox headquarters would offer the surrounding areas, I can see that I've won him over with the facts and figures Elle and I have been painstakingly working on round the clock.

"The property is currently in family trust, which is being handled. Once that's been done, I will offer a small portion of the overall plot to Fox as a long-term lease, maintaining family ownership as well as presence on site."

"You intend to live here and run the company as well? Bloody brilliant, I do say."

He scans the paperwork and then the land surrounding us once again. I give him the moment to visualize it the way I do, the positive impact a Fox HQ2 can have, not just for me, but for London.

His lips press together, and I can tell he's impressed. "Excellent presentation, Colton. Do the same for the entire council, and I don't foresee your having any issues with your zoning changes. Especially with you at the helm." He looks at Elle for a moment, as though debating what he's about to say. "If it were an American company coming in and placing one of their own at the top, I'm not sure they'd go for it. But with your name attached, the history of the Estate returning to its grandeur under its heir, you're an absolute shoo-in"

I dip my chin in acknowledgement. "Thank you, sir."

BACK AT THE HOTEL, I WANT NOTHING MORE THAN TO MAKE LOVE TO Elle. Especially after our rather revealing day, but she's a wicked taskmaster who won't let me rest. Not that I want to rest, exactly, but at least take a break buried to the hilt inside her.

"Not yet. Call Gary and Debra before they head home for the day. I'll go . . . get ready."

The light in her eyes is naughty, and I know she's up to something, which only makes me want to follow her into the bedroom more. But she shuts the door in my face.

I stand there, nose to the wood, shocked at her audacity. And delighted at her cheeky boldness.

Sulking a bit, I do as she bade and call the US office. "Hi, Gary, what do you have for me?"

"Quite a bit, actually. I spoke with Roger, working as your liaison—not a Fox representative, to be clear."

"Of course. I understand and appreciate your attention to detail." I know Gary's walking a fine line, helping me personally while maintaining his own standards professionally, all the while, keeping his contract with Fox at the forefront.

"Thank you. So, Roger says the trust is pretty clear-cut. If I may speak frankly?"

I hum an agreement, and he soldiers on.

"To be honest, you should've done this ages ago, Colton. Once you turned twenty-one, the property was available to you exclusively as part of your grandfather's will. Even if you weren't going to do anything with it, the Estate should've been under your purview for the last several years. But because you didn't pursue it, it fell under a larger trust, an umbrella, if you will. Edwin Wolfe is primarily in charge of that umbrella in practice. There's nothing he can really do to stop you from taking ownership of it, though. It's yours. It always has been."

Wow. So many thoughts rush through me. It's mine. It's always been mine. Dad can't stop me. I'm going to make this dream a reality, in London, with Elle at my side.

I'm going to succeed. Not that I care in the least about showing off to my father anymore or to prove myself worthy of his love. But for myself, for Elle, and for our future.

"Thank you, Gary. Truly, I can't express how much I appreciate your help on this."

He chuckles. "You're quite welcome, Colton. Glad to hear you say that, actually, because changing gears . . . I do hear London is quite a lovely city. Perhaps I can come across the pond, as you say, and help you get HQ2 up and running when the time is right?"

"Abso-fuckin'-lutely, Gary. That'd be brilliant." I know my accent is thicker with excitement, but I don't care.

"That means yes, right?" Gary replies, but he heard me loud and clear.

We hang up, and I make calls to Debra and Helen.

Debra graciously receives the high praise I heap on her for her drawings, expressing gladness that her blueprints helped sway the council representative. She needs minimal leadership, mostly telling me her next steps in pricing out the plans.

Helen is almost giddy when she answers my call. "Mr. Wolfe, it's been better than expected without you here. I mean . . . not that we, that *I* don't miss you. But nothing I haven't been able to handle, sir."

She gives reports on several projects and how she's addressed them, correctly at every turn. Operations are running smoothly under her guidance, and she and Miranda even handled a shipping issue that could've been a hassle with ease.

"And Tom Givens?" I question, the only potential concern I'm left with.

"Who?" Helen says smartly, then giggles. "He tried to come in and throw his weight around a bit, but I set him right. I heard through the grapevine that he's tossing about the idea of retiring *early*."

I smile at that too. It would not be an early retirement for Tom since he's over seventy. In actuality, he should be enjoying his days with his grandchildren, taking up a hobby, maybe, not trying to be a big shot in a situation where he's allowed himself to become obsolete with his lack of growth. It didn't have to be that way. Allan Fox is getting on in years too, but he's constantly learning, exposing himself to new ideas, and welcoming the march of time and progress. Tom simply sat on his laurels, which he can happily do at home in his easy chair. He's earned that luxury.

We should all be so fortunate.

"Well, if he retires before I return, make sure to send a bouquet, please. Or a plant, perhaps? Something he could care for while home."

"On it, sir."

Of course, she is. "Thank you, Helen. I don't know what I would've done without you, these last years or this last week."

"Fallen on your *arse*, is what." I love it when she uses my British lingo back at me, speaking to the early days when we could barely understand one another at all, though technically, we were both speaking English. "I expect the same consideration as I adjust to London life."

"What?"

"Well, I don't know what you'd do without me, so I've been making plans to move with you. And no, that wasn't a question. I won't let anyone else fill that role, Mr. Wolfe." She's professionally respectful using my formal name as she tells me what-for.

"I would be delighted to have you aboard, Helen. In fact, I think you'd get along with my Nan. Peas in a pod, you are."

We hang up after a few more updates, and I sit back on the couch, my hands locked behind my head.

I'm doing this. Everyone back in the States has virtually declared me the winner in this race, even wanting to follow me across the pond. It feels good, amazing, actually. And I want to celebrate, dance about the room, perhaps the way Elle did when we arrived.

But no. I want to open that door and celebrate with her. Not just this professional success, though it is what I've worked tirelessly on for so long, but to celebrate us. A much bigger and more important achievement.

I've captured her heart, and she, mine. And that's the greatest success of all.

I knock on the wooden door, smirking at the oddity. It's my door, it's my hotel room, but it's not any longer. It's ours, and I can't wait to see what my daring girl has gotten up to while waiting for me to do her bidding.

"Come in."

I fuckin' hope so, I think.

I open the door slowly, letting the anticipation build. And then I see her.

She's draped across the center of the bed in blush-colored lingerie that makes her look nude but somehow is sexier than just bare skin. It must be the thigh-highs, which she knows I adore.

"Fuckin' hell, Elle," I whisper.

She stretches luxuriously, highlighting the curves and swerves of her lithe body. "Good reaction. I told you Tiffany would pack me everything I'd need for any situation. Now, come here." She beckons me with a finger, but it's her eyes that draw me in.

I'm dropping bits of clothing on my way to the bed, which is more her messy habit than mine, but right now, I just need to be bare with her.

I perch over her, my fists denting the fluffy bedding on both sides, our bodies aligned and legs intertwined, but I hold us separate. It takes every ounce of willpower I have.

"Tell me. What's the dare this time?"

She bites her lip seductively. "I've been thinking about that while I waited for you. This time, I think I don't want any dare at all. Just you and me, doing whatever we want. No rules, no challenge. Just free to be us."

I freeze, searching her eyes. "I think that's the most daring thing you've ever said. I love you."

She says it back, but it's mumbled against my mouth as I drop my weight onto her gently, pinning her beneath me with a kiss. It's a soft, sweet sipping at her lips, memorizing her taste again and again. Because I know what I want, and she did say for us to each do *whatever* we want.

I let my kisses follow the line of her jaw to her ear, where I can't help but suck her lobe into my mouth. Eventually, she writhes, wanting more, and I whisper into her ear.

"Put your hands up and hold the headboard, love. I'm going to lick and kiss, suck and nibble every fuckin' inch of you."

"Yes, sir." There's a tease there, but she does as I order, her hands slipping between the mattress and headboard as she carelessly knocks the pillows out of the way. I grab one and slip it beneath her hips, lifting her up like a smorgasbord for me to feast upon.

"Beautiful." Just the one word, but goosebumps break out along her flesh. I chase them, kissing from her wrists at the top of the bed, across her breasts, down her belly and legs, to her toes, which makes her giggle. I think her previous declaration of no-feet had less to do with our putt-putt activities and more to do with . . . "You're ticklish!"

She squirms, laughing and smiling, and while I file the information away for future fun, I move back up her long legs to where we both want my tongue.

I lick her clit, teasing and suckling the nub gently at first and then more intensely as she gets closer to coming. But I hold off, edging her. "Wait, not yet, love."

I do it again with my fingers slowly grinding in and out of her, rubbing her G-spot the way she likes. "No, still not yet."

"Ugh, you're killing me, Wolfe." The whine of my last name makes me chuckle because I know she's not mad, but she lifts her hips, putting her pussy back to my mouth in a silent order.

I let my fingers dance across her center, from her clit to her pussy, gathering her honey. And then I move lower, finding her tight asshole. She clenches against me at first, but I make slow circles with my finger against her ass and my tongue against her clit, and she relaxes into it.

"Let me in, Elle. You've let me into your heart, which is a much riskier thing. I promise to make it feel good." The dark promise is a low murmur as I keep up my ministrations.

Slowly, I press in millimeter by millimeter, and she takes my finger into her ass. "Good girl, love. That's it, relax and let me in your sweet arse. One day, maybe you'll let me fuck you here too?"

She clenches tight at my words, and at first, I think she's revolting against the idea, but then she bucks and I realize that just the thought of me shoving my cock into her ass has her coming. "Fuck . . ."

I slam my mouth back over clit, sealing tight around her as I suck the nub and batter my tongue against it. All the while, I'm slowly fucking her ass with one finger and dreaming of the day she lets me fuck her there too.

"Colton!" Her calling out my name as she comes hard feels

like the greatest part of my day, and I take no mercy on her. I push her through her first and then straight into another orgasm as I slide the fingers of my other hand inside her pussy to work her G-spot.

She comes and keeps coming, her pussy soaking me as she quivers. "Fuck, fuck . . . yes . . . don't you dare stop!"

I wouldn't dream of it.

I'm not sure there's a count for how many times she comes, more like just a clock ticking away the minutes, but eventually, she goes boneless, sagging into the fluffy bed the way she always does after a good orgasm. I take it as a sign of a job well done on my part. On a sigh, she says,

"Holy fuck. Unicorn . . . rainbow sprinkles . . . what the . . . new bar."

I have no idea what she's saying, but it all seems good, so I roll with it. "Stay just like that."

With her hips lifted on the pillow and legs spread wide to make room for me, I line up with her messy pussy. I balance on one arm, guiding my cock through her cream, but when I slide across her clit, she jerks.

"Sensitive. Just get inside me."

"Yes, ma'am." I agree in one heartbeat and thrust into her with the next. Her walls grip me tightly, and I almost start pounding into her fast and hard, chasing my own orgasm that's so damn close. But I don't. I ease in and out, slow and steady, feeling every inch of her cling to my cock. "You feel like heaven, love."

Her eyes fly open, meeting mine clear and happy. I don't know that I've ever made anyone truly happy, just by being myself. Not like Elle.

I've seen her search for me when she enters a room. She wants to hear what I think and feel and is most attracted to me when we're doing the silliness of nothing. She's rare, and I intend to appreciate every bit of time I have with her, praying for more every chance I get.

Her hands leave their headboard hold and cup my face, keeping my eyes on hers. "I love you, Colton Wolfe."

I groan and fall. Into her, into a black abyss of her warmth, into us. It feels good. It feels right. It feels like forever.

CHAPTER 29

ELLE

*L*ast time I'd sat around with the entirety of Colton's family, it'd been shockingly loud and threat filled. A major contrast to today, where everyone sits primly and properly, as though indifferent strangers.

Edwin sits at the head of the table once again, his lawyer to one side and Eddie to his other. The posturing seems so painfully purposeful to put Colton at a disadvantage. Colton sits beside the family lawyer, eschewing his brother's side, which puts Roger, Colton's attorney, at Eddie's right.

And of course, all the women—Mary, Nan, Lizzie, and me— sit in cushy armchairs, in the room but not at the big boys' table where we can actually be a part of the discussion. It would piss me off, but realistically, this is Colton's chance to shine and he needs no support. He's ready for this, and it's been a long time coming—to go head to head against his father. Finally.

Edwin begins. "Let's get this over with. I have more important things to attend to."

Of course you do, I think with an eye roll that matches Lizzie's. Nobody wants to sit around a table when it's such an obvious admission that you've lost your bluff. I swear I see Mary flinch, but Nan seems to be fighting back a small smile at the whole thing. Perhaps being over here isn't as bad as I thought. At least I can read the room, study reactions as Edwin and Colton handle their business.

"Of course, Mr. Wolfe." The family lawyer, a wiry old man

with whiskers coming out both his ears and his nose, says obsequiously. He smooths his hands down his suit front and then picks up a stack of papers, tapping them against the table.

"As we've discussed, the trust for this specific property, colloquially known as the Estate, was bequeathed to Master Colton Wolfe upon his grandfather's demise. As the trust was never enacted subsequent to Colton's twenty-first birthday, the property fell under the larger family umbrella for management. It is my understanding that Colton would like to pursue his ownership at this time?"

"Yes, Mr. Hamish. That is correct. It seems I was uninformed as to my rights upon my twenty-first, but effective immediately, I'd like to exercise them for the Estate."

Eddie looks to Edwin again, an ugly sneer on his face, which seems to have last been shaved days ago. "Father, do something about this. You promised."

"Quiet, Eddie." Edwin's hiss is sharp and unexpected. To Eddie, at least, because he plops back in his chair, arms crossed over his chest as he slouches.

"Bloody prat, swooping in like a vulture and taking what's not his." Eddie pouts and mumbles under his breath, but everyone hears him.

Colton gives in and addresses Eddie. His eyes are sharp, his tone razor-laced. "If anyone has taken what is not his, it's you. You've spent your entire life as the golden boy just because you were born first—which was no accomplishment on your part, I might add. I am not the black sheep Father has always made me out be, but you are certainly not the saint he paints you as, either. In a way, I pity you because his coddling has resulted in your utter lack of ambition, simply gallivanting about like a sodding fool while his neglect and abuse, in turn, have shaped me into something he never anticipated."

Colton's eyes cut back to Edwin. "Someone who can take him on, challenge his standing, and topple the pedestal he precariously perched himself upon. Because I'm clever, but also because I will work my bloody arse off for it."

"Enough!" Edwin bellows, his palms slapping the table. "Let's get this done without the trip down memory lane. I don't need your judgement, boy."

The lawyers have been sitting quietly, no doubt used to

275

family rows over inheritances. But at the order, they get to work, reading out the paperwork line by line.

"Initial here and here," Mr. Hamish tells Edwin. "And you here and here," he says to Colton.

Roger confirms Mr. Hamish's instructions, and Colton reads it as well before initialing. They continue line by line, page by page, delving into thick legalese I'm glad I don't have to understand. It's not just that it's lawyer-speak, but it's British laws and inheritance formalities, both of which seem seriously complex.

I watch the whole exchange in horrified wonder. How did it get to be this way? I turn to find Mary with silent tears trailing down her face, but her chin is held high, not caving in.

I dig in the purse at my feet, having kept it in favor of handing it over to Alfred in case we had to make a quick escape. "Here." I offer her a tissue. I don't pity her, not after the tea fiasco and not when she's let this inequity between her sons go on unfettered, but it's simple human kindness to offer a tissue to a crying person.

She takes it without comment, though I think I see something like shame in her eyes. Perhaps she's a bit lost on how it got to be this way too?

Lizzie leans over and whispers to me. "So, Coltie taking over the Estate and building a headquarters here. That means he's moving home, right?"

I peel my eyes from the lawyers virtually holding court over the powerhouse men to meet Lizzie's eyes. "Yes, it does."

"And you too?"

I nod slowly. "Is that okay?"

Lizzie and I got off to a bit of a rough start, with her thinking I'd be a barrier between her and her beloved brother. But I'd like to think we've worked some things out. Encouraging her to stand up to Will and stand up for herself felt like bonding to me. Lizzie is important to Colton, and therefore, she's important to me. I only hope she can see that.

"Of course! I've always wanted a sister, and damn near anyone would be better than my wanker brother." Her voice is quiet, but Mary and Nan both hear her.

Mary breaks into fresh tears again, but Nan reaches over, patting Lizzie's hand comfortingly. Then Nan looks up and she winks at me. I have no idea what that's about. The poor woman's family is virtually imploding around her. I wonder again if she's either smarter than she seems to be or completely daft, to borrow one of Colton's words.

"Are you sure you feel like going out? I know you want to celebrate, but we can stay in if you'd like." I would honestly be fine with either option, especially because I'm not sure what's going through Colton's mind.

He did it. He took ownership of his family land, which is step one of his proposal for Fox. But whether that comes to fruition or not, and I have every belief it will, he'll have proven his point to his family that he is a success and be able to live here in London proudly. I know he wants to watch out for Lizzie and Nan, and even Mary, to some degree, though I fear she's a lost cause.

"No, I've kept you locked away in your castle tower for too long. You deserve to see London." He presses a soft kiss to my lips, sealing the promise.

I throw my arms wide. "Not exactly a bare, cold tower for this princess. There are like ten pillows on the bed and room service, you know?"

"I know, but I have plans for you. Something special."

"A surprise?" I know my voice has gone high-pitched, but I can't help the excitement as I jump around like a toddler dosed with espresso. "Where are we going? What should I wear? Are we going to dinner at Buckingham Palace?"

Colton laughs, his smile so wide that the dimple I haven't seen in days pops out. "No, not dinner at the palace. I'm rich and have connections, but that's a whole different pedigree. I won't tell you where, but you should definitely wear a dress and heels. Dress for a night on the town."

I squeal and run for the bedroom, closing the door. "Don't peek! I want to surprise you when I'm ready." I swear I hear him chuckle at my antics, but I don't care.

I have a surprise date in London with a British hottie who loves me. Whose life is this?

Mine! I think, and my feet tap a happy dance into the bathroom so I can hop in the shower.

I take extra care with my hair and makeup and slide a white

dress over my curves and thigh highs. Oh, you can bet I'm wearing those because whatever Colton has planned for tonight, I have plans of my own too. Orgasms. Lots of them.

I step out to the living room of our suite to find Colton waiting in a dark suit. He looks edible, and I think he feels the same way about me as his eyes devour me.

"Stunning, love. Truly stunning."

I'm struck with an urge to curtsy, but knowing that I'm not particularly adept at it, I fight it. Instead, I glide across the room to Colton and he wraps his arms around me. He leans in for a kiss, but I turn my head.

"Nope, date first. Don't mess up my lipstick."

I'm teasing, but he growls and kisses my neck, ending with a quick nibble to my ear. "Let's go."

Oliver pulls up to a landmark even I know. The London Eye. A giant Ferris wheel with glass pods offering views over London that can't be matched.

Oliver opens the door, and Colton escorts me to the entrance. "Do we need to buy tickets?"

"Mr. Wolfe. Lovely to see you tonight, sir." The attendant smiles politely, gesturing for us to follow him.

I gape at Colton. "Apparently not. What did you do?"

The doors to a pod open, and I'm blown away. My belly flops like a fish, not at the potential for going high over London, which ordinarily would be a bit scary, but at the sight immediately before me.

There's a table set for two right by the glass windows. My hands go to my mouth, zero cares to my carefully applied lipstick now. "Are we having dinner here? I didn't know they did that!"

The attendant chuckles. "We don't, ma'am."

Colton nods to the man, and the doors slide shut behind us. Colton takes my hand and leads me to the table, pulling out my chair for me. "Thank you." He sits across from me, and I can't take it any longer. "Spill it, Wolfe. What exactly have you done here? Because this is . . ."

I look around us at the fancy white tablecloth, what seems to be fine china beneath silver domes, white wine already corked, and fresh roses in the middle of the table. Then my eyes trace to the view through the entire surrounding of windows, watching all of London appear before my very eyes. And finally, back to Colton himself.

"This is amazing."

His smile is cocky as shit. He knows he's blowing my mind. I'm not a girl who needs all the bells and whistles—I mean, we had fun playing putt-putt, for fuck's sake—but I'm not going to pretend I'm not as giddy as a schoolgirl at this degree of opulence. It might not be needed, but it's so, so appreciated.

"It's nice to know people sometimes. I rented out the entire pod for three revolutions, no interruptions. Just you and me and London. This is my 'thank you' for *everything*."

I smile at the deeper meaning to his words, so much tied up in them—our work, our relationship, our future.

"I mean . . . shit, you could've just gotten me a Macy's gift card, you know. I'm a simple girl."

"Miss Stryker, there is nothing simple about you."

It's the best compliment I think I've ever gotten. Not because he thinks I'm complicated but because he took the time to figure me out.

"Shall we?" He pours me a glass of white wine and removes the cloche from my plate, setting it aside.

We eat and watch the sun get closer to the horizon as Colton tells me bits and stories about London, some anecdotes about buildings here and there, and a bit of British history, which sounds better in his honeyed voice than any history teacher I've ever had.

He opens a small, lidded ice bucket and pulls out a delicate saucer. "What's that?" I ask curiously.

Colton sets the dish in front of me. His lips are doing that twitchy thing, and my brow raises in anticipation for another surprise. He removes the lid, announcing, "Pineapple sorbet."

My bark of laughter isn't the least bit ladylike, but Colton seems delighted by it nevertheless. "Plans for a blowie later?"

"It's called a jobby. You'll have to work on your slang if you're going to move here. But perhaps I'm thinking of how especially sweet you'll taste on my tongue? You did tell me that pineapples are rather useful both ways, did you not?" Colton licks his lips as if he can taste me already.

"You don't have to tell me twice." And with that, I scoop a

too-big bite into my mouth. A second later, though, I hiss. "Shit, brain freeze!"

His laugh is one of utter delight at my dorkiness, and he saves me from myself by pulling me to my feet and leading me to the glass. Pressed up against the railing, the windows surrounding me, I can see everything.

"That way, far off in the distance, is the Estate. Can you see it?" Colton's breath is hot on my ear, and I don't think the Estate is even visible from here. He's just trying to keep me distracted from the dirty things he's doing to me.

His hand slides up my thigh, squeezing my waist in tempo with the kisses he's trailing down my neck. "I dare you . . . to pull your dress up and let me taste you right here."

I laugh. I can't help it. "It's all glass!"

"So?" Colton steps behind me, his hard cock nestling between my cheeks. I gasp, and his hands guide my hips to grind against him. "You want it too. The thought of being surrounded by glass excites you, doesn't it?"

I hum, not agreeing or arguing. "There's fantasy and reality, though. Very different things."

"I'll be fast. You sucked me off in under fifteen minutes. I can get you off faster than that. We'll have time before we get back to the ground. No one will be the wiser . . . except we'll know."

Oh, shit. Excitement zings through me, standing every nerve in my body on edge. I still don't answer, but he knows. He can read me like a book.

"Bend forward."

And so help me, I do. I fold over the railing at the waist, my hands pressed to the glass to help me arch. The chill of the room brushes over the backs of my thighs as Colton pushes my dress up. He groans when he sees the thigh highs, and I silently congratulate myself on the good choice. I sway my hips a bit, trying to rush him.

I look back to see him dropping to his knees, a god worshiping at my altar with hungry eyes. He pulls my panties to the side, and the first touch of his tongue to my lips feels so good my eyes close.

"Eyes open. I want you to know where you are the whole time, Elle."

I nod, blinking hard before I'm able to focus on the view in front of me. All of London, with Colton between my thighs.

He licks me fast and hard, diving right in as though he's acutely aware of the time limit he put on himself. I climb higher and higher, my moans echoing back from the glass. "Oh, my God . . . now!"

I buck against Colton's mouth, my eyes slipping shut as I come, but I don't care, too lost to pleasure to even notice.

"Mmm," Colton groans.

As I come down from the high, I blink lazily. Suddenly, a flash catches my eye, and I shake my head, but another flash gets my attention. Squinting, I see a drone hovering right outside the pod, and I realize that we've crested the circle and are now almost at the platform . . . which has a crowd of people on it.

"Colton?"

Colton stands up and looks over his shoulder, his face going white when he sees the group. "You've got to be bloody kidding me."

The pod doors open, and I see a familiar elegant woman, her long brown hair in perfect curls over her shoulders. Beside her, a man stands in shock, and a little girl hides between them.

"Run!" Colton yells, grabbing me by the hand, and before I know it, we're sprinting as hard as we can.

Oh, shit. I think I just had sex in front of royalty.

CHAPTER 30

COLTON

"Fine choice of evening activities, sir," Oliver says as he jerks the wheel on the car to the left and we whip around a turn. "I haven't had this much adventure since . . . oh, never mind, forget I said anything."

"You didn't say anything!" Elle exclaims near-hysterically as she looks behind us.

Distantly, I wonder what qualifications Oliver has for this type of driving. Chauffeur duty is one thing. This is quite another.

"What in bloody hell is going on?" I growl as I wipe at my face with my pocket square. Elle and I are a mess, clothing askew, and we barely made it past the shocked security, who luckily were prepared for an external threat, not two people bursting forth from a London Eye pod and trying to escape. We just managed to jump into the back of the Ghost before Oliver pulled away, quickly merging into traffic, using it as a disguise.

That hasn't stopped the paparazzi from chasing us, though. I haven't been newsworthy in London for years, but someone seems to have a long memory.

"Today is the young Princess's birthday," Oliver explains from up front. "Right turn!"

He yanks the car in a slewing skid to the right, and Elle is thrown against me, where I hold her as Oliver starts to smooth things out.

"What are we going to do?"

"No way to lose them in this heap," Oliver says as a photog on a motorcycle comes streaking next to us just to prove his point. "Even in London, a Rolls Royce is pretty bloody noticeable."

He's right.

"I'll call ahead to the Rosewood. They are well-versed in celebrity stays, and while I'm not that type of famous, they should be able to handle our coming in hot."

"Do it." Oliver's bark sounds military-esque, an order I follow.

The front desk attendant who answers hears the barely restrained panic in my voice and immediately goes into emergency mode. Admirably, she handles everything with calm efficiency.

"Yes, I understand. Arrival in approximately two minutes."

I repeat the instructions to Oliver and he nods sharply. I get the feeling I could've told him anything from pull over and hide to drive onto a moving airplane, and he would've been able to handle it without breaking a sweat.

"Get ready. You get out of the car and get inside the hotel. The final turn is coming." Oliver pulls in with squealing tires, and hotel security rips the door open, ushering Elle and me into the building. "Oliver?" I ask the hulk who's pushing us deeper into the hotel.

"We'll handle it. No worries, Mr. Wolfe."

I take him at his word and continue following his lead—into the elevator, up to our suite, and inside in one big rush. Once behind the closed door, he pauses. "Safe, sir. Please stay put until we give you the all-clear."

Elle is pink-cheeked and wide-eyed, but her voice is steady. "How long do you think that will be?"

The hulk shrugs one shoulder, as if lifting both broad ones would take too much effort. "An hour, a day, a week? Hard to know. Depends on who you are and what you did." He quickly holds up a hand. "No need to explain, sir. Call the front if you need anything."

With that, he's gone and we're alone.

Elle and I lock eyes. Shock, fear, horror mixed with wild abandon, disbelief, and last but not least . . .

Laughter.

It's not right, but it bursts forth despite being inappropriate.

"Oh, my God! I can't believe that happened! What the hell did you get us into?" She smacks at my chest, reminding me of her previous stint with swatting at me. "Rule three, Colton! Rule three! Are we going to jail? What are jails here even like? Are there firing squads?"

I grab her hands and quiet her with a kiss, knowing that I still taste like her. "We're in trouble, for sure. But no jail time. We definitely fucked up, but only a minor break of rule three. Probably . . . maybe?"

She glares, knowing I'm blowing smoke. "Indecent exposure, lewd acts in public, sex in front of royalty." She ticks them off on her fingers, and when she says it like that, it does sound especially bad.

But for now, we're safe. And that's what matters.

THE KNOCK ON THE DOOR IS UNEXPECTED, ELLE AND I LOOK TO EACH other questioningly.

"You think a paps got up here?" Elle asks quietly, as though they might hear through the heavy wooden door.

It's been a solid twenty-four hours of misery. The paparazzi did follow us to the Rosewood, and when they were denied access, they promptly set up shop out front to wait for us. I have no doubt their resolve is stronger than our own.

To make matters worse, as the photos hit the morning papers and social media online, with both mine and Elle's names boldly listed, an angry mob had joined the reporters.

British sensibilities are rather loose, especially when whatever misdeeds you do are behind closed doors. But apparently, public snogging in front of the royal family is worthy of a near lynching.

They're calling for Elle's head, labeling her an 'American whore' when there's room in the headline and a 'tart' when there's not. Both are painful judgements that sent her to tears. And they're heralding my return to London as the 'Wolfe in black sheep's clothing.' Not nearly as deeply slicing, but a ruination of my family name in a place where it's always meant something, even with Father and Eddie's own misbehaviors.

They've been smart enough to stay off the front page, at least. Unlike me.

The knock pounds again, and I point to the bedroom. "Go in there so you're out of sight, just in case."

Most people would cower, be willing to send me to the front lines to save themselves. But not Elle. Though she's stepped to the bedroom, she stays in the doorway, ready to pounce and have my back if needed. Her jaw is tight, her fists are clenched, and she looks ready to war.

Fuckin' badass ball buster. I love her.

I peek through the peephole but see nothing. I slowly crack the door open and a tiny woman pushes her way in, slamming the door behind her. "Nan?" I blurt out. "What are you doing here?"

Elle steps out of her ambush point when she hears me. "Nan?" she repeats.

Nan looks from me to Elle and back again. "Ah, young love." She cups my cheek as though I'm nowt but a boy before smacking me none too gently. "No time. They're coming. Just nod and be quiet for once in your life, Colton. Maybe apologize, though I know you're not sorry."

She looks around the room as though searching for something, and fresh worry strikes me. "Nan, are you okay? Who's coming?"

Another knock on the door. This one hard and commanding.

Nan looks me in the eye, and with a harsh hand, mimes zipping her lip and throwing away the key before pointing at me. In a blink, she shoves Elle into the bedroom and closes the door, the lock clicking an instant later.

What the fuck?

This time when I look out the peephole, I see three men. I can't avoid this, no matter how much I'd like to, so I open the door. "Father, Eddie, Mr. Hamish, please come in."

Dad pushes through the door as though I didn't just invite him in, making himself at home on the couch. Eddie helps himself to a top-shelf whiskey and then perches on the arm at Father's side, and Mr. Hamish finds an armchair that puts him out of the line of fire between my father and me. Smart man, Mr. Hamish.

"Bloody right bastard you are, Colton. Couldn't even keep

your wanker in your pants until you got to the car like a normal bloke?"

The vein in Father's forehead is already pulsing dangerously, but Eddie smirks behind his glass, thoroughly enjoying seeing me raked over the coals. For the first time, perhaps, I actually deserve it.

"For fuck's sake, you've dragged my good name through the mud and your mother won't be able to show her face at the club ever again."

"Oh, yeah, Mum's been a sobbing mess over the news all day. Don't fancy she ever thought she'd see her baby boy on his knees in the Eye, huh, Coltie? Those American tarts are just so scrummy, though, aren't they? Couldn't wait for taste of that biscuit." He winks at me like we're chummy blokes.

Father growls. "Shut up, Eddie."

Eddie looks as though he's been shocked with a cattle prod. Guess Father's never said that to him before? Well, welcome to the club, brother.

"Father, I'm certainly embarrassed this has gotten so blown out of proportion, but it will blow over. Mum will be fine, accepted back into the fold of her bitchy biddies, not that I care in the slightest. And your name will stand for what it's always stood for." I don't elaborate, knowing that I can't and won't say a single pleasant thing about my father's blowhard reputation.

"Out of proportion, you say? Well, perhaps you'll care about this. I spoke with Baron Berkman this morning. It seems that the council is rather apprehensive at rezoning the Estate for *someone like you* to lead an American company to our shores." His cocky smile is razor sharp.

"What have you done?" I demand.

He examines the well-manicured nails of his right hand. "Well, you were correct that the property was yours all along. As it sits now. But you need permits, and they'll be denied. You need rezoning to bring your Americans here, and it'll be denied."

His shark eyes meet mine, victory in their dark depths. "Mark my words, boy. That land will not see a single blade of grass changed until long after I'm dead and gone. You may own it, but you will never be able to use it. Unless you'd like to live in the drafty house as it sits? Though I do believe I could get it condemned if you tried that."

I'm about to explode, beat my own father's arse with my bare hands. Or at the least, verbally fillet him.

He can't do this. But he has.

He shouldn't be able to, not after all the hard work I've put in and the bright future I envisioned here. But he's all too willing to swipe that away like bothersome crumbs of toast from the breakfast table.

I hear something in the bedroom, a thud as if something fell to the floor, and I'm reminded of Nan's crazed ramblings as she came in.

I don't know what she was talking about. Hell, I don't know if she knows what she's talking about half the time.

But of anyone in my family, I can trust her.

So I grit my teeth so fuckin' hard I think they might crack. "You've had your victory lap. Well played. Now, please leave."

He blinks, disappointment showing in the lines around his lips as they press together. But he stands, pulling on the lapels of his jacket. "Very well. I won't say it's good to have you home. In fact, please go back to the States as quickly as possible. Let us true Wolfes pretend *this* never happened."

He says *this* as though he means me.

I swallow thickly, only my love for Nan holding my tongue. Father brushes past me, walking out the door with a straight back, showing only satisfaction in his belief that he was right about me all along.

Eddie swallows the three fingers of whiskey in one gulp, slamming the tumbler to the table with a loud, "Ahh." He purposefully bumps me as he walks by. "Bye, Coltie!"

Schoolyard taunts of years past paint his tone, as if not a single day has gone by. For him, perhaps they haven't. He's still the juvenile bully he's always been. Last but not least, Mr. Hamish walks by. He has the manners to look chagrined . . . at my behavior? At my father's? At Eddie's? It matters not.

Once they're gone, I close the door and call out, "They're gone."

Nan and Elle open the bedroom door slowly. Nan comes over to me straight away, patting my cheek a bit too hard. "Well done, Coltie. Now, I'm off. But remember, I was never here."

She opens the door before I can ask any questions, looking left and then right. She sneaks out to the left, opposite of the way

Dad's entourage went, on her tiptoes with her shoulders scrunched down. As if that would do anything to hide her. She's wearing a crisp black pantsuit, black hat, and sunglasses, for fuck's sake. She's like a picture-perfect version of a rich old lady other than the cat burglar posturing.

Elle shrugs when I turn back to her. "She didn't say anything, was leaned up to listen at the door with a glass. Which she dropped, on the rug, thankfully. Did you know that Nan curses like a sailor? At least, I think she was. It was a lot of mumbling, but I'm pretty sure I caught the gist."

I smile, but there's no happiness to it. Not even Nan's antics can cheer me up now.

"What are we going to do?" Elle asks. "We have tickets to fly out tomorrow, but I can move them up if you want to get out of here? Do you think we can get out of the country?"

I roll my eyes, an approximation of Lizzie's habit, which makes me miss her already. "They won't hold us here. We're not captives. But yes, let's go back to the States."

I don't say home, though I suppose that's true. But in just the short time of this extended week, London had truly started to feel like home again. And I'm running away from home . . . again.

CHAPTER 31

ELLE

"Come to Tiffany, honey." She holds her arms out, and if I had the energy, I'd run to her. But I don't, not after the long flight where a flight attendant asked Colton and me to sign her latest edition of some rag tabloid. So I shuffle across my living room, dropping the handle of my suitcase as I go, and fall onto the couch, where she wraps me up in her arms.

"I'm so sorry, Elle. So sorry." She pats my head, motherly-like as if I'm a little girl, and though I know I should chafe at that, it feels too comforting to complain. "Where's Colton?"

I sniffle a bit, fighting back tears even though I feel like they should be totally drained dry by now. "He went home, said he had some work to do. I could've gone with him, but I just needed a moment."

"Yeah, sure. That makes sense. You two are okay though, right? I mean, you were talking serious stuff about him. This didn't change that?" She sounds hesitant to even ask, like I'm a fragile bomb about to detonate in her hands.

I nod. "We're fine. I love him, he loves me. I'm just embarrassed. He's angry. His dad screwed him over on the property. The whole project is done for. Hell, I don't even know if he'll be able to live there if he wanted to."

Tiffany's mouth falls open. "Shit, that's a messed-up family. You'd think they'd want him home. A major VP, bringing his kajillion-dollar company along for the dog and pony show."

I bite my lip, not wanting to break Colton's trust. "It's not like that. I don't want to spill his tea, but it's . . . his family's not like that."

Thankfully, Tiffany doesn't push the matter further. "You know what you need?"

"A time machine so I can go back and not get photographed getting eaten out in front of royals?"

Her laugh stings, even though I'm the one making jokes about it. "Can I say I love that you didn't say you wanted a time machine to go back and not get eaten out, but just to not do in front of the royals? That's good thinking there, girl. Real specific to the actual problem."

She taps her temple and winks at me in praise. "And probably means that Colton's tongue is just as good as his BBC. But no, I was going to say ice cream. I bought some for you when you said you were coming home."

She gets up, letting me fall flat on the couch when she's no longer supporting my leaning position. Sophie takes advantage, jumping onto my chest and bumping me with her tiny pink nose. I scratch behind her ears, burying my face into her fur.

Tiffany reappears with a pint of ice cream and two spoons. "No! Don't do that to her!"

I snort and do it again to be bitchy. "She's my fur-baby. Get your own."

Okay, so maybe I'm still a bit salty about how much I missed Sophie while she was loving on Tiffany as though I never existed.

Tiffany laughs. "No, I'm not being stingy with her. That damned monster got into my bag and found my shimmer powder. She somehow dumped it on the floor and then rolled around in it like a pig in mud. I had to vacuum it up and give her a bath, but she's still pretty . . . uh, shiny."

Tiffany points at my face with one of the spoons.

"Do I have it all over me?" Her grin is a definite yes. "You gave my cat a bath? How badly did she hate that?"

Tiffany tilts her head. "Surprisingly, not so much. At first, she was a demon, clawing and hissing. But once I got her submerged and waterboarded a little, she was fine and dandy. She tried swimming around in the tub, and I think by the end, she thought it was like a kitty spa."

I try to imagine that, but can't. I also don't care enough about shimmer powder on my face to actually wipe it off. But I definitely grab a spoon and commandeer the pint of ice cream for myself.

I pull the lid off and slide my spoon across the top layer where it's a little melty. That's the best part, and Tiff's letting me have it without a word. Goes to show how bad she thinks all this is too.

Mouth full, I tell her, "I don't want to talk about me anymore. What's going on with you? At the office? With Ace? Distract me."

Her wry brow says, 'Are you not entertained?' but she does catch me up on what's been going on at work, which is mostly the same things that were going on before I left. Ricky is flirting with Miranda on the daily now, but they haven't had an official date. The phone rings, copies get made, and there's been plenty of chatter about the HQ2 sites.

"I don't want to jinx it, but I think Ace might've turned a corner too. After you left, I didn't even go home for several days. I just couldn't, you know? Though I know that sounds bad."

She shakes her head sadly and I give her the pint. She needs it more than me right now, but only for a minute. Because sex in front of royals trumps asshole brothers.

"It was a bomb, Elle. Trash everywhere, a sinkful of dishes, a dent in the sofa where he sits, Kevin going stir-crazy, and I don't think he'd even flushed the toilet. He wasn't expecting me, so thank God for small favors, I didn't catch him jacking off or anything like that."

Her whole body shudders. "No showers either, for days. My apartment smelled like teenage boy, homeless guy, and dog shit. I couldn't pretend it wasn't disgusting. There was no hiding it, not that I felt the need to, but it was really bad. I think he was embarrassed. I don't know what made it different that day, maybe just how bad it was? But he seemed like he was looking around, seeing his situation with fresh eyes."

"What happened?" I hate to hear about Ace having such a hard time, but I am thankful that my problems are at least superficial. I mean, who really cares about consenting adults going a bit too far in public when there are real people with real problems? Okay, so the kid seeing it is a serious complicating factor that icks me out majorly, but hopefully, she has no idea what she saw.

"Nothing at first. I got the things I went by for and just left.

But he called me yesterday, before all the stuff happened with you and Colton. He asked me to come by, actually invited me over to my own apartment, which I thought was pretty hilarious."

The resting bitch face says she didn't laugh a bit. "But I went. And he'd cleaned. Just a little, but there was room for him to sit on the couch—he flipped the cushions around so there wasn't a dent—and the armchair didn't have a single dirty shirt on it. And he apologized, said he's getting help."

"What kind of help?" I take the ice cream back and shovel a big bite into my mouth because I know she's going to take it again.

And yep, she reaches for it and licks around the rim where the drips are threatening to spill over. "Therapy, I think. He said his girl fucked him up good. Apparently, she was pregnant and told Ace it was his. He had this whole dream life planned out, with them getting married and having the baby. He was saving up for them, just really happy to be a husband and a dad. She had the baby, playing the odds right up until the end, but when the little boy was born, he knew it wasn't his kid."

"Oh, shit!" Sadness at Ace's loss, not exactly of his child but of his dream, weighs me down. "Poor Ace."

"He even told her he'd stay, raise the baby as his own, and marry her. She said no, that the other guy said he would marry her if he turned out to be the dad. Ace left her and what he thought was going to be his kid at the hospital and came to my place. That's what's been eating at him. But he's getting sorted out, taking care of Kevin and cleaning up after himself. Therapy, I guess, and he mentioned that he wants to find a new job here, and an apartment too."

"Wow, good for him. I can't imagine how you pick up the pieces and go on after that, but I guess it makes sense why he's been so scattered. Tell him to let me know if I can do anything to help."

"Will do. I think he's gonna be okay, though. It'll take some time, but he'll get there. Even if I have to force him."

We eat in silence for a few minutes, staring mindlessly at whatever's on the television. I couldn't tell you what it is since I'm not really paying it any attention.

"Have you talked to Daddy since the news broke?"

I'm too tired to even bother with correcting her, but I hold up my middle finger.

"Really, go over and talk to him. He deserves that, at least. Otherwise, he's going to find out in line at the grocery store when he sees his little girl getting some. Want me to go with you? I can act as a buffer. He can cry on my shoulder about where he went wrong with you and I'll tell him that we both did our best to keep you from making bad choices, but some kids just can't be stopped." She tsks, shaking her head sadly.

"No. I do need to go, but you're staying here. Far away from Dad."

"Fine." She pouts, crossing her arms, but then she reaches for the ice cream. "But you're not getting my Ben & Jerry's then."

"Tell me one thing first, baby girl. Did that asshole take advantage of you in any way? Of course he did. He's your boss." He answers his own question, not giving me a moment to answer.

"Dad, dad. Listen to me, please." My plea seems to get through to him because he quits ranting about the 'British bastard' and focuses.

"He didn't take advantage of me. We got carried away, which wouldn't have been a big deal if not for the whole royalty thing, but . . . I love him, and he loves me. And we want to be together, even after all this."

I'm holding my breath, my chest stretched to capacity with hopes, prayers, and too much carbon dioxide buildup. But I don't dare breathe. Not until I hear what Dad has to say.

"You love him? He loves you? What does this have to do with HQ2?" Dad looks so confused and runs his hands through his hair, messing up his perfectly slicked hair.

He got a haircut while I was gone, I think idly. It's longer on top and shaved underneath, trendy and fashion-forward. And I wonder who I can set him up with again. Maybe it's the daughter in me who just wants to see her dad happy, or maybe it's the woman in love who wants everyone to feel this joy, but Dad deserves someone. No names come to mind right now, though, unfortunately.

"Nothing. We just fell in love despite our rocky start."

Oops, didn't mean to say that. I bite my lip, hoping Dad doesn't ask questions, but he seems to think I was referring to Colton leveraging me as a pawn on the project. "Definitely hard to overcome telling someone flat-out that you're using them. I hope you made him work to prove it?" Dad's eyes narrow as he pins me in his gaze, looking mean, but I know it's a front. Mostly.

"I did. Made him play putt-putt on our first date—the gross, old-school kind."

Dad's eyes go wide. "Putt-putt? Colton Wolfe?" He laughs, slapping at his thigh. "Well, I'd have liked to see that, I think."

"And he made me bungee jump. It was terrifying, but so cool. I have the video from that, if you want to see?"

I'm excited by how easily Dad's taking this. I thought he would lock me away in his spare room and throw away the key, just letting me out for exercise in the yard like a dog. Or a prisoner.

But he's talking like this is almost totally fine.

Until he cringes. "Think I'll pass on videos and pictures for a while, actually, baby girl. I've seen *more* than I want to."

And now it's my turn to cringe. Talking about sex with my dad is probably on the short list of conversations I never want to have. Ever.

"I'm sorry about that, Dad. I know it's embarrassing."

He hugs me to him. "Elle, we have been through so much, the two of us against the world, but you're growing up and I know that. We talked about your period when it was time for that, we talked about how to say no and be safe, we talked about experimenting in college, we talked about hopes and dreams. There is nothing I wouldn't talk about with you if you needed to. But remember, you have Tiffany too, and she's probably a better person for you to talk about your . . . uhm, sex life with at this point."

He whispers *sex life* like it's a dirty word, which makes me laugh. But he's right. Even as a dad, he never shied away from anything, especially not like my friends who had moms to go to about that stuff. Dad was on the ball, always.

He had a basket of pads and tampons in the bathroom for me well before I started, and yep, he taught me how to use them. I don't know how he knew, and I was too red-faced and dumbstruck to ask at the time, but he learned so he could teach me. Same when he bought me condoms along with a mini fridge for college. He never questioned it, just sent a fresh box with every care package. Real-life practicality went hand in hand with the bigger life lessons with him.

He's the absolute best. And I'm still not ready to discuss my boyfriend eating me out. Just a hard no on that conversational front, always will be.

"Oh, by the way . . . that lesson on saying no and being safe?"

Dad's brow raises. "I thought you said Colton didn't take advantage? Do I need to have Billy and Ricky have a talk with him? They'd definitely be onboard for that." Dad punches the air a little like he's shadowboxing.

I chuckle, knowing he would if I gave the slightest indication that Colton had overstepped. "No, not that. I met Colton's sister in London. Her name's Lizzie, and she was having a particular problem with a neighbor boy. I taught her the same skills you taught me. Worked like a charm."

I grin proudly, both of myself for sharing the lesson and of Lizzie for being the brave badass to actually do it.

Dad beams, proud of himself too. "Well, you tell Lizzie that if she has any more problems, I'm sure Billy and Ricky would love a trip oversees to handle some business."

"Sure thing, Dad. Will do."

CHAPTER 32

COLTON

*H*eading into the office, my gut is tight. Not nerves, exactly, but resolution. Today is going to be an utter destruction of everything I've built professionally. I will have to stand tall under curious gazes, hold my tongue as sharp barbs are volleyed my way, and most importantly, not let my temper control my fists.

That's my biggest concern as I enter the lobby and see Billy and Ricky waiting for me. Billy is keeping watch on the door from one of the sleek leather couches, and Ricky is chatting up Miranda. She doesn't even pretend to get to work as I come in. My power is that depleted.

Actually, perhaps she's just that engaged with Ricky? Her eyes are sparkling and locked on his like laser beams, and her body is leaning dangerously close to him. Even from across the room, their chemistry is explosive. Not exactly workplace appropriate, but I'm certainly not one to disavow workplace relationships, now am I?

"This way, Wolfe. Daniel's waiting to see you." Billy's order is only slightly softened by the Vanna White arm gesture as the lift doors open. If I wasn't certain my odds of surviving the trip up a couple of floors were fifty-fifty at best, it might even seem kind. But then again, he just maneuvered me to the back of the square cage and strategically placed him and Ricky in front of the doors. There was definitely no kindness intended in his moves.

We ride up silently, or at least I'm silent. Billy and Ricky are virtually screaming at me, but only with their eyes and popping knuckles. I hear them loud and clear, though.

Billy does the same arm trick at Daniel's door, though I go in willingly. I'm not an arse who will run from this. He's a protective father, and I've made his daughter front-page tabloid news. He's got the right to rip me a new one. Billy closes the door, and Daniel, who's been staring out the window overlooking the canyon, turns to face me.

"Colton. Sit."

"Daniel." I should stop there. If we were on equal footing, I would, so that he would throw the first pitch and I could adjust from there. I'm willing to give him the advantage this time, though. For Elle. For us.

So I don't stop. "I am sorry, truly sorry, for the pain and embarrassment I have caused Elle. I never meant for anything like that to happen."

From behind me, I hear a snort and can't help but turn around. Ricky's eyebrow, just one of them, is raised nearly to his hairline in question. *You sure about that, bucko?* that brow says.

To Daniel, I explain carefully. "Obviously, we both meant for certain things to happen. I meant that I didn't intend for the entire globe to be included in our private matters."

Daniel waves his hands. "Stop. I've already talked to Elle about that part. And I don't want to talk about my little girl's 'private matters' ever again."

Thank fuckin' God. Because it's not something I want to discuss with her father, either. But there are other things . . . "If things were different, I'd be coming to you man-to-man for your blessing—" Three growls sound out around me. "But understandably, now does not seem to be the time."

That seems to settle them, but only slightly. "What is it the time for, then?" Daniel bites out.

A hard question, one I don't have the best answer to.

"All I know is that I love Elle and want to be with her." Blunt, brutal truth is all I can offer.

"Be honest, just you and me," he says, forcing out every word. "Did you use my daughter to hurt me?"

I try to find the right words and hesitantly explain. "I knew when I found out her name that having her with me would gum up your mental gears. I didn't plan on using her as anything beyond that, though. She was to be a distraction for you, simply by her presence on my team, and I was bluntly upfront about that. Did you intend for her to sabotage me?"

Daniel reluctantly nods. "Not to harm you, but I did ask her to give me some inside info if she heard anything, an early scoop so that I could counter you if need be."

"I see."

The silence stretches out, but Daniel doesn't relax. He turns back around to the window, looking out at the fog surrounding the building for a moment, then turns back. "Do you care for her? Truly?"

"With all my heart."

He grunts, but I think I see the tiniest softening of his jaw. I choose to take it as a hopeful sign. "Does this mean you'll be coming to Tennessee with us?"

"Yeah, one big, happy family." I turn behind me, not sure if Billy or Ricky made the comment. Their blank expressions give zero clues.

I stand and offer my hand to Daniel. "I haven't lost the HQ2 proposal race yet."

His grip is hard, a punishment for so many things. "I'm going to destroy you. May the best man win."

EVEN THOUGH I'VE BEEN ON THE BOARD FOR A FEW YEARS NOW, THE boardroom has an intimidating feeling to me. Part of it is that with its sterile glass table, brushed steel chairs, and white walls, I feel like I've just stepped into some science fiction medical exam room. The other part is the overwhelming sense of power within these walls. While the room might feel modern, the suits sitting around the table are old-school, strategic, power-hungry types. It's not a dig. I'm one of them myself.

Except today, that power has all been stripped from me. Perhaps not formally, not yet. And I was talking a big game with Daniel, but there's no escaping this. I overplayed, both with the HQ2 site and with my behaviors that have painted Fox unfavorably, not just in the UK but in the US. Seems tabloids are gossipy about the royals the world over.

I sit in my usual place, midway down the long table, the large wall of windows at my back. Usually, they give a sense of grandeur. Today, I feel boxed in, even with the sky stretching out above the canyon. Especially with the gray fog rolling in over the horizon like a warning squall.

Allan calls the meeting to order and then summons me by name. "Colton? Would you like to make your presentation now?"

I dip my chin, feeling the pitying looks of the other board members weighing on me as I stand. All but one. Daniel Stryker, who still looks more angry than sympathetic.

"Ladies and gentlemen, before I discuss the HQ2 proposal, there is another issue I'd like to address." I swear I can see them lean forward, hungry for any salacious gossip they can get their greedy hands on.

"While in London, I was photographed in a particularly compromising situation with another Fox employee." Heads turn to Daniel, who is clenching his teeth so hard there's a bump of muscle appearing and disappearing above his jaw. He said he didn't want to discuss this ever again, but I have to clear things up or it'll hang over not only my head but Elle's. "It was certainly unintended to bring a spotlight to Fox Industries, and to me and Miss Stryker, and for that I wholeheartedly apologize. I won't go into the details of my relationship with Miss Stryker beyond that it is consensual, and at no time did I grant her unfair advantage over any other employee in this company."

I pause, taking a deep breath and letting my jump over that first hurdle settle, because it's a big one. And I went in already stumbling, clipped it, and took a header, right in the middle of the race in front of the whole crowd.

Surprisingly, no one asks questions. At least not yet, but I'm sure they're coming. Allan stays quiet too, and I take it as a sign to continue.

"As to my HQ2 proposal . . . if you'll recall, I suggested London for a global presence to grow Fox. I still feel like that is the best course of action, and if you'll review the information included in the binder in front of you, you'll see the tax breaks, economic benefits, profit margins, and more to support that. However, my site visit did not go as planned."

I scan the table, but not a single eye is on me this time. They're all flipping through the pages of the binders of information Helen printed out. Elle and I worked hard to compile our case all week, and it's solid. Except it's all predicated on using the Estate as the headquarters' site. And a flawed foundation makes the entire proposal iffy at best.

"The proposed site was a location I would have easy access to, because it belongs to me."

The bomb drops and eyes return to me. The shock is apparent. These are intelligent people, and they know the scope of the site and a rough estimate of land costs in London. Even if they weren't familiar, it's all spelled out on page twenty-three for them in black and white.

"My family has owned the property for generations, and it has been held in a trust, but my grandfather left it to me. Honestly, I wanted to prove to myself, my family, and to this company that I had the bollocks to bring Fox into the next generation. The opportunity seemed so perfect, like it was there for the taking. I intended to coordinate a long-term land lease with Allan to make the site the most attractive option. I truly felt, and still feel, it is a perfect location for the next phase for Fox. A global expansion. And I do have full ownership of the property."

Interest piques, but I'm about to knock it all off the table.

"However, the land needs to be rezoned and must have council approvals for the changes to allow Fox to come in and build. And while I did have council support, the recent bad press has changed that. The council is now refusing to make these changes, making the land virtually useless."

Allan sits back in his chair, one ankle crossed over his knee. With narrowed eyes, he challenges me. "So, what's next for a London proposal? Are you giving up?"

I look at the aerial view of the Estate on the front of the presentation binder. I could just give up. It's probably the smartest plan to play closer to the vest for a bit after such a huge failure. I need time to lay low, lick my wounds, and regroup.

I dare you . . .

I hear Elle in my head, not even a complete challenge. Maybe just daring me to be daring.

And so I do. I dare big and hard, with huge risk and very little potential for a win. Because it's what my heart and my gut say to do.

"No, sir. Not giving up, Allan." I shake my head definitively. "This property is not the right one with its current restraints. But there must be others. Sites that would not have the restrictions my land has but that would offer the same incentives and benefits." I'm pleading my case here, in the truest sense of the word.

Allan is unswayed. "But you don't know where this fictional site might be, or if it even exists. Correct?"

I sigh. "No, sir. But with more time, I will find it. I promise you that." I look around the table, meeting each board member's eyes. "I promise each of you that. I just need time."

"Is that everything?" Allan asks. He's not being cold, exactly, but he's not his usual warm and friendly self. I can see the writing on the wall.

"Just that I'm sorry I botched this up with my bad actions."

"Very well. Please sit, Colton. Daniel, are you ready to discuss Tennessee as an option?" Allan's smile feels like the final nail in my coffin.

Daniel gets up, walking to the front of the room. He meets each board member's eyes for the briefest of seconds but glares long and hard at me. I blink first, letting him have the victory.

His presentation is solid. He even addresses the globalization angle and how that progress can be handled and intensified while staying stateside.

He's going to win the selection for HQ2. I can see it, feel it, taste it. And so can he.

London won't stand a chance when I don't even have a proper site to propose, just a pipe dream and hopes.

"Thank you, Daniel." Allan's friendly handshake and smile with Daniel as he wraps up only seem to secure the inevitable. Daniel sits down and Allan addresses the entire board.

"Two interesting proposals. I'll open the floor to discussions and questions."

There's only a few, mostly for Daniel, though I'm asked about my parameters for finding a new potential site.

Allan's assistant interrupts. "Sir, excuse me, but there's a conference call you need to take." She points to the screen behind Allan, the one where the two cover sheets are displayed side-by-side.

"Can it wait, Janet? We're in the middle of something here."

"She insisted. Rather vehemently."

With that, Janet steps into the conference room to fidget with the projector.

CHAPTER 33

COLTON

"*N*an?"

"Good morning, America!" she sing-songs "I always wanted to say that, thought I'd never get the chance, but here we all are. Well, I'm here and you're there, but I'm sure you get my meaning. Made it by the skin of my teeth, I did. Not that I've had those in ages." She sounds delighted and happy. And slightly mad hatters.

Nan is sitting in a green leather wingback chair that dwarfs her, making her seem like a small child. She's got on a navy suit jacket and a necklace with a brooch twice the size of a two-pence coin. Her hair is perfectly coiffed and her eyes are bright.

All of which might be perfectly normal, except that she's on the telly in the board room of the American company I work at while I'm making apologies for fucking up. And every board member is looking from her to me, me to her, with varying shades of confusion and amusement.

Perfect. Just what I need. Another nail in the coffin of my time at Fox. I went off to stand on my own two feet and faltered massively. And now my Nan is somehow stepping in?

Sinking into the floor, or maybe jumping out this wall of windows behind me, is the only thing that can save me now.

Allan looks to Janet, who shrugs. She's done her part, I suppose, got the tech up and running. *Yeah, thanks for that, Janet!*

"Excuse me, ma'am. I'm Allan Fox of Fox Industries. And you are . . .?" He trails off, the epitome of polite expectation.

"Dorothy Seymour, of the London Seymours. And that rascal's grandmother. Oh, the stories I could tell about that one!" She chuckles and shakes her head. "Always a smart boy, my Coltie. Straight As without even studying, beat his brother's arse a time or two." She whispers out the side of her mouth as though sharing a secret with Allan alone, but the entire room hears. "Eddie deserved that, though, for sure. I made fifty pence on that fight, wagered with Alfred, I did. He's the house assistant, you see. Did you know he graduated with honors from Oxford? Coltie, not Alfred, of course. But I'm sure you knew that from his CV. Yes, my Coltie is such a good boy."

Her eyes find me, full of love and joy. The rest of the board is bordering on abject horror at her rambling outburst. I'm again contemplating jumping out the window. Though they're probably locked and secure for just such an urge. Maybe I can walk out with my head held high, fly over the pond, and ask Nan face-to-face what the fuck she's doing?

No time for that, though. "Nan, what are you doing?" I beg her to stop with a glare, but she can't, or doesn't, see it.

Allan smiles. "Lovely to meet you, Ms. Seymour. I did know that about Colton, quite an impressive resume he came with. But I'm afraid we are handling some rather serious business here and I'm not sure this is the time to wax poetic about his attributes. Perhaps we could discuss these things privately at a later time?"

Dear God. Allan is playing nice with Nan, placating her like you do the crazy people who assault you on the London Tube to beg for coins.

Nan waves her hand at him. "Oh, pish posh, don't call me Ms. Seymour. That was my mother, and I'm much too young for that nonsense. Call me Nan like everyone does." She smiles congenially like this is a kind offer Allan should thank her for. "And we have some business to conduct, Mr. Fox, so perhaps we should get to it."

Nan is mad, but perhaps it's in the best of ways? One can only hope, I suppose.

"And what business is that, Ms. Sey—" At her pointed glare and pressed lips, Allan corrects himself. "Uh, Nan?"

"The Estate, of course." Nan's brows drop together, scanning Allan as he might be the daft one. "I'm sure Coltie's told you about the land and his desire to build a new headquarters of your company here. And I rather like the idea, seeing as it gets my boy home to me. Along with his sweetie, Elle. I do like that girl. Did you know she taught my granddaughter how to kick a boy in the bollocks?"

Her expression glazes over, going distant for a moment, before returning. "Yep, I do fancy Elle, too. Anywho . . . getting your little company here on the Estate gets my boy to me, and his sweetie with him, so I consider that a win all the way around, wouldn't you?"

"Nan, please. I did explain about the Estate and that while I do own the land now, the council will not approve the zoning changes, so it's a moot point. I've suggested that we consider finding a secondary site in London—"

"You'll do nothing of the sort, boy. There's nothing in London that'll work like the Estate, anyway."

If I could reach through the telly screen, I would shake her. Hug her, and then shake her, and then hug her again. A secondary site is my only move in this proposal race, and she just torpedoed it.

Allan's lips press together, losing all patience for whatever shitshow this is. "Well, I do thank you for your candor, Nan. If that's the case, perhaps we'll continue on with our other option and build out in Tennessee."

Nan leans forward, too close to the camera, and all we see is a close-up of her eye. She's got a dried-up eye bogie that makes me blink hard as I recoil. "Are you daft, man? I just said the Estate is perfect."

She didn't say that at all. No one argues with her.

"Here, maybe this will help. Mr. Hamish? You're up. Make these American blokes see the good sense their Mums didn't bless them with."

And now she's insulting Mr. Fox. Bloody brilliant, Nan.

Mr. Hamish comes on screen, perching on the arm of Nan's leather chair uncomfortably. He waves awkwardly, but he at least seems professional in his proper suit and tie.

"Hello. I'm Harold Hamish, an attorney for the family. Perhaps I can help clear up any . . . misunderstandings?" He looks to Nan, not saying that she's nutters, but we're all thinking it.

"Allan Fox. Please do explain, Mr. Hamish. Quickly, if you can."

He nods and clears his throat, holding up a piece of paper. "I've been the family attorney for decades, my father before me and my grandfather before that. It was my grandfather who originally wrote this particular trust. It seems Colton Wolfe inherited the land upon his grandfather's passing, but until recently, it was being managed under the larger family trust. Colton's activation of his rights under the trust had me taking a second look and visiting with Ms. Seymour . . . I mean, Nan."

Her angry face melts back to glazed happiness.

But she interrupts Mr. Hamish. "You're taking too long to tell it. I'm going to die of old age before you get to the part about Coltie coming home and giving me grandbabies."

My head thunks to the table. It doesn't make what she just said disappear, so I do it again for good measure. *Thunk.* Nope, still happened.

"Nan." I'm begging, pleading for her to stop.

She winks at me as if having the time of her life. "So Mr. Hamish brought some things to my attention about the trust, or shall I say *trusts.* We're rather wealthier than God himself over here, and it does get tiresome trying to manage things. Mary, that's my daughter, was supposed to be handling things because she's my heir, but she's got a rather poor constitution, that one." She shakes her head sadly. "Not sure where she gets it from because her father was stout stock and I'm perfectly willing and able to fight for what's right."

She smiles a shark smile at Allan. "Like now. With Mary not doing things properly and letting Edwin . . . that's her louse of a husband and Coltie's father . . . run roughshod over good sense, I'm taking back ownership over the whole lot of it."

Her words don't sink in at first. But slowly, they start to make sense, just a little, to me.

You see, our family money, the one that gives us station, power, and relevance throughout London, comes from the Seymour side of the family tree. From Nan.

Mum married Father, who came from what was an upper-crust family to be sure, but it was nothing like her own family. He suddenly became the big-shot power of the family, putting Mum in her place and taking control of everything. I never questioned it as a boy. It was just how marital dynamics worked to my mind because of their parental example. Mum lunched and did charity business, and Father ran the business side of things.

But it was never his business to run. It was Nan's. And before that, her own father's. He was the one who got the contract during World War II that changed everything for our family, turning riches into utterly massive wealth.

"I'm of sound mind and fit body, so I'm doing it my own self. With Mr. Hamish's help, of course. Oh, and I'm hiring a private manager to assist me because I'm much too busy with my roses for all that daily nonsense about facts and figures. I mean, who cares about the stock market closings?"

Lots of people, Nan. But it's a small percentage of the family portfolio, so we can basically play the stock market like most people play quarter slot machines.

"But Mary, and by extension, Edwin, will no longer get their greedy little paws on my Papa's money. Well, I'm not a monster. Perhaps I'll give them an allowance. Hold it over their heads the way Edwin did everything he gave my Coltie." She looks rather gleeful at the prospect.

I stand up, needing her attention, needing to stop this hope from blooming inside me if I'm misunderstanding. "Nan? For fuck's sake, spit it out already. What have you done? The council . . ."

She waves at me, her hand dropping at the wrist like 'oh, them.' As if the town council is nothing but fodder. "Edwin has friends in high places, rest assured of that. And it seems he leveraged that to make sure you wouldn't get the approvals you need. What he forgot is that I've got friends in even higher places, and hell, half of his friends prefer me over that old blowhard, anyway. So they were quite happy to make me happy, which left Edwin's threats as useless as he is."

Allan jumps in at that. "Are you saying that Colton owns this property dead to rights, and you've worked it so that the restrictions he's said will hamstring us are no longer an issue?"

Nan rolls her eyes, and I wonder how much time she's been spending with Lizzie. On a sigh, she says, "That's what I said at the beginning. Build your little company headquarters here and bring my Coltie home to me, and his Elle, too, and we're all happy." She looks to Mr. Hamish, speaking quieter but not nearly quiet enough. "I said that. Is the man daft? I'm worried about Coltie working for a man who can't understand basic business."

If she wasn't giving me, and Allan, the golden goose on a silver platter, I'd be worried he'd take offense. As it sits, his face is damn near beaming, seemingly happy to let Nan insult him and call his life's work a 'little company' if it makes good business sense.

Allan turns back to the table, clasping his hands in front of him. "Ladies and gentleman, I think we've heard two rather interesting proposals on where to take Fox Industries in the next phase. Shall we vote?"

We don't even need to. The direction is readily apparent, and if anyone was considering raising their hand for the Tennessee option, Nan's dagger-filled glare surely had them second-guessing their vote.

"That's majority," Allan decrees.

Actually, that's not true. It wasn't a majority vote. It was unanimous, even Daniel raising his hand for Fox to build HQ2 in London, though I know it had to kill him . . . to lose the HQ2 race and because he knows that Elle will go to London with me.

"We'll adjourn for now, though I'd like to speak with Colton and Daniel. And you as well, Nan, if you can wait one moment? I'd like to hammer out the details of this deal while we're all here. Mr. Hamish, let me call for our corporate lawyer too."

"Gary England, Allan. He's been instrumental in this proposal and is very familiar with the ins and outs of the trust and British law at this point."

Allan nods to Janet, who's been standing off to the side, watching the whole circus in case of technical difficulties. "Can you fetch Gary for me, please?" She nods and virtually runs from the room. I have no doubt that she's already spreading the gossip along the vine as she goes. By the time we leave this room, the whole company will know . . .

. . . that my family is richer than God himself, according to Nan.

. . . that my father is an arse who tried to stop me from succeeding.

. . . that Nan rushed in to save me and might be utterly mad.

. . . that I'm expected to move to London, run HQ2, and have grandbabies with Elle.

. . . that I couldn't be happier about any of it.

And I don't care who knows it. *Share it all, Janet! Save me the trouble, please.*

I do take the quick moment while Allan and Janet speak to turn to Daniel, though. "You voted for my proposal? Why?"

Daniel tilts his head. "I'm competitive by nature. And like your Nan, I'll fight for what I think is right. It wasn't about besting you, or not entirely about it, at least. I truly thought Tennessee was right for Fox, for all the reasons I explained in my own presentation."

His pause is painful, making me lean forward in anticipation. "But . . . ?"

"Until I heard your full proposal. HQ2 belongs in London, and you belong at its head as Regional President." He offers me his hand, and I shake gratefully. There's still a bit too much squeezing, jockeying for dominance, but it's in good-natured fun. Mostly.

He uses his leverage on my hand to pull me forward, growling in my ear. "I voted for London, but I'm still not sure about you for my daughter just yet. She's all I have, and if you hurt her, I will kill you."

I lean back, putting precious inches between us so that if I need to, I can at least get a punch in. He's glaring at me hard, but there's the slightest light in his eyes. A light that looks shockingly similar to his daughter when she knows she's won and can't help but gloat about it, at least a little bit.

But he's lost the HQ2 race, so what has he won? Perhaps some happiness for his daughter, and he knows it.

I wink. "I dare you to try."

His lips quirk, fighting the smile he wants to flash as he tries to maintain his badass persona. I give him the absolute truth so that he can smile freely. "I will never hurt her. I love her. And if I do, I'll gladly stand still so you can kill me slowly and painfully."

He does smile at that. "Deal."

CHAPTER 34

ELLE

"*Again, I'd like to offer my utmost apologies and beg forgiveness from the Royal family,*" Colton says from the television in his penthouse apartment. "*There are no excuses for my behavior, and I'd like to reiterate that Miss Stryker is entirely blameless in the entire incident.*"

"*Is it true that you're moving home to London, Colton? Bringing not only your sweetie but an American company with you?*" The *Good Morning, Britain* host is digging for dirt, hoping for first run at some juicy gossip.

"*I'm not at liberty to discuss business matters, but yes, I am coming home. And I'm bringing Elle with me.*"

Even through the screen, he looks like a man in love. And that has been our saving grace in the media circus. It's one thing to badger someone over sordid acts. It's quite another when Colton and I have stood up and apologized profusely, stating that we are in love and were celebrating.

It seems 'we got carried away' settles quite a few feathers as new lovebirds who are committed to one another and to London. Who knew the British were so enamored with love?

Or at least that's how I'm choosing to see it. Colton is a bit more practical and thinks they've just all done some public snogging and are feeling 'right jammy they weren't the ones caught with their arse in the air.'

Luckily, it also seems that the princess didn't see as much as we feared. She was fitted for glasses just a week after the whole incident and debuted the chic pink frames at a belated birthday celebration. Thank heavens for small favors.

Whatever it is, I'll take it because I do not want to see my O-face on the cover of a tabloid ever again.

Colton's voice calls out from the kitchen. "Turn that thing off. I don't want to hear myself playing nice again."

I don't do it right away, instead freezing the frame so I can appreciate just how gorgeous he is. Back when he used to walk past my lobby desk, I thought he was the big, bad Wolfe and wanted him to eat me up. Now, I can see the many facets of him. Yes, he is a monster in the boardroom, and even occasionally in the bedroom. But he's also the little boy who needs some assurance sometimes, the serious man who needs an injection of fun, and the one who holds my heart with tender care.

"Busted!" he calls out, coming into the room with a tray, which he sets down on the coffee table. I quickly turn off the television in favor of the treats he's brought. He's got a decadent spread of cheeses and slices of meats, strawberries, and tiny bits of toasted bread crackers for us to celebrate his proposal win. It's a small, at-home celebration, just the two of us, which feels right after all the hard work we put into it. Even if Nan was the true savior. "Hope you're hungry?"

"As a horse," I say, stuffing a cracker, cheese, and meat stack into my mouth all at once.

His brows jump together. "Are horses particularly hungry? Like compared to say, a cow or a sheep? What makes horses so starved?"

I laugh, spewing crumbs everywhere. "I don't know! It's just a saying."

He nods, eyes dancing. "Ah, more of these American idioms so obsessed with animals."

We both laugh, falling back onto the couch. I kick my feet a bit, accidentally knocking the edge of the tray like the graceful swan I am. It spills his tidy display of dinner into a mess of food. "Oops! My bad."

He shakes his head. "It's quite alright, love. I'm finding I rather like a bit of your brand of crazy in my day. And my night. It's all still edible. You just have to search a bit to find what you want." He demonstrates by exaggeratingly looking for a slice of cheese to add to his cracker-meat stack. There are at least four slices of cheddar right in front of his face that he purposefully overlooks in favor of looking under my shirt.

"Definitely not any cheese there. But there might be a little something you could nibble on." I lift a brow, daring him.

He shoves his own unfinished stack into my mouth. "Hope you got enough, horse. Let's go." He stands, pulling me to my feet as I try to chew the too-big bite.

"Diff yu juss call me a horf?" I say, or try to say. I swallow and try again. "Did you just call me a horse?"

Colton smiles so big his rarely seen dimple pops out. I'm a lucky bitch because I get to see it all the time. It feels like my own secret.

He shrugs. "You did first. Hungry as a . . ." he leads me. Before I can smack him, he bends down to toss me over his shoulder as I sputter. "Tally-ho!" he yells, spanking my ass.

From my upside-down vantage, I bite his cheek through his cotton sweatpants. "Don't call me a ho too!" Truthfully, I don't care in the least. He can call me whatever he wants because I know where he's going as he takes the stairs two at a time.

He's getting a workout today, and we haven't even started.

As he tosses me onto our tennis-court-sized bed, I scissor my legs, already feeling the heat building there. "Hey, Colton?" He's shoving down his pants, rock-hard cock in hand as he looks at me.

"If I'm a horse . . ." His lips quirk, doing that no-smile thing that tells me he's laughing on the inside. "Then I dare you . . . to ride me hard all night long."

"Fuckin' hell, Elle. Tally-fuckin'-ho!"

He grabs my ankle, pulling me to the edge of the bed and spinning me around so that my head hangs off. With his cock right in front of me, I lick from his balls to his crown, enjoying his hiss as a sign of my good work. "*Yes*, suck me, love."

He slips into my mouth, into my throat easily at this angle, and I moan against him. His hands pull at my nightgown, gathering it up to expose my body to his eyes, his hands.

He plucks at my nipples, and I arch, begging for more. With a groan, he folds over me, shoving my legs wide so he can lap at my pussy. The new angle pushes him deeper into my mouth, and I almost gag, but he sucks my clit hard and I cry out. The distraction and cry are exactly what I need to open my throat and let him in comfortably.

We work each other like that, him in my mouth and his mouth on me, getting closer and closer to the edge. Of the bed, and of coming. But I know he won't let me fall, except into bliss.

"Arr-vung," I say around his cock as I spasm. He loses his pace for a second but picks back up, his fingers blurring across my clit.

As I float back to earth, I realize he's fucking my mouth hard and fast. His thighs go tight under my palms a split second before he fills me with his cream. I swallow and swallow, fighting gravity to keep it all.

With a shudder, I hear him growl, "Wow."

I preen, pleased with myself, but pretty damn pleased with him too because my whole body is tingling with what he did to me. It's rainbow-coated unicorn sprinkles every time with him.

He pulls out of my mouth slowly, helping me sit up.

"Oh, fuck, hang on."

So blowjobs, or jobbies, as I've taken to calling them too, can be messy business. Saliva dripping from the corners of your mouth, eyes watering, and cum everywhere if it's too much, too fast. And that's when you're right side up and it goes down your chin. Upside down, it goes the other way.

I've got tears in my hair, spit going up my cheeks, and I'm pretty sure I just blew a snot bubble.

I don't care in the least. Sex is sloppy, sweaty fun if you're doing it right. Colton offers me a warm, wet washcloth, and I wipe my face as he strokes along my skin . . . across my collarbone, down my arm, and back up to trace my neck. I know where he's going. Ear lobe loving man. Sure enough, he holds it between his thumb and forefinger, rubbing it like most men would appreciate a hundred-dollar bill.

"What did you say as you came?" he says softly. "I wasn't sure you were okay, but you damn near chased me with that hungry pussy."

I grin behind the washcloth. "It's sort of an inside joke. It just came out unintentionally."

His brows knit together. "What did you say?"

"I'm arriving?" I say, knowing I'm blushing ten shades of red. "It's a British thing, right?"

He laughs, but I'm not sure he gets the joke because he says, "You Americans are quite funny sometimes."

But it's not Americans. It's the British who crack me up, with their properness and fancy pinkie-finger tea parties, who curse like sailors and talk about snogging all the time.

I think they're pretty perfect. Or at least Colton is. And Lizzie and Nan, too.

CHAPTER 35

COLTON

"*Y*ou can't come," Elle tells me seriously. She's shaking her head and holding out a hand, palm to me, to emphasize her point.

"I'm invited, I swear it. Actually, he invited *me* and then told me to bring you." I take that hand, pressing a kiss to the back of it.

Her eyes narrow as she pulls away from me, both hands going to her hips. "My father, Daniel Stryker, invited you to lunch? And not just *any* lunch, but to Frankie's Burger Hut? That's what you're telling me?"

Her eyes scan me like a lie detector, but I don't know why.

I mean, yeah, it's a little unexpected for Daniel to call out of nowhere and invite me to lunch, and maybe my first thought was that it was an ambush attack before I drag his little girl halfway across the globe. But then he'd said to bring Elle. With her there as a witness, I don't think even Daniel would kill me.

No, he'd do it quietly, with an airtight alibi in place. Smart, methodical, strategic man. He's awesome, a right role model for me to aspire to follow and certainly better than my own father.

"He did. And I'm not going to be late, so get some clothes on." I swat her ass and she balks.

"Get naked, love. Get dressed, love. Make up your damn mind, Wolfe!" she rants, but she heads to the bedroom to pull on clothes.

Hopefully, she goes for one of the outfits Tiffany helped her organize toward the front because that would definitely be faster than the mess of things she stuffed near the back of her side of the closet. I'd questioned her need for a hot dog costume at first, but Tiffany had slapped her hand over my mouth and shook her head gravely, telling me to not even try because greater people than I had failed that mission. I'm pretty sure she meant herself, or at least I hope so, because I don't want to think about other guys having ever been in Elle's closet.

I wait by the front door, controlling my tapping foot by willpower alone as I check my watch for the sixth time. "Elle?" I dare call out. I will not be late to this lunch, especially if it's as big of a deal as Elle's making it out to be.

I can't wait any longer. I follow her upstairs to find her still naked, leaning over the bathroom counter to put her makeup on.

"Love, we have to go." I'm risking beheading and I know it. I only pray that Daniel will understand that it's his daughter making me late, not my own disrespect.

"We're fine. I'll be ready in a jiffy."

"What's a jiffy? Is that fast?" I ask, looking at my watch again. "How about this . . ."

I scan her luscious body and glance to the closet behind me. "I dare you . . . to let me pick out your outfit." It's a double win . . . one, I can get her to hurry up, and two, I can choose what I'm going to take off her later.

She begins pulling her hair up into some twisted thing I know will end up with a scatter of bobby pins on the nightstand later. "Okay," she says.

Yes. Thank the fuckin' Queen Mary!

I don't look at the pictures of outfits Tiffany spent hours compiling because even if I found a suitable one, I'd then have to find the actual pieces somewhere in here. In this . . . I won't say mess, but . . . chaos?

I look along the bottom edge of the clothes, looking for a hemline that falls a bit longer. There!

I pull out a black dress that I absolutely love on Elle. The one she likely already knows I'm going to select for her. Not only because it looks lovely on her with its silky softness that skates over her skin, but because the tiny spaghetti straps mean she can't wear a bra.

Usually, that sexiness does me in. And later, it will. But right now, it's one less piece of clothing she has to get on so we can get out the damn door.

I gather the fabric in my hands and hold it low. "Step in."

Elle lifts one leg and then the other, and I slip the dress up her body. I hold a strap out, noting the knowing smirk as she feeds her arm through. "Done? Ready?" I ask.

"You forgot panties." She's done with her hair, at least, and turns to head toward the bedroom.

"No, I didn't." I toss her over my shoulder, grabbing her sandals as I go out the door.

"Colton!" she yells from upside down. "I am not meeting my dad for lunch with no underwear on. No bra is bad enough!"

The lift takes us down quickly, but not quick enough. I don't even get to enjoy the view of the city, too busy keeping ahold of Elle as she squirms, smacking my ass with her cat fight, don't-hurt-a-bit swats.

I drop her semi-carefully into the Lotus, taking special delight that the dress slides up, exposing a long length of her thigh. "I dare you to."

She sputters, going still and quiet in an instant. Her arms cross over her chest. "I hate you sometimes, Wolfe."

I set her sandals at her feet. "Here, you can put these on while we drive."

"You're going to regret this, you know?"

Fuckin' hell, I hadn't thought that far ahead. Had only thought about this getting us out of the apartment and to lunch as quickly as possible. But I can see that light of challenge in Elle's eyes. We might be on time, and she might be wearing my favorite dress, the one I can't wait to take off her later, but damned if she's not going to drive me crazy with her lack of a bra and knickers.

While we're having lunch with her dad and I'm trying not to look like a lovesick fool who wants to snog his daughter.

"Hey, Dad!" Elle says in greeting, kissing him on the cheek. "I'm going to go order for us. Be right back."

She starts to go, leaving me alone with Daniel. Don't get me wrong, I'm not scared of the man, but this isn't the professional version of our relationship we've worked out. This is personal, and okay . . . I'm a little scared.

"You don't know what I want." It's a ploy to stall, but Elle just grins over her shoulder.

"I dare you . . . to let me pick. Chili, bacon, and jalapeños, right?"

She's gone, too far away to catch her unless I want to make a scene by yelling. Daniel laughs, pulling my attention back to him.

"She's kidding, right? That sounds disgusting."

His face falls into anger. "That's my favorite burger you're smack talking."

I pale, just as I suspect he wanted, and he laughs again. "Just kidding. That sounds like heartburn on a plate. I don't eat this shit anymore, too old for greasy burgers, but it's always been our place. I think I singlehandedly got Frankie to add black bean burgers to the menu so that I could eat here with Elle and not have a heart attack."

We both look over to the window where Elle is ordering our food. Frankie's Burger Hut is a small, hole-in-the-wall place with dirty picnic tables outside under an awning, paper towels on wooden dowel stands, and what appears to be a fox mascot. Frankie the Fox. I get it. But the painting is half-worn and his eyes give him a glazed look, almost making him look . . . high? Well, okay, then.

"How did you end up with this as your place? It doesn't seem quite like you."

Daniel smiles, lost to the past. "Elle, of course. Frankie's used to have commercials on Saturday mornings during cartoons. There was a jingle the animated fox sang, something about Frankie's being frankly the best. It was awful, and Elle used to sing it constantly, begging to come see the fox. For a while, I had pictures of her next to that painting, like a growth chart as she got taller, older."

I can see what she means about this being their place, and I suddenly feel out of place even though I was invited.

Elle reappears with three baskets of burgers, balancing them all easily, much to my surprise. She's not exactly known for being graceful, after all.

"Stryker special for Dad, BBQ gut blaster for me, and a basic for you, Colton. Figured I'd start you off easy so you didn't get too scared."

I look down at Daniel's, which is stacked with thick slices of tomatoes and avocado and wrapped in lettuce leaves instead of a bun. Then to Elle's, which is a mess of brown sauce, bacon slices, and I think I see an onion ring peeking out from inside the burger? Finally, to mine, which is a pretty standard cheeseburger with lettuce, tomato, and onion. I feel grateful for my basic burger and say, "Thank you."

We begin eating, and I can't help but smile as Elle picks up her monstrosity of a burger with two hands and takes a huge bite, getting sauce along her cheek. I hold up a paper towel, but she shakes her head. "No sense in cleaning up now because I'll only get messy again with the next bite. I'll clean up when I'm done."

Daniel laughs. "She's yours now. No returns, no exchanges, no backsies."

Elle growls, spitting out a tiny bit of burger, but she catches it with her thumb, shoving it back into her mouth. My brows raise. I can only imagine her at a proper tea.

Somehow, she swallows her bite and turns to Daniel. "So, what's up, Dad?"

Daniel sets his burger back in his basket. "Actually, I have ulterior motives for lunch today. Both with work and with you two."

I bristle. Daniel and I have made peace over the last few weeks as Elle and I have returned to work and the set-in-stone plans for HQ2 have gotten underway. But I haven't forgotten, nor has he, that the peace accord is tenuous and predicated on my not fucking up, or fucking over his daughter.

Or fucking his daughter, but I am doing that quite often. We just don't speak of such things, nor do we do it in public anymore. Ever again.

Dares be damned, we're strictly behind-closed-and-locked-doors types now.

"I spoke with Allan Fox yesterday. He's quite pleased with how the London project is going, looking forward to sending you overseas, in fact. Doesn't seem to give two shits that he's sending my girl too."

Oh, fuck. Is Daniel going to come to London? I mean, technically, Allan could choose my proposal of the London site and then still assign someone else to be Regional President. Say, Daniel Stryker, for example?

"You don't say." My voice is tight, the few bites of burger sitting in my belly like stones.

"Seems he's rather excited to go back and forth between the US and the UK, take the wife on a grand tour of Europe."

His eyes lock on mine, holding me in place.

"But to do so, he wants a bit more freedom. Said he wants to ride the Tube wherever it may lead, though we both know he won't step foot in the Tube. He'll take a chauffeur every mile of the way."

I think of Oliver instantly. "I know a great guy who could help get Allan and his wife anywhere they want to go."

We're tap dancing, shuffling around something, but only he knows what.

Daniel nods. "But to have that freedom, he'll need someone to not only handle the London HQ" —his chin lifts, indicating me— "but someone to handle US operations too." That smirk is pure victory.

"You, I take it?" I say with a smile. I'm not mad. It's a rather bloody brilliant solution.

"Yes, so you'll be Regional President and I'll be CEO."

"Dad! That's awesome!" Elle yells, getting several tables' attention. She leans over, pressing a BBQ-sauced kiss to Daniel's cheek.

He chuckles, wiping at the smear with his paper towel. "Thanks, baby girl. Looks like I'll be your boss, after all. And Colton's, too."

Threat and delight mix together in a perfectly veiled statement. Well fuckin' played, Daniel.

I hold out a hand. "Congratulations, Boss."

"Thanks, Son." The nickname is a shock, a blessing on my relationship with his daughter, at the same time telling me to get my arse in gear.

If Elle's leaving the nest and moving overseas with me, renovating what will be our home, and making a life with me, I'd better fuckin' make it official. Fast.

EPILOGUE

ELLE

"You can't go. I simply won't allow it. Or I know . . . I dare you . . . to stay right here with me." Tiffany acts as though she's found the hidden switch that will enable her to win her way.

She's sideways across a chair in the living room, head lolled back and legs bent over the arm.

"Tiff, we've been through this. I've been going back and forth from the US to London for half a year now while we got the site built and ready. It's time." She pouts, her bottom lip poking out adorably. I grab it, much like Nan does your ear if you piss her off, and wiggle her face back and forth. "You're going to be fine. You've got a great apartment—"

"Because I stole yours."

"Taking over the lease," I clarify. "You've got an amazing car." That one hurt, but shipping Cammie overseas was ridiculously expensive. It was cheaper to just buy a new car once in London, and as Colton reminded me, he was richer than God and could afford to buy me any car I wanted. But Cammie's going to good hands, at least, now that Tiffany knows how to drive a stick.

"Again, stole yours."

"Bought it free and clear at a slight discount. A bigshot job that you earned." I dare her to disagree on that one. Colton's exit led to a large amount of shuffling as some people chose to follow him to London.

It meant that Miranda moved up to the executive floor as an

operations leader, filling in some of the oversight roles Colton had previously managed. The management ones that were beyond Miranda were handed off to other VPs. And that rearrangement put Tiffany into Miranda's old role. She's the front desk supervisor now, in charge of Megan and two other new girls.

Tiffany doesn't hide her haughty arrogance. "I am a badass boss. And at least now, I don't have to see Ricky and Miranda making out in the copy room. My best guess is that they're sneaking off up on the fifth floor." I bet she's right but don't throw Ricky under the bus.

"Ace is doing well with his new job, and Kevin graduated from obedience training with flying colors." Actually, Kevin's going to doggie school was life-changing for him and Ace. Turns out, Ace is really good with dogs when he's not wallowing in self-pity. He started his own doggie day care and training business and has clients all over the city. The multiple daily walks have helped him lose weight and feel great, he says. I think he likes the small dogs a lot too, a pseudo-replacement for the baby he thought he'd have.

"Have you seen his latest pup? It's the tiniest little thing, named Dumbledore. He's going to do great things," she intones. I don't know if she means Ace or the dog.

"Maybe you can take Dumbledore? I bet he won't suck your soul while you sleep, at least." Oops, I overplayed. Tiffany pouts again. "I know you love Sophie and take such great care of her when we're going back and forth, but she's my baby."

"She'll have to go into quarantine before you can bring her into the UK," she whines. "Poor baby will be so scared." I raise one brow at her theatrics. "Fine, she'll probably have all the other quarantined animals bowing down to her reign of terror. But I'm going to miss her. I'm going to miss you." She crosses her arms over her chest, that lip making a reappearance. "Nope, you're not going."

I sigh, playing the only card I have left. One I don't want to play at all, but desperate times call for desperate measures. Besides, I don't think it'll really matter. "Dad will still be here."

Tiffany's eyes brighten and her lips twist in evil glee. "That's true. Daddy and I will both be here, all alone without you. He'll need comforting, and so will I . . . we can cry on each other's shoulders. And if things get carried away from there . . . well, who could blame us?" She shrugs as if it would be a totally unintentional oops for her to seduce my dad.

I point a manicured finger at her. "Keep your too-young paws off my dad, Tiff. No-go zone. Girl Rules remain in effect."

She nods, not agreeing in the slightest but wanting to seem as though she does. "Oh, of course. I would never, Elle." She even crosses her heart, kissing her finger and holding it to the sky in promise. Which would be reassuring if she didn't follow it up with a damning question. "But just in case, should I sign the cards 'Love Dad and Mom' or 'Love Dad and Mum'? You're going all British, you know, and as your stepmother, I want to respect that."

I growl, dumping her out of the chair and to the floor. "I hate you sometimes." I don't. I never do, not even when she's pushing my buttons like they're nuclear defense controls.

She pops up, laughing, and hugs me tightly. "I love you too, Elle. And I'm going to miss you like crazy."

I squeeze her even tighter, not wanting to let go. I might've been trying to convince her it was going to be okay here without me, but I was just as much trying to convince myself.

I give her one last dare. "I dare you . . . to live large and recklessly every day without me here. Maybe wear clothes that don't match just for the hell of it, get a tattoo of the artist's choice without peeking, and be open to all the great things coming your way. Because you deserve each and every one of them, Tiff."

We're both crying now, big, fat, ugly tears. "Gah, don't do that to me! I was doing okay," Tiffany says, though both of us know she wasn't doing fine at all. She wipes her cheeks, holding me at arm's length. "You too. I dare you . . . to create something magical over there in London. A fairy tale life and love better than you could've ever imagined."

And those all too familiar friends bubble up inside me, anticipation, excitement, and restlessness. I'm ready for this, to be with Colton in a new country, with a new role at the new headquarters, in our new home.

"ELLE, DEAR, HOW LOVELY TO SEE YOU." MARY'S FALSE WELCOME

and delight at seeing me unexpectedly are just that . . . fake. But I've gotten rather adept at the play-nice-while-cutting-sharp British style.

"You too, Mary. How are you?"

I don't need to ask. I already know because Nan keeps us apprised on every little thing. I swear, that woman knows gossip from one side of the city to the other within moments of anything happening.

Because of Nan's gossipy ways, I already know that the trusts are doing exceptionally well under their new professional guidance. In fact, with Helen here now to help Colton at the office, Nan has been grooming me to take over her liaison role with Mr. Hamish and the private manager, wanting to keep it in the family without allowing Edwin access through Mary.

Oh, yeah. I'm in the family now.

Colton and I had a small ceremony on the front porch of our newly renovated home at the Estate. Dad and Tiffany flew over, and we coordinated so that Mr. and Mrs. Fox could see the grand opening of HQ2. Lizzie was a flower girl, even though she's technically too old for that, but she rather got a kick out of throwing flower petals at Colton. It had been lovely and small and private. The exact opposite of the large, public spectacle Mary would've wanted to show off to her snooty friends, but it hadn't mattered because she hadn't been invited.

I do wish that Colton and his mother would make peace, but she's chosen to stick by Edwin for now. We'll be here, waiting with cautiously open arms, if she ever decides to reach out.

As for Edwin and Eddie, they're constantly chafing against the allowance Nan has set them on, begging for more when their blustering demands don't net what they want. Truthfully, Nan is more than generous, ensuring that Mary and Lizzie are well-kept but not giving in to childish tantrums for trips to Paris with Eddie's tart of the day.

"I'm well. Very well, I suppose," Mary answers generically. "How's Coltie? I haven't heard from him in so long."

I smile, not sure if she truly missed him or if it's a dig at his not acquiescing to Edwin, and by default, her. Truthfully, it doesn't matter and I answer honestly.

"He's very well, actually. Fox is up and running, and he's

serving as Regional President, with a full staff. He's happy. We're happy."

Okay, so maybe I'm a little more than adept at playing nice while cutting deep. My words all sound like the humble brags Mary and her ilk are so accustomed to, but I know exactly how hard it is for her to hear about Colton's good fortune. She bet on the wrong horse and lost big.

Really big. She lost her entire family. Something I can sympathize with.

"That's good, quite brilliant," she says, a waver in her voice. "And you? If Colton has a staff, what are you doing?"

I place a hand on my flat belly, knowing this will be the sharpest wound of all and hoping it will be the one that removes the cancer that is Edwin Wolfe from her still-beating heart while there's a chance.

"I'm doing very well, thank you for asking. Growing the next generation of Seymours and politely disagreeing with Nan over whether we should name the baby after her grandfather. Neville is a lovely name, but it's rather outdated, don't you think?"

Her eyes are shining, hope and pain mixed in equal measure. "Seymour? Don't you mean Wolfe? Though I suppose Neville Wolfe isn't much better, is it?" She titters.

I'm surprised she doesn't know. Shocked, actually. Even if Nan or Lizzie didn't tell her, news spread along with our wedding announcement. You see, when we married, I didn't just take Colton's name. We both changed our surnames . . . to Seymour, in honor of Nan and her family tree. She'd been right touched and had even cried, blasting Colton and me both for ruining her mascara.

"We're Seymours, Mary. Colton and Elle Seymour. I thought you knew."

The tears overflow, and I feel the first bit of hope that maybe she'll come around. "I guess I'd say something about returning to his roots, but his name has always been Wolfe. Until now, I suppose."

I take her hands hesitantly, not prepared for this degree of familiarity with her but feeling like it's the right thing to do. "He's a wolf through and through, but he's a Seymour by blood. So are you, and this baby will be too. You could meet him or her, if you'd like?"

Testing, teasing, hoping, praying. This is more delicate than any dare I've ever completed.

She nods. "I think I'd like that."

"Would you like to call Colton? I'm sure he'd love to hear from you." I hold up my phone, pressing his name, and when he answers, I tell him there's someone who wants to talk to him.

When I hand Mary the phone, I feel those same old feelings. Success, accomplishment, and even power. Not over Mary, but over the ability to create our own destinies. I get the feeling she's starting a new one right now.

I'm a wife, soon to be a mother, a US transplant in the UK, a daughter, a friend, a daredevil, and a tornado of chaos. But even so, I got my happily ever after.

Maybe Mary can too. I wonder if my dad would like her?

Thank you for reading! I hope you enjoyed the story and had a some good laughs! Don't say goodbye to these characters just yet though. Want to see where they are just over a year later? Grab the extended epilogue here or go to my website at laurenlandish.com and click on The Dare.

EXCERPT: MY BIG FAT FAKE WEDDING

VIOLET—FIVE MONTHS AGO

*T*his can't be happening. He can't be leaving me.

Not now.

Not ever.

My heels click across the hospital floor as I race down the hallway. I'm in such a panic, the words blaring over the PA system hardly register from the blood rushing through my ears in a dull roar.

"Code blue, room four! Code blue, room four!"

I nearly trip over my own feet as I break into a shuffling run, boomeranging for the nearest patient room. I swear my heart is going to explode when I spot the correct door and burst inside to see . . .

"Nana!" I exclaim as I see my grandmother, Angela Russo. She looks up from where she's hovering like a hen over my grandfather. The scowl on her face highlights the parentheses of wrinkles around her lips, making her worry immediately apparent.

My grandfather, Stefano, looks up at me, his unusually pale face widening into a huge smile. But even with the happiness blooming, I can tell he's worn out, aged decades in the short time since I last saw him.

"My beautiful little flower, Violet!" he sings, his Italian accent coming through as he holds his arms out to me. "I knew you would come. Come here so I can give you a kiss!"

"Oh, Papa, I was so scared!" I say, rushing into his arms and collapsing into a ball of relief. "I dropped everything and came as soon as I heard."

Papa looks over at Nana with a triumphant wink of his eye as he rubs my shoulders. "See, Angie? This one loves me the most. Do you see any of our other granddaughters here?"

"That's because you've scared them all away with your crazy stories," Nana growls, but there's an undercurrent of affection for the man who is both a thorn in her side and her everything.

Papa laughs and squeezes me with a fierce strength that belies his shrinking frame, raining kisses down upon my forehead. I feel comforted, enveloped in his familiar scent, leather and spicy meats . . . masculine and comforting. For a moment, I forget the direness of the situation as he rocks me back and forth in his arms like I'm a child or the one in need of comfort, though he's the one in the hospital bed.

But the moment is fleeting as reality slams back into me, and I rise to my feet to ask Nana in a rush of words, "What happened? Is he going to be okay? How long has he been like this?"

"The old fool was working out back in the summer heat after I told him he should take it easy and come inside," Nana says with a frosty scowl at Papa, but her voice softens as she speaks, revealing how frightened she really is. "I found him lying face down in the dirt."

"Papa!" I say in admonishment. "You know you're not supposed to be taking on a heavy workload, doctor's orders. Why didn't you listen to Nana?"

Grandpa waves away my worry with a bony hand. "I don't see what the fuss's all about. A man has to work, and I'll do what I need to until the day they put me six feet under. I just tripped and had a little fall, that's all." He says it like he believes that to be the truth.

Nana gives me a sour look that says, 'That's definitely not what happened.' "He passed out—" she begins.

"I fell and was getting up before you came squawking like a worried hen, making things worse," Papa interrupts. "So, I decided to lie back and let you do what you were going to do. You shoulda done the same for me."

"Nonsense!" Nana snaps. "If I hadn't found you, who knows what would've happened?"

"Nothing." Papa dismisses Nana with a nonchalant shrug.

"I'd be fine, maybe about to pass out from eating some of your overcooked pasta—"

"Why, you old bast—"

"Bah! Hush, woman, you worry too much. I'm more likely to drop dead from all of your hen clucking than I will from a little heat."

Their bickering is comforting in a twisted way, the camaraderie of being together for decades and knowing which buttons to push to get a rise out of each other but also which ones are entirely off limits.

He pulls a long cigar out from the side of his bed and offers it to her. "Here. Calm yourself and have a stogie." The shit-eating grin on his face says he knows he's poking the bear, and I realize he's giving her something to focus on besides worrying about him. He's a slick old fox, I'll give him that.

Nana snatches the cigar out of his hand, brandishing it as if it's a weapon. "Have you gone *pazzo*? They don't even allow smoking in the hospital. And really? A smoke when you're supposed to be recovering?"

"Sure, why not? I'd rather have a smoke than act like a *pagliaccio*!"

Nana throws her hands up in frustration, the cigar flying from her hands in a perfect arc that ends in the trashcan. If she wasn't so riled up, I'd give her a round of applause, but as it is, I'm staying out of their battle. For now, at least. "Oh, *fanculo tutto*! You're impossible!"

"I know." Grandpa tosses me a mischievous wink meant to lighten the mood. "That's why you married me. You like the challenge."

The two continue to bicker as I look on fondly, feeling a sense of relief. Whatever happened to land Papa in the ER hasn't robbed him of his feistiness, so it couldn't have been too bad, could it?

It's a particularly hot summer, and it's not uncommon for the elderly to overheat when they underestimate the weather. Maybe he's right and this is all a lot of fuss for nothing. He just needs a slap on the hand to follow the doctor's and Nana's orders a bit better, and everything will be fine.

Even as I tell myself that, I know it's wishful thinking and childish hopes. A girlish desire to deny the mortality of a man who has always seemed larger than life to me. Deep inside, I know he's no more immortal than the rest of us, but even so, I need to know this isn't going to happen again. I love him too much to lose him. Especially not now, and if I had my say, not ever.

After being reassured several times by Papa that he's fine, I excuse myself from the room to let him and Nana bicker themselves out.

In the hall, I run into a man wearing a long white coat and carrying a binder with Papa's name on the spine. His name tag says *Dr. Lee*, and he has an aura of calm control that seems to relax me immediately.

"Are you Violet?" he asks before I can say anything, giving me a warm smile.

I nod. "I am. How'd you know?"

He grins. "Your grandfather wasn't concerned in the least about his health and has been talking about you since the moment he came in, telling anyone who'll listen about his granddaughter. If you didn't know, he's quite fond of you."

I smile. "That definitely sounds like him. Can you tell me what happened? I'm not sure I trust his version of events."

Dr. Lee's expression turns solemn and the energy around him shifts, making me instantly nervous. "It appears that, due to the heat and overworking himself, your grandfather's blood pressure dropped and he lost consciousness."

"That's what Nana said. So, if we can keep him from overdoing it, he's going to be okay." I say it definitively, like I'm adding tying him to his recliner in the air-conditioned living room to my to-do list.

Dr. Lee tilts his head, his lips pressed together. "Well, as I explained to Angela and Stefano, we're waiting for tests to come back for a more complete picture, but I don't need the tests to tell me that his heart isn't in good shape. It hasn't been in quite some time."

Oh, no.

"But he's stable now . . ." I say, like I'm refuting his medical knowledge with only the power of my hope.

"I'm sorry to be the bearer of bad news, Violet, but . . ."

The growing look of sorrow and despair in Dr. Lee's eyes says everything, and I'm forced to grab ahold of a wall rail to keep from falling.

No.

It can't be.

It just can't.

My worst nightmare come to life.

"How long does he have?" I ask through the lump in my throat. The words sound surreal, like someone else is saying them.

"At his age, it's hard to say," Dr. Lee muses, shrugging his shoulders. "Anything I say is at best an educated guess. Six months? A year, maybe? But he's a stubborn mule who refuses to follow orders, which complicates things. To be honest, he could go at almost any time if we can't get his heart to function properly and him to be compliant."

His words, an awful confirmation of what I feared most, hit me like a sucker punch to the gut, the air leaving my lungs in one forceful gust.

Six months to a year? Or less?

How can Papa, the only father figure I've ever known, the man who practically raised me from a pigtailed toddler to adulthood, the man who could take on anything the world threw at him and live to tell about it . . . have such little time to live?

In that moment, all the should've, could've, and would'ves flash in front of my eyes. It's as if everything I expected to experience with Papa has turned into a puddle that's evaporating quicker than I'd ever considered.

But the worst part is, the one thing he's wanted to see the most is likely to never happen, and that looms like a dark umbrella over my breaking heart.

When's my beautiful little flower getting married so I can walk her down the aisle?

To say marriage is a huge tradition in my family is like saying a tsunami is a little wet. An understatement of such magnitude, it's laughable, especially for my grandparents, who look forward to the next generation of weddings with teary smiles and proclamations of the continuation of their legacy with another branch on the family tree.

Hell, most of the women in my family are married off before they're old enough to drink alcohol. In fact, I'm probably the only woman in my family, at age twenty-six, who isn't married with a wagonload of kids.

Due to my busy career, I've been single for as long as I can remember, although I've always dreamed about having this big fairytale wedding. I used to use Nana's curtains as a makeshift veil and Papa would pretend to walk me down the aisle. I want him to do that for real, hold my hand as I greet my husband-to-be, bless us with a marriage as long and happy as his and Nana's has been, and see that I've finally grown into the woman he always told me I could be. Successful, loved, happy.

Now it's never going to happen.

As if sensing my tormented thoughts, Dr. Lee adds, "If there's anything you need to say or anything important left for you to do with your grandfather, I'd do it very soon. Now if you'll excuse me . . ."

Gee, thanks for the guilt trip, Doc.

Whatever else the doctor says fades off into the background as I watch Nana and Papa bicker through the glass window, happier now and blissfully unaware of the countdown looming.

In that moment, denial surges and I clench my fists.

This can't happen. I won't let it.

Six months to a year?

I can make it work.

Suddenly determined, a feeling of resolution washes over me as a plan formulates in my mind.

Don't worry, Papa. I'm going to find myself a husband so you can walk me down the aisle on my wedding day before you leave this earth . . . if it's the last thing I do.

VIOLET

"I still can't believe it!" I squeal, wiggling my fingers and watching my engagement ring flash as the overhead lights reflect on the diamond's faceted surface.

Having already heard this once, or maybe two dozen times, my two best friends sigh but rally with the appropriate oohs and ahhs, even throwing me a bone of another "Congratulations, girl!"

My lifelong bestie, Abigail Andrews, and Archie Hornee, my

interior design assistant, are basically saints for putting up with me at this point. "Colin and I are getting married!"

Archie arches one perfectly sculpted eyebrow and presses a palm to his black T-shirt-covered chest, which is most definitely manscaped. Ever the sarcastic ball of sass, he deadpans, "Dear, we know." He continues the performance by pulling a Vanna White, slapping a big fake smile on his face and gesturing widely to the roomful of wedding gowns surrounding us. When he finishes, his face goes right back to his usual blank 'fuck off' mode.

As if we'd be at a wedding dress shop for any other reason. Lord knows, Abigail and Archie aren't looking to get married, and obviously not to each other since Abigail lacks a rather important piece of the perfection that Archie is looking for, a never-ending appreciation of his special brand of hilarious, off-the-cuff, don't-care-about-being-politically-correct, catty-bitchiness.

So nope, not for them, for sure. We're here for me! I can't believe it's really happening.

It's been five months since Papa's diagnosis, and what a busy five months it's been.

Initially, I thought there'd be no way I'd ever get married before his heart gave out. After all, his doctor had painted a grim picture with no happy ending.

But despite the odds, Papa has miraculously held on long enough for me to reconnect with an old high school fling and get engaged after a whirlwind romance where we both said we wanted the whole nine yards—wedding, marriage, kids. Luckily, since Colin and I already had a history, it wasn't starting at ground zero, and instead, we moved quickly after a short get-to-know-you-now phase. He's a really good man, and I think we can be happy together.

Serious relationship, party of two . . . here! I think, adding a shimmy to my ass as I raise my hand, peering at the weighty sparkle resting there again.

But despite my excitement, the rows of gorgeous gowns, and two friends with a sharp eye for fashion, I'm currently trying on what has to be my twentieth wedding dress. Ride or Die Bride, an edgy bridal shop that calls itself the *Number One Bridal Shop for the Modern Badass Chick*, is failing to deliver a dress that is *The One*.

They've got everything from fairy tale princess to woodland nymph to Vegas stripper, mixed in with classic beauties covered in expensive lace and hand-sewn beading. My dress is here, I know it is. But in the three appointments I've made, I haven't found it. Yet.

I need *perfection*.

It has to be. Everything about my wedding has to be perfect in order to do it right for Papa.

"I'm so happy for you!" Abigail declares, rushing forward and pulling me into a fierce hug. A moment later, I feel another set of arms wrap around me, Archie's, and I'm encased in a group hug.

"Hey, guys!" I gasp as I feel my bridal shapewear corset, a marvelous invention that gives me the perfect hourglass figure, squeeze me to within an inch of my life. Any more and I swear it'll crush my ovaries. "I know you're both excited for me, but I can't breathe!"

No one told me trying on wedding dresses and getting the right shape could be this painful. I thought it was come in, try on a few dresses, and after a few twirls and happy tears, be done.

"Shit, sorry!" Abi and Archie exclaim in near unison. As Archie jumps back, Abi tries to loosen my corset but fails as there's too much dress fabric in the way. "I forgot how tight we had to pull it to get you into this thing."

"I'd blame it on the pa-pa-pa-pasta!" Archie sings, doing a not half-bad riff on *Blame It* by Jamie Foxx, while measuring my curves through fingers held in a square like he's a cameraman looking for my good side. His puckered lips and sharp brow remind me of Zoolander, and I'm waiting for him to say something about 'Blue Steel', but it doesn't come.

Still, I can't help but burst into laughter at his antics then gasp as the corset tightens even further. *Shit, is this damn corset alive?* "Hey!" I rasp, leveling a stern finger Archie's way and defending the curves I was blessed with through a particularly short and fierce round of puberty. "I'm half Italian. Pasta, pizza, lasagna, and red wine are a way of life for me, okay?"

With zero apology, he traces my shape reflecting in the mirror, which is admittedly a little fuller looking in this unflattering white taffeta ballgown that's a definite no-go. "No one's commenting on your curvy figure, love. There damn sure ain't nothing wrong with a little a junk in the trunk. Just look at Kim Kardashian." He waits a moment and then adds under his breath, but still loud enough for Abi and me to hear, "Only in America can someone turn an ass and a sex tape into a multi-billion-dollar family empire!"

The next gown is wrong too, and the one after that is even worse.

It's a sparkly number that somehow makes me look like a constipated fairytale princess. Too New Jersey, if that makes any damn sense, and as a half-Italian, avoiding *any* Jersey Shore comparisons is vital to me.

Which probably means I'll have to come back another time to try on even more gowns. Abi and Archie might kill me if I make them sit through this again, but I need their help and want someone to celebrate with when I do find *The One*.

Because I will.

Against all odds, I found a husband-to-be, a venue with an opening for our short-notice ceremony and big reception, and I will find a dress that makes me feel special for my big day.

Abi adjusts my bra straps, beaming at my reflection even though she already told me this dress is ridiculous and Archie made a rather harsh comment about my being ready for Wedding Day: 90s Vegas Style with the amount of bling thrown on this thing.

"When do you want to come check out the invitations?" Abi chirps. She co-owns a local specialty floral boutique and is handling all of my flower arrangements personally. But as my maid of honor, she offered to do the invitations as well.

Shit.

"Oh, yeah, sorry! I've been so busy with work and dress hunting, I totally forgot about that! When do you want me to come by the boutique to see them? Colin and I have a breakfast date tomorrow morning to talk about the wedding, so we could rearrange and come by the shop instead. But Archie and I have a job lined up right after—"

"With Bitch-ella, the Ice Queen," Archie interrupts with a mutter that I can't really disagree with, but I give him a side-eye that begs him to at least try to be professional about the client.

"So, we'd have to be fast," I finish.

Abi purses her lips thoughtfully as she places her hands on my hips, moving my body slightly to the side and staring at my shape in the mirror. "No way. You two do a breakfast date, and we can figure out a time when it's not a rush. Tomorrow's Friday, so maybe we can do it after work and then grab drinks?"

I nod, ignoring the flutters of butterflies in my stomach. I don't know why I'm so nervous all of a sudden. I mean, yes, there's a lot to do and not much time to do it in, but everything's going to plan, just like I hoped.

Papa.

Colin.

The wedding.

I should be on cloud nine. Yet, these butterflies don't feel like good, happy flutters. More like a tornado of responsibility, expectations, and nerves.

Abi turns me, eyeing me thoughtfully. "You good? Everything all right, Vi?"

I don't want to bring down the mood or start examining the questions in my head too closely, so I play pretend, telling myself that slightly cold feet are normal. After all, getting married is a big deal and not one to take lightly.

"I'm fine. It's just this damn corset!" I say with a grimace, grabbing my sides. "After I meet with Colin tomorrow, everything should be good to go." I look between the both of them, spreading my arms out to the side and twirling across the showroom stage in my dress one last time. "Final verdict?"

"Not my favorite," Abi says, shaking her head.

"I agree," Archie co-signs. "It's totally giving me *Tangled*, meets the *Little Mermaid*, meets *Cinderella* vibe, but like they all became dancers on the Vegas strip. Emphasis on the strip."

"Gee, thanks, Arch," I mutter sourly. But funnily enough, I agree with his assessment, although my terms were a little less . . . animated and crude.

Archie winks at me. "You're welcome, sweet cheeks."

"Don't worry, Vi. We're going to keep looking and find the perfect dress that'll knock Colin flat on his ass!" Abigail's assertion settles me slightly, helping me focus on the issue at hand . . . my dress. If I can just find that, everything else will be smooth sailing.

"Yeah, turn that frown upside down!" Archie adds, pushing at my cheeks with two fingers. He looks deep into my eyes, and I'm expecting some sweet words of wisdom, but I should know better with Archie. "Just think, before you know it, Colin won't have to bag it up anymore, and you'll get to feel the *real* thing. How big we talking here?" He holds his fingers a few inches apart, spreading them to indicate a bigger and bigger appendage, but it's seeing the whites of his eyes growing as I don't stop him that does me in.

"Oh, God, you're too much!" I groan, forcing his hand down and chuckling.

Come on, girl. Everything is going to work out. It has to.

"I'M CALLING OFF THE ENGAGEMENT."

The words hit me like a freight train, a grenade launched directly into my heart.

When Colin told me he wanted to meet with me this morning, I was under the impression it was to discuss the details of our wedding, plan who we were inviting, what DJ we were going to use, etc.

Never in a million years did I think it would be to dump me.

"Violet?" Colin asks, noticing that I've gone completely rigid, my latte frozen inches away from my lips and my half-eaten bagel in front of me.

Colin Radcliffe. My fiancé. *My ex-fiancé,* I correct with a wince. *Fucking rat* is what my mind is yelling loudly.

Dressed in a gray, freshly pressed, tailored suit, Colin's blond hair is styled and parted, and he's gazing at me with expectancy, as if I'm supposed to burst into hysterics, crying and making a scene worthy of Hamlet.

But I'm frozen, thinking WTF?

Why?

And . . . why now?

But wondering the whys won't do me any good. Colin's obviously thought this through and wants to end it all.

Doesn't matter that I just spent weeks trying to find the perfect wedding dress.

Doesn't matter how much I want the fairytale wedding.

Doesn't matter that my Papa won't get to walk me down the aisle. Maybe never.

None of it matters to him.

In a hit that's even more impactful than Colin's words, I realize that none of my thoughts on this betrayal have anything to do with us, our relationship, or our love. *Love?*

Do I even love Colin?

Stupid me thought I'd make it work using a checklist for our compatibility.

Both career-oriented people. Check.

Former lovers. Check.

Both matured and ready to settle down. Check and check.

Boy, was I wrong on that last one.

"Violet?" Colin presses again, this time reaching across the table and placing his hands atop mine.

Suddenly, I feel queasy, and I have to fight back the urge to throw up in his lap.

"I know this has to come as a shock to you, but I'll cover the lost deposit on the wedding hall and every other expense associated with our engagement so you don't have to worry."

Just like I thought, he's already planned his exit strategy, as if our wedding, our marriage, was some business transaction. For him, maybe it was. For me? I don't know, I realize. Maybe this is what the buzzing butterflies have been trying to tell me?

"Why?" I ask simply, battling down the surge of nausea.

Colin licks his lips, lips that I once enjoyed on my neck, on my breasts, on my most sacred of places.

"Violet, you know I adore you, and you're beautiful, smart, and kind, but . . . I don't think I'm ready for marriage." He stares at me again, rubbing my hands as if waiting for the crying hysterics he knows must be coming.

He definitely wants a show, just not too much of one. That perfect balance of greedy hunger for drama, tampered with the knowledge that he doesn't want to look bad.

That's why he picked the coffee shop, I realize. Cold and calculated. The Radcliffe way. In public, he knows I'm not going to go fully emotional, batshit crazy or really even make a scene. It's not my style.

But he does want to see me shatter into a million tiny pieces, and he wants an audience while he does his dirty work.

I've been ignoring it, something I could easily do with our quick whirlwind relationship, but I can see it clearly now that he's serving it up on a platter like a Thanksgiving turkey.

Everything is a façade with him. Image and reputation reign supreme.

I bet he thought I'd fit some corporate wife checkbox. Which would be so hurtful, except that I guess I was doing the same thing with my own checkboxes.

This was doomed from the start.

When I don't muster even a single teardrop or argument, he continues, "We're both so young, and hell, we haven't even had sex in over three weeks." His tone is accusatory, like it's my fault we've been so tired that sex has seemed like one more thing on the ever-growing to-do list.

He keeps digging at the wound, pouring salt in a steady stream into the bloody mess of our relationship. "We're both so busy with our jobs. You have that decorating thing you do that you love so much, and it takes up so much of your time, and I'm really busy at Dad's company, kicking ass and making deals. I . . . I just think we're at two different crossroads in our lives."

The decorating thing that I do? Fuck off.

Out of all the things he said, insulting my job pisses me off the most.

And I could argue against so many of his points, letting him know that everything he said was bullshit.

But I'm not going to because, simply put, I don't have time for this shit.

And I realize . . . I don't care. Not about Colin.

I'm such an idiot. But it was all for a good reason.

Sorry, Papa. I tried.

"Fine," I say simply, pulling my hands away from his before taking off my engagement ring. "Here. You can take this back, too. I don't want it."

I place the ring on the table and slide it across toward him, resisting the urge to throw it in his face or shove it up his nose, not wanting to give him the satisfaction of an emotional outburst. The huge diamond rock in the center sparkles against the light, catching the eye of several women sitting around us.

I swear some of their heads turn like *The Exorcist* to get a better look as they realize what's happening, their eyes as big as saucers as they gawk at the size of the ring.

One of the women even leans so far forward to get a better look that she jostles her steaming hot coffee, spilling it on her hand. But instead of crying out at what I know has to hurt, she quietly blots at it, blowing cool air across her hand so she doesn't miss a single moment of the Colin and Violet Breakup Show.

"You know," I say as I grab my purse and slide on my Gucci shades, ignoring the commotion of googly-eyed stares and growing whispers from women around us, "It was really good to reconnect after so long, Colin. And we tried to make it work. It didn't. Thanks for everything."

My words are clipped and to the point.

If he's going to break off our engagement like this, I see no reason to drag it out with some long ass monologue that'll amount to nothing in the end, anyway.

Finished, I begin to rise from my chair, but Colin grabs my arm, holding me in place, his jaw slack in surprise.

One of the women watching suddenly decides that's her cue and claps her hands sharply, interrupting our scene with one of her own. "Boy, you'd best let that girl's arm go. You had your moment, and a queen like that is better off without a twat-stain like you."

Several people gasp at her language and volume, but Archie has me corrupted to not even blink at that level of crudeness. Thankful for the support, I look over to her and offer a weak smile of appreciation. For his part, Colin scowls but loosens his grip. Still, he's not done.

"Wait a minute now, Vi. You're not even going to try to talk about this? After all we've been through?" His voice has an almost whine to it, confirming what I expected.

He wanted me to break down and beg him not to leave me.

In front of a fucking audience.

Like he's some golden goose prize that I would debase myself to possess.

Well, he can kick rocks.

I won't give him the satisfaction of a show.

I shrug nonchalantly. "Nope."

"Look, Vi, I know how much our getting married means to you. I get it, you're pissed and upset. I would be too, but can we please not end things on bad terms? You don't have to act this way—"

"We're *fine*," I say, disengaging my arm from his grasp and rising to my feet. "Besides, you're right. It's probably for the best."

Colin's lips work for several seconds, at a loss for words. Like he can't believe this didn't turn out how he expected, me in a crying puddle at his feet.

He clenches his jaw, showing that he's actually getting angry. "Violet—"

"'Bye, Colin."

Ruffled, Colin straightens his collar and clears his throat, trying one last tactic, gesturing at my half-eaten food. "Will you just sit down and finish the bagel, at least?"

Turning away, I toss over my shoulder, just as casually as he tossed away our relationship, "No time. I gotta go to work . . . and do that 'decorating thing'."

My single cheerleader stands up, her arm circling in rally. "That's right, girl. Strut it out of here and own the world." She sneers at Colin, more emotionally invested in this than even I am, and isn't that pitiful?

She's my only supporter, though. Every other woman in here is judging me as unworthy of keeping Colin. All they see is a handsome guy in a suit with a flashy diamond ring . . . back on the market.

I imagine Colin will be collecting numbers by the stacks before he even walks out of the coffee shop.

Well, they can have him.

I get into the cab and far down the block before the tears come. Not for Colin, not for the decimation of our relationship, but for Papa and for the little girl I once was, and still am to some degree, who wants to make her grandfather happy.

Read the entire book here. Or search My Big Fat Fake Wedding on Amazon.

ABOUT THE AUTHOR

Standalones
My Big Fat Fake Wedding | | Filthy Riches | | Scorpio
Bennett Boys Ranch:
Buck Wild | | Riding Hard | | Racing Hearts
The Tannen Boys:
Rough Love | | Rough Edge
Dirty Fairy Tales:
Beauty and the Billionaire | | Not So Prince Charming | |
Happily Never After
Get Dirty:
Dirty Talk | | Dirty Laundry | | Dirty Deeds | | Dirty Secrets
*Irresistible Bachelor*s:
Anaconda | | Mr. Fiance | | Heartstopper
Stud Muffin | | Mr. Fixit | | Matchmaker
Motorhead | | Baby Daddy | | Untamed

Made in the USA
San Bernardino, CA
21 May 2020

72112379R00195